FELLSIDE

By M. R. Carey

The Girl With All the Gifts
Fellside

FELLSIDE

M.R. CAREY

orbit

www.orbitbooks.net

ORBIT

First published in Great Britain in 2016 by Orbit

1 3 5 7 9 10 8 6 4 2

Copyright © 2016 by M. R. Carey

The moral right of the author has been asserted.

All characters and events in this publication, other than those clearly in the public domain, are fictitious and any resemblance to real persons, living or dead, is purely coincidental.

A CIP catalogue record for this book is available from the British Library.

HB ISBN 978-0-356-50358-5
C format ISBN 978-0-356-50359-2

Typeset by Palimpsest Book Production Ltd, Falkirk, Stirlingshire
Printed and bound in Great Britain by CPI Group (UK) Ltd, Croydon CR0 4YY

Papers used by Orbit are from well-managed
forests and other responsible sources.

MIX
Paper from
responsible sources
FSC® C104740

Orbit
An imprint of
Little, Brown Book Group
Carmelite House
50 Victoria Embankment
London EC4Y 0DZ

An Hachette UK Company
www.hachette.co.uk

www.orbitbooks.net

To Louise. To David. To Ben.

If I lived a thousand years I could never love you enough.

PART ONE

WHO BY FIRE

1

It's a strange thing to wake up not knowing who you are.

Jess Moulson – not thinking of herself by that name or any other – found herself lying in white sheets in a white room, overwhelmed by memories that were predominantly red and yellow and orange. The colours merging and calving endlessly, out of control, billowing heat at her like she'd opened an oven door too quickly and caught the full blast.

Someone had just been talking to her with some urgency. She remembered the voices, low but coming from right up against her face.

Her face . . . Now she thought about it, her face felt very strange. She tried to ask one of the women in white who came and went why this was, but she couldn't open her mouth very far, and, when she did, she wasn't able to make anything happen beyond a few clicks and rasping sounds which hurt her in coming out.

The woman leaned in close and spoke very softly. She was younger and prettier than Jess but still managed to wear an air of authority. For a moment, Jess didn't even have any kind of reference point for what this person might be. A nurse or doctor

3

seemed most likely, but in the utter disorientation of those first few minutes it seemed possible that she was some kind of nun – that the crisis Jess was going through, against all the evidence, was a crisis of faith.

"You won't be able to talk for a few days yet," the woman told her. "You shouldn't even try. There was a lot of damage to your lungs and the tissues of your throat, and they won't heal if you put strain on them."

Nurse then, not nun. The damage was to her lungs and throat. Her soul might well be intact, although it didn't really feel that way.

Jess made a shrugging gesture with the arm that didn't have a drip in it. She wasn't shrugging the information away; she was trying to ask for more. But the nurse either misinterpreted the gesture or ignored it. She walked on without another word.

Jess was left feeling not just frustrated but afraid. The nurse's expression as she looked down at her had been very strange. There had been compassion there, but also something that looked like reserve or caution. Did Jess have some disease that was communicable? But in that case, why get so close?

She didn't worry about it for long though. There was something in her system that was pulling her endlessly towards sleep. She gave in to it – a surrender that was repeated on and off through that first day. Her conscious periods were short. Her sleep was shallow and haunted by whispers in what sounded like many different voices. Her waking brought the same questions every time as she clawed her way up out of the darkness like a swimmer hitting the surface just before her lungs gave out.

Where am I? How did I get here? Who's thinking these thoughts? What was before this?

It wasn't just the one nurse who was careful around her. They all seemed to have their issues. Jess kept hoping that one of them would answer the questions she couldn't ask. It seemed like this should be something that got covered in Nursing 101. If a patient wakes up from severe trauma, you start by filling her in on the

4

basics. "You've had a very nasty accident," say, or "You were mugged and rolled and left for dead outside a tube station."

Almost a clue there. A thousand memories twitched at those words. Tube stations had been a feature of her life, so London was probably where she lived. But there was nothing in her mind to back up either the accident or the mugging hypothesis. There was just a hole – the outline you might leave if you cut a paper doll out of a sheet of newspaper and then burned it or threw it away. She wasn't Jess for now. She was the suspicious absence of Jess.

When she did start to remember, she got that same sense of blank confusion all over again, because she was only remembering earlier awakenings. The first day hadn't been the first day after all. She had been here for much longer than that, drifting in and out of consciousness, living in a single fuzzy moment that was endlessly prolonged.

The earlier wakings had been different from the more recent ones. Her disorientation had been overwhelmed back then by desperate, uncontainable hunger. She was an addict (when those memories came back it was in an almost physical surge, as though her compressed mind were snapping back to its accustomed shape) and she had needed a fix. Had needed to feel okay. One time she had pulled herself out of the bed and crawled most of the way to the window, drip and all, intending to climb out of it and slip away down to the Hay Wain on a heroin run. Through the window there was a view of sky and tall buildings – no way of knowing how far away the ground was. But Jess had been prepared to try until the women in white embargoed the idea.

Remembering all this now brought the craving back, but it was dulled. Manageable. The hunger wasn't strong enough to pick her up and shake her. It just sat in a little corner of her mind, politely requesting attention.

That in itself was scary. With the memories of her addiction had come another set of memories, pushed to the surface of her mind by the force of some internal pressure. She'd got clean before, just once in her life, and the process had been a dark streak of misery obliterating days and weeks. If she'd been through cold turkey again, lying in this bed, then she must have been here for a very long time.

The weird feeling in her face frightened her too. It was as though her flesh didn't belong to her. As though someone had given her one of those cosmetic masks made of fragrant mud and then forgotten to scrape it off after it hardened.

On the third day she tried to sit up. Women in white came running and pushed her down again. "I want a mirror," she told them in a bellowed murmur like the world's worst stage prompt. "Please, just bring me a mirror!"

The women in white swapped uneasy glances until one of them reached a decision. She went away and came back with a tiny compact from someone's handbag. She held it so Jess could look up into her own face looking back down at her. It was a nasty shock, because she really didn't recognise it.

This wasn't the amnesia. She knew what her face should look like, and what she was seeing now wasn't it. Oh, it was a reasonable facsimile that would fool a stranger – and when it was at rest it didn't look too bad. Well, yeah, actually it did. There was thick swelling around her eyes as though someone had punched her a whole lot of times. The skin was taut and shiny in places. And she was fish-belly pale, as if she'd spent a year or two living like Osama Bin Laden in a cave in the side of a mountain.

But when her face moved – when she tried to talk – it turned into something from a nightmare. The right side of her mouth was unresponsive, deadened, so the more animated left side tugged and twisted it into a parade of grimaces. The symmetry disappeared, and you realised that it had never really been there at all.

"Okay?" the nurse holding the compact asked. Gently. Probing the wound.

Jess couldn't answer. There wasn't any answer that covered how she felt.

Some of the recent past came back to her in her sleep that night. The whispering voices were still there, as though a hundred

6

conversations were being held in the space around her head. With them came a sense of vulnerability, of lying exposed in some big open space. She wasn't alone: a multitude surrounded her, invisible. So many that there wasn't enough room for them all to stand: they were folded around and over her like hot treacle poured out of a pan.

Jess hadn't dreamed since she was a child, but images came and went nonetheless. She held her face – a tiny version of it – in her hands, and then parted her fingers to let it drop. Again and again. Sometimes when it dropped there was a rustle or a tinny clatter from far below her, sometimes no sound at all.

Then the fire came, rising up in front of her.

Climbing in at her mouth.

Nestling inside her.

She woke shivering in the warm hospital room, chilled by her own slick sweat. A breath was caught halfway up her throat like a solid thing, and she had to spit it out piecemeal, in quick, shallow gasps.

"What happened to me?" she croaked at the nurse who came to take her temperature and blood pressure in the morning (smell of breakfast heavy in the air, but Jess was nil by mouth so the smell was as close as she was going to get). "There was a fire, wasn't there? Tell me. Please!"

"You should—"

"I know, I know. I should get some rest. But I can't until I know. Please!"

The nurse stared at her for a long time, hanging on the cusp of saying something. But all she said finally was, "I'll ask the doctor." She tucked Jess in, folding the stiff cotton sheets with the brusque efficiency of an origami black belt.

"Please," Jess whispered again, saving it for when the nurse's face was bent down close to hers. She thought it might be harder to say no at that range.

And it seemed she was right. "Yes, there was a fire," the nurse said reluctantly as she smoothed out the last creases from the sheet.

"Where . . . was . . .?" Jess asked, feeling only a few hot twinges in her throat this time. As long as she limited herself to mono-syllables, she could ace this conversation.

"Your flat. Your flat caught fire when you were inside. When you were . . . not able to move."

When I was high, Jess translated. I set my flat on fire when I was high. Who does that? Only someone intent on ruining them-selves and everyone around them.

Her mind treated her to a slideshow. A resin statue of a Chinese dancer with a flute. A lampshade shaped like a hot-air balloon with two waving fairies in the gondola underneath. Her folk CDs. Her books. Her photo albums. All gone?

"How . . . bad?" she asked.

"Very bad. Really, you should try not to think about it. It's not going to help you to get well."

The nurse retreated quickly. It seemed to Jess that she wanted very much to get out of earshot before she was made to field any more questions.

And at that point another slide clicked into view.

John.

His face, his name and a sense of what the face and the name had meant. Oh Jesus, if John was dead! Panic flooded her system, only to be followed a moment later by a wild and slightly nause-ating surge of hope. If John was dead . . .

She sat up before she even knew she'd decided to. She couldn't sustain it though, and slumped right back down again, sick and dizzy.

She had to know. She husbanded her strength so she could ask, and tried to shore up her non-existent stamina with an exercise regime. She could only hold her weight on her elbows for a few seconds before falling back on to the sheets, but she worked on it at intervals through the morning, determined each time to beat the previous time's total.

Consultants' rounds were at eleven. The doctor walked past Jess's door without slowing, followed by a bustling line of medical students who – each in turn – peered in with big round eyes as though Jess was a model in a porn shop peepshow before hurrying on to rejoin the crocodile.

Right then.

God helps those who help themselves. Jess hauled herself out of bed and slid her feet down on to the floor. She worked the cannula out of her wrist and let it fall. The loose end drew a ragged red line across the white sheet.

It wasn't easy to get vertical, but once she did, she was able to translate her drunken sway into a forward march just by picking the right moment to raise a foot and put it down.

She headed for the door at action-replay velocity, taking about a minute and a half to cover twelve feet. Getting through the door was more of a challenge, because she accidentally knocked it with her elbow and it started to close on some kind of spring mechanism. She had to lean against it to keep it open as she negotiated the narrowing gap. Then she was through, the door swinging to behind her, and for a moment she thought she was free and clear. But that was because she was looking to the right and the swelling around her eyes left her with no peripheral vision.

From her blind side a hand came down on her arm, just below the shoulder – not heavily or tightly, but it stopped her dead all the same. A voice said, "Ms Moulson, I'm going to have to ask you to go back inside."

Jess turned. It took a lot of small movements of her feet. The woman who was facing her now was not in white, but in midnight blue with a bright yellow tabard. She was a policewoman, no taller than Jess but a fair bit stockier and more solid, and presumably (unlike Jess) not so weak that a stray breeze would knock her over. Jess sagged, checkmated in a single move.

And appalled and confused all over again. Why was there a policewoman here? Was she under guard? And if she was, did that mean that she was under protection or under restraint?

That was such a big, yawning chasm of a question that it eclipsed, for a few moments, the question of what had happened to John.

9

"Why?" she croaked. That was a little vague, but it would have to do.

The policewoman frowned. She had dark, freckled skin that made Jess flash on the memory of her own face in the mirror – her unnatural pallor, like something that lived under a stone.

"You're under arrest. Didn't you know that?"

She did now. That had to count as progress. She managed another "Why?"

The other woman's expression changed, but only for a moment – a cloud of doubt or concern drifting across it and then disappearing as quickly as it had come. "For murder, Ms Moulson," she said. "The charge against you is murder."

She closed in on Jess, as though she intended to herd her physically back into the room. Jess stood her ground, more out of bewilderment than belligerence. Murder? she thought. Whose murder? Who am I supposed to have . . .?

"You'll have to go back inside," the policewoman said. "I shouldn't even be talking to you. I'm the one who's meant to keep other people from talking to you."

"Who . . .?" Jess panted. The corridor was yawing like a ship at sea. She couldn't move, although she might make an exception for falling down.

The woman's hand came out and took her arm again. She leaned past Jess and pushed the door open – effortlessly, one-handed. Jess could have thrown her full weight against it right then and that feeble little spring would have been too much for her. "Please, Ms Moulson," the policewoman said. "Go back inside now. I'll tell your lawyer you're awake, the next time he calls."

But Jess had come way too far to back down. "Who?" she whispered again. "Who . . . dead? John? Was . . . John?"

"Your lawyer will fill you in," the policewoman promised. But when Jess didn't move, she sighed heavily and shrugged. "It was a little boy," she said. "A ten-year-old. It looks like it may have been an accident, but that's not for me to say. You set the fire, and the charge as I understand it is murder."

10

She had both hands on Jess's arm, one above and one below the elbow, and was trying to turn her around. But no part of Jess was communicating with any other part now. Her upper body moved, her hips twisted, her legs stayed exactly where they were.

There was only one ten-year-old boy who she knew even vaguely. His name popped into her head from nowhere, and her lips shaped it although no sound came.

Alex.

Alex Beech.

She was aware of falling. But the floor, when she got to it, recoiled from her as though she was something unpleasant to the touch.

2

Alex Beech was the boy upstairs.

Upstairs where, exactly? It began to drift back into Jess's mind in clotted, disconnected pieces.

The first piece looked like this.

Coming home late one evening from the bookshop where she worked to her flat in Muswell Hill to find this skinny little kid sitting out on the stairs – the flight that led up from her landing to his – dressed in a vest and underpants. Feet bare in the November cold, on stone steps that were chill even in summer. His blond hair was darker underneath, as though he bleached it. And his face looked too small to sustain that crazy, free-form mop.

"You okay?" Jess asked.

The boy nodded but didn't speak.

From above him came shouts in two different voices, bass and soprano. The door of the upstairs flat was closed, but the phrase "always been your fucking problem" came through clearly in a falsetto yell. That was the mother. Then "Don't start! Don't you bloody start!" from the father.

Jess hesitated. You couldn't invite someone else's kid into your flat, could you? Certainly not without letting their parents know.

However innocent your motives were, it wouldn't fly. She almost talked herself into it but chickened out. She made cocoa instead and brought it out to him. Chocolate flakes and marshmallows. All the trimmings.

The next time she looked out, he'd gone. The mug was where he'd been sitting, on the seventh stair from the bottom. It was empty.

That first encounter set the tone for all the others. They were allies of a sort, but they only ever met in no-man's-land. On the stairs. And they only ever talked about banalities.

"How was your day?"

"It was okay."

"You want some cocoa?"

"Yes please."

Apart from that, she followed Alex's adventures at a distance. Heard his mum and dad cursing him out – seemingly whenever they took a break from cursing each other. She knew his name was Beech because their mail lay out on the table in the hall some days, waiting to be picked up. And she got the *Alex* from a thousand shouted commands and reprimands.

"You've got a pet," John said the first time he saw the boy. "Did he follow you home?"

"That's not funny, John."

"I'm not laughing. Honest, Jess! I think it's cute. What does he eat?"

She had to admit that she didn't know. But the next time Alex camped out on the stairs, she brought him a sandwich as well as the cocoa. "It's cheese," she said. "I don't know what you think about cheese. But it's there if you want it."

He seemed to think that cheese was acceptable, by and large. He ate the sandwich, apart from the crusts. And their relationship entered a new phase. Jess thought of it as comfort and supply.

Still no talking, though. Just "How are you?"; "I'm fine." She thought about sitting down next to him, striking up a proper conversation. So is school going well? Do you have a favourite sport? A best friend? Do your parents only shout at you or do they hit you too?

"You want to keep your distance from that," John warned her. "I mean it, Jess – it's trouble you don't need. If he tells you he's being abused, what are you going to do? Call the police? They'll start looking into us too, and find out we're using. We'll go to jail."

John still called Alex her little pet, but he didn't laugh any more and there was a nasty edge to his voice when he said it. He seemed to feel that the whole thing had gone beyond a joke.

Jess went ahead and had the talk with Alex anyway. John Street wasn't her conscience. He was the anti-Jiminy Cricket, always egging her on to darker and crazier things. This time she decided to pretend she had a better angel.

"Only once," Alex said when she asked him if his dad ever got physical with his reprimands. Jess had no idea what to do with that. She suspected that one smack or punch always led on to n, where n was a large number. But it wasn't exactly a smoking pistol. Not enough to justify an anonymous tip-off to child services, or an ugly altercation on the upstairs landing. And her batteries were low in every way that mattered. If there was a confrontation, she would almost certainly lose.

She gave Alex her number – made him put it into his phone. "If you ever need someone," she told him, "you can call me. Or just come down and knock on the door. I'm usually home."

It didn't ever happen. And after a while she forgot about the promise – forgot she'd ever even made it. The addiction was lying like an iron bar across her brain right about then, and it was getting worse with each day that went by. Alex was one of the last things to go, but he faded out in the end along with the rest of the world. She went sailing away to a sunny, squally island where the population was three: herself, John Street and heroin.

At first, that was as far as Jess's memories would take her. But she kept on dipping her bucket into that deep black well and hauling up more and more details. When the psychiatrists appointed by the court to test her mental faculties asked her what she could remember, she tried her best to tell the truth, but the truth changed from one session to the next. She could see in their eyes that they thought she was faking her amnesia.

Then her lawyer (also court-appointed, set in motion by the magic of legal aid) arrived like a fox in a henhouse and sent the psychiatrists packing. His name was Brian Pritchard. He was exactly Jess's height, which made him quite short for a man, and grey-haired, even though he couldn't have been more than forty-five or so. The hair read almost like a statement – of gravitas and moral rectitude. "My client isn't ready to talk about these traumatic events," he told the shrinks in cold, clipped tones. "And by God you'd better not try to use those assessments in court if you haven't got a consent form to go with them!"

But they did have a consent form. Jess was signing everything that was put in front of her, collaborating with every legal process, being as helpful as she could. That was what innocent people did, and she was sure in her heart she was innocent.

Pritchard did not approve. "You've been arrested and charged," he told her waspishly. "In an ideal world the police would still be vigorously pursuing their inquiries, but we don't live in an ideal world, Ms Moulson. If you hand yourself to them on a plate, they will take you and pick you apart and wipe their fingers clean with the laws of evidence. And in the meantime they will not be exploring any other possibilities, because exploring other possibilities takes effort. So please, as a favour to me, treat everyone who *isn't* me as your sworn enemy until your trial is over."

Jess glanced at the man who had accompanied Pritchard on to the ward. A skittish little junior solicitor or clerk whose role was to hand his boss pieces of paper when they were needed and who scarcely ever spoke. When Jess met his eyes, he blushed and looked away.

"Oh, I don't mean Mr Levine," Pritchard said. "You can treat him as landscape."

On that first visit, Pritchard took Jess's statement about the night of the fire without comment or question. On the second, the next day, he brought her some newspaper articles and print-outs from internet blogs in order, so he said, to give her a better idea of what she was up against.

Inferno Jess: "I know nothing!"
The woman at the heart of tragic ten-year-old Alex Beech's death is being treated at London's Whittington Hospital both for her physical injuries and for memory loss. Yet doctors have found no evidence of brain damage or psychological trauma.

Pritchard seemed to be trying to provoke her into some kind of response, but all Jess could give him was exhaustion and despair, occasionally peaking into dull amazement.

"They might as well just come right out and call me a murderer!"

"They'd be very happy to," Pritchard said. "But they're mindful of the sub judice laws. Most of them use the word 'alleged' quite liberally. Alleged murderer. Alleged crime. The magic ingredient in unfounded allegations. Some have taken to calling you 'the Inferno Killer', in quote marks. They have a star witness, by the way. You should brace yourself, because it's going to get unpleasant."

"Who? What witness?" But she knew.

John. John Street. Of course.

"Don't let that prey on your mind," Pritchard advised her. "I think he's their weak link, to be honest. I'm delighted that they're leading with him. I'm sure we'll get to the truth. Now let's go over that statement of yours and see which parts of it are fit for purpose."

Not many, it turned out. Time and again the lawyer took Jess to task for stating as truth things she could only know by impli-cation. "You were out of your head for large parts of the evening, yes? Then please don't make assumptions about what you didn't see and couldn't hear. Your role here is to state the facts. Let me worry about the truth."

"They're the same thing!" Jess protested, but Pritchard shook his head.

"The facts are in the outside world. You can verify them with your senses or with objective tests. The truth is something that people build inside their heads, using the facts as raw materials. And sometimes the facts get bent or broken in the process."

"I'm not going to lie," Jess said.

"You misunderstand me. I'm not asking you to. I'm asking you to stay with the facts, where you're on safe ground, and stop lunging off towards something dim and distant that you're thinking of as the truth. That's a dangerous voyage, and you shouldn't try to make it alone."

Jess didn't argue, but only because she wasn't up to the effort. She wasn't good for much of anything right then. Up in the facial reconstruction unit of the Whittington Hospital in Archway, surrounded by people who mostly maintained a professional deadpan, she felt like a prisoner in a tower made out of other people's words. Alex was dead. That little kid, who never caught a single piece of good luck in his life, was dead. And they were saying she did it.

She couldn't even protest her innocence. Saying you didn't do it and saying you didn't remember doing it were two different things. She was sure in her own mind that something else had happened. Any one out of a million something elses. Alex had fallen down the stairs. His parents had killed him and then gone looking for a scapegoat. He'd killed himself. She wandered in her mind through the maze of these possibilities – and believed in none of them, because in her mind, Alex Beech was still alive. Still keeping up his endless vigil on the stairs. Nothing else made sense to her.

She had an unreliable temper (when was there ever an addict who didn't?) but almost always when she got angry it was with herself. For cowardice, passivity, lack of backbone. For being so woefully short on what her Aunt Brenda (*oh Brenda, I need you now!*) used to call stick-to-it-iveness. True, she had hated John in recent times, and often wished him dead. But wishing without doing was exactly her speed. Surely you couldn't become a murderer without knowing it. Maybe you could forget the act because of trauma or madness, but you couldn't forget the intent. If it had ever been there, it would still be inside you, in your head or your heart, and a thorough search of the premises would find it.

Jess carried out a lot of searches, came up empty and went into the trial still believing in herself.

Over the space of two weeks, that belief was inexorably demolished.

3

These were the facts, which the prosecution established in a brisk and businesslike manner. There had been a fire. In Jess's flat, which was number 16 Orchard Court, Colney Hatch Lane, Muswell Hill. It happened on an evening when only two people were in the flat – Jess herself, and her boyfriend, John Street.

Jess had been at the epicentre of the blaze (you only had to look at her face to know that). She had lain there until the firemen came in and carried her out. She probably would have died from smoke inhalation except that the drugs had sent her so far under she was hardly breathing.

Street had been injured too, requiring skin grafts to his badly burned hands. He got his injuries beating at the flames to put them out – trying to quell the blaze.

The fire didn't have a natural or accidental origin. It was set on purpose. The crime scene investigators, who came in while the ashes were still hot, had traced it back to a metal wastepaper basket. One of these experts gave evidence in court. He was young, personable, straight out of a TV crime show. "Someone had filled the basket with papers, drenched the papers in lighter fluid and dropped a match in on top," he said, describing the actions in the air with his hands. "Then the basket itself had been tipped over."

"In an attempt to spread the blaze further and faster?"

"Objection," Brian Pritchard interjected. "That's interpretation."

"Sustained," the judge agreed.

The Crown prosecutor didn't seem troubled. "My learned colleague," he said, "is trying to leave open the possibility that the fire could have caught by accident. In your opinion, is that a genuine possibility?"

The CSI expert shook his head. "Absolutely not."

"And why is that?"

"We were able to trace the chemical residues, and that gave us the spatter pattern from the lighter fluid as it was poured out. It was poured in a series of wide arcs around the wastepaper basket, extending up to five feet in each direction. So whoever was pouring it was not trying to start a blaze in the wastepaper basket itself. They were using the wastepaper basket to set the flat on fire."

Jess experienced the first vertiginous moment of doubt. She remembered sitting on the floor with that wastepaper basket gripped between her knees, its mouth a blurred and wavering circle into which she was dropping . . . what? Something slick and cold that she had tried to tear but couldn't, so she'd had to settle for crumpling and twisting and folding.

"Photographs," John Street said when it came to his turn on the witness stand. "Jess was tearing up photographs of the two of us."

"And why was that?" the prosecutor asked him in a completely unconvincing tone of surprise.

"We'd been arguing about . . . well, about nothing really. Nothing much. We'd shot up earlier in the evening."

"You'd taken heroin?"

"Yes."

"You're both addicts?"

"Yes. And the hit wasn't . . . wasn't anything much, and Jess

20

got crazy. She wanted me to go out and get some more, but we didn't have any money . . ."

Some of this was raising answering echoes in Jess's mind. Not the argument: there had been so many arguments, it was hard to zero in on any one. And not the ache of the incomplete fix: there had been lots of those too, as their need grew and their ability to feed it diminished. But that night's high had seemed to her to be as deep as an ocean.

What she remembered was the photographs. Her dream (not a dream, she didn't dream, just an image, just a thought) of holding her own face in her hands crystallised now into an actual memory. And the reek of lighter fluid, the slimy feel of it on her fingers. The doubt she'd felt earlier congealed into something like terror. She wanted to deny the things that were being said about her, but the memories trapped her, hemmed her into a space even tighter than the tiny dock in which she sat. It was as though there was a second trial running in parallel with the real one, in which she was the witness and the defendant and the judge. She was trying herself, and her defence didn't hold up at all.

"Mr Street has testified that you set a fire in your flat on the night in question. In the wastepaper basket. Do you deny this?"

"No, I . . . no . . . no."

"And is Mr Street correct about what it was you burned?"

"Yes."

"Photographs of the two of you together."

"Yes."

The bare truth. No equivocation. The only way of establishing what had really happened was to follow the trail all the way to the end. If she lied or swerved away, she might improve her chances of being *found* innocent, but not of actually *being* innocent. The one without the other was no use to her at all.

"Then your relationship with your boyfriend – with Mr Street – wasn't going well?"

"No. Not very well. We kept on arguing. And . . . fighting. We fought. I mean, he . . . John . . . he used to . . . hit me."

21

"Hit you? Physically abuse you? Did you report any of these assaults at the time? Tell friends what was happening, or family?"

"No." *We didn't have any friends. And I couldn't make Brenda any more unhappy than she was.*

"But you went to your doctor, or to a hospital? An A & E? Your injuries were documented?"

"No." *He wouldn't let me go. He didn't want anyone to see. And he knew where to hit me so it didn't show.*

"Well, let's confine ourselves to the verbal altercations between the two of you. There's at least some consensus that they actually occurred. You argued about drugs?"

"And other things." Everything, really. Nothing was too small for their mutual resentment to catch on and scrape against. Every chance word was a declaration of war. Mostly it wasn't drugs at all, and it wasn't love. It wasn't even *you hit me, John. You're supposed to love me and you keep hitting me!* It was *you didn't pull the chain, the last Mars bar was mine, you said that sarcastically, it's your turn to go to the shops, this place is a tip, can you at least open a window?* Because that's what you do when you're heading for a brick wall and accelerating. You pounce on trivia. The things that really matter can't be said and don't have to be. They're lying like submerged rocks under the spray and froth of everything you do say. Everything you shout and scream and snarl.

"And how did you feel on the night of the fire?"

"How did I . . .?"

"About Mr Street. About your relationship. How did you feel?"

"It's hard to say."

"But if you had to put it in a few words. In one word, even."

"I felt . . . trapped." That wasn't new. But it had been strong that night. Stronger than usual. The urge to get out of a relation-ship that had become abusive, dangerous and desperate. To push John out of her life and be herself again. When she tore up the photographs, it had started with that impulse: they were photo-graphs of her and John together, and she was trying to rip him

22

from her side, as though some weird voodoo might translate that act into reality.

She saw Pritchard in his seat at the defence table, staring down at his files and shaking his head slowly from side to side. But the word was out and she wasn't sorry. It was the truth. The truth was her refuge. If she told the truth, everything would come out right.

But it didn't. It just kept on getting worse.

The ninth day of the trial was the hardest. That was when Alex's parents gave their evidence. They both worked, the father as a bus driver and the mother at the snack counter of the Muswell Hill Everyman. Two or three nights out of every week, depending on the vagaries of their shifts, Alex came home to an empty flat, warmed up his own dinner in the microwave and put himself to bed. The night of the fire was one of those times.

"So Alex was alone that night?"

"Yes." Tears ran down Mrs Beech's red, scrunched face. "I'll never forgive myself. Not ever."

Alone. And most likely asleep when the smoke started pouring up through the floorboards of his bedroom. He woke up already choking to death. He might have made it out of the flat, but either he couldn't find his way in the suffocating pall, or he was just too weak from the smoke damage to get that far. He crawled into the polythene playhouse that was still in his room although he was too old for it now and never played in it. He died curled up on the floor, the molten plastic weeping white-hot tears on to his exposed flesh.

That was where the prosecution rested, more or less. The defence did their best, but Jess was briefing against them now. Her memories of the fire agreed on every point with the scenario the Crown's lawyers had so eloquently and persuasively laid out. She told the truth, and damned herself.

She'd been moved out of the Whittington by this time into the remand wing at HM Prison Winstanley. The cell was half the size of her room at the hospital, but Jess liked it better. Nobody came near her. Nobody saw her. She was sinking into herself, like someone sinking into quicksand in an old movie. She didn't welcome interruptions to that process. Well, maybe *one* interruption. But Brenda was ill. She'd been taken into hospital a week before Jess for multiple herniated discs, and she was still there. Still more or less unable to move. She couldn't attend the trial and she couldn't visit, but she'd written a dozen or more letters to Jess to tell her to be brave, to have faith in herself. That was Aunt Brenda's universal prescription, and Jess loved her for it. It implied that there was something there to have faith in.

She was on suicide watch. Impassive guards watched her closely, like priests, for any signs of incipient despair.

And she had considered suicide. She'd thought about it lots of times, in the way of someone taking stock of all their options. But leaving aside the hurt it would cause to Brenda, it would be so hard to do. She would have to think of something in the bare, featureless cell that could be turned into an implement. She would have to get past her own instincts and her own cowardice. And she would have to do it before the guards noticed what she was up to and came running to stop her. There was no way. If there was a way, they would already have thought of it and put a stop to it.

On the eleventh day, she argued with Brian Pritchard and tried to dismiss him. She wanted to change her plea to guilty. Pritchard told her – almost angry, almost as though he cared – to pull herself together and think it through.

"How can you know whether you're guilty or not if you don't remember anything? Give yourself the benefit of the doubt, and give me a little room to work in." Pritchard had already told Jess his own opinion, which was that John Street's evidence didn't hold together. Street was hiding something, and he should be pressed hard until he gave it up.

Jess let her not-guilty plea stand, but Pritchard didn't get his wish. He started his very robust cross-examination of John Street at 3 p.m. on day twelve. On day thirteen, Street failed to present himself at court. The skin grafts on his hands had delaminated from the healthy tissue surrounding them and he had had to go back into surgery. Pritchard requested that proceedings be suspended, but he was standing in the path of a juggernaut. By that time, nobody in the courtroom believed that Jess was innocent, least of all Jess herself. The judge ruled that Street's evidence was substantially complete, and that no purpose would be served by a delay. Pritchard glanced at Jess in the dock, saw the resolve in her eyes and let the point go.

The judge's summing-up to the jury was short and to the point. "The Crown's opting to try Jessica Moulson for murder may seem puzzling or contentious to you, given that she never intended to kill Alex Beech. The argument is that she formed the intention to kill *somebody* – her partner, John Adam Street – and therefore that she cannot offer in mitigation the fact that she killed somebody else. Her actions, if you accept that they were her actions, led directly to the wished-for outcome, except that the fire she set consumed the wrong life. There are a great many legal precedents for calling Alex Beech's death an accidental manslaughter rather than a willed murder. But changes to the Police and Criminal Evidence Act in its most recent incarnation allow the court to frame it as a murder. That is not a paradox. It is the law as it now stands."

The jury stayed out for the whole of one day and part of the next, but when they came back the verdict was unanimous. Guilty.

Jess was way ahead of them, as far as that went. When the terrible word was spoken, her first thought was, What took you so long?

4

Brian Pritchard came to Jess's remand cell to say goodbye. She was allowed to receive visitors in her cell because her injuries put her in the category of disabled prisoner. The lawyer sat in the cell's only chair while his clerk, Levine, had to stand.

Jess was lying on her bunk. She didn't try to get up. She felt at this stage as though even a slight movement like that was more of a commitment to life than she wanted to make. She was conscious of Levine's eyes on her the whole time, except when she looked back at him. Then his gaze would shoot away in a random direction. Pritchard hardly looked at her at all: just the occasional glance, after which his eyes would go back to the floor or to his own hands, folded in his lap.

"For the record," he told her, "I still think we could have won."

"Really?" Jess asked tonelessly.

"Yes, Ms Moulson, really. With a different jury. With Street chained to the witness stand. With you in a different frame of mind."

Jess couldn't sympathise with his regrets. She had none of her own, at least as far as the verdict went. It was hard even to be patient with him. "If justice was served, where's the problem?" she demanded.

Pritchard tutted. "Justice? Justice is even more problematic than truth. It's an emergent property of a very complicated system."

"I don't know what that means," Jess said wearily.

She was trying to shut the conversation down before it got started, but Pritchard clearly wanted her to understand. He raised his hand, tilting his flat palm to left and right. "It means that it's neither an ingredient in the pie nor the pie itself. It's the smell that rises up out of the pie if you've cooked it right. We don't aim for justice, Ms Moulson. We perform our roles and justice happens. You didn't perform your role very well, if you don't mind my saying so."

Jess thought she was done with emotion in the same way she was done with words, but anger surged inside her and she couldn't push it down. Pritchard seemed to blame her for the outcome of the trial – as though everything she'd said and done had been intended purely to inconvenience him. To a lawyer, everything was sideways on and skewed by parallax. There was no point in trying to make him understand how simple this was to her. But the words came out of her anyway.

"I killed a child."

"You don't know that," Pritchard said.

"I do know it. They proved it. And Alex . . ." That was as far as she got. His name dragged her under, and she had to fight for air. The clerk, Levine, took a step towards her, but there was nothing he could do besides stand there and look concerned.

As an addict, she'd lived for so long in a place where nothing mattered, where she had no anchor. If there was any real feeling in her life at all, it had been that tenuous connection, that futile compassion for the scrawny kid on the stairs who'd barely spoken to her. Killing John would have been bearable. Understandable. Killing Alex Beech was a different thing altogether. There was no coming back from that. She wouldn't even want to live in a world where you could come back from that.

"Pending your appeal, Ms Moulson," Pritchard said, "I'd like you to take it as a working assumption that *nothing* has been proved yet."

"I'm not making an appeal."

Another gesture, this time waving the inconvenient words away. "Well, I believe you'll change your mind on that, once you've got past this current crisis of self-loathing. You haven't seen Fellside yet."

Fellside was the titan prison up in Yorkshire to which she was now being sent, freeing the remand cell at Winstanley for its next resident. Jess knew nothing about the place apart from its name. Unlike Wormwood Scrubs, say, or Dartmoor, or Pentonville, it was a name that carried no associations for her.

"Is Fellside so terrible?" she asked Pritchard, trying for an ironic tone.

"All prisons are terrible," Pritchard answered with po-faced seriousness. "High-security prisons are generally more terrible than the rest. And private prisons are the worst of all. Profit and public service make very bad bedfellows."

He told her a lot more about Fellside – explaining why, to him, it did count as an especially terrible place. Jess barely listened.

"I'll be fine," she assured him. If Fellside was terrible, Fellside was where she belonged.

Pritchard picked at a loose thread on his jacket, his mouth tugging down at the corners. "It's your decision in any event," he said. "I can't lodge an appeal against your wishes. But it's my duty as your legal adviser to tell you that you have excellent grounds for an appeal and it would be a mistake not to lodge one."

"I think my biggest mistake was to let you represent me," Jess said. She was being rude to make him leave, him and his last-puppy-in-the-pet-shop-window clerk, but it didn't have any immediate effect.

"We're not obliged to like one another, Ms Moulson," the lawyer said. "I'm your legal representative, not your friend. And I'm aware that you didn't choose me. But I'll fulfil my role as I see it until such time as you discharge me from—"

"You're fired," Jess said. "Thank you. For everything. But now you need to go away."

"That's not a decision to make on the spur of the moment," Pritchard observed.

"I'm not making it on the spur of the moment. I made it when I saw you in court. I don't want you to be my lawyer any more. If I decide to make an appeal, I'll go with someone else. A different firm. I won't use you."

Pritchard gave a heavy sigh. He stood, still calm but a little on his dignity. "Well then," he said, "I believe that concludes my business here. But please let me know if you change your mind."

"I won't."

Levine knocked on the door. He was still darting glances at her. Pritchard bowed his head like a man in prayer as he waited in silence for the guard to come and let them out.

After they were gone, Jess lay very still on the bunk with her eyes closed, trying not to panic. She'd thrown away her parachute deliberately: she didn't want to be tempted to try to use it. But it was still frightening to lie there in the dark and feel so very much alone.

5

Throughout this time, Jess's sleep was still disturbed. Whenever she closed her eyes, she felt her tiny cell dissolve away, leaving her lying out in the open in a place that was vast and endless. An unseen multitude moved in front of her closed eyelids: shadows so faint you could barely see them, but so many that they coalesced into an endless darkness. At the limits of her vision, everything broke up into turbulence and chaos.

And still there were the voices. The whispers that had troubled her at the hospital were louder than ever now. She had always assumed they were talking about her, but when she could actually make out the words, she didn't feature in them at all. They were fragments of wishes, regrets, laments.

I shouldn't have
if he
my only
never even saw

Jess's dreamscape contained no actual dreams. The last time she'd dreamed anything she could remember on waking, she must have been six or seven years old. But now her troubled sleep was strewn with the jagged shards of other people's broken lives.

It was a punishment her subconscious mind had picked out for her, and she knew she deserved it, but it wrought badly on her nerves.

She had one other visitor at Winstanley: her Aunt Brenda, who was to all intents and purposes her only living relative. Her father was out there somewhere, but in so many ways Barry really didn't count. Brenda came in on two sticks, looking way too big in the narrow cell. The chair creaked ominously as she lowered herself into it. She brought fruit and chocolates, as though Jess was still in hospital rather than in jail, and apologised for not coming sooner.

"There were reporters on my lawn," she said. "Lots and lots of them. I didn't want to go out and talk to them about you, so I hunkered down and waited."

Brenda didn't bother to mention the other factor – that her surgery had left her still in pain and about as mobile as the average barnacle. She looked older and a lot more tired than when Jess had seen her last, her hair showing streaks of white at the sides and her shoulders slightly stooped. The injury to her back had taken a lot out of her, and the surgery had taken even more.

"It's okay," Jess said, hugging her with great care. "I'm glad you're here now." Brenda's friendship, Brenda's love were precious things to her, and all the more because they weren't built on any closeness between Brenda and Jess's mother, Paula. The two sisters had drifted out of touch a long time before Paula died, mostly because of arguments about Barry. *You should kick him out. Change the locks. Tell the police the next time he comes around.* Brenda took no prisoners and asked for no quarter.

And presumably she had also had to work through her own feelings about her niece accidentally killing an innocent kid. But she tried not to bring that up, the same way you might avoid the word "cancer" in a cancer ward.

"How are you coping?" she asked instead.

"Not all that well," Jess admitted. She told Brenda about her bad dreams. The whispers in the dark and the sense that she wasn't alone.

31

"Like your nightwalks," Brenda said. Her face creased with concern.

"My what?"

"Your nightwalks. When you were little. Don't you remember?"

"No, I really don't. Wait, yes. Do you mean all that crazy stuff I did with Tish?"

Tish had been her imaginary friend. They had wandered together through lots of half-baked fantasy landscapes based on *Where the Wild Things Are*, *One Monster After Another* and the Faraway Tree stories. Jess had laboured hard on those adventures, working out the details while she was still awake and trying to carry them with her over the threshold as she dozed off.

Brenda winced visibly. It seemed her back was still giving her problems. "No, no," she said. "Not Tish. I meant the other times. When you said you could walk into our dreams."

"I don't remember that at all," Jess said.

"Oh, you were adamant about it. When your mum asked for details, you told her you'd seen her on a big ship. She asked you what she was doing on the ship and you said she was shooting a bird with a bow and arrow."

"That's from *The Ancient Mariner*."

"Yes, it is." Brenda nodded. "And you had never read that poem. You were only six years old. But Paula was reading it for her Open University course."

"Then I must have heard her reading it out loud."

"Perhaps you did. But she was a little shaken up all the same because she'd had a dream about it that night. It was just a coincidence, obviously, but it really did look as though you'd managed to open up her head somehow and take a look inside."

"I don't remember any of that."

"Well, it happened. And then a few weeks later, when you were staying the night at my house, you did it again. You told me you'd seen me dancing with Gene Kelly."

"Had we just watched *Singin' in the Rain* by any chance?"

Brenda laughed. "We'd watched it a month or so earlier, so I

32

suppose that was a lot less spooky. You used to visit me a lot back then. I don't know why I dreamed about Gene Kelly that night though. Maybe we talked about him, and that was why he was on both our minds. But then there were your angels."

"My angels?"

"They stood around your bed at night, you said."

"Angels stood around my bed?"

"Well, no, it wasn't exactly that, was it? You had to go and visit them. That was how it worked. They lived in what you called the Other Place. Which was like the seaside except that it was all on fire."

Jess felt a slight tremor at the back of her mind: a tectonic shift which was small only by virtue of being very far away. She had no recollection of seeing these things but she remembered talking about them. The words had a tautness to them. Some big, submerged memory hung below them like the weight on a plumb line.

"Mum got angry," she ventured.

"Well, she got scared, I think. This all seemed very real to you, and you were talking about it all the time. About the angels, and about being able to see what was going on in other people's heads when they were asleep. You did sound very convincing, I must say. You said you kept losing your way and you were scared you might get stuck there one night in this Other Place. None of us knew what to make of it. Paula took you to a child psychologist in the end. NHS. You were on the list for ages before the appointment came through. With . . . no, I don't remember her name."

Jess did. It had bobbed to the surface of her mind, unlooked for and unwelcome. "Carter. It was Dr Carter."

Brenda tapped her forehead with one finger, admonishing her poor memory. "That's right. She saw you loads of times. She was saying at first you might have a . . . what was it? An incipient psychosis. But she changed her tune. In the end she just said you had a really active imagination and there was nothing to worry about."

33

Jess remembered the doctor now: a smiling, grandmotherly type, with her hair in a sugarloaf bun, but she asked about a million questions and the smile stayed on her face no matter what her voice did, so in the end it didn't mean anything.

She remembered lying. Hiding. Saying what she thought would go down best. Because every kid knows when they're in trouble just by reading the faces of the adults around them. Every kid gets an instinct for when to lie low. She gave her name, rank and serial number. She said she was okay. She said she made it all up. How could the sea catch fire? That was just crazy talk!

All the while gauging from Dr Carter's face how this was going down. Triangulating into a sweet spot defined by nods of the head and minute variations in the intensity of that everlasting smile. Dr Carter's final diagnosis was that Jess's night-time escapades were signs of mental health rather than mental illness. "When a child's life hits a crisis of any kind," she told Paula Moulson briskly, "they've got to have a refuge from it. Or if not a refuge, then a workaround. I'm not prying, but has there been something like that going on for Jess recently? Some sort of upheaval?"

Paula just nodded. She'd married an upheaval, and he was home right then on an extended visit.

"Well then," said Dr Carter with an expansive shrug. "You should be thankful that Jess is able to play these conflicts out in her mind rather than in reality. This night world of hers seems to be a place of turbulence and confusion – an internalisation of those same forces as they appear in her daily life. The imagination is a plastic power, Mrs Moulson. A *shaping* power. We make the things we need. And then when we don't need them any more, we set them aside. All you have to do is to let that happen."

In other words, Jess was off the hook. She went home, got into bed and pulled the covers up over her head.

She trained herself out of dreaming, because every time she dreamed, she woke up in a panic. It was a sad time. For one thing, she remembered missing Tish very badly. But more dreams meant more sessions with Dr Carter, more interrogations, more time being smiled at. For months she woke up four or five times a night, dragging herself from the Other Place by main force.

Then she didn't have to any more. The dreams stopped coming. She slept with her head under the covers all the way into her teens, woke up remembering nothing. And the angels . . .

The angels went away and didn't come back. Tish didn't come back either. Maybe they all just got tired of waiting for Jess to come out and play. She could barely remember now what her nightly journeys had been like. They had been very real to her at the time, she knew that much. But she'd forgotten almost all of this. She remembered Tish, but mainly as a story she'd been told about herself rather than an actual presence. She'd been very young, after all. When you're a kid, pretty much anything can heal over and leave no scar.

Aunt Brenda changed the subject. "You were in the papers every day," she said. "They were coming out with terrible things about you, Jess. Some of these people who call themselves reporters . . ."

She went off on a rant about journalistic ethics, which Jess knew was intended as a show of solidarity. The substantive point – Alex – couldn't be contested, but it was some comfort to know that her aunt was on her side and wanted to lift her mood.

Finally Brenda put her hand on Jess's arm. "It was the drugs," she said. "It wasn't you. You're not capable of hurting people, Jess. Not on purpose."

But Jess knew she was. Everyone was. It was basic human kit.

"I'll come and see you," Brenda promised. "Up there. It's a long way, but I'll come."

"No, you won't," Jess said. "You're not even to try until you're better. But I'd love it if you could write."

"Of course I will. Every week. And as soon as I'm up to making the trip, you'll see me there. No arguments."

They embraced and Brenda left, trying not to let Jess see that she was crying.

I've let her down so badly, Jess thought. *There were never very many people who were willing to think well of me, and I smacked them all in the face.*

It felt right then as though that was what she'd been doing all her life.

6

Jess went to sleep still thinking about those old nightwalks, those dead angels. Perhaps that was why, for the first time since her childhood excursions, she dreamed. Real dreams, not bodiless whispers. Dreams where she walked and moved, saw and did things.

In the most coherent of the dreams, she was lying right there in the remand cell when her phone started to ring. She looked around for the phone but couldn't find it. She was dimly aware, even in the dream, that her phone was with the rest of her effects in a police lockbox somewhere. It seemed logical, all the same, that it should be trying to make its way back to her.

But she didn't find it in the bed, or on the table, or in the locker (without a lock or even a door) where prisoners were meant to stow their meagre belongings. So she went looking elsewhere. She opened the door of the cell and stepped out – into the lobby of her flat in Muswell Hill.

She climbed the stairs to her own landing, which was dominated by a huge, ugly mirror mounted on the wall directly across from her door. She could see that she was casting no reflection in the mirror, which she took to mean that this was a temporary visit. She wasn't coming home to live just yet.

(It burned down. Didn't it burn down?)

Alex Beech was sitting on the next flight of stairs, in his usual spot. He looked the way he had when she saw him last – or at least, the last time she could remember seeing him. Wearing an Arsenal T-shirt that was too big for him, most likely a hand-me-down, and a pair of denim shorts out of which his spindly legs protruded like the two halves of a wishbone.

Jess plopped herself down next to him and they sat in slightly uneasy silence for a little while. Not perfect silence: the ringing of the phone continued from somewhere very nearby, muted but distinct.

"I'm sorry," Jess said at last. "I'm so sorry, Alex."

Alex didn't answer, or look at her.

"I didn't mean to hurt you," she ventured again. She put a hand on his arm. Or she tried to. Her fingers slid right through him as though he wasn't there.

That was when she realised – with dream logic that came to her fully formed – that she was dead. It wasn't Alex who was burned up in the fire: it was her. And he was still waiting there for her, would wait always, but she would never come.

And that was why her phone was ringing, she suddenly knew. She had told him he could call her. He was doing that right now. If she could find the phone, she could pick up and they could talk, at least. And maybe he could tell her the way back so she could come to him.

She left the boy's side and went into her flat. The door was standing open, the hallway empty. She always left her phone on the bedside table when she slept, and death was a lot like sleep. It seemed that it even came complete with dreams. The ringing got louder and she knew she'd guessed correctly.

When she went into the bedroom, the phone was right there on the table. John was lying in the bed, eyes closed, chest rising and falling in a slow, shallow rhythm. The ringing didn't wake him. The phone couldn't reach into his sleep, his dreams, because it was only meant for Jess.

She reached out to pick it up, but the skin on the back of her neck prickled. Someone was behind her.

She turned slowly, and they were there. Thousands of them. Naked, with their arms at their sides. In order to accommodate them, the room had ceased to be a room. All that was left was the bed and the bedside table and the angle of two walls, standing now on a wide, flat foreshore that stretched as far as her eye could see.

They were almost all women. The few men stood out by contrast. They all had their eyes closed. Their faces mostly wore similar expressions of blank indifference although a few looked sad or troubled. They were not watching Jess: they had no idea that she was there. In fact, she knew, each of them had no idea that any of the others were there. For all each of these women knew, she stood alone. Only Jess could see them all.

As she had seen them when she was a child. Perhaps they had looked like angels to her then simply because they had no clothes on. The only naked bodies she remembered seeing as a little girl were those of Christian saints.

The phone hadn't stopped ringing all this time.

It took an effort to turn her back on the silent assembly, but she did. She picked up.

"Alex?"

Just static on the line. No voice that Jess could make out, although the crackle and hiss rose and fell with the inflections of a voice.

She tried again. "Alex?"

There was a voice there, but it was so far down she could barely make it out. She closed her eyes. That was dangerous, given that the whole place might burst into flames at any moment, but it felt like it was vitally important to take this call.

"Who's there?" she asked.

"Who's there?" someone else asked at the other end of the line. Not an echo. She was almost able to identify the voice.

"It's Jess," she said. "What do you want?"

The voice answered but the static spiked and peaked right over the words, drowning out most of them. She heard *fire* and *lost* and something that might have been *a frame* but was probably *afraid*.

"You don't have to be afraid," Jess said. She was still thinking that this might be Alex, although it didn't sound like him. "I'm here if you need me. I'll always be here."

"How?" the other voice whispered. The static had cleared, but the volume had dropped away with it to the limit of what she could hear.

"How?" Jess repeated. "What do you mean?"

"How . . . ?"

Then silence.

Then, "How did . . . ?"

A storm of static, so abrupt it seemed that the ether was trying to snatch the words away before they reached her.

But they did.

"How did I get here?"

The voice was hers. She was talking to herself. But that didn't mean she had an answer.

7

How did I get here?

It was impossible to say.

Unless by hating something you straightaway started to turn into it. As though your hate was a sort of magnetic field, turning you around like a compass needle, dragging you into a new shape like iron filings.

Jess's father crashed and raged in the maze of her childhood memories like an intermittent minotaur. "Where's my fucking coat? Did you take money out of my pocket? Did you hide my shoes? What's the fucking kid looking at? Are you telling her lies about me?"

Addiction. Addiction was the real monster here. And young Jess knew, watching her parents, that you could get addicted to anything. Barry Moulson was addicted to alcohol, and Paula Moulson née Ketterbridge was addicted to him. It didn't matter how many times Baz turned up, took command of Paula's pay packet, raided their pathetic savings, pawned the TV and then hit the road again. The next time he appeared, Paula's arms would still be wide open.

In school and then in college (maths and physics, combined honours), Jess steered a course as far away from all that bullshit as she could get.

"You want to smoke some weed?"

No.

"Pop an E before we go into the club?"

Actually, I don't.

"The sex will be way better if you snort some bloom."

Thanks but no thanks.

The first sip, the first drag, the first pill . . . that might be all it would take. Better not to start than to start and never stop. "It's okay," her friend Kit said to her at the end of her first year at Durham. "Everyone thinks you're a frigid prude, but they're way too scared to say it out loud so it all balances out, you know?"

But it got seriously unbalanced in year two. That was when her mother got sick. Not-ever-getting-better sick. Sick with cancer – first of the liver, then of the everything. Seriously? Barry floats his organs in sixty per cent proof, and Paula's liver goes? Clearly there was no God, no justice, nobody at the switchboard. The universe was a badly written soap opera where every plot twist strained credibility just that little bit further.

Jess went to her pastoral supervisor, explained the situation and dropped out of uni.

"You don't have to do this," her mother protested. "I'm not an invalid, Jess!"

But you will be, Jess thought. And in any case, their time together had become something that could be counted. That needed to be counted. She didn't say any of that. What she said was, "Durham is six hours away, Mum, and the train ticket costs ninety quid even with a railcard. And I can pick up again from right where I was. I want to be with you, just until you're all right again."

The huge lie making it impossible for Paula to protest against the smaller one. They hugged and cried, and nothing more was said.

In fact it took three years for Paula to die. Four rounds of chemo, three operations, an endless drip-drip-drip of bad news followed by worse news followed by outright disasters. Jess had never regretted her decision. She was with her mother at the end and her being there made a difference. Everything Paula did – moving, talking, blinking, breathing – brought a little gasp of pain, but she didn't die alone and she didn't die afraid. She went into the dark with Jess holding her hand. Holding it so tightly that for hours afterwards it felt as though they were still touching. Still together.

So no regrets, ever. But she couldn't just pick up where she'd left off. This was the second time around so she wasn't entitled to a student loan. She would have to save up the money for her tuition fees and her living expenses – a tall order when the economy was tanking. She got a job at Half the Sky, a feminist-slash-ecological bookshop on Caledonian Road, and started to put a little by.

Broke her collarbone in an accident at the shop involving a stepladder.

And made a brand-new friend.

"This is about managing the pain," the doctor told her. "Oxycodone is a very powerful analgesic, so it's not to be abused. These are controlled-release tablets. You take them twice a day, and they sustain what we call a resting level of the drug in your system throughout the next twelve hours. We'll review in a week's time."

Where have you been all my life, oxycodone?

Jess was in ecstasy. Some of that was not feeling the physical pain from her injury. The rest was not feeling anything else. There was an old ache inside her that forgot to ache when she was high.

She lived on oxy and fresh air for three months. But then the prescription ran out and she crashed. It was impossible to hide, like a disfiguring illness. Like a bereavement. "I need your mind to be here as well as your body, Jess," her boss, Susan, warned her. "No point turning up for work if you're just going to sit there." "You need me to fix you up?" her colleague Nicola asked. "Seriously, what do you need? I can get it."

Nicola Saunders was only at Half the Sky one day a week. The rest of the time she worked in the pharmacy of a private hospital. "You want oxy," she assured Jess, "all you've got to do is ask. There's no need to suffer."

There was no need to suffer. Money would buy her perfect happiness.

"Not that I'm doing it for the money," Nicola said. "I'm doing it for you." She took the money anyway though, and her prices went up on a regular basis.

"You want to try something stronger? Drop one of these just as the oxy kicks in – you won't believe where it takes you."

Jess stuck to the devil she knew. "I don't care about the thrill," she told Nicola. "I'm just in a bad place right now, and it helps."

"Oh sure, I get that. It's temporary relief, absolutely. It's not, you know, a lifestyle thing. You can always stop."

And Jess knew she could. Any time. But somehow at the moment of decision she found herself popping a tab anyway. And the moment of decision was coming on her with a quickening tempo. In the aftermath of a fix, she felt a blissed-out calm. A few hours later she started to get ragged around the edges. Bad nerves gave way to irritation, and irritation was the tip of an iceberg that shelved off steeply towards gnawing anger for anything that was between her and her next hit.

Barry's voice came back to her. "Let's open another bottle. The party's just getting started. Come on, Paula, name me one single thing that looks better when you're sober!"

That was what gave her the strength, in the end, to kick the habit. She knew that dance so well. It had been part of her life for as long as she could remember, not constant, but refreshed and rediscovered whenever Daddy came calling.

She fought her way out of the trough. Not cold turkey or anything like it. She eased off slowly over the space of a couple of months, buying the same amount of the drug from Nicola every week and measuring her progress by how much of each blister pack ended up in the bin.

She got clean. It was the hardest thing she'd ever done.

Then at one of Nicola's parties, she met John Street.

And finally took delivery of the disaster her whole life had been preparing her for.

8

Jess woke to find herself already sitting up, her heart hammering. The dream was gone, the normal world was back. But only up to a point.

She knew that the normal world was a dream too. You could wake up from it any time you liked.

They had taken her belt and her shoelaces. They had fastened a thick plastic cover over the light fitting so that she couldn't smash it and expose the wires. They had fixed a camera to the ceiling of her cell so she could be monitored for her own good whenever the authorities saw fit.

But there was one door they couldn't lock. Their jurisdiction ended at the surface of her skin. As long as she could kill herself without any props, tools or external assistance, there wasn't a damn thing they could do to stop her.

And she could, of course.

It was basic human kit.

PART TWO

THE HARDEST TIME
TO BE ALIVE

9

Fellside prison was a private entity, wholly owned by a security company that went by the name of *N*-fold. *N*-fold had only just climbed on board the correctional bandwagon, and its board of directors was very mindful of the PR implications of their latest prisoner. While the paperwork was still in process, they went into conclave with an extremely select and highly expensive group of human rights lawyers. This was two full weeks into Moulson's hunger strike, which she'd started in the remand cells at Winstanley right after her conviction. The media had got wind of it two or three days in and made a mighty noise about it, embellishing their accounts with choice titbits which had to have come from one of the remand wing guards or trusties.

Then on the morning of Moulson's transfer from Winstanley, the directors sent their in-house expert up to the prison on a fast train out of King's Cross to tell the governor, Save-Me Scratchwell, what his options were. She told him they were limited.

"We've looked at this from a lot of different angles," she explained. "And we've taken legal advice from top people in the field. We've decided to let Ms Moulson die. That's going to be the most straightforward course and, from a legal point of view, the most easily defensible."

The governor had come by his nickname because of his evangelical zeal. And being a religious man as well as a company-owned one, he was deeply divided about this whole Moulson situation. He was also frankly unimpressed with the legal expert, who dressed like a fashion plate and looked as though she was barely out of law school.

"Just let her die?" he echoed. "Really? Surely in today's world there are interventions. Regimes . . ."

"There are the same interventions there always were," the expert told him. "The nutritional mix and the delivery systems may have been refined in various ways, but forced feeding is still basically putting a tube into a person's stomach – either through the nostril or directly through the torso – so you can pour something down it. And it's still illegal."

"But if it's to save a life, it's got to be justified, hasn't it? I believe I read in connection with Guantanamo Bay that they have a policy of—"

"Yes, they do, but it's illegal there too. There's broad agreement that it's a form of torture. International agreement. Since 1975, if someone tries to starve themselves, and they're of sound mind, you've got to let them do it. The only way you'd get away with force-feeding them is if you could prove their judgement was impaired."

Scratchwell thought that through until he found the unexcluded middle.

"Which very definitely is not going to happen," the expert said as he opened his mouth to speak. "If you were to get a psychiatric evaluation done on Jess Moulson now, and if it gave even the smallest indication that she was in an abnormal state of mind, it would cast doubt on the guilty verdict. Her solicitor would call a mistrial and the Crown Prosecution Service would get very seriously upset. Frankly, governor, it would be an embarrassment for us. And the timing would be extremely awkward.

50

We're currently negotiating a new raft of government contracts, all of which depend on our being seen to do a good job here."

Scratchwell was starting to feel really unhappy about all this. It had the look of a no-win situation. "But if Moulson dies here at Fellside – on my watch, so to speak – surely I'm in breach of my duty of care. Especially if I didn't take any steps to make absolutely sure she's in her right mind. What if we're sued? What if I'm charged with manslaughter?"

"That's vanishingly unlikely. And you'd win the case."

"If a burglar can sue a householder when he falls through a skylight . . ."

"Bodine versus Enterprise High School. The burglar didn't win; the school settled. And that was in America."

"You said there was international agreement . . ." Scratchwell began.

"On force-feeding, governor, not on every possible wrinkle of the law of tort. Believe me when I tell you that you can't be sued for your failure to do something you'd have been legally barred from doing in the first place."

The expert raised both hands, miming the scales of a balance. "On the other hand, if you respect Moulson's wishes and allow her to die, you can devote yourself to making her comfortable over that time, and you can talk openly to reporters about exactly what steps you're taking to lessen her suffering. That may sound cynical, but I suggest you think of it as the lesser evil. You can fight Moulson or you can work with her, and if you work with her you can do some visible good.

"Of course, the moment when she dies is still going to be a critical time for you, and there could be control issues."

"You mean riots."

"We can't rule them out. Everyone knows a death is the perfect inciting incident. But we've quantified the risk as low on the basis of three factors. One: Moulson killed a child. So the emotions stirred up by her death probably won't include outrage or a sense of injustice. Particularly since – factor two – it's suicide. She wants this."

"And what's factor three?"

The expert shrugged. "Nobody ever gets to meet her," she told Scratchwell. "You don't release her into gen pop at all. She'll most likely be dead in two months anyway."

The governor boggled a little at this sting in the tail. Isolating a prisoner pre-emptively could usually only be done when there was an immediate security risk which outweighed the prisoner's rights to humane treatment. It was a breach of a great many different statutory regulations and guidelines. "Solitary?" he exclaimed.

"I thought you didn't use that word here. But no. I'm talking about medical withdrawal, not punitive. Your infirmary has a quarantine unit, doesn't it? You put Moulson in there. If she's serious about dying, she'll soon be needing continuous medical supervision. You'll just be starting that process early. It's all about keeping a low profile, governor. The main aim is not to excite commentary or prurient attention any more than is necessary."

Scratchwell's uncertainty still showed on his face. "You shouldn't overthink this," the expert advised him. "Moulson's needs are best met by accepting the choice she's made and facilitating it."

"Facilitating her death?"

"Absolutely."

10

Jess was transferred from Winstanley to Fellside by private ambulance. The accommodations on board were so luxurious, she almost expected an in-flight movie.

She didn't eat, of course, although food was available. But there was a bottle of water by the side of her gurney and another set up in some kind of cradle over her head. The second bottle had a rubber nipple attached to the business end which Jess could reach just by turning her head in case she was too weak to stretch out her hand. She wasn't – not yet. Two weeks into the hunger strike, she could still sit up and even walk a few steps unaided.

There were about a hundred diagnostic devices to measure her vital signs, a remote for the gurney which let her sit up just by pushing a button and three nurses whose whole purpose for being there was to make sure that Jess didn't experience a single moment of discomfort. Two of the nurses had been hired from the same private hospital that provided the ambulance; the third, Patience DiMarta, was a Fellside staffer.

Patience was one half Portuguese, the other half West African, but her accent was broad Yorkshire. She stood a head taller than the agency nurses and ordered them around with an easy authority.

She was brisk and cheerful, not fazed by the weirdness of the assignment. She told Jess that her preferred way of working was no nonsense on either side. That deal would hold as long as Jess behaved herself, and would lapse if she made any trouble.

"I haven't eaten any solid food in fourteen days," Jess pointed out, her voice weak and a little slurred. "I won't make trouble. I don't even remember the recipe for trouble."

Patience nodded approval. "Then we should be fine," she said genially. "You've probably noticed we've got a guard right here too. That's Ms Andrea Corcoran, and even though you're weak and sick, she'll beat you like a carpet if you misbehave."

The guard was sitting on a fold-down seat at the rear of the ambulance. Stocky and red-headed, she looked like a bouncer at the door of a nightclub. Except that she had a Jilly Cooper novel in her lap and only looked up from it long enough to acknowledge her name. "Whatever DiMarsBar just said is bollocks," she commented tersely, and went back to the book.

Patience made sure Jess was strapped in, then gave the all-clear to the driver. "D'you want anything to help you sleep?" she asked Jess as the ambulance eased into motion. "It's a long way, and some of the roads once you get up on to the moors are what they call unadopted. That means they're mostly rocks and holes."

"No thanks," Jess said quickly. She didn't relish the prospect of bumps and jolts, but she was already spending half of every day asleep and that was more than enough. Bad dreams weren't a novelty any more, they were her constant companions. Every time she closed her eyes, she'd find herself back in her burning flat looking for Alex, knowing that if she didn't find him in time, he was going to die. Knowing that if she turned her back, those silent women would be waiting there with their closed eyes and their slack, expressionless faces. No. No more sleep, thank you very much.

Apart from the dreams, she felt as though she was getting better rather than worse. The first few days had been terrible. Her stomach had screamed out for what it was being denied, not letting up for a moment. And that physical discomfort had somehow translated into a sense of panic. The walls of the cell had closed in on her. Her heart had raced and stuttered like a stalling car.

But instead of intensifying, those symptoms had faded. Jess didn't even feel hungry now, except in a very abstract sense. She remembered food in the way that you might remember a wonderful holiday from a few years ago. She had bad headaches, it was true. She was as weak as a two-year-old, her breath stank like a dead goat and her muscles ached. All of that was bearable.

It was only the nightmares that really got to her. If she could kick those, dying wouldn't trouble her too much.

Most of the trip was a lot smoother than Patience had suggested. Then once the road did start to get rough and bouncy, the agency nurses released a couple of bolts on the gurney which lifted it up onto shock-absorbers. There was almost no pain.

"It's a pity you can't sit up and look out of the windows," Patience said at one point. "Fellside is quite impressive when you see it from a distance, across the moor. Almost beautiful."

The guard, Corcoran, who'd been reading Jilly Cooper without a break all the way from London, glanced up a second time at this point. Judging by the look on her face, she might be prepared to take issue with that word.

"What's it like close up?" Jess asked.

It was meant as a joke, feeble as it was, but Patience took the question seriously. She thought about it, one eyebrow crooked up a little.

"Different," was all she said.

11

Different was a good word, carefully chosen. Certainly there wasn't much beauty on display when the ambulance doors opened and Jess saw Fellside for the first time from the inside.

The first thing that registered as the gurney was lowered to the ground was the inside of the prison's perimeter wall, rearing high above her. Tangles of razor wire stood on the top of it. They looked a lot like birds' nests, or like birds' nests might look if birds were made of steel and fed their chicks with rivets.

She was in a vehicle bay of some kind. It was a warm day, but the high wall cut off the sun and plunged the whole place into premature evening. She remembered Pritchard telling her that thousands of women lived here, but at least in this corner of Fellside there was total silence. For all Jess could tell, it might be just the five of them left after some inexplicable holocaust had swallowed up the rest of the human race.

"We'll take it from here," Corcoran told the agency nurses. "You swing around by the visitors' gate, drive up to the barrier and show your passes there. There's no going out through this one."

As the ambulance pulled away, the guard turned her attention back to Jess. "Well, since we're back in the Land of Bad Things . . ." she said. She unhooked the handcuffs from her belt and used them to fasten Jess's right wrist to the steel rail of the gurney. It was the first time Jess had been cuffed since her trial. Bile and claustrophobia rose in her throat, but she kept her face expressionless.

"Sorry," Corcoran said – not to Jess but to DiMarta, whose nostrils had flared a little when the cuffs went on.

"Are we good now?" Patience asked with icy politeness.

"We're good," Corcoran said.

The big nurse wheeled the gurney across the bay, out into an open space that allowed Jess to see the prisoner wings for the first time. She could see now that Nurse DiMarta might have a point. The prison's main buildings were tall and graceful, each painted in a different colour of the rainbow. Knowing what those blocks of concrete and glass really represented, Jess felt a weird sense of dislocation. Their prettiness felt like a calculating lie. The smile on the face of the tiger.

DiMarta steered the gurney through a set of double doors into a corridor painted like the main blocks in joyous primaries and pastels. Corcoran walked alongside, her trashy novel now stowed out of sight in one of the many pockets of her uniform. "Do you want me to take a turn with that thing?" she asked – possibly to make up for the handcuffs, which seemed to have rubbed the nurse up the wrong way.

"Oh, and here she comes again," Patience said. "Let me push the trolley. Let me bandage that wound. Let me perform the operation. Demarcation, petal. You'll get me in trouble with the union." Her face was still a little set, but her tone was bantering. If the handcuffs hadn't been forgiven, they weren't going to be an issue between the two women.

They moved Jess through a whole lot of different places, most of which she didn't get much of a look at because she was on her back and staring at the ceiling.

Processing seemed to go on for ever. Jess's civilian clothes and effects, taken from her when she was first signed in at Winstanley, now had to be handed over into the care of the Fellside authorities. The clothes, Jess knew, were the ones she'd been wearing on the night of the fire, so if they were ever given back to her, all she was going to do was to throw them in a bin or finish the job and burn what was left of them. What else was in the bag? Her mobile phone, which she now associated with her bad dreams and never wanted to see again. Keys to the ruined shell of her flat. A wallet full of maxed-out credit cards. A Fossil watch, the glass cracked across from the heat or from some unremembered impact.

All my worldly goods, she thought. Pity I never made a will.

Fellside's induction process didn't bend to accommodate the new inmate's special circumstances. Despite the fact that she was wearing nothing but a hospital gown, Jess was thoroughly frisked. Then she was wheeled into a smaller room, where a female guard put on a pair of latex gloves and gave her a cavity search with the aid of a plastic speculum. They hadn't felt the need to search her bodily orifices at Winstanley: perhaps they'd already done it back at the Whittington Hospital while she was still unconscious. The guard did her best to be gentle, but the humiliation was more or less total. Her right arm pinned in place by the handcuffs, Jess had to lie on her side on the gurney with her pelvis raised and her legs awkwardly spread like a baby having its nappy changed. Except that a nappy change was non-invasive. DiMarta stood by through this process with her muscular arms tightly folded, radiating disapproval.

"You do know she's come in from another prison?" she asked the guard.

"It's standard procedure, Patience."

"It's stupid, that's what it is."

They kept Jess parked in the little room for a while longer. After a few minutes, they wheeled in a TV on a big portable stand and plugged it in. Apparently there was a video all newcomers were meant to watch, and Jess had to watch it, the head end of the gurney ratcheted up to a comfortable forty-five degrees. It showed the view she'd failed to see as she was driven here – the prison from the other side of the moor, perched on the dizzying edge of Sharne Fell with the rock escarpments falling away from the base of its walls like the folds of a dress. The brightly coloured towers of the prisoner blocks rose over the sparse moorland like some lost suburb of Disneyland.

A gravelly, avuncular voice extolled the virtues of the N-fold corporation and its extensive contributions to human happiness. "The Fellside Correctional Facility for Women stands on the edge of the North York Moors National Park, in the valley of the River Leven – a place of great scenic beauty. Against this idyllic backdrop, three thousand women form a community committed to a practical ideal of rehabilitation."

"I hate the voiceover so much," Corcoran said gloomily. "If I ever meet that smarmy bastard, I swear I'll do time for him. Probably right here."

Jess mostly let the words wash over her, but she marvelled at the perfect dislocation of form and content. This was like videos she'd seen for timeshare apartments, full of staged shots that oozed insincerity. Smiling inmates reading books, working in kitchen gardens, turning pots. A craft village behind a fortress wall. *Where do I sign up?*

"Our prisoner wings commemorate women's achievements in a range of fields, from science to politics. Designed by award-winning architect Roger Lawley, they foster a sense of space and freedom rather than confinement. The centrepiece of each building is the commons, an open space of four thousand cubic metres which serves as both a recreation room and an assembly point.

"It's not called that," Corcoran muttered, clearly still resentful about having to sit through the video.

"What?" Jess asked.

"It's not called the commons. Ever. They've all got their own names for it. In Franklin they call it the farmyard. In Elion it's the bucket. In Goodall, where you're going, it's the ballroom."

"Why the ballroom?" Jess queried. She could see that Corcoran wanted to be asked.

"First day the place was open, someone tore a pair of pink pompoms off a hat and threw them down from the fourth-floor walkway. They got stuck in the anti-suicide nets, and someone said they looked like a pair of testicles dangling there. Hence, the ballroom."

The video was showing each of the blocks in turn now in a free-flowing montage of serious but deeply content faces.

"Blackwell wing . . ."

"Butlins," Corcoran translated.

"Curie . . ."

"Cunt House."

"Dietrich . . ."

"Daffy Duck. That's the psychiatric wing."

"Elion . . ."

"Hellhole."

"Franklin . . ."

"Wanklin."

". . . and our maximum-security wing, Goodall."

"The State of Grace."

"That one sounds okay," Jess murmured.

The guard shook her head slowly, leaning forward to turn the sound down as the credits rolled. "You haven't met her yet."

"Haven't met who?"

"It doesn't matter," Corcoran said. "You'll find out."

After that, there was a visit from the governor. Ordinarily Jess would have been taken to his office, Corcoran told her, but the gurney presented logistical problems, so he came to her. He stepped into the room right after the induction video ended, as though he was the next item on the bill, and stood in stiff silence until Corcoran realised what he wanted and relinquished her chair to him.

Governor Scratchwell was a tall, gaunt man with high cheekbones hollowed out underneath, so his face was a visual mnemonic for the prison itself – perched up on a precarious cliff, remote from the world. His welcome speech to Jess, though, was all about

60

engagement. Moral rearmament. The importance of faith in a wide, shallow, almost meaningless sense where the articles of faith never had to be stated. Jess was aware of the governor's unease at being in the same room with her. He seemed to be using the dry, abstract words as bargepoles to fend her off with.

"My door will always be open to you," he assured her. "I want you to believe that the most important barriers here are the ones you've built within yourself, and we will work with you to break them down."

Jess had no idea what that meant, but Scratchwell didn't invite questions. He just made his speech and left.

It seemed that the formalities were finally over. Jess was grateful for that. After the cavity search, she was half afraid she might be due for a cold shower and a delousing.

Instead she was taken up to the infirmary in the service lift, which was as big as a room. Once the lift doors closed, Corcoran took out her key and undid the cuffs.

"Now that it's just us girls," she said.

The infirmary was on the fourth floor of the admin block, and took up more than half of it. It looked and felt like a hospital A & E. White light from overhead strips fell on white tiles and beige linoleum. The only primary colours were in the posters on the walls: WHEN YOU SEE THIS, WASH YOUR HANDS. GET SERIOUS ABOUT YOUR HEART. CROSSING YOUR FINGERS WON'T STOP GONORRHOEA.

The reception area was also a consulting room. A meds cart was parked against one wall and steel-fronted cabinets lined two more. Handwritten sticky labels listed the contents in a neat, meticulous script that was way too small for Jess to decipher.

The place was deserted. DiMarta looked all around as though she expected it not to be. She frowned.

"Can I leave you to it?" Corcoran asked.

"Did you look at the paperwork?" DiMarta shot back, answering a question with a question. "This prisoner is high security." Glancing at Jess, she added, "Sorry, petal, but you are. Sylvie was meant to

61

be here, but I suppose she was called away. My shift ends in ten minutes and I can't stay on without a chit. You'll have to hang on until she comes back." DiMarta had seemed pretty cavalier about the rules earlier, but apparently this one actually meant something.

Corcoran shrugged. "Still got my book," she said. "I'll survive. If Dennis comes after me though, you better back me up."

DiMarta wheeled Jess through into the main ward (not the quarantine ward, as the governor had instructed – that memo had got lost in transit somewhere) and transferred her quickly and expertly from the gurney to a bed. She wrote up Jess's chart, offered her some pain relief again, was refused again and made her exit.

Corcoran had stood in the doorway this whole while. She retreated back into the reception area now, after telling Jess to call if she needed anything. "Not that I can give you anything. But I can stand around and commiserate."

She pulled the door to, and things went really quiet. Most rooms have some sound in them, a hum of air conditioning or gurgling in the pipes, which you're not aware of until silence lets it through. The infirmary was truly silent. It was restful at first: Jess closed her eyes and tried to sleep.

But she opened them again almost at once. She had a weird sense that somebody had just come into the room. The silence was different now: it had become the non-sound of somebody standing very still, holding their breath.

"Hello?" Jess murmured. She thought it might be Corcoran coming in to check on her, but if it wasn't, if she was imagining things, she didn't want to drag the guard away from her book and look like an idiot. Nobody answered.

But she couldn't settle after that. The feeling that she was being watched stayed with her. It was a little like the feeling Jess associated with her dreams – except that this wasn't a multitude, it was only a single presence. And unlike the dream women, it was definitely watching her. The sense of focused attention was disconcerting, almost claustrophobic. And it intensified the longer it went on. She didn't know how much more of it she could bear. She was going to have to sit up, although she wasn't sure she had the strength to do that. She was going to have to see for herself that she was alone.

But the spell was broken very abruptly. A commotion started up in the reception area outside. Raised voices. A woman sobbing, another telling her to hold still. Corcoran's voice said, "Holy fucking Jesus!" and the crying rose to a wail before it fell away into half-vocalised moans.

Nothing after that for a long while. Then Corcoran held the door open and a woman was led through, supported by a nurse who wasn't DiMarta. "You've got some company," Corcoran told Jess. She said it lightly, but her mouth was set in a tight line.

The woman the nurse was supporting was the first Fellside inmate Jess had met. She was a strange sight in a lot of ways. She wore a bright yellow tracksuit, cinched at the waist with a wide black belt that was sewn into the fabric all around. Her face was pale but suffused with red blotches, her short blonde hair plastered to her cheeks with sweat. She walked with a slight stoop, head ducked below her rounded shoulders. She looked a fair bit younger than Jess, but her face was etched with old traumas and tragedies. Her hands, held out stiffly in front of her, were encased in massive boxing gloves.

No, not boxing gloves. They were thick bandages wrapped many times around something rigid, probably splints, that kept the hands flat.

The woman was on the short side, but the nurse was shorter still and as thin as a rake. Her pinched face showed she was carrying most of the weight here. She walked the woman past Jess's bed to the next one along, where she laid her burden down. She pulled the blankets back and brought a cotton gown from a cupboard.

"You want me to help you undress?" she asked, still a little breathless. She hadn't looked at Jess up to that point, but now she

63

did – with a slightly aggrieved expression as though to say, "You see how hard other people have it?"

"It still hurts," the blonde woman whimpered.

"The painkillers haven't kicked in yet, McBride. It will get better. You want me to help you undress?"

"I – I think I'll just lie down for now." The blonde woman rolled on to her side and curled into a ball, but with her hands held out so they didn't touch the rest of her body.

"Okay then," the nurse said. She transferred her attention to Jess. There was a second's pause before she turned, a sort of gathering of herself. "What about you?" she demanded. "Any problems here?"

Jess shook her head, carefully and slowly, because sudden movements made it ache.

"Good," the nurse said, flexing her wrists like someone who'd just come out of one stand-up fight and was about to wade into another. "Let's not have any." She stepped back through the double doors, which swung to behind her.

"Sleep well, ladies," Corcoran said, and followed her out.

The blonde woman moaned low in her throat.

12

Shannon McBride's big mistake had been to rip off the Q box.

It wasn't that there was anything worth having in there. There really wasn't. It was stuff that had been brought in as gifts for Fellside inmates but had then fallen into a sort of unofficial escrow either because the inmate in question had been released or because the visitor's name had dropped off the approved list.

None of that really mattered. What mattered was that by custom and practice, the stuff in that box was earmarked for Harriet Grace. Grace sat at the top of Goodall wing's food chain where most illegal enterprises were concerned, and she policed her borders with a certain judicious fanaticism. So nobody ever touched the Q box, even though it sat out in the open in the visitors' room where a lot of people could get to it.

Grace had no personal use for the tawdry little gewgaws in the box – a sorry flotsam of hair slides, chocolate bars, shampoo bottles, out-of-date magazines and homemade cakes. Her credit at the commissary was infinite and her cell was a cave of wonders. But there was a principle at stake, and when Mr Devlin, the shift supervisor, told her that the box had been rifled, she took it personally. "Get me a name, Dennis," she told him. "I'm not letting this lie."

The Devil was in Grace's pocket, and in a number of places that were even more compromising than that, so he went away and did as he was told. He got his snitches to ask around, not about stuff that had been stolen – the whisper line usually shied away from fingering people for specific crimes – but about stuff that had been given. Who was suddenly being way too generous? Who felt snubbed because she'd seen some cool stuff being handed out and hadn't got a share?

Shannon McBride's name popped up like underdone toast. An impromptu search turned up about two thirds of the stolen bits and pieces stowed in all kinds of random places around her cell. In her locker, under her mattress, inside her mattress, in a scraped-out place under a loose tile – everywhere.

Devlin wrote up the theft in the daybook and told McBride to expect a spell of punitive withdrawal, which meant solitary. That was the euphemism introduced by Governor Scratchwell as part of a drive to improve morale by giving unpleasant things innocuous names. But solitary was the least of McBride's problems now.

Grace didn't sit on the matter for long. That was never her way. At six the same evening, the ground-floor corridor was closed off at both ends, and the Devil sent the duty officer off to the fourth floor's solitary cells to check all the locks and light circuits for an invented fault.

And Grace held court, right there in front of everyone, in the big open space at the heart of the building's ground floor. The ballroom.

A lot of people there felt that McBride deserved some kind of comeuppance. All the same, they were nervous. They read Grace's mood and it was volatile in the extreme. It was never safe to be around her at times like this, and if it hadn't been a three-line whip, enforced by Big Carol Loomis and the even scarier Liz Earnshaw, they would all have been somewhere else.

McBride was brought in and she stood before Grace, who had set up her judgement seat right in front of the TV. Normal service was clearly suspended for the duration.

66

"You know what you did," Grace said, putting on her no-bullshit voice. "Everybody else here knows it too, but say it anyway."

Unlike her two favourite enforcers, Grace didn't have a physical presence that was in any way frightening or intimidating. She looked like Santa Claus's slightly slimmer sister, with a face that flushed easily and a habit of sighing after she moved, as though she was about to make some jokey reference to "these old bones". What made her scary was her reputation for never forgetting a slight and never bothering to make a distinction between great things and small. If you pissed her off, you pissed her all the way. There were no stopping points along that road.

McBride was scared shitless, but she was on the spot and there was no running from it. She was surrounded – by unwilling witnesses who also served to kettle her in with her persecutor.

"I didn't take that stuff, Grace," she said in a shaky voice. "I just found it."

Grace considered this pathetic defence for a moment, and perhaps that got McBride's hopes up because she started to stammer out some story about how she saw a packet of biscuits thrown into the animal feed tub behind the prison farm and followed a trail to the pig stall, where behind a bale of straw, like the Wise Men finding the baby Jesus . . . McBride had a very big mouth and not much up on top of it, so she kept on adding twiddles to this pointless fantasy to see if they improved it. That was very much her way: she clung to her stories the way some people clung to more physical and tangible addictions. Finally Grace stopped her by putting a finger to her own lips. *Hush.*

McBride burst into tears and said yeah, okay, she ripped off the Q box. "I didn't mean to do it," she snuffled. "I just was weak, Grace. I thought I could sell some of it for a hit. Then I knew I couldn't, because I'd get found out, so I was going to put everything back the way it was, but I couldn't get into the room to—"

"Put it down there," Grace said. She wasn't talking to McBride: she was talking to Big Carol and Jilly Fish, who had just come into the ballroom with two big plastic bags full of stuff. They put the bags right in the middle of the big table that had been made by pushing all the little tables together.

There was a quickening of interest around the room, like a breath all the women there took turns to let out, because it was obvious what this stuff was: it was the stolen goods from the Q box, which Mr Devlin had taken back but had then clearly passed on to Grace.

Grace stood up. She walked right past McBride, who had to step aside for her, and on over to the bags, which she upended so all the little bits and pieces went sprawling across the table: jewellery, snack foods, comic books, home-recorded CDs, jokey little souvenir statues and framed photos and a hundred other things, most of them with their in-process labels still attached by elastic bands.

"Sit down here," Grace said to McBride, pushing a chair in front of the table. And McBride, still crying a little, did as she was told. As she sat down, Liz Earnshaw stood up.

Liz was a big woman. Every bit as tall as Big Carol although not as broad: her body and face were gaunt, the bones of her elbows very visible (she cut the sleeves off all her prison-issue sweats as soon as they were issued). But one look was all it took to make you realise you shouldn't mess with that, shouldn't go any nearer to it than you had to. Earnshaw had no control at all, no limits, no off-switch. She was half crazy, full of fury and violence the whole time and one bad word away from burning up like a match. But she'd come to Grace's attention at some point and Grace had given her an official role in the Fellside political economy, which was that she hurt the people who Grace told her to hurt.

So now, seeing Earnshaw come lumbering up to the table, McBride made a little noise that was halfway between a sob and a groan. She knew this was going to be bad.

Earnshaw squatted down next to the table, and another one of Grace's little helpers handed her a hammer. It wasn't a big sledge-hammer or even a claw hammer that a carpenter or mason would use. It was a pin hammer with a slender shaft and a dainty little head. They were used in the ceramics workshops sometimes to break old pieces of clay down into brickbats so they could be recycled, but there was no way on Earth that one of them should be out here in gen pop. There were a lot of different safeguards in place to make sure that couldn't ever happen. But when you've got a senior warder tucked into your knicker elastic, checks don't always check and balances don't have to balance.

"So this is the deal," Grace told McBride. "You go ahead and try to swipe three things off the table. Whatever you think you can reach. Lizzie is going to stand by with the hammer and try to stop you by hitting you in the hand whenever you go for anything."

A wave of rustles and murmurs went around the room, a gathering of tension. Grace was well aware that all of this – this very public spectacle of pain and humiliation – might constitute going too far. But she had decided that "too far" was the right distance to go.

"Have you got that?" she asked McBride, in a gentler voice.

McBride nodded to show that she understood. And the show commenced.

It might seem that a woman of Earnshaw's size should be slow, but nobody who'd ever seen her move would think that.

The first time, McBride managed to fake her out. She twitched her right hand then drew it straight back again, while with her left she snagged a scarf whose trailing end was very close to her. Liz swung with the hammer and the Formica table rang like a gunshot. Its bright yellow surface now bore a perfectly circular indent. McBride's hand didn't, so that was one up to her. A cheer went around the room: as a spectator sport, this might not be so bad after all.

But McBride had caught a piece of beginner's luck, and after that it evidently had other places to be. Liz had her eye in now.

There were no more cheers. A ragged chorus of gasps and sighs the first time McBride took a hit, a strained silence the second time. The silence persisted, punctuated by the sound of the hammer falling – not booming percussion but dull, meaty thwacks – and McBride's yelping cries of shock and pain as she snatched her hand back.

For a while it looked as though McBride's score was going to stay at one. Then she got lucky again, managing to snag a mug with her thumb (all of her fingers now being broken). It was a Happy Mother's Day mug, and she only came away with the handle. The business end of the mug got shattered by the hammer. But Grace – the final arbiter – said that still counted.

McBride didn't get lucky again. After ten minutes or so, it was clear that she never would, because you've got to have functional hands to pick things up.

But from Grace's point of view, things were going swimmingly and the object lesson was all she'd wanted it to be. She was slow to register the changing atmosphere in the room – the way the tenor of the silence shifted and congealed. After a while, though, it was impossible to miss it. The set, stolid faces. The hands gripping knees, not moving. The eyes flicking away, each time, from the terrible moment of impact.

The ringside audience was not enjoying this. Whether or not they thought McBride had earned her punishment, they didn't appreciate – as they should have done – her being called to account. Grace felt a surge of annoyance, but she suppressed it. These women were tough, some of them almost as tough as she was. They understood the judicious application of force, and whatever they felt about it now they would surely agree later that this was fair. Or if they didn't, fuck them.

There was a window – quite a long interval actually – when she could have intervened. Tempered justice with mercy. Put a different spin on the evening's entertainment. She was frankly just a little bit tempted. But where does that sort of thinking get you, really? More often than not, on the other end of that descending hammer.

There was even a moment when Liz Earnshaw, whose hands had never yet shaken no matter what grisly business they were

70

engaged in, glanced across at Grace with a questioning frown as if she was looking for the order to stand down. Grace didn't give it. She gestured to Liz to carry on, and Liz – after a near-subliminal hesitation – raised the hammer again and brought it down.

There wasn't much further to go in any case. A minute later, two at the most, McBride threw up, keeled over and passed out from the pain. That was game over, lesson learned and sermon preached. Grace got up and walked out, deliberately not looking back or saying a word to anyone. She'd already said everything that needed saying.

She left the contents of the boxes where they were, scattered all over the table. But nobody took anything. That was part of the lesson too.

As soon as Grace was gone, with Big Carol and Earnshaw in tow, the Goodall women rose in a collective surge. Lorraine Buller took charge (which was no surprise), sending a couple of women off to get towels and water, a couple more to bring a bottle of TCP from her cell.

"Should we report an incident?" Pauline Royal asked. Po had been a civil servant out in RL and had earned a three-year stretch for writing large cheques to herself out of departmental funds. But now that she was in prison, as if to make up for those old transgressions, she was a stickler for the rules.

"Don't be stupid, Po. We clean her up a bit first. And wake her up a bit. If we take her to the guard post now, she won't have a clue what she's saying."

"All right," Po muttered. "Keep your hair on."

Buller's anger was mostly at herself. She'd wanted not to be here. Had thought about organising a boycott of Grace's kangaroo court, but as always she stopped just shy of open opposition to Grace. Buller was tough and almost fearless, a biker bitch in a previous life with more sins on her conscience than half the block, but she had children and grandchildren in the outside world: hostages to fortune. Grace knew no limits and respected no rules.

71

If you stood against her, you had to lock down and take what came.

By the same logic, McBride couldn't talk to a guard right now until she'd got her story straight. If she blurted out Grace's name, she'd get into worse trouble. The kind of trouble that led to not getting up one fine morning because your throat had been excavated with a Stanley knife.

The other inmates had formed a sort of honour guard around the unconscious woman. Not that there was anything to protect McBride from now. The proceedings were over and Grace wouldn't be coming back. But everyone who felt like Buller did, which was most of them, wanted to put down a belated marker to show that their hearts were in the right place even if the rest of their guts were deficient.

"She's a mess, look," Kaleesha Campbell muttered. "She could lose that finger altogether. This is just wrong."

"Tell that to the Bride of Frankenstein," someone else suggested.

"Lizzie Earnshaw's not that fucking hard."

No, Buller thought. Just hard enough, really. Hard enough and sharp enough to be a shiv in Grace's manicured hand. Two or three women of the right temperament could take Lizzie down easy. And Grace would pick up another shiv and go right on cutting.

The women came back from their errands. They revived McBride with a sponge dipped in cold water. Wiped the grit and dirt out of her wounds as best they could, Po holding on to her while she whimpered at the sting of the disinfectant. They made sure she could count how many fingers they were holding up. They made sure she had something to say to account for the damage. And then Kaleesha went along to the guard post and told the duty officer, Mrs Lessing, that there had been an accident. A bad one.

Lessing took one look at McBride's hands and called the infirmary, bringing Nurse Stock at a flat run. Stock could see that Shannon's injuries were going to need more extensive treatment than the prison's infirmary could provide. They were probably serious enough to justify calling Dr Salazar at home and getting him to authorise an immediate transfer to Leeds General, but Stock was a woman who enjoyed the reassurance of routine and hated to step outside it. She signed McBride into the main ward for the night. Salazar would be clocking in again at 6 a.m., which wasn't that long, and he was paid more than she was precisely because his job description included making the tough decisions.

Stock took charge of McBride and led her away – with the aid of two female warders – to the infirmary, where she found that another patient had been admitted in her absence. This was Jessica Moulson, whose arrival had been the source of locker room gossip for weeks now.

The Inferno Killer. Only a few hours into her sentence and already hard at work on her escape attempt.

13

McBride was tripping a little, partly from the very powerful pain-killers she'd been given and partly from the pain that they were failing to kill. She thought she was hallucinating Jess, whose reconstructed face shone in the light of the overhead fluorescents like a porcelain mask and whose eyes, after so many days without food, had the ghost-panda stare of a junkie on the morning after the bender that should have finished her.

Jess's clothes were wrong too. She'd transferred from Winstanley wearing a remand prisoner's grey cotton shirt over a white hospital gown – but that colour scheme was meaningless in Fellside, where your clothes were absolutely determined by your status. Like all the other women from G block, McBride wore high-security yellow with a black sewn-in waistband. Maybe the Goodall inmates were meant to look like wasps. They were definitely meant to remind anyone who saw them of things that were toxic and had to be handled with care.

So McBride found it hard to process this weird apparition. "Oh, are you fucking sick?" she muttered, addressing her own subconscious mind. Because it was as though she'd invented a sort of imaginary friend for herself, and she couldn't understand why she'd made her be a botched ghost of a woman with a messed-up face.

Jess didn't have any answer to that, so she went for a question instead. "What happened to your hands?"

McBride didn't answer. She rolled over to face the wall, covering her eyes with her bandaged fingers. She fell silent apart from her shuddering, uneven breaths.

The exhaustion of the long journey overwhelmed Jess with unexpected suddenness. When she closed her eyes, she felt a jolt as though something heavy had slammed shut. She fell headlong into sleep.

Sometime in the night, McBride started to cry. The pain meds were wearing off and she knew she wasn't going to get any more until morning. She was a known junkie and her word on matters of pharmaceutical need wasn't good. But it wasn't just the pain: it was the fear too, and the memory of her own helplessness. Even, a little bit, it was the shame of having stolen all those things from women she knew, many of whom had treated her well at one time or another.

The sound of her sobbing dragged Jess from a deep pit of sleep. But it only dragged her partway: a fug of unreality clung to her as she looked around her for the source of the sound. Perhaps she was dreaming again. She had the sense that she'd often had in her hospital room and in the remand cell at Winstanley that the room was a lot bigger than it should be.

Someone was crying. She convinced herself it was a boy's voice. She must be back in her own bed, and Alex was out on the stairs, half naked in the cold. He was waiting for her but she hadn't come.

The moment she moved, her mind began to reorientate itself. She knew, as she stood on shaky feet, that this wasn't Muswell Hill but somewhere else. But she couldn't shake the feeling that it was Alex who was crying and that he still needed her even though she'd let him down so badly.

The journey to the next bed was only two steps. The hardest

part was lowering herself down without falling. She could see the outline of a body in the dim glow that was filtering into the ward from the lighted reception area. She stroked Alex's hair and whispered reassuring words. Just sounds really, just telling him she was there. When that didn't seem to help, she took him in her arms and held him as he sobbed. She even sang to him. Whatever came into her mind: snatches of lullabies and hymns and pop songs.

The realisation that it was a woman she was holding came slowly. She might have pulled away, but by that time Shannon's gulping tears were slowing and the convulsive movements of her chest were coming at longer and longer intervals. It seemed she was taking some comfort from the embrace.

So – even though this still didn't quite feel real – Jess held the other woman until she slept. Then she lowered her back on to the bed as gently as she could. Her hands were shaking from the unaccustomed effort, barely able to take Shannon's scant weight.

She had to sit for a minute or so, gather her strength, before she returned to her own bed and pulled the covers back over herself. The room still seemed too big, and too open. A breeze drifted through it: a breeze that carried no scents but was heavy somehow with the weight of its own journey. She could see the walls, but they looked as thin as curtains.

Shannon was aware of everything that had just taken place – of the singing, the warmth of an adjacent body, the soft hands stroking her hair. She had no idea who was doing it, and she accepted it mainly because it had to be a dream. A sweet voice shining through the hazy half-light of the fentanyl, wrapping itself around her pain so the sharp edges of it didn't cut her any more.

A woman's voice? Or a boy's?

14

Sylvie Stock missed this show because none of her furtive glances into the ward coincided with it. There were a lot of glances though. She'd already seen Jess Moulson's face when she brought McBride on to the ward, but she kept wanting to see it again. She was drawn to it by a prurient curiosity.

She'd followed Moulson's case in the tabloids, on the TV news and on the *Daily Mail* website, where it had sparked dozens of discussion threads. The prevailing opinion there, which Stock had both expressed herself and "liked" when other people said it, was that Moulson's face being burned off was proof that God cared about the fate of little children and that his justice was always working.

But she hadn't really meant that even when she said it; it just seemed to be the right language to use when you talked about evil. Stock was a rationalist and an atheist. Most of the time she saw the world as a big machine where things just played themselves out. Anonymous forces, impersonal powers, action and reaction, cause and effect. It would be comforting to live in a world that had order and purpose in it, which she supposed was why so many people pretended they did.

If anything, that little boy's suffering proved that there was nothing. Nobody watching over us or giving a shit. A loving God wouldn't let that happen to a child. Stock's husband Ron, who was Catholic, said that we were sent down into this world to make our own souls, which was why Jesus was a carpenter. Only our souls were made not out of wood and nails but out of the good or bad things we did. Stock wanted to know how that could work when some kid could be burned to death in his sleep before he had a chance to do anything, good or bad.

No, it was all just words. You lived. You died. You chose whether to be God or the devil to the people around you. By becoming a nurse, Stock had declared her allegiance. So had most of the people she treated here at Fellside, only they'd made the opposite choice.

Finally she gave in to the nagging impulse and went through into the darkened ward with her pocket torch, moving as quietly as she could. She didn't shine the torch directly into Moulson's eyes, but on to the pillow beside her face. Moulson was deeply asleep by this time, her features twisted into a slight frown, as though she was trying to remember something.

Seen from this close up, her face was deeply disconcerting. There was no one feature that stood out as ugly or wrong, but the assemblage just flat out didn't work. And Stock had read that Moulson had had seven operations to get her to this state, so it made her mind reel just a little to think of what she must have looked like before. She noticed the high-gloss shine, so unlike the look of real, healthy skin. She felt an urge to touch it and see what the texture was like.

She suppressed that urge with difficulty. She suspected that if she were to touch Moulson's face, the next thing she'd do was punch it.

She went back to her desk and her eventless vigil. But she was imagining the Inferno Killer sunk in peaceful, painless slumber.

It's not right, she thought. It's not right at all. Somebody should do something about that.

15

Liz Earnshaw didn't dream.

She didn't even know, really, what dreams were. When other people talked about all these stories that played out in their heads while they were asleep, she thought it sounded like bullshit. But any time when she was particularly troubled, she saw Naseem Suresh's face behind her closed eyelids. It wasn't a dream because Naz didn't say or do anything. She was just there. And she seemed to still be there, somehow, after Liz woke up.

On the night of Shannon McBride's punishment beating, this happened three times. Each time, Earnshaw sat up in the over-heated dark, staring at the wall until the image faded. Each time, she muttered, "I'm sorry, Naz," then lay down and closed her eyes again, trying to find her way back to the imageless void that was where she went to at night. It wasn't McBride she was apologising for, obviously. And she didn't kid herself that Naz could hear her.

Either way, when the wake-up sounded, Earnshaw's eyes were already wide open.

She was very comfortable with violence, but mostly she hurt people in quick, furious, focused ways. The protracted torture of McBride had been unusual, unsettling, and now it was hard for her to put it out of her mind. She could summon the memory into the muscles of her right hand, like the ghost of a real sensation: the solid, shuddering impact of the hammer into McBride's flesh and bone, again and again, changing gradually as the bones broke and the flesh was tenderised.

She kept her ears open at breakfast for news of how McBride was doing. A word or two would be enough. That she was coming back on block. That Dr Salazar had fixed her up and passed her as fit. That her pulped hands had been perfectly, seamlessly restored.

But there was no talk at breakfast. Not in Earnshaw's vicinity anyway. Whenever she approached a table, all conversation muted, as though she was a living, walking volume control.

She had better luck in the yard, where earshot went further than eyeline. She could hear drifting clumps of conversation as she threaded her way through the crowd, but the clustered, informal debating groups seemed to have other things on their minds. Picking up a word here and a sentence there as she lumbered around, Earnshaw eventually pieced the story together – if you could call it a story.

Some woman with a weird face like a porcelain doll was up in the infirmary. Rowena Salisbury, the canteen trusty who took meals over to the women on the wards, said it was Jess Moulson. The Inferno Killer.

A few women swore or spat on the ground at the sound of that name. Most kept their own counsel. In the outside world, guilt and innocence tended to be seen as two completely separate things, like the on and off positions of a light switch. Earnshaw didn't know much, didn't think much about things she couldn't touch or see, but like anyone who's ever stood up in a courtroom and answered that question – *How do you plead?* – she knew instinctively that people's consciences were tricky and complicated geography. Like an old canal that's had so many things pitched into it over the years that you can't see the bottom. It's definitely not clean, but who's to say which particular bit of junk belongs where?

So she didn't say anything about Moulson or have an opinion on her. But she heard McBride's name mentioned at last, and turned in that direction. She forced her way into a ring of women who were in no way pleased to see her.

"So how is she?" she demanded. "McBride? Is she back on block?"

Everyone went silent and serious for a moment. As though maybe they thought Earnshaw didn't have a right to ask. "Salazar has been Skyping Leeds General," said Luanne Kingston. "He's thinking they might have to drive her over there. Nobody's heard anything else yet." You would think to look at Luanne's solemn, anxious face that she'd never cosmetically rearranged her husband's bit on the side with a broken bottle. You would think Luanne was a saint.

"Nobody's heard?" Earnshaw repeated. "Then why were you talking about her?"

Another short, frosty silence before Luanne caved again. "Jess Moulson sang her to sleep. So Shannon said, anyway. She told Rowena about it when she brought the breakfast in."

"Moulson? The murderer?" It sounded unlikely, and McBride was known for her stupid stories. This was probably just more of the same. "Moulson sang to her?"

"Apparently, yeah."

"And who gives a fuck?"

Luanne's face took on the expression of someone who's holding back from saying a lot of different things. "Nobody," she said.

"Right," Liz agreed, and moved on.

She couldn't settle to anything. This wasn't one of her on-call days but she checked in with Grace to see if she might be needed. She wasn't. Dima Juke and Roz Jacobs were already propping up Grace's door, and since this wasn't a day when anything was coming in from outside, Grace was unlikely to find herself short-handed. Earnshaw went in and asked anyway, getting the answer she expected.

"We're fine, Lizzie," Grace told her. "You just relax and have a day off."

Which sounded great but wasn't really in Earnshaw's repertoire. She didn't read. Didn't do drugs or religion. Wasn't in film club or AA or the farm rota. Hadn't had a girlfriend since Naz died. She had no leisure activities except remembering, and she really didn't feel like remembering right then.

"I could tidy up a bit," she suggested.

Grace looked at her as though she had offered to do an exotic dance. But maybe she saw something in Earnshaw's face, because she nodded. "All right, go on. If you want to. But keep it quiet while I meditate."

Grace meditating looked like Grace sprawled on a chair with her legs open and her eyes shut. Liz tiptoed around her, half-heartedly moving things from one end of a table or shelf to the other and then putting them back again. There was nothing to tidy. Grace had a place for every item she owned.

Liz started to slip into the past. She didn't want to, but she did. She saw red. Blood soaked into streamers of trodden-down toilet paper. A crêpe-paper heart. The knuckles of her own hand, raw and ruined, after she'd punched the wall of her cell a hundred times.

"What did you say?" Grace asked.

Earnshaw's thoughts scattered. "Nothing."

"I thought you said you were sorry."

"No."

Grace sighed. "All right, Lizzie, enough of this. You're not my maid. I've got a better job for you."

"What do you need, Grace?"

Grace went over to the bookcase and took out a notebook. A fancy Moleskine that looked like a real book out of a library. "Last page," she said, handing it over to Liz. "Bad debts. Go and see how many you can turn into good ones."

Liz took the book with a big surge of relief and gratitude. "I'll shake them up a little," she promised.

"I'm sure," Grace said.

"Grace?"

"Yeah?"

"Will McBride's hands be okay?"

"Of course they will. McBride's half-Irish, Lizzie. She was raised on that shit."

The lilt of Grace's voice and the grin that went with the words told Liz that that was a joke, so she laughed. And laughing about it made some of the bad feelings recede. She went out with a much lighter heart to do Grace's bidding.

16

The next morning, the infirmary was in top gear. Dr Salazar was there for his early clinic and Patience DiMarta – "no nonsense on either side" – was back on as duty nurse.

Completing McBride's transfer to Leeds was Salazar's first order of business. Her hands were in a horrendous state, and she was likely to lose at least one finger, maybe two. Even splinting so many broken and pulverised bones went way beyond Sally's expertise. Beyond Sylvie Stock's too, very clearly: Sally undid her barely adequate dressings carefully and replaced the splints and bandages as best he could, but it was only a stopgap. McBride had to be moved, and quickly.

"And this was an accident?" he asked her. His tone was incredulous. He couldn't help it.

"A table fell on me," McBride mumbled.

Salazar turned her right hand – the worse of the two – very gently, so they could both see her knuckles. "These marks," he said, pointing, "look like separate impacts. And they're not even coming from the same angle. If a table—"

"It was just an accident, Sally," McBride said. "My own stupid fault. Lots of people saw it."

Salazar let it go. Once he would have pushed further. Taken the names of the other women who were supposed to have witnessed this accident and then questioned some of them to see whether their stories agreed. He might have filed an incident report. Even gone to the governor and asked for an investigation.

He didn't do any of those things any more. Experience had beaten all that right out of him. But he still thought about doing them, as if to remind himself how big a gap there was between where he was and where he ought to be.

After the prisoner escort arrived and took McBride away, Salazar asked DiMarta to make up the quarantine room while he questioned Moulson (in one of her brief periods of full consciousness) about things like what day of the week it was and where she'd been born. He had to establish that she was of sound mind because otherwise – by some weird logic that had a lot more to do with law than medicine – her decision to kill herself couldn't be allowed to stand.

Moulson passed on all counts. Salazar felt he didn't do too badly either, in that he maintained his best bedside manner the whole time he was talking to her. Moulson's face was like nothing he'd ever seen. Just like Sylvie Stock the night before, he tried to imagine what her injuries were like before she was operated on. They must have been terrible because reconstructive surgery had become something pretty close to magic in the last decade or so. You could grow new skin from stem cells and restore muscle function with microvascular transfers. If Moulson had received all these treatments and still looked the way she did, her face must have been burned to the bone.

But whatever she looked like, Salazar could find nothing wrong with her cognitive apparatus, therefore nothing to justify intervening in her slow-motion suicide. He and DiMarta had Moulson moved out of the main ward into the quarantine room (as per the governor's instructions) by eleven o'clock. He asked Moulson if she'd consent to a visit from Fellside's non-denominational pastor, Sarah Afanasy. Moulson declined, politely but firmly.

85

The quarantine ward was a little secure space all by itself, like a solitary cell in the heart of the infirmary. The pastor would have had to make a house call, because Moulson wasn't going anywhere, even if she changed her mind about dying.

But she didn't. She was still totally lucid when she was actually awake, and she refused – politely – all sustenance except water. DiMarta left her with a plastic pitcher and two plastic cups.

To Sally, the two cups seemed a bizarre touch. "She's not going to be entertaining anyone," he pointed out, joking.

The robust DiMarta was just a little outfaced for a moment. "You know," she said, "I didn't even think about it. It's just automatic. Fill the jug, set out two cups. Isn't it funny how much of what you do is . . . you know, not thinking about it?"

"The power of routine," Sally agreed. He was very much aware of the phenomenon – of options silting up, doors rusting shut. Sometimes it seemed to him that every time he came to the point of a decision, it was pre-empted by a decision he'd already made years before. "We're like robots, really. Not sophisticated ones, just kids' toys. Moving in grooves that are already cut out."

DiMarta was shocked. "I didn't mean anything that depressing! I just meant that it's easy to go into autopilot without realising it."

Salazar protested that that was what he'd meant too, but he'd soured the conversation. He had no gift for banter.

He looked down at Moulson, who had fallen asleep again. Unable to think of anything to say that would lift the mood again, he fell back on physical comedy. He set out the two cups, filled both of them and pantomimed introducing Moulson to an imaginary guest.

DiMarta laughed out loud, but then clapped her hand to her mouth. "That's not good," she said between her fingers.

"What? What's not good?"

She pointed to the two plastic cups. "That's how you call the *Coco*. By pouring a glass of water or wine in front of an empty seat."

86

"And what's the *Coco*, exactly?"

"A monster that eats children and then takes their shape."

"Lovely. This is a Portuguese thing, is it? I didn't know you were superstitious, Patience."

DiMarta shrugged her broad shoulders. "Autopilot," she said. "I grew up with it. Every night my mother told me to go to bed without any fuss, or the *Coco* would come and get me."

"And here you still are."

"Yes. But I didn't make a fuss. Or set a place at the table for ghosts."

Salazar looked in on Moulson throughout the day. She came and she went, but generally she wasn't strong enough to talk even when she was awake. He tried anyway, making meaningless conversation just to show her that he was there and to remind her that she was too. The worst thing about death was that it tended to be lonely, even when there were people around you. And this death was likely to be lonelier than most.

Starvation, in Sally's purely theoretical understanding, was a complicated proposition. There was no smooth progression to it. It came on you bumpy and discontinuous like a cart bouncing over rocks. He talked it over with Patience, who would probably have to carry as much of the burden as he did.

"Starving isn't abstinence from one thing; it's abstinence from a whole lot of things. Mostly people only think about the big, obvious ones."

"Calories."

"Right. No calories, so you've got no energy to move. And no proteins for cell repair. But there are so many other things your body needs. We're very complicated engines, Patience. We've got to have chloride for our stomach. Iodine for our thyroid gland. Electrolytes for our nervous system."

"I don't like thinking of a human being as a machine," DiMarta tutted. "I wish you'd use a different metaphor."

Sally registered the objection, but it was the only metaphor he had. "So all those different parts of you are going to have their own different emergencies, which will just come whenever they came. And then eventually you'll reach catabolysis. You'll start to feed on your own fat and then on your own muscle and tissue: your body will try to break itself down for parts."

"I imagine it stops hurting at that point," DiMarta said doubtfully.

Sally was going to do his best to make sure it didn't hurt at all. Moulson had refused treatment, but he was allowed to give her pain relief, and since she was dying anyway, the sky was the limit. All the same, he wasn't looking forward to seeing any of this, or managing it.

But it was part of his job, and he would do it to the best of his ability. At least, he hoped he would. He knew his own failings very well, and one of them was cowardice. There might well come a point when he was tempted to look away.

17

"A letter for you," Nurse Stock said.

She set the cream-coloured envelope on Jess's bedside table. Then stood and stared at it as though its presence there disturbed her in some way.

Most of the nurses treated Jess with wary detachment but Stock seemed to have an intense interest in her. She came into the quarantine ward quite often, even when there was nothing specific that she needed to do there, but almost never spoke a word.

"Thank you," Jess murmured. She waited until the nurse finally went away before she opened the letter.

It was from Brenda, of course. And it wrung her heart, which was otherwise beyond wringing by this time. Jess had written to her aunt to explain about the hunger strike. It was one of the hardest things she'd ever done, but she couldn't bear the thought of letting Brenda find out from the TV news. Brenda who had been her second mother, both before and after her real mother died. Who had called her *my little jelly mould*, and then *my lovely Jess.* Who had always loved her, no matter how unlovable she became.

This was Brenda's response. *Don't put out that precious light, Jess. Whatever they say you've done, don't throw yourself away. Not for someone else's idea of crime or sinfulness. You know what you've done and what you haven't done and you've only got to answer to yourself, not to them.*

But that was precisely the problem.

Jess used the controls on the bed to lift herself halfway upright. She had a pad and a pen, which Nurse DiMarta had ordered from the commissary on her behalf. She used it now to scrawl an unsteady, spidery reply.

Don't come to me. Don't be hurt by me any more. I love you so much, but this is the best way for me. Don't cry.

She sealed the letter, addressed it and put it on the table. The postage would be taken from her commissary credit, which was rapidly dwindling towards zero. But then again, so was she.

She fell asleep again, despite the harshness of the ward lights, and dreamed of nothing. Her next stop and final destination.

Sylvie Stock collected the letter and took it downstairs to drop it off in the box next to the admin station.

All mail from patients in the infirmary was handled in this way. It wasn't special treatment exactly. Still, it rankled with her to be running errands for a child murderer.

She tore the letter up instead and flushed it down one of the staff toilets. It was a tiny thing, but it gave her a little transgressive thrill that she carried with her for the rest of the day.

"Could you please leave the lights off?" Jess asked Dr Salazar the next day or maybe the day after that. "They hurt my eyes."

"I need them on when I examine you," Salazar told her.

"I know, but . . . the rest of the time. When I'm alone."

He did as she asked. And after that, there were no days or nights. There was just the darkness where she lived, and the signal flares that blinded her every time the doctor or the nurses came and vanished with them when they went.

90

Dr Salazar was dosing her with tramadol, because moving and swallowing was starting to hurt her now. The tramadol dulled the pain but it also made her dizzy and nauseous whenever she moved her head even slightly. It skewed her time sense too, unless that was a side-effect of not being able to see the sky any more.

Doing time, she thought inconsequentially. As though time were a drug.

If it was, she might have dosed herself more carefully.

18

"So this piece you've got in the infirmary," Grace said to the Devil. "Moulson. What's going on with that?"

She'd only just finished Devlin off about five seconds before and he was still out of breath, but he was used to Grace snapping back into business as usual right after sex, so he rolled over and lay back with his hands behind his head as she lit herself a cigarette. He could afford to relax. Liz Earnshaw and Big Carol Loomis were on duty at the door, and nobody was going to come in and interrupt them. Even if another warder came looking for him, they'd know better than to look under Grace's skirts.

"She's killing herself," he told Grace with massive distaste. "The one way she can do it without any kickback. A hunger strike. We've just got to sit and watch, apparently."

"It's a protest?" Grace demanded, ignoring Devlin's bitching as she usually did. The man had a lot of grievances. He lived in a world where everyone he met was keen to cheat or insult or disrespect or disobey him, or at all events to get away with something. He was, in his own mind, the bastion of order and the bastion of not taking any shit. Grace found him pliable to a fault as long as she didn't attempt to challenge this cosmology.

That was part of what she liked about Devlin – or approved of, at least. There was almost nothing to him that you couldn't take in at a glance. *Thug* was the first thing you would think when you saw him, and you weren't likely to see anything later that would make you doubt your judgement. He was big and broad across the shoulders, kept his bullet-head meticulously shaved. More than anything else, he was hard. That was the impression he gave anyway; as though if you cut into him you'd find the same solid, massy substance all the way through.

That was the one place, though, where appearances did deceive. Devlin was a bully all right. Bullying, in Grace's opinion, was a big part of who he was. But he had a sentimental streak too. He liked to believe that his junior warders were loyal to him, that the inmates respected him, that he was an emotional pivot for people he mostly treated with brusque disregard. To be loved and understood was the core of his fantasy life, which maybe went some way towards explaining how things worked between him and Grace. He saw an intimacy where she saw an alliance.

He considered Grace's question and shrugged – not irritably, because he was still comfortably post-coital, but dismissively. "No. She doesn't think she was hard done by. Her lawyer asked if he could come in and talk to her about an appeal, and she said she didn't want to see him."

"Then what is she doing?"

"I don't know. Got a bad conscience probably. She pleaded not guilty, but she fell apart at the trial and pretty much admitted she killed the kid."

Grace didn't have anything to say to this, but privately she thought that anyone who'd let themselves get destroyed by a sense of guilt was probably better off dead, and certainly wasn't worth wasting any sympathy on. Guilt was one of the things she knew about but didn't understand. It seemed to be as much use as hen's teeth. If something was done, it was done. If you didn't intend to do it, it wasn't on you; if you did, you lived with your choice.

So Moulson was a queasy curiosity to her. But that was all she was, and the talk soon turned to other things. Grace had three new couriers to train up for drug runs, all with court appearances in the next couple of weeks. She wanted Devlin to arrange pick-ups for them. It was a lot of work, and it involved a lot of arguing back and forth about names, dates, times, locations and amounts. It was a pity they'd already had sex. This stuff got them both cheerful and excited again. But Devlin had a shift handover to deal with and he'd been in Grace's cell for forty minutes already. Forty-five was a limit they'd agreed on a long time ago, and they stuck to it.

Devlin put his uniform back on, Grace giving his cock a squeeze before he put it away. Mixing up business and pleasure again, she let him in on a thought she'd had. "I think we could afford to up the volume."

Devlin was far from enthusiastic. Grace had known he would be: that was why she'd waited until he was leaving to say this. The Devil preferred a quiet life in which money and gratification came to him easily, without his having to reach for them. "Where?" he demanded. "We've got the whole block to ourselves now. There's no competition, Grace."

"I'm not thinking of Goodall – I'm thinking of Curie. Dizzy gets out in two weeks. There's an opportunity there."

She waited for Devlin to start nit-picking. She knew what the objections were, and she had answers for all of them.

He started out with the most obvious one. "What about Hassan and Weeks?" Those two were Dizzy Disraeli's prison daughters, and they were almost certainly planning to pick up her distribution network after she was released.

"That's why we're having this conversation now," Grace said. "I'm thinking that Hassan and Weeks might get themselves into some trouble. Bad enough so you have to throw them in solitary for a week or two . . ."

Devlin smoothed out his shirt while he thought this over. "That's going to take a lot of arranging. Don't get me wrong – I can do it. But it will cost. And who's going to sell for you? If I shut Dizzy's tap off, yours has got to be up and running or there'll be blood on the walls."

"I've got some people in mind." Grace ran through the names she'd come up with – Ellen Heinz, Sue Calvie, Jasmin Sullivan, a couple of others. But she could see from Devlin's face that he was still more focused on the spanners than on the works.

"You'll need someone to carry the stuff in," he pointed out. "I can't walk into Curie. Not regularly. Not with a pound of black up my shirt."

"That's the big issue," Grace agreed. "Do you know any Curie screws we should be talking to?"

Devlin shook his head emphatically. The six prisoner blocks at Fellside were independent republics and the rackets mostly didn't run between them. Grace could understand his reluctance to play recruiting sergeant: that kind of conversation would require him to show his before the other parties showed theirs, which would be a substantial risk.

And speaking of risk, Devlin now named another one. "What would we do about Kenny Treacher?" Treacher was Dizzy's supplier – a man with a very bloody reputation. Grace had seen the man a few times when he came in to visit Dizzy. She thought he looked like someone who would kill you without changing his facial expression, which even at rest was like a crab-apple that had tried to eat itself.

Treacher had known Dizzy before she went to jail, but his most intense relationship was with Dominica Weeks, Dizzy's daughter, who he'd met while she was inside and according to rumour was going to marry as soon as she was out. He couldn't be bought off or brought on board. He would already have plans in place to ensure a smooth regime change once Dizzy passed the baton. Taking Hassan and Weeks out of the equation would leave him temporarily with no handholds, so he couldn't stop someone else moving in and stealing his customers. But he wouldn't like it much, and he might try to stir up trouble afterwards if he thought he had a chance of undoing the done deal.

"You let me worry about that," Grace said lightly. The truth was that any reprisals Treacher launched would most likely be confined to the lowest rungs of the ladder. She was happy to accept collateral damage there. "You just think about mules. Ask around if you can. It's really got to be a screw who carries the stuff through. One with a few years on her too, if we can manage it."

"Want to specify hair colour?" Devlin grunted.

"Blonde, Dennis. With big wide eyes. People who look like angels get an easy ride."

Dead on the forty-five-minute mark, Devlin stepped out of Grace's cell, walking between Earnshaw and Loomis, who stood facing front like the Beefeaters at the Tower of London. He adjusted his tie and checked the hang of his trousers to make it very clear he knew that they knew what had been going on inside the cell, and that he didn't give a shit. Then he strolled away with his accustomed swagger.

Big Carol mimed the act of fellatio until Earnshaw's blank stare unsettled her and she stopped.

19

News about the murderess who'd decided to die spread quickly around Fellside.

And quickest of all in G block, where Shannon McBride (back from Leeds General with nine fingers, splints and pins all over her painstakingly repaired hands, and at least a month's exemption from work details) provided the perfect vector of transmission. She felt as though Moulson was her property, at least on a narrative level, and it hurt her to think of other people building where she had the initial stake. So she told anyone who'd listen to her about how Moulson had sung her to sleep, and how Moulson's voice had this weird hypnotic power. It was an old story by now, but it still had some currency – especially from the horse's original and genuine mouth.

Shannon told it in the commissary to add some spice to a bland corn-beef hash. Her audience was drawn from the second floor of the block, her cellmates and posse. Po Royal was there, and her girlfriend Kaleesha, the G block librarian. So was Hannah Passmore, the only lifer on the second floor. Hannah didn't really belong in this peaceable and literary bunch, but she had bunked with Po back in the day and they still looked out for each other.

"Maybe that's how she killed that kid," Po said. "Sang him to sleep and he never woke up."

McBride thought that was pretty amazing, and normally it would be something she'd be very happy to weave into her story. But it made Moulson into a monster. When she thought back to that terrible night, what she remembered most of all was the way the pain had seemed to be unbearable right up until Moulson touched her, and then it had faded right away.

Well, that and the fact that she'd sort of mistaken Moulson for a boy at one point, or thought there was a boy in the room, or something. But that part was confusing and it didn't seem to go anywhere, so she left it out.

Shannon thought about stories she'd heard when she was a kid about scary women who sang, where the power was in the singing and you were much better off not listening. Sirens and selkies and suchlike. She didn't want to put Moulson in that company. But maybe Moulson could have some of that power without being bad.

"She does have a really weird voice," she admitted. "It sort of gets into your bones and vibrates."

"If she's got a vibrator, I want twosies," said Kaleesha. That comment got her a dig in the ribs from her cellmate and lover. "You stay bloody clear of it, you dirty bitch!" Po admonished her.

Hannah Passmore shook her head sombrely. "Singing," she said with distaste. "What's she got to sing about?"

"Maybe she can't help herself," McBride suggested. She was embellishing freely now. "Her eyes were sort of glazed over. It was like she was in a trance or something. Like the song was just going to come out of her no matter what she did."

"What did she sing?" Po asked her. There had been lots of things, but the only one Shannon could remember was "Time After Time" by Cyndi Lauper. That bathetic detail just fell to the ground and lay there, and she made a mental note to make it something different next time she was asked. The song really wasn't the point, when all was said and done. The point was the story

– or rather, getting a reaction to the story. She was more than happy to adjust the finer details to meet her listeners' needs and preferences.

What Shannon liked about stories was the attention they got her, and the way the stories kept on going around after she'd started them. It made her feel like she was plugged into the life of Goodall wing – like she was the belle of the ballroom. In other ways, she knew, she was strictly marginal. She'd been that way long before she got to Fellside. Her family had disowned her as soon as she got herself arrested – well, as soon as they found out the charge was drug dealing – and her fiancé had dropped her like a shitty stick. Nobody ever visited her and she never got any letters. The space she'd left behind her in the world outside had closed again without her in it. So she told stories, and for as long as she had an audience, she convinced herself she had friends.

Then after the night of the Q box trial, she suddenly did. Women who'd never had time for her before were stopping by her cell to talk or offering her a game of Connect 4 or gin rummy in the ballroom. So she offered up her stories, which were really all she had in the way of conversation, and rubbed herself up, purring, against the luxury of an audience.

Moulson was a good story and Shannon polished it to a high gloss with many iterations. She could never be entirely certain, though, what response she was going to get. Very few of the Goodall women took the tabloid verdicts on the Inferno Killer at face value. But they knew a child had died, and they didn't take that lightly. For Moulson to die in her turn seemed like a reasonable outcome.

Some people, of course, were a lot more pragmatic about the whole thing. Harriet Grace, for example. Word was that she'd opened a book on how long Moulson would last. For anything longer than six weeks, the odds topped off at a hundred to one. But there wasn't anyone in Fellside who took that bet.

Shannon really hoped that Moulson would change her mind

and live. She wanted that for a lot of reasons. It would give her a chance to say thank you to her for helping her through those dark hours.

And being so very unlikely, it would make a much better ending.

20

Another week went by, and Jess stuck to her guns.

She was dying by inches and ounces. But she'd crashed through the pain barrier in the third week, and now most of what she was feeling was coming to her dulled and deadened. Apart from when she swallowed or tried to talk, which was agony because of the fungal infection under her tongue.

"I can treat that," Dr Salazar had told her when he turned the edge of her tongue with a depressor and found the livid, swollen flesh. "There's no reason why you have to suffer."

He'd actually said it more than once. The last time, he'd almost pleaded. Jess could tell that it distressed him to sit by and watch pain that he could do something about. But she didn't know how strong her willpower was. Worse things would be happening soon. If she said yes to treatment now, how could she trust herself to say no later? And if she stopped being able to say anything, would she have set a precedent without meaning to?

It was better to just ride it out until none of it mattered any more.

The tramadol helped, not so much by easing the pain but by erasing whole stretches of time. The effects of the drug had intensified as her body mass got less and her system got weaker. Now, whenever Salazar or one of the nurses gave her a shot, it was as though she were a cork being shoved deep into black water. She would rise again slowly, slowly, to find a different nurse on duty and half a day gone.

One time, when she came back to herself after one of these immersions, she had the strong conviction that she wasn't alone in the room. It was like her first night out on the main ward, only even stronger. Someone was moving behind the head of her bed. She waited for whoever it was to come into her line of sight, but they didn't. They just kept moving back and forth behind her – the footfalls light and uneven in a way that made it hard to imagine what the owner of the feet was doing. Skipping? Dancing? Pushing something along the floor with no hands?

She might have risked a hello, but she knew what it would feel like if she moved her ulcerated tongue. She waved instead, a half-hearted ghost of a movement where her hand barely left the sheet.

The footsteps stopped right at her shoulder and the bed-frame creaked as it was touched. The unseen visitor sniffed loudly – the liquid sniff of a nose that needed to be blown – and then there was a chafing sound at the limit of audibility; Jess imagined a hand rubbing a face, or someone scratching an itch.

The longer the silence lasted, the less likely it seemed that the other person would break it. And now the silence was complete, which made Jess wonder whether she'd heard anything at all. Perhaps this whole experience was an artefact of recovering from the oblivious kiss of the painkillers.

But she felt something now: a stirring of air against her cheek. The visitor was still there, and close enough that she could feel their breath on her face.

She turned her head very slowly to lessen the jarring of unused muscles.

There was nobody there, and nothing at all behind the bed. The bed was pressed right up against the wall, the headboard actually fixed to it. The space in which those footsteps had skipped up and down didn't exist.

21

"So you're saying she's running out of road?"

Devlin was sick of Salazar beating around the bush. Sick of standing in the infirmary and sweating his balls off because the admin block had no air conditioning and the heatwave just went on getting hotter. He wanted a straight answer. But Doctor fucking Feelgood here was still shying away from giving him one.

"All I'm saying is that she's reaching a crisis," Salazar repeated for about the tenth time with a shrug of his sloping shoulders. "The next forty-eight hours are going to be crucial."

"Crucial?"

"Decisive."

"Shit! You're just using ten different words to say the same frigging thing. Is she going to die or not?"

The doctor winced, his eyes flicking from left to right and back again to avoid focusing on Devlin's face. Devlin knew Sally for a pussy. The kind of pussy who hated making a stand on anything, even if that just meant stating a categorical opinion. There was an irony in that, because Sally's huge, potato-shaped bulk made him seem imposing and permanent. And once upon a time there had indeed been some doggedness to him. Now he was a man who mostly ducked out of the way before you could come at him, just like he did now.

"I'm not having that conversation," he told Devlin.

"Yeah, you are, Sally. Otherwise we'll have another conversation about dipping your paw into the honeypot. We could bring the governor in on that one."

Sally had gone through a brief period of borrowing from his own stock. It was when his wife, Leah, was dying from cancer and he'd used the drugs to give her a softer landing than she would otherwise have had. Devlin had found the evidence in the form of an invoice the doctor had thrown away after working up a convincing fake with a bottle of correction fluid and a photocopier. Devlin now had both the original invoice and the doctored copy in a file in his office. He'd kept Salazar's secret, but he called in the favour on a regular basis. It hadn't let him down yet. He was confident that it never would because it was only one half of a perfect lock. The other half was Naseem Suresh, who Devlin never mentioned at all because he knew he didn't have to.

"Speaking of self-medication," he added, driving his point home in case that needed doing, "what have you got for me?"

Salazar went to the secure cabinet, unlocked it and came back with three pink and white packets of pethidine. Devlin pocketed them without a word. He'd had an intermittent habit ever since he got to Fellside – or rather, ever since he took up with Grace – but he was way too sharp to fall over the diamorphine event horizon. Pethidine, taken half a tab at a time, was like a long, slow fuck, and he got along with it just fine. He knew from daily observation that heroin didn't have nearly such good manners.

"Okay," he said, happy that the natural pecking order had been duly established. "Joking aside, give me a time of death for that bitch."

But Salazar still seemed reluctant to commit himself. "Moulson is weakening fast now," was all he'd say. "She's probably going to

104

have a major organ failure in the next few days, and I won't intervene unless she asks me to. But if she asks . . ."

Devlin was puzzled. "I didn't think she was talking any more."

"No, she isn't," the doctor admitted. "It would be difficult for her. Her mouth is in a very bad state. But she's still aware of her surroundings, at least some of the time. It's not impossible that she might say a . . . a word or two, or make some gesture that I could interpret as asking for an intervention."

"A gesture you could interpret?" Devlin piled the words up high with disbelief and contempt.

"Yes."

"Well, here's a thought for you, Sally. Don't."

"Don't . . .?"

"Don't interpret. Let nature take its course."

The doctor stood on his dignity, but it didn't add as much to his height as he might have hoped. "I'm the best judge of my own responsibilities, Dennis. I'm employed by the prison but I work for my patients, like any doctor does."

"Well, that's what I'm asking you to do, you fucking idiot. This is what she wants, right? And the governor told you not to interfere. I'm just telling you the same thing."

"But if she changes her mind . . ."

Devlin put his hand on Salazar's shoulder – a little bit like a father, even though Salazar was ten years older than him.

"Help her to stay strong," he said.

Sally didn't say anything. But there was something in his face that looked a little bit like defiance. Devlin didn't leave it at that anyway. He leaned in close, his hand still gripping tight onto Sally's shoulder.

"You remember what happened the last time you decided to stand up and be counted?" he growled.

"Yes," Sally said. "Of course I do."

"We're not going to have a repeat of that, are we?"

The doctor blinked very rapidly a whole lot of times. "Well, that would be unlikely," he said. "This is . . . this is not a comparable situation."

105

That was when Nurse Stock walked into the infirmary, and she walked in softly enough that neither of them noticed her.

"You just remember this, Sally," Devlin said. "The woman you've got in there killed a kid. She fucking cooked him. In a perfect world, she'd get what she gave that little boy. She'd go out baked and basted like a Sunday roast. People like you, all you think about is your own good intentions. You see a pain, you put some ointment on it. You see a disease, you prep a needle."

"I don't see what you're getting at, Dennis," Sally said quietly. His eyelids were still going like a semaphore.

"What I'm getting at," Devlin said, "is that some people *are* the disease. You're not doing any good by keeping them alive; you're just adding another layer to the shit we're all walking in."

"Nobody is a disease. That's a vile thing to say."

Devlin shook his head in sorrowing contempt. "Well, never mind," he said. "If she hangs on too long, maybe I'll come on over with a plastic bag and close the betting myself."

He turned then, and saw Stock. He didn't seem even a little bit worried about being overheard. There weren't many people at Fellside whose pricked-up ears Dennis Devlin needed to worry about, and Stock wasn't one of them.

"Hey, Sylvie," he greeted her. "Talk some sense into this moron, would you?"

He walked out, leaving Dr Salazar gathering up the pieces of his fractured dignity. As he walked away, he heard Sally say, "That man is a bully, pure and simple. Pay him no mind, Sylvie."

He didn't hear what Stock said. But he was pretty sure he knew what she was thinking. He thought of her as someone very like himself who wouldn't bear fools gladly and could always tell one when she saw one.

22

Stock was PD that night. Primary duty nurse, in charge of the infirmary until Dr Salazar signed back in again at eight the next morning and relieved her. And through the watches of the night, Devlin's words worked away inside her.

Stock was a woman of strong and mostly conservative convictions. She disliked gays and immigrants and any other people who in her opinion asked for more than they deserved. Despite her atheism, she liked the moral seriousness of religions and religiously minded people. She felt they sat in the right corner on most social issues.

And one of the issues that oppressed her most was the abuse of children. She thought Jimmy Savile was a worse man than Hitler had ever been, because at least most of Hitler's victims had been able to fight back. What could a child do when a grown-up hurt them? Nothing.

She brooded about the sex offenders in the closed unit in Dietrich block. She never got to meet them because Dietrich was a kingdom within a kingdom. It had its own medical staff geared up to the specialised needs of lunatics and monsters. That was probably for the best: if a paedophile took some damage, for example in a punishment beating, Stock didn't know if she could bring herself to fix her.

There might be a riot at Fellside some day. In riots, Sylvie knew, all kinds of scores got settled. The protection that was routinely provided at the taxpayer's expense for the child murderers and the child rapists meant nothing when the walls came down.

But that was a distant prospect. In the here and now, under her care this very night, there was Jessica Moulson, the Inferno Killer. With the blood of a child all over her hands. And Devlin's soliloquy to Dr Salazar was hanging in the forefront of Stock's mind like a permission slip from a teacher.

Her only intention was to put her finger, very lightly, on the scales of justice. Nothing more than that. And she denied to herself that she was even doing that much. Her first sins were sins of omission. She was meant to apply Vaseline to Jess Moulson's lips every two hours to keep them from drying and cracking any worse than they already had. She didn't bother. And when Moulson's water bottle emptied – the one with the teat on it so Moulson could take nourishment like a baby without moving her head – she didn't refill it.

But those small things unlocked something bigger inside her – and even though what she was doing scared her badly, she did it anyway. When she took Moulson's temperature, she jammed the thermometer in under her swollen tongue with unnecessary force. And when it came time to give Moulson her pain meds, she handled her a lot more roughly than she needed to.

She lifted Moulson's wasted leg and turned it, looking for a likely vein. She bent the leg sharply outwards like someone who was about to joint a chicken, gripping it too tight at the knee and the ankle. She was aware of how easy it would be to pull the tibia out of its socket. The woman's muscles were basically string at this point.

She pulled back from the horrific thought, pretended it hadn't excited her. She had her job to do and she would do it. She was a professional.

She found a vein at last, right up in the groin area. Evidently Moulson hadn't got that far, back when she was using. Stock had seen heroin addicts with track marks everywhere on their bodies. She'd once treated a prisoner who'd blinded herself in one eye by shooting up into her sclera. And she'd known another one who used to inject into her tongue, using dental floss to strap off. Nothing surprised her any more. She'd gone into nursing to relieve pain, and at Fellside all she'd seen was people committing atrocities on their own flesh. She hated it.

She scrubbed the inside of Moulson's thigh with antiseptic and prepped the hypo. She was using a multi-dose bottle of tramadol, so she slid the tip of the needle through the rubber seal and drew up the dose.

Then she put the needle to Moulson's groin and drove it in. As with the thermometer, she pushed a lot harder than she needed to, not intending to injure Moulson but almost imagining that her hatred would communicate itself somehow through the needle's point. She sank the plunger in as though she was detonating a bomb.

She didn't realise her mistake until she withdrew the hypo and the blood started to well up out of the pinprick wound. The dark blue-purple was suffused with a brighter, richer red. And it was coming too freely, running down Moulson's thigh and dripping on to the sheet before Stock could get a towel to it.

That was wrong. Very wrong, in a very specific way. She must have delivered the dose of tramadol into Moulson's artery.

Stock bit down hard on her lower lip, but an involuntary moan forced its way out anyway. For a moment she was literally paralysed with horror. This was a terrible thing to have done – the kind of mistake that could end your career. More than that, it could end a life.

The thing that made arterial injection so dangerous was that it caused a massive concentration of whatever medicine you were injecting to be delivered very locally, to the tissue that was perfused by that particular artery. The tissue of Moulson's upper leg and thigh would swell and her blood flow would be massively disrupted. The pain would probably be short-lived, measured in minutes, but it would be incredibly intense. In the longer run, there'd be a serious risk of gangrene because some of that super-swollen, blood-deprived tissue would die. If enough of it died, the leg would have to be amputated.

Of course there might not even be a longer run. Moulson could get a blood clot and die of a heart attack in the next few minutes.

Stock backed away from the bed, her left hand clamped around her right wrist as though it now took both hands to hold the empty hypodermic. Her mind was full of clamouring alarms, and the impulse to run was almost overpowering. She couldn't run. Moulson's blood was flowing down over the marbled grey skin of her upper leg. The stain on the sheet was expanding outwards, a nearly perfect circle. Irrelevantly, out of nowhere, Stock remembered her husband Ron reading aloud from the Old Testament. Moses splitting the rock, and the water coming forth in great abundance.

She pulled herself together as much as she could. She ran and got a T-pad from the first aid cabinet and brought it back to the bed, although it felt like someone else's body she was moving. She pressed her thumb against the insertion point while she tore the packet open with her teeth. The pad was soaked with tranexamic acid. It ought to stop the bleeding.

She held the pad in place for a full fifteen minutes until her thumb ached from the constant pressure. Moulson was twitching and whimpering in her sleep, little tremors running through her body. But the drug was keeping her under, even though she was registering the pain through the narcosis.

I have to get away, Sylvie thought. *I have to get out of here, right now. I can't stay in this room.*

A part of her knew that running away wouldn't help – that this would come back on her no matter what she did. But an animal panic filled her now. She did what she could to clean up.

Changed Moulson's gown and then the sheets, her hands shaking as though she had some sort of palsy. She took the blood-soaked T-pad and its packet through to reception, dropped them into a sharps envelope and stuffed them well down in her handbag. She couldn't take the sheets. They'd have to go into the laundry the next day, at the bottom of a bag where they might not be noticed.

She got as far as the door.

But that was where reality reasserted itself. She stopped with her hand on the handle, at the end of an invisible tether of conscience and fear and pragmatism. She really had no choice but to wait this out.

And hope that Moulson didn't die, even though death was what she had deserved.

23

A memory, taken out of context.

Or maybe the needle slipping into her thigh *was* the context. Bringing back more consensual injections in what (in spite of everything) probably counted as happier times.

"I don't know," Jess said.

"What don't you know?" John's mouth was quirked up into a grin. As though he already had a good idea what she was going to say, and wanted her to say it because it was going to be hilarious.

"I'm clean," Jess told him. As shorthand for a lot of other things.

They were sitting cross-legged on the floor, with the lights down, the TV playing without any sound and soft music on the iPod. The track was "The Trouble I'm In" by Gavin Rossdale, which didn't feel like a good omen at all, but they'd shared a curry, two King Cobras and a tub of Cherry Garcia. Now John wanted to share something else, and he seemed to want it badly.

"If you're clean now," he pointed out, "that tells me there was a time when you were using. You've done it before."

"Not this!" Jess protested. *This* was a little plastic baggy full of China White. *This* was Not Kansas, was way beyond anywhere she'd ever been. She tried to explain. "I was on oxy for a while.

It took me a long time to get off it again. Heroin . . . Honest to God, John, that's not my thing."

He was still grinning. "You know what the active ingredient in oxycodone is, Jess?"

"No."

"It's diacetylmorphine. The exact same thing that's in heroin. You were already on opiates. This isn't any different. Except that the way I take it, you don't get so much of the dangerous stuff. You just get a quick high. Look, I'll show you."

There was no ligature, no spoon, no syringe. "None of that shit. That's mental!" John liked to hot-rail using the glass tubes that florists sell single roses in. He demonstrated, heating the white powder with a Bic lighter until the inside of the tube filled up with creamy white smoke that seemed almost as solid as mashed potato.

He took a hit himself, then held the billowing tube, the white kaleidoscope, out to her. "Come on, babe," he murmured. "Don't leave me here on my own."

Memory and longing betrayed her. She let him put the tube up against her lips. She breathed in. A shallow breath at first. But the second one was deeper. And from there, by slow and inexorable degrees:

the needle

the first time he hit her and said he was sorry

the first time he hit her and explained why it was her fault

losing her friends

losing her job

burning the house down

murdering Alex Beech.

Jess was aware of the needle going in, but thought she'd dreamed it. The little prick of pain that promised pleasure, an artefact of a past that had to be gone for ever. She'd been floating in and out of consciousness for days now, and she couldn't tell any more where her dreams ended and the real world began. It was all one long pilgrimage through a slough of synaesthetic porridge.

113

The one reliable thing in that bleary universe was the fall and rise that came with each dose of tramadol – the dip into profound darkness, where everything was sweet but barely there, and the gradual return to a more negotiated place of dull aches and neural static.

When this dose hit her system, it felt at first like the familiar welcoming descent, and Jess surrendered to it in much the same way she'd once surrendered to the saccharine sting of heroin. But this time was different. She sank down with jolts and jars, as though she were pushing her way through a crowd – and then, although she didn't stop falling, something else was falling through her. Lots of somethings, red-hot and razor-tipped.

The pain swelled and swelled to a terrible, impossible pitch. She kept on tumbling, end over end. How could anything hurt this much?

She wanted to cry out but she couldn't even do that. This was an interior place where things like sound didn't really exist. There was only the one feeling, filling every corner of the world. She was a snowball in hell, rolling and rolling, cocooned in more and more thicknesses of whatever it was that was hurting her.

This place didn't look like how she imagined hell, though. She fell through a roiling chaos of shapes and forms that exploded out of each other and then folded back in again in an endless cycle. There were faces in there, and hills, and meandering hallways. Shifting, hurtling mazes of something and nothing and then something again. Gravity and perspective lurched and plunged from moment to moment, filling her with a sort of bodiless nausea.

It was a place of infinite size. It had no edges or borders. But after a long, long time – hours or ages – something else loomed up ahead of her. Or perhaps below her. It was a dark and ragged circle, as perfectly black as the moon occluding the sun. She was going to fall into it, whatever it was. Even in a dream world, that yawning absence terrified her. It looked like death.

Jess tried to reach out an arm to grab something to slow or stop herself, but she had no arms. She had no body. She was only a point of view, flying like a comet through silent immensity.

But a point of view implied eyes, and if she could have eyes she could have hands. This was a dream, right? In a dream you could have anything, be anything. Give me hands! she thought desperately, and she felt an attenuated prickling where hands might be, or come to be.

It was too late to take that experiment any further. She'd drawn level with the black circle, which was both bigger and closer than it seemed, and shot right on into it, into a shaft of unrelieved dark. The ocean was gone. There was nothing around her now but emptiness. Emptiness and pain.

And acceleration. The pit had its own gravity. It laid claim to her. It was bringing her to its bosom with invisible hands and she couldn't fight it.

I can, a voice said. *Hold on.*

Something laid hold of her, pulled at her from above. The touch was feather-light at first, and unavailing. The pit refused to let go.

But so did this newcomer. It turned and angled Jess. Twisted her. A little at a time, but persistently, repeating the movement again and again. She was being dragged sideways. Buffeted by contradictory forces. The terrible momentum she'd built up was burning away in shuddering waves that danced and drove through her.

For a moment it seemed that she came to a halt in mid-air as those forces found a balance. Then she was moving downwards again, or at least it felt like down.

And landed, with a surprising jolt of impact, on something solid that supported her.

Jess's immediate instinct was to throw herself flat, but there was nothing for that instinct to act on so she just stayed where she was.

Which was where, exactly? There was no way of knowing. No way to tell if she'd just been rescued or taken as prey.

The one thing she was sure of was that she wasn't alone. She felt the same sense of close and intense scrutiny that she'd felt on her first night in the Fellside infirmary, and many times since.

The thing that had taken her was watching her now and had been watching her for a long time. She was defenceless. Terror filled her like a cup and leaked away again just as quickly because she was nothing. She couldn't hold anything, not even an emotion.

Jess had seen a movie once where the hero took his gun apart to clean it and then heard the footsteps of approaching assassins. Over a soundtrack of pounding drums he struggled to put the dismantled weapon back together in time to defend himself. There were no drums here, no sounds at all, but that was what she tried to do now.

What Jess was building for herself, though, was a body. She might be attacked at any moment, but she built outward from the core because that seemed the right way to do it. She made herself a heart – not a beating heart, because for all she knew she might be dead, but a heart that was her centre of gravity.

She hung a head above it, like a hat on a hook. Eyes and ears in the head, so the abstract space was darkness now and the strained pause was silence.

Legs dangling down until they touched the ground – which had no warmth, no cold, no smoothness or roughness yet to speak of, but it was below her and so it was ground.

She turned a full circle, moving her notional feet in tiny increments.

She reached out with her imagined arms. Resistance on the right-hand side; nothing on the left. It seemed that the place where she was standing was a narrow ledge of some kind, buttressed on one side and not the other.

She was ready now. Ready to defend herself.

I'm not going to hurt you.

The voice was no voice at all. It arrived in her mind without travelling through the air. Even so, it had volume and tonality. It was high and light, like a child's voice or a young woman's.

What – what – what – ? Jess thought and tried to say. She had forgotten to put a mouth in her face, so nothing happened. But whatever was out there heard her anyway.

Nothing, it said.

The question Jess had been trying to frame was, *What do you want?*

A mouth has a tongue. Teeth. Lips. A palate. All those things are needed before you can start to make and shape sounds. Jess tried to get the parts in the right sequence, knowing that even if she did an immaculate job, she would still be missing the magic ingredient, which was breath.

In the meantime, since this thing could read her thoughts, she asked, *Why?*

Why what? the other demanded.

Why did you help me?

There was a long silence. The unseen other was circling her: she knew that, because the pressure of its gaze upon her shifted as it moved. There didn't seem to be any room on the ledge for anything to go around her, but maybe whatever she was talking to could walk on air, glide through rock. The rules were different here. Jess turned too, scared of being outflanked.

You said hello to me.

Jess's mock mouth moved, her mock tongue stirred together soft-edged gobbets of sound. Nothing intelligible came out. *I said what?*

When I saw you, in the white place. The hospital place. You said hello to me. Most people only see me when they're asleep. You saw me when you were awake. It was nice. It was nice to be seen.

It was nice. That was what a child would say. But what would a child be doing here, in this inexplicable abyss? What did it say about Jess's mental state at this point that she had dreamed a child into her nightmare to share it with her?

Show yourself, Jess thought. *Let me see you.*

No. Quick. Categorical. The other was just as wary as she was, just as slow to trust, for all that it had saved her. What had it saved her for? Or from, for that matter?

The hole goes on for ever. People who go in don't come out again.

"But I – then how can I—?" She was speaking with her mouth this time. The sounds hung in the air, rough-hewn and shapeless.

117

You'll have to climb.

Jess had no idea how to do that. Her new-made body was a flimsy thing, unsuited to serious effort of any kind. Her real body was back in the real world, a great distance away in a direction she didn't even have a name for. And climbing out of the pit would only be the start of a long and arduous journey. Surely it would be less effort just to wait here until she woke?

And she wanted to know who her rescuer was. She wanted that very much. A strange presentiment had come to her, the outline of a thought that she was almost afraid to acknowledge.

She tried to mount an ambush. She imagined a light, hanging in the abyss above her, pushing back the darkness. She strained her freshly minted heart with wishing for it. And the darkness slowly thinned from black to grey.

The other was gone in an instant. She knew because she was no longer watched. The bubble of its attention had burst against her skin.

The light blossomed too late, like a thin and faded sun in this fathomless night. The feeble glow lit Jess, though she cast no shadow (she was scarcely more than a shadow to start with). It lit the ledge she stood on, an arm's length wide. It lit a rock face beside her, rusted brown like old blood.

The other was gone. She was alone in her dream.

24

Jess waited a long time for something to happen. For the voice to return, or for morning to raise her up on its back and carry her home to reality. But at last, when it became clear that neither of those things would happen, she climbed.

It was easy enough, at least at first. The rock face was rough and pitted and offered a million handholds. And before she started, she put some effort into refining and improving her imagined body. You couldn't walk without muscles and sinews. You couldn't cling on to outcrops without fingers and thumbs, or step up on to ledges and escarpments without toes and heels. She equipped herself with these things, pleased at the way her dream flesh responded to her thoughts.

But the downside of having a more realistic body was that it experienced realistic wear and tear. Though the pain that had brought her here had faded now, Jess was soon tired and aching from the ascent itself.

She climbed for hours. She climbed for ever. The rock wall didn't change and neither did the abyss. Nothing stirred that infinite column of air. Nothing moved here apart from her.

She knew she was dreaming, but she couldn't make herself

wake up. She thought about allowing herself to fall again – testing the limits of dream logic by letting the pit take her. She found she was afraid to do that. She was also afraid of losing her way at the top of the shaft and wandering for ever without finding her physical body again. That was ridiculous, of course. "For ever" could only mean until morning came and it was time to be given her next round of meds.

But it didn't feel like that. It felt as though waking up might turn out to be a challenge. Perhaps she wasn't asleep at all but in a coma.

Or insane.

Or dead.

With that thought she ran out of wall. Her spidering fingers touched nothing but empty air above her. She hauled herself out on to a plateau of black rock that was as smooth as glass. It was only a few steps wide. Beyond that there was nothing but chaos: clashing waves of colour and shape and formless light like a constant explosion. She felt a tidal pull dragging her into that sensory spew. She tried to look away from it, but it was everywhere.

And he was waiting for her there. Although he'd fled when she tried to catch a glimpse of him, he'd paused here at the rim to see her emerge. All Jess could make out was a slight figure crouched on its haunches, a smear of shadow backlit by garish immensity.

"Let me see you," she whispered, but her gaze kept flinching downwards at the ground. She saw him in momentary glimpses, smeared by the movement of her own eyes.

He didn't answer or move. She took a step towards him, and then another. Focusing on him alone, ignoring the monstrous storm of images.

He got to his feet and for a moment she thought he might run. But he didn't. He stood quite still as she walked towards him. His hands were at his sides and his head was bowed, looking at the ground.

She drew near to him. So slowly! She wanted to put off as

long as she could the moment when that face looked up and saw her. But there was no choice and nowhere else to go.

He didn't wait for her to reach him. While she was still about ten paces away, he raised his head to look at her, but his face was mostly lost in moving shadow. His features wavered like pondweed in a sluggish current.

It made no difference. She knew, had known all along, whose face she was going to see. She steeled herself in advance for the shock, but it was wasted effort.

She sank to her knees. Dream or death or delirium, she couldn't face this. She waited for him to speak, to accuse her or perhaps to sentence her. He still said nothing. He was wearing the same vest and shorts he'd had on the first time she saw him on the stairs outside her flat. His face wore a serious frown that made him look, for a moment, a lot older than he was.

Something heaved inside Jess like a sob, but it found no exit. "I'm sorry," she said, just as she had in that earlier dream. "I'm so sorry, Alex." Her voice sounded hollow and dead in her own ears.

What for? the boy asked.

"For . . . hurting you." *Killing*, she meant. *For killing you.* But the word wouldn't come.

I don't remember that. Was it a long time ago?

She had been in hospital for eight months. The trial had taken three weeks, and then she'd waited in the remand wing at Winstanley for another seven. Almost a year. For a ten-year-old, almost for ever.

"A very long time."

I don't think I know you. But you don't have to feel bad about it, as long as you're sorry.

She knew that she knelt within a dream, was talking to a dream, but the words still overwhelmed her. She couldn't find any answer.

She risked another glance. Alex was looking at her with eager interest. He even flashed her a momentary smile. He seemed pleased that they'd got through the awkwardness, as though his

121

agony and his death were things that could be set aside as long as the proper social rituals were observed.

This is where I live, he told her. *Where do you live? You should probably go back there now. The big hole isn't safe and I mostly don't come here.*

"I live . . ." Jess gestured vaguely to one part of the horizon and then another. "I'm in prison because of . . . what happened. I don't really have a home any more."

But you should go back to where you were before.

"I don't know the way."

I can take you back to where I first saw you. It's easy to get lost until you're used to it.

He held out his hand for her to take. Jess raised her own arm, a mere slab of substance, graceless and thrown together. They touched. His fingers closed around hers.

Grief and shame filled her and poured from her. She sobbed out her heart on the black obsidian. Alex watched her sadly, in silence, as though he'd seen a world of suffering and had run out of words to answer it.

"I'm sorry," she said again.

You told me. Come on. We have to go now.

She climbed to her feet. He was tugging at her hand, pulling her towards the exploding world which surrounded the pit on all sides. For some reason, the thought of going there filled her with dread – as though there might be something waiting for her that was worse than what she'd already endured. Something that would break her down in pieces if she even saw it.

You can close your eyes, Alex said. *I know the way.*

She did as he said. She let him lead her, eyes screwed shut, away from the pit into the dazzling lightnings of his world. Sometimes his other hand touched her elbow to turn or steady her. When she hesitated, he whispered reassurance.

They might have walked ten miles or a thousand. Time and space meant nothing here. There was nothing but the textureless ground under her feet and the soft touch of Alex's hands. If she walked through any medium at all, it was through his gentleness.

Almost there. Just another step.

But she didn't want to take it now. Though this dream had started off in agony, the thought of waking from it back into Fellside prison, into what her life had become, seemed like a terrible prospect. Most of all, she didn't want to leave Alex.

It was nice to meet you too, he said with guarded politeness.

"Perhaps you could come back," she hazarded, her homemade heart beating like a hammer. "I'd like . . . I'd love to see you again, Alex."

I don't think so. It's noisy here. And too bright. I mostly stay where it's dark and quiet.

When she didn't answer, he prompted her again. *You have to go that way. It's not far. Try it.*

Jess turned from him and stepped forward, still with her eyes closed against the glare and the sickening motion. One more step, he'd said. And that was all it took. She went back into her body, which lay open and ready to receive her.

She woke herself with weeping that tore the shrivelled membranes of her throat. When she remembered that night afterwards, that was always what came back to her first. The taste of her own blood, welling up in her mouth and spilling down her chin.

It was just a dream, but it had felt more real and more solid than anything since the trial. The blood made sense. It was as though she'd broken her fast on razor blades.

25

Jess's loud, half-strangled sobbing brought Nurse Stock running, in something of a panic. She slammed the room lights on with the heel of her hand, the sudden glare pinning Jess to her pillow like a beetle to a board.

Stock was unusually solicitous. She brought a beaker of water for Jess to drink, examined her throat with a speculum and mixed up a weak antiseptic paste for her to swallow, washed down with more water.

"Those lacerations will probably heal by themselves," she said. "I think. I'm sure they will. But I'll leave a note for the day team to check them. Dr Salazar will know what to do. And there's always more systemic pain relief if you need it."

Jess read the time from Stock's watch as the nurse fussed around her. It was two o'clock, presumably in the morning. It felt as though whole days must have passed, but Nurse Stock had been on duty when she fell asleep and it seemed that this was the same night. She settled her head back on the pillow, drained and almost numb. The light was still hurting her, but sheer exhaustion made the pain bearable. "I'm going to change this pillowcase," Stock was saying, almost babbling. "It's soaked from your sweat. I think you must have had a . . . a fever that broke in the night, or . . ."

The next time Jess woke, she was alone in the room.

She dozed again. Nurse Stock was back, pulling the covers down to examine her.

Alone.

Stock taking her temperature, pushing the cold tip of the digital thermometer into her ear.

Alone.

Alone.

Alone.

Some time passed. Maybe it was a day. And another night. It could have been anything.

It was dark again, apart from a band of sunlight spilling in at the half-open door. Patience DiMarta walked across Jess's line of sight, left the room and closed the door behind her.

Alex coalesced out of the sudden dark, like stirred milk coming to the surface of a mug of coffee.

For a second or two, Jess could only croak. Her mouth gaped open but her injured throat wouldn't make any other sounds. Her feet kicked spastically, out of rhythm, pushing her backwards up the bed. Her heart beat at her ribs just once, with the force of a hammer blow. Then it seemed to stop, as though it had wedged itself tight in there and couldn't get free again.

She threw up her hands to hide him from her sight, but she was too weak to hold them there. Gravity dragged them down and the boy was still standing at the foot of the bed, solemn, staring, only mildly interested in her terror.

I need to talk to you, he said.

26

He came back every night, and every day.

He wore her down by infinitesimal degrees.

Jess knew he wasn't real, couldn't be real, but Alex refused to let that matter. He was with her every minute. Pale in the daylight. Bright against darkness, like a fresh tattoo.

And every time she surrendered to the weakness of her body, the failing of her organs, he dragged her back. To wakefulness. To life.

There was no refuge.

"You're not here," Jess croaked at him. Jagged, incomplete sounds. Sounds made of broken breath. But he understood her.

Where am I, then?

"In my mind. In my memory."

"Did you hear that?" Nurse DiMarta asked Dr Salazar. "She's wandering in her wits. She just said so." Jess had forgotten they were even there. They came and went like shadows now. Only the other shadow was real. Only Alex. "Probably a mercy. I don't think it will be much longer."

"Then why is her heart rate so steady?" Salazar murmured.

They moved back and forth around her, taking measurements,

exclaiming, occluding Alex and then revealing him again and again. He didn't move. He stood in the shadows at the far end of the room but he was as clearly visible as though he was in bright sunlight. Or perhaps it was the light of a fire she couldn't see. In his bowed head and pursed lips there was a boundless patience.

She slept and woke. Alex still waited.

"All right," Jess whispered, giving in at last. "What?"

I changed my mind.

"About . . .?"

You said you hurt me, and I told you I didn't care.

He leaned over her. Jess flinched back, her upper body sliding further up the headboard, but there was nowhere to go. You couldn't escape from madness, and clearly she was mad.

Oh God, she was mad. And talking to the ghost of the boy she'd killed.

I don't think you did kill me. That's what I wanted to tell you. That's why I came back.

He was right beside her, his face leaning down to look into hers. She turned her head away. "Burned . . ." she tried to say, although what came out wasn't words. "In a . . . fire . . ." In her dream or hallucination, or whatever it was, he'd been able to read what was in her mind. She let the images form there. The waste-paper basket. The bedroom. The smoke. The horror.

I didn't die in a fire!

"But . . ."

I didn't. Listen to me. There might have been a fire. I suppose there was if you remember it. But I must have been dead before I burned.

Alex held up his left hand, fingers spread, then pointed to his right eye and cheek. *There was a woman. She hurt me, here and here. Hurt me with sharp things. And then she killed me.*

The dead boy frowned – the same solemn expression he'd worn in her dream. *I was wrong*, he told her. *It does matter. I was alone for a long time and I forgot. There was nobody to talk to, so I forgot. I didn't know who I was or what had happened to me. But then you talked to me and it made me start to remember. Now I want to know*

127

the rest. There was a woman who hurt me. Not you. I'd know if it was you. And there were other things before that. I want to know. It's horrible not knowing. It's almost like not being here at all. If you feel sorry for what you did, you've got to help me.

But you're not real, Jess thought. *You can't be real.*

I'm as real as you are! And I brought you back. I was kind to you.

He stepped away from the bed, glowering at her now with something like indignation. *There's nobody else I can ask. Nobody else sees me when they're awake. So if you don't help me, I'll never know. I'll be stuck not knowing for ever.*

I can't, Jess protested. There was no point in telling him again that he was a hallucination, a fitfully firing neuron. He wouldn't believe her. *Alex,* she said instead, *if there was some way to help you, I'd do it. But you're dead, and I'm dead too. I can't do anything.*

Yes you can! The boy's fists were clenched, his face twisted with anger and frustration. *You can see me and you can talk to me. And you can talk to other people. Somebody must know!*

His expression changed – becoming calmer, but also filling with a frightening resolution. *I know about you wanting to die, Jess. I saw you thinking about it a lot of times. But I'm not going to let you die until you've done this first.*

He turned his back on her and walked away. She could see him for a long time getting smaller and smaller, as though the cramped room was a corridor that stretched halfway to the end of the world.

Jess. It was the first time, alive or dead, that he'd ever called her by her name. It burned behind her red, itching eyes the way a brand might burn on her skin.

27

Grace lost a packet when Moulson rallied.

It wasn't a little bit here and a little bit there: it was a single massive payout to a dozen or so long-shot punters when Moulson hit the six-week mark with a heartbeat, a pulse and a full matching set of vital signs. Grace paid out in the ballroom that evening. She handed over the money without a murmur, as a bookie was bound to do, but the muscles in her jaw got tighter and tighter until Big Carol Loomis became seriously scared and tried to deflect the lightning with a change of venue.

"Look at this," she said, pointing to a poster on the wall. "Film club is showing *Angels with Dirty Faces*. 'Top of the world, Ma!' You want to go watch it, Grace?"

Grace turned to stare at her with flinty eyes. "*White Heat*," she said.

"What?"

"'Top of the world, Ma!' is the last line in *White Heat*. *Angels with Dirty Faces* has Cagney dying like a coward to stop impressionable young kids from following in his footsteps. No, Carol, I don't want to watch it. But I want you to. And when you're done, you can write me a fucking review."

Loomis weighed up many possible replies, but settled on a nod. She kept her face carefully expressionless as Grace walked away with her empty cash box dangling from her hand.

Dr Salazar witnessed Moulson's return from the dead with mixed emotions. He was amazed and overjoyed when he saw that she was rallying – an instinctive response arising out of a fuzzy but firm conviction that life was better than no life and that his job was to push as hard as he could in the right direction. But as a professional, he was mystified and almost affronted. How could this thing have happened? How could it be continuing to happen in front of his eyes?

Nurse Stock, who was actually the first to see the change in Moulson's condition, had a more straightforward and primal reaction. When she told Sally about the spike in the readings, she was whey-faced and terrified, close to breaking down. The whole time Salazar was examining Moulson, she was babbling away to him about how she'd made a mistake with Moulson's meds. She should have reported it, but it was late and it was dark and she didn't realise . . . and on and on.

Sally saw exactly what mistake she'd made: the violent purple bruise on Moulson's thigh made it clear as day that Stock had injected the last dose of tramadol into the artery instead of the vein. Moulson ought to have died, or at the very least gone into a cardiovascular crisis.

It wasn't an easy mistake to make with the femoral artery. It was a big target, whether you were trying to find it or (which was much more likely) avoid it. Stock had almost killed a patient through the kind of blunder you might expect from a first-year med student. A sloppy first-year med student with a happy-go-lucky attitude. The initial mistake was compounded by her not reacting properly to the sudden rush of blood that must have occurred as soon as the needle was withdrawn. Instead of seeing this for what it was – proof positive that she'd pierced an artery – Stock had just staunched the flow and walked away.

And now she was watching him, tense and rigid, as he inspected

130

the damage. She was waiting for the axe to fall. But Salazar had a problem with axes. Evil had to be identified and extirpated, obviously. But he'd flinched from that test before, when the evil was a lot bigger. Stock most likely had just made a mistake, and who was he to judge another human being's failings when he was such a desperate mess himself?

She was waiting for him to say something.

"Better get another bandage," he muttered. "This one is soaked."

Stock made a small, unidentifiable sound and retreated. When she came back with the bandage, Salazar stood aside and let her change Moulson's dressing herself. He thought he ought to say something, but he couldn't think of anything to say.

"I'll give her the tramadol from now on," was what he finally came up with. "We'll change the schedule so I can do it last thing before I leave."

Stock mumbled something he didn't hear. It was probably just, "Yes."

"All her meds," he said. "Leave them to me."

When Moulson asked to be fed, he took care of that too. The hypertonic drip, then the solids. He bought baby food from a chemist's in Fletchertown on his way to work and fed her that, cold and straight out of the jar. The prison canteen wasn't geared up to making nutritious meals for people with heavily ulcerated mouths.

Moulson got to spend six more days and nights in the quarantine unit. The nurses were pretty punctilious about her dosage now, especially Sylvie Stock, so she spent a lot of that time in carefully regulated tramadol sleep. Way too deep for dreams.

Then when she woke up, she was in muggy, gluey tramadol withdrawal. Not too much of an ordeal for someone who'd gone cold turkey from heroin, but more than enough to take her edge off. She didn't know where she was, and wherever it was, she felt like she was melting into a puddle.

All this while, she was putting on body mass like she was on steroids. Patience DiMarta weighed her three times a day with

131

awe and delight: she was recording Moulson's immaculate resurrection on a graph that she'd pinned up on the wall next to the bed. When Dr Salazar asked her whether this was a clinical tool or a motivational one, she just said, "I know a miracle when I see one."

Nurse Stock felt much the same way and kept on avoiding Moulson as far as she could. She felt like Moulson had been brought back from the brink on purpose to accuse her, and she was waiting for the other shoe to kick her in the stomach. If this was a miracle, it was a miracle that was aimed right at her.

Meanwhile in the prisoner wings, the whisper line was still humming, still digesting the astonishing fact of Moulson's recovery and the associated fact of Grace having to pay out on her book. Each of those two miracles substantiated the other one. Moulson was a very hot topic, and Shannon McBride's story about meeting her in the infirmary was once again much in request.

Shannon was more than happy to oblige, expanding her little turn into a one-act play. But she was still casting around for a theme, so the details changed a lot from one rendition to the next. Sometimes she had Moulson singing a recognisable song, but most times the song was in some weird foreign language Shannon couldn't identify ("Cyndi Lauper? No! Where did you hear that?"). Sometimes Moulson stroked her hair, or her brow, and Shannon drew strength from the touch. And sometimes – the best version, after a lot of scene-setting about how dark it was and how she couldn't be certain if it was a dream or not – Moulson was cuffed to the bed, but the cuffs fell away when she stood up and came over to where Shannon was crying on her bed of pain. *Don't be afraid*, she said, and started to sing . . .

Most of the Goodall women at this stage still held to the facts of the case. This was a kiddie killer, after all. Not a paedo, which would have put her beyond every pale there was, but still close enough to the lowest of the low that you could measure the gap with your hand. They liked a good story – who doesn't? – but they didn't believe that God would choose Jess Moulson as His servant, no matter how hard up He got.

Moulson did choose God though. Or at least she went for the initial consultation. She told Sally when she was able to talk that she'd had a change of heart. She wanted to see that pastor after all.

Jess liked Sarah Afanasy a lot, almost in spite of herself.

The non-denominational pastor didn't look very much like a spiritual adviser. Jess's mental image of a priest was of someone thin and pale, halfway out of the body into the spirit, and that was what she thought she needed. Pastor Afanasy was built to a more roly-poly body plan, and she seemed wholly comfortable with that. Instead of clerical robes, she wore black jeans, red plimsolls and (although she was well into middle age) a T-shirt with anime characters on it.

"Oh wow, they keep it hot in here, don't they?" she said as she dropped herself down without ceremony into the visitor's chair next to Jess's bed. Her voice had a slight transatlantic lilt to it. "What do I call you? Is Jessica okay?"

"It's Jess," Jess said.

"Jess. I like that. And you can address me as 'your holiness'. What can I help you with, Jess?"

Jess smiled dutifully at the joke, but she didn't have a ready answer for the question. What kind of help was she looking for here? And how could she describe what she didn't understand herself? She tried to push past the blockage by stating the obvious. "I did a terrible thing," she said.

The pastor nodded. No jokes now. She was instantly serious. "And it's weighing on your mind?"

"Yes."

"I heard about your hunger strike. Was that your way of saying you were sorry?"

"It started out that way."

"And you really wanted to die?"

133

"Oh yeah." It was the simple truth, and Jess said it with no self-consciousness. It was all she'd wanted. "But then when I was very close to dying, I thought . . . I saw . . ."

"You thought that there might be a reason to live after all."

Jess considered. That *was* what Alex had offered her. And the answer was surely the same even if she was hallucinating him. If all of this was just her own mind trying to find a loophole, scraping around at the last moment for a get-out clause.

The answer was the same, but the verdict couldn't be. Either she'd found a reason to live or she was lying to herself on so deep a level that she'd effectively lost her mind. And it seemed so obvious when you looked at it like that. This was exactly the wish-fulfilment fantasy she would have chosen for herself. That Alex wasn't dead. Or if he was dead, that he still needed her somehow, however little sense that made . . .

But the counterargument was staring down at her from the wall next to the bed. DiMarta's neat, fussy little line graph charting her inexplicable weight increase. *I know a miracle when I see one.*

Pastor Afanasy didn't seem to expect Jess to confirm or deny. At any rate, she carried on after the long pause as though Jess's silence was an answer in itself. "There's something I need to tell you," she said, "whether you want to hear it or not. Contrary to what you might think, you can't make up for something bad you've done by killing yourself. In fact there's almost nothing you can do by killing yourself except make the people who love you unhappy." Jess thought of Brenda and felt a moment of nausea – a disgust with herself that pushed her back towards despair. "If you're genuinely troubled, genuinely penitent, you've got to try to do good things going forward. Whatever you think God wants from you, whatever you think his plan is, that's the only deal that makes any sense. You understand me, Jess?"

Jess made a non-committal sound, half laugh and half sigh. She didn't. She didn't understand at all.

"He never asked you to die," Afanasy persisted, with a harder edge to her voice. "Nobody did. That was you shutting down because life was hurting you too much to bear. The very best you can say about it is that you were pouring good money after bad – making an awful mistake even worse. It wasn't ever going to do anybody any actual good."

There were lots of answers to that. That doing good was something she'd never managed yet, and it was probably way too late to start. That Alex's parents might get some crumb of comfort from the blunt equation of an eye for an eye. That at least she was making damn sure she never fucked up again.

But it was all irrelevant. What counted was what came next.

"If there *was* something good I could do . . ." she said. "If I could help somebody . . ." But she couldn't finish the sentence, still less start to explain it.

"What?" Pastor Afanasy prompted her.

"No," Jess said. "I don't know. I don't know anything."

"Then give yourself the benefit of the doubt," the pastor suggested. It was exactly what Brian Pritchard had told her to do, only he'd been referring to things in the past, and Sarah Afanasy was talking about the future.

Which made Jess wonder for the first time whether she – or Alex, for all the seeming finality of death – might actually have one.

28

Another night, another dream. A banal and ordinary one this time. Jess was playing hopscotch in the playground of her primary school. She was her nine-year-old self, acutely conscious of the dental braces she was wearing and the new shoes she was supposed not to scuff.

She woke to find Alex sitting cross-legged at the foot of her bed. Actually he wasn't quite touching the bed. He hovered an inch or so above it, casting no shadow on the crisp white coverlet.

Something dark and curdled rose in Jess's mind where her unbelief touched her fear, and both refused to dissolve. If Alex was a figment, just her own guilt wearing a dead child's face, then she was mad and lost. If he was real, then she was penned in with a monster, something utterly impossible and wrong.

No, I'm the monster, she told herself. Not him. Anyone who hurts a kid is a monster, whether they meant to do it or not. Cling to that. If there was one wrong, sick, unnatural thing in this room, it was her. And whether Alex was real or not, this was her penance, dangling within her reach. She could grab for it or she could go down into the ground as she had intended, with nothing done. Nothing changed or atoned for.

I like your uniform, Alex said. He said it loudly, even though he wasn't speaking aloud. She had the sense that he was trying to change the subject, though not a word had been spoken. *I had a black blazer with a red badge. There was a goat and a flag and* dum spiro spero *underneath.*

In her dream, Jess had been wearing the blue blazer and skirt of Heathcote Road County Primary.

"I want to help you," she said in her rusty, closed-for-repairs voice. "I don't know if I can, but I'll try." She was eliding a lot of things, including *I have no idea if you're really here or if any of this means anything but maybe, if there's a God, he sees me trying and that somehow counts.* She could have said those things but it seemed easier to let them slide for now.

The dead boy smiled. *Thank you, Jess!*

"You want to know . . . what happened before the flats burned down? This woman who hurt you – you want to know who she was?"

A vigorous nod. *And why she hated me. And where my friend went.*

"Your friend? You never mentioned . . ."

It was something else I only just remembered. There was a girl who was my friend and another girl who hated me.

"A girl, or a woman?"

Alex frowned, visibly turning that question over in his mind. *I don't know,* he admitted at last. *I remember it lots of different ways. I think before I forgot it I dreamed it a lot, and where I live now dreams are the realest thing. I see her as a woman and I see her as a girl.*

"Your own age?" Jess hazarded.

How old am I?

"You were ten when you died." Putting it into words made her mind rebel all over again against the craziness of it all. She was diving down the rabbit hole with her eyes wide open. There might not be a bottom.

Then probably older than me. But I don't know.

Which was hardly surprising, Jess thought bleakly. If he was a child, or the remnant of a child, then his perspective was limited by a child's understanding of the world. If he was a fantasy of her own making, then everything he said was meaningless and it all came down to some happy daydream of making amends. Either way, she was on her own.

Or maybe not. Not entirely. If she reopened contact with her lawyers, told them she'd changed her mind about lodging an appeal, there might be a way to get them to take another look at the events that had brought her here: the fire, and Alex's death.

It was better to believe, she realised, suddenly and all at once. If she believed, then she would have Alex with her, for a while at least. She'd have that solace, and perhaps another chance to prove that she could be the friend he needed. All she'd lose, even in the worst-case scenario, was her mind, and what the hell else was she using it for?

Pastor Afanasy's words came back to her, and now she could open up her arms and embrace them: this was a much better deal than dying.

Wherever it might lead, she decided she would take it.

29

Dennis Devlin was very unhappy about the collapse of the Jessica Moulson book. Grace had tasked him with keeping track, through Salazar, of the stages of Moulson's decline so that she could adjust her spread of odds accordingly. The Devil had done his best to meet this brief, and had had to work hard at it on account of Salazar's reluctance ever to call a spade a fucking spade. When Moulson lived, it seemed to Grace that there had to be a problem with the quality of her intel.

Devlin felt much the same, only where Grace blamed him, he blamed Salazar. And in due course he paid the doctor a house call. He found Sally up in the infirmary with Sylvie Stock, Sally filling in order forms for his pharmacy while Sylvie changed bedsheets. He was no judge of atmosphere, but he was pretty damn sure he hadn't interrupted a love-in.

"You're wanted in Franklin," he told Stock. "Stay there a good long while." She took off without a backward glance. As soon as she was gone, Devlin told Sally how unhappy he was with how the Moulson thing had worked out.

Sally was apologetic, which was right and proper, but he was defiant too. "It was a miracle," he said. "A little way outside my remit, Dennis."

"No man can serve both God and Mammon, Sally. Moderate your fucking language."

"Well, what would you call it?" the doctor demanded, slightly wild around the eyes. "She was right there, on the edge. Her weight had dropped to five stone. She had a thready pulse and her blood glucose was about one third normal. Below that, even. I would have said she had a day left at best before either her diaphragm gave out or she went into cardiogenic shock. And then—"

"Don't say a miracle happened," Devlin warned him.

"Well, something happened. And it's not something I can explain. She came back. Looking at her vitals now . . . it's like it's not even the same person."

Devlin felt that *something I can't explain* equated to *something that's not my fault*, and he didn't agree at all. "I went on your word, Sally," he said, grabbing hold of the doctor's lapels and pushing him back against the racks of the drug cabinet. Bottles of pills and tubes of unguent spilled on to the floor as Salazar tried to squirm sideways out of his grip. "And I passed your word along to Grace. Now look at this. We're all out of pocket because you can't do your job."

"I told you," Salazar protested. "I told you I couldn't give you a definite yes or no."

"You told me you might be out by a day or two. You didn't say she might live to draw her fucking pension!"

Salazar was about to say something, maybe something about Moulson not being out of the woods yet, but Devlin didn't let him. He slammed his fist into the doctor's stomach.

Salazar sank to his knees with a hiccup of shock and pain.

Devlin could get behind the shock at least. He was shocked too. He had no idea until he did it that punching Sally was even an option. But he hadn't minded how it felt at all, and he was ready to repeat the experience if Sally offered him a good excuse.

Gripping a handful of Salazar's hair, Devlin tilted his head back so they could go on talking face to face. "You let me down," he said, his voice level despite his drunkenly sloshing emotions. "I asked a simple favour, Sally, and you messed it up. Just so you know, we're not friends any more."

Salazar was trying to splutter out explanations and protests and more explanations. He wasn't making too much sense, and in any case, Devlin wasn't listening. Suddenly, coming out of nowhere in the same way that sucker punch had come, he'd had an idea. A really big one. It filled his attention wall to wall for a few seconds.

He'd cut loose on Salazar in a moment of weakness, his frustration getting the better of him. Perhaps it went deeper than that though. Perhaps he was trying to prove something to himself – that he was as big a man in his domain as Harriet Grace was in hers.

But thinking that through reminded him of Grace's little problem with regard to Curie wing. He had been using Sally all this time as a personal and private resource, deliberately keeping him out of Grace's eyeline. No matter how well he and her ladyship got on, he preferred for Grace not to know about his other little solace, the pethidine, and where he sourced it from. The day he put his balls in the palm of anyone's hand and invited them to make a fist would be the coldest day hell ever saw.

But Sally as a drug mule had an almost irresistible appeal. The doctor could go wherever he liked, whenever he liked. He mostly preferred not to, of course – left it to the nurses to run the satellite clinics in the prisoner blocks while he sat up here in his little make-believe ER and counted bedpans – but he could change all that whenever he chose to.

When you came down to it, who was better suited to dropping off drug shipments than a doctor? It was genius – the solution to Grace's short-term problem, and in the longer term, the kind of asset you could build an empire on. Sally would kick, of course, but he didn't have it in him to kick hard. Not these days.

Devlin let go of Sally's hair and stood back. Sally scrambled to his feet.

"Fix yourself up," Devlin told him brusquely. "Go on. You're a fucking mess. What time do you finish your shift?"

Salazar wiped away tears with the heel of his hand, which was shaking. Devlin watched him work out the not-so-complicated sum of what he would do next, the correct answer being nothing. He couldn't complain about what the Devil had just done to him because that doctored-by-a-real-doctor invoice was a hostage for his good behaviour. He couldn't wield the axe because it would bounce back in his face and split him in two.

"What time do you finish?" Devlin repeated. "Are you deaf?"

"S-six o'clock," Sally said.

"Come over to Grace's cell when you're done. No, wait. Come over right after lunch. Write it up as a medical visit. Say she's got menstrual cramps or something."

Salazar didn't seem thrilled at this prospect. He groped around for an excuse, came up with exactly the sort of feeble bullshit he was generally known for. "With menstrual cramps she'd just come into clinic."

Devlin breathed out through his teeth – half of a laugh bolted on to half of a sneer. "Something else, then. Dealer's choice. Just be there."

"For what?"

"A job opportunity."

"I've already got a job!"

"Yeah." Devlin conceded the point. "You do, for now. And if you want to keep it that way, Sally, you'll do what you're told and whistle while you do it. If you make me come and get you, I'll be in a really shitty mood."

Devlin headed for the door, but he stopped to look into the quarantine ward. Moulson was sleeping there, her breathing low and steady. Her cheekbones still stood up like the poles of a collapsed tent, but there was some colour in the skin around them.

"Clueless little bitch," Devlin growled. "She can't even kill herself right."

After Devlin had gone, Dr Salazar tucked his shirt back in and tried to hide the fact that Devlin had torn a button off it.

142

He was still crying. He couldn't make himself stop, even though he knew that Stock might come back at any moment and see him. Every time he managed to wipe his face dry and get his features composed, it would just start up again.

It was the humiliation more than the pain. And the fear, which of course was the most humiliating thing of all.

He knew he didn't have a choice. Some fights you'd lost before you ever got into them. Devlin and Grace. If you tried to touch one, you were bound to get both on your back. They held each other up like some scary religion with two mighty pillars.

Salazar could remember not being afraid of them, or of anything. But then two tragedies had fallen on him out of a clear sky. Two deaths. The first was an inmate, but his thoughts shied away from that now as they always did. The second was his wife, Leah. She had been his courage and his wisdom and his strength. She had all those virtues, and when Sally walked out of Fellside each night into her arms, he had bathed in them and got his own supplies all stocked up.

Sally was open-eyed about his idolatry. He'd known Leah was seeing someone else in the last years of their marriage, and though it had hurt him, he'd got over it. He was nobody's idea of the perfect lover, or the perfect husband. Whatever she was giving (or taking) elsewhere, she'd always given him everything he needed. One of his deepest regrets was that he'd never thought to wonder what she needed until it was too late to ask.

30

Governor Scratchwell wasn't the kind of man to overplay his own authority. He was well aware that Moulson recovering consciousness was a huge deal-changer, and therefore not a situation he should treat as a freestyle event.

He called the legal expert on the number she'd left for him, and got a different legal expert with a much more abrasive manner. When Scratchwell told expert number two that Moulson was awake, he said he was aware of that. His tone suggested it was somehow Scratchwell's fault, but his words were more equivocal. "You did everything in your power to give Moulson a painless and dignified death. Now she's reconsidered and you'll respect that too. Release her into gen pop."

"But . . . is that wise?" Scratchwell ventured. "She's very high profile now, because of all of this. And the nature of her crime . . ."

"Which is murder."

"The murder of a child."

"With no sexual assault. We're not seeing her as a high risk to your normal running, Mr Scratchwell. Not any more."

Because it's not you that's risking it, Scratchwell thought bitterly. He couldn't explain about the book that had been run on Moulson's survival. Officially he didn't know about it, because knowing about it would have required him to shut it down – to push against an aspect of Fellside's ecosystem that he kept well away from. But he knew that it had happened, and that as a side-effect it had kept Jessica Moulson as a trending topic in the prison throughout the six weeks she'd been on death watch. To release her now, with everyone watching, with the rumour mills spinning at maximum velocity, felt like tempting providence.

But his corporate bosses weren't exactly giving him a choice. He was going to have to cut Moulson loose and live with whatever happened next.

The one thing Scratchwell could do was to have a word with the most experienced supervisor on Goodall. Tell him to keep an eye on Moulson in case she made trouble or had it made for her.

Half the male screws at Fellside were perverts or incompetents, and any Venn diagram would show a large overlap between the two. But Dennis Devlin was a man you could rely on.

And Jessica Moulson would be as safe in his care as in God's own pocket.

PART THREE

STATE OF GRACE

31

Everybody had their own version of Harriet Grace's origin story. Like thunder or earthquakes, she seemed to require an aetiological myth. Shannon McBride's was the connoisseur's choice though. She'd stolen it wholesale from Mr Devlin, who she'd overheard in conversation with two of the G block guards, and she preserved all his idioms and intonations. It was far and away the best thing in her repertoire, but she was careful about when and where she told it. If word of her recitals ever got back to Grace and Devlin, the Devil would probably hurt her worse even than Grace would, because he'd have his own hurt coming in due course.

"She did it twice," Shannon would say. "That's the thing you've got to know about her. Two times over she made herself. I mean, like, literally out of nothing.

"She didn't have rich parents or a good education or any of that stuff. All she had was, you know, her belief in herself. Her belief that she could do it.

"She grew up in Churchbeck, and let me tell you in case you didn't know, Churchbeck is not Manchester. It's not even Bury. It's just one of those places where factory workers used to live in Dickens novels and shit. And Dickens isn't hiring any more."

That always got a laugh, and though Shannon herself didn't actually get the joke – or know who Dickens was, for that matter – she was happy to take the credit. With the scene set, she would lean in close as though she was imparting great secrets. "Grace went to one of those massive comprehensives that they made by collapsing a whole lot of little schools all in together. She had a bad time of it, no doubt. She got beaten and bullied and bent all out of shape. I know you wouldn't think it now, but she was the victim back then. Mostly because she was really weird-looking. She had a thing."

If nobody asked the obvious question, Shannon would wave her hand across her face as though she was trying to mime something that was too hard to describe in words. The words of this legend might be Devlin's but she added the stage dressing herself, and she was good at it. Sooner or later someone would play straight man for her. "What kind of thing?"

"I think they call it a facial cleft. But there's lots of different kinds and she had one that was way out there. Crazy. Like, her lip and her nose were all folded back into her cheek, sort of in a pleat. She couldn't even talk properly. They called her Frogface. And nobody would touch her or get too close to her in case they got the Frogface Curse.

"But she was really clever, even then. All the kids who were picking on her in the playground, she beat them all when it came to her grades and all that stuff. She came out with a fistful of A-stars, even though she was off school half the time having all this surgery done. They can't fix a facial cleft all at once because the bones of your face don't all grow at the same speed. So they've got to do it a bit at a time.

"And in the end they made her beautiful. She's still got these little tiny scars – under her hair and along the line of her jaw – but you can only see them if you get in close and look really hard, and who's gonna be up for that?"

Shannon tended to rush through this part of the story fairly quickly in case anyone asked her how she knew about Grace's

150

scars, or came up with questions about the surgery that she couldn't answer. If they asked about the exam grades she just said airily that you could look that stuff up online.

"So now here she was with a new face and a new job, and she was on top of the world. She was working down Bury job centre. Setting up interviews for all the little snots who used to give her grief. She made them dance, from what I heard. Oh yes.

"Anyway, that was how she got into all the people-trafficking stuff. It was only what she doing already really, except with illegal immigrants. She was hiring them out for building sites or crop-picking or whatever and taking two-thirds of the pay-off for herself. Making money hand over fist."

This was the cue for a dramatic pause. The audience knew the punchline, because here was Grace doing a twelve-stretch in the middle of nowhere. How are the mighty fallen. And risen again. But they didn't know the precise mechanism, and in some ways this was the best part, so Shannon drew it out.

"It was Operation Gary that fucked her. What, you never heard of that? It was after all those cockle pickers drowned in Morecambe Bay. They set up a special task force to stop people from doing what Grace was doing.

"But she might have got away with it if she hadn't taken on a partner. She was never all that great with computers, and it was slowing her down. She needed someone who could run ads on the 'Help to Work' website and stuff like that. Match up supply and – what's the other one? – demand, yeah, when she had a dozen illegals in the back of a van doing nothing.

"So she took on this nice young man. Stephen Menzies. He did all that stuff for her. Did some other stuff for her too, if you know what I mean. Scratched her back and oiled her crack.

"Only Menzies was a police grass. He was part of this Operation Gary, and he got all the dirt on her and then gave evidence against her when she was arrested. She got twelve years, with deferred parole. Plus they stripped out all her bank accounts and took her house off her and everything. Illegal enterprise, whatever they call

151

it. They left her with the clothes she stood up in. Banged her up in here.

"I know what you're thinking. It takes time to bounce back from something like that. And it does. It took Grace about a month. From the moment she came in here, she was looking around her and seeing how it all fitted together. All the rackets. The big operators – there were three or four of them back then – they thought she was nobody. First-timer and all that. They didn't pay her any attention. Until she walked right up and took it away from them.

"It's all about what you believe in, and what Grace believes in is Grace. And nobody else, not any more. She never forgets and she never forgives. Once she had it all sorted in here, she went back and dealt with a few bits of old business."

This was Shannon's favourite part, which was why she always saved it for last. "She hired these two blokes. Johnny Satchell, who used to be the bouncer at Electric nightclub, and this ex-squaddie, Peter something or other. A real head case, he was – scariest man you could ever meet. Grace paid for twelve hours of their time. Top dollar, but she said she wanted their best work.

"The clock started when they knocked on Stephen Menzies' door. Saturday morning, eleven o'clock. She knew he'd be in, and he was. All by himself. And by God, she got her twelve hours' worth."

32

Dr Salazar had his audition with Grace sitting on one of the comfortable chairs in the privacy of her cell. It was a great deal more luxurious than his consulting room.

Devlin had warned him not to say a single word about their private arrangement regarding his pethidine habit, and Sally didn't. In fact he barely opened his mouth at all: between fear and shame, he was an elective mute.

Grace seemed to be fine with that. Sally felt she mainly wanted to be listened to, not to listen. "This is a new venture for us," she said, leaving the *us* undefined. "We've got total control of the market here in Goodall, so if we're going to expand at all, we've got to move outwards into the medium-security blocks. You understand?"

Sally nodded.

"Now Mr Devlin thinks there might be a part for you in all this, doctor, and I value Mr Devlin's opinions. But you haven't always been in my corner. Two years ago you were making serious trouble for me, and I had to get serious with you in return. I'm sure you remember that. The thing is, it's okay to try something like that once, when you don't know any better. But I wouldn't want you to try it again. I'd want reassurances. I won't ask for promises, because promises don't mean anything. I just want to hear you say that you've learned your lesson and you won't do anything stupid."

"I have," Sally said. "I've learned my lesson."

"And . . .?"

"And I won't do anything stupid." The words came out easily and brought no increased unease. For Salazar, just being here in this situation was the functional limit of degradation. The speed of light. If you hit the speed of light and accelerate, you can't go any faster.

Besides, anything that came out of his mouth, any promise he made, was automatically a lie. He was going to give in his notice as soon as he finished his shift tonight. Walk away from Fellside and never come back. Grace wouldn't chase him. And Devlin wouldn't inform against him once he was gone – not when there was nothing to gain and a risk that he might inform right back.

Grace studied the doctor's face for a while before going on to outline what it was she wanted from him. "We don't currently have many friends in Curie. None of the guards over there are on my payroll. That will change, but to start with we need someone who can go in and out freely and make drop-offs to my dealers there. It's a seed crystal, really, that we can grow from. Have you got any questions about any of that?"

Sally shook his head.

Grace's sunny mood took a slight dip. "You should have lots of questions. Where? When? What? Who? I haven't given you any of the details. Are you even listening to me, doctor?"

"Yes," he assured her.

"Then . . .?"

"I'd . . . like some details."

I won't do it, Sally told her in the safety of his mind. *Talk all you like, it won't make any difference.*

But as he shouted that discreet defiance, his thoughts hit an image that momentarily derailed them. Water. Blood. Toilet paper.

154

One upturned eye, whiter than bleached cotton, fixing him with a stare of reproach or warning. His throat constricted. He winced and closed his eyes, trying to drive the awful memory away. Grace and Devlin didn't seem to notice.

Devlin was saying now that Sally's drop-offs should be piggy-backed on a weekly clinic in Curie – either a new one or one of the existing ones. "I like that," Grace agreed. "But it shouldn't be a straight handover."

"Why not?" Devlin asked. "Why complicate things?"

You can't make me, Salazar thought.

"If our dealers sign up for the clinic, week after week, their names are on a list. There's a paper trail. And as an added compli-cation, Sally – no disrespect, doctor – gets to see who he's delivering to. Much better if he leaves the package somewhere for them to pick up later. Double blind means nobody is compro-mised. Nobody can trick up anybody else if they get caught themselves."

I won't do it.

"What about the meditation room?"

"Nice. I think we can make that work."

They ignored Sally for a while, talking over his head about weights and dates and logistics. He waited to be dismissed, and in due course Grace told him he could go.

"Just one final point, doctor," she said when he was halfway to the door. The Columbo moment. He wanted to be gone, to get the complicated process of fleeing underway, but he had to stop and turn around.

"Yes?"

"That previous time that we were talking about, when you tried to make trouble for me. You remember how it came out?"

"Of course."

"You were still alive when it was all over. Not everybody was that lucky."

"I said I remember." A tiny, forlorn flash of irritation, gone as soon as it arrived. "I do, Grace. I remember."

155

She nodded, unperturbed. "Well, the same thing would happen this time too. If you let me down again. The exact same thing."

Salazar didn't understand for a moment what it was she was saying. "But," he said, "there isn't anyone . . ."

"No. Nobody who's directly involved. But I'm told that you and Nurse DiMarta have a nice little platonic friendship going. So I'd probably start with her."

Salazar went back to the infirmary. It was empty that day: Moulson had been discharged the same morning. He sat at his desk with his hands in his lap, silent and still, as his mind fitted itself around the contours of his new role and terms of employment.

It was funny, in a way. If his life were a comedy, ending up as a drug mule was the one beat nobody would see coming.

And if it were a tragedy, likewise.

33

Jess was released into gen pop with as little fanfare as could be managed. A screw collected her from the infirmary and walked her across the rec yard to Goodall. It was Corcoran, the guard who had escorted her in the ambulance from Winstanley. She cautiously congratulated Jess on still being alive.

"Not according to plan, right? But there are some things you can't really plan for until they happen. Or don't happen. You know what I mean?" They walked along in silence for a few moments, then Corcoran said, "The truth is, this place can be awful if you make enemies. And IMHO, the worst enemy you can make is yourself."

Jess was still purging the tramadol out of her system. She was as shaky on her feet as a two-year-old. She responded to this homespun wisdom with a weak nod of acknowledgement. She got the point. But that ship had probably sailed.

The usual way into the block was via the ballroom, but Corcoran's brief was to ease Moulson into her new quarters without raising a ripple. She unlocked a door at the back of the building and they went in through a service corridor that led directly to the east stairwell. A sign on the door read: THIS IS NOT AN EXIT EXCEPT IN CASE OF FIRE.

Goodall wing had a bouquet which, after the antiseptic purity of the infirmary, was so rich and complex it was disconcerting. Jess tried to work out its ingredients. Air freshener. Institutional food. The hot-iron tang of sweat just before it turns sour and awful. Old sheets left folded for years at the back of an airing cupboard. People. Overwhelmingly it was the smell of people shut in together, rubbing each other smooth year after year like stones in a sack.

Corcoran held a door open for Jess, pointing the way up a metal staircase. The centre of each tread had been worn smooth and slightly concave by thousands of feet. Pritchard had said that Fellside was a recent build, but people were like oceans. When oceans set to work, mountains fall and are broken down to make beaches.

A babel of voices assailed Jess's ears as they ascended, but Corcoran had worked out their approach with a view to stealth. Though close at hand, the ballroom was invisible. Only that wash of voices told Jess how near she was to a new universe.

Corcoran took her up to the second floor and along an open walkway. The ballroom was on their left, but they stayed close to the wall on the right. They stopped at a door marked 239, Lorraine Buller's cell. Buller's old roommate, Cyndi Souk, had been downgraded from high to medium security and transferred to Curie wing. "Might happen to you some day," Corcoran told Jess. "If you keep your nose clean. Nice life in Curie. Unlimited visits. Access to the farm and the plant nursery. Even conjugals."

Having painted this idyll on the noisy air, she said goodbye and good luck and left Jess to make her own introductions. Jess went into the cell, not sure if she should knock. A middle-aged woman with a blonde buzz cut was stretched out on the top bunk with the Penguin Classics edition of *Middlemarch* in her hands. She was dressed in the same yellow and black tracksuit that Jess was now wearing. Her heavily lined face looked like an artist's rough sketch that had been overworked, every spare inch shaded in or cross-hatched. The pale blue lines of old tattoos peeped out at her wrists.

She glanced up from the book and gave Jess a nod, civil but distant.

"Moulson? I'm Buller. You're bottom-bunking. And I get the sink first in the morning. I've got three years on you and that's the way it works. I don't like singing when I'm trying to read, and I don't like bad farts that come without a warning. If there's anything you don't like, you'd better tell me now."

Jess shook her head.

"What, there's nothing you don't like? Nothing at all? It was a serious question, love."

"People laughing at their own jokes," Jess hazarded. That had been John Street's prejudice rather than hers, but it was something to say and it seemed to be acceptable. Buller made a face that translated as *each to her own* and returned to her reading. Jess sat down on the cell's only chair, slowly and carefully so as to reduce the jarring impact when she settled herself on the mottled plastic seat.

"This is free association time," Buller said. "Just so you know. It's the one time when you don't have to stick in the cell. You can go out on the yard or sit in the ballroom."

"I'm fine here," Jess mumbled.

"Well, I can understand that," Buller said. "Nice and quiet. Nobody shouting at you. But if you want a word of advice, you should show your face. They're going to shout at you sooner or later. Then they're going to lose interest and go and shout at somebody else. Hide your face and you're probably only feeding the fire." She glanced across at Jess for a moment, then gave her attention back to George Eliot. "My opinion anyway," she said.

Jess sat for a while, thinking it over and gathering her strength. Finally she got up and headed for the door.

"Good luck," Buller muttered as she passed.

Jess got as far as the railing right outside the cell door. She rested her elbows on it and stared down into the ballroom. Gradually one woman after another noticed her and looked up at her until the entire ballroom met her gaze. Everyone in Goodall knew who

159

she was, and that she was coming on-block that day. There was considerable interest in her, some of it hostile, some detached and even a little (mostly because of Shannon McBride's narrative skills) that was inclined to be positive.

Jess didn't know about any of that, but her instincts screamed at her to retreat from all this scrutiny, which she couldn't read and didn't want. She certainly couldn't bring herself to go down and mingle. She was stuck out there on the walkway like a soldier in no-man's-land.

But suddenly she felt a hand slide into hers. She looked down to see Alex Beech standing next to her, his face on a level with the third bar of the railings. He didn't say anything, but a little strength ran out of him and into Jess, trickling through their clasped hands the way cool water trickles down your throat.

In the infirmary, when he'd first come to her, her fear had shut out all other emotions. Here, where she knew no one, he was the only familiar face and she felt a rush of relief and gratitude to see him.

I didn't want you to forget me. You thought I was a dream before. I'm not. I'm not a dream and you've got to keep your promise.

"I know that." Jess tried to keep her lips from moving too much when she spoke. She was talking to a ghost who nobody else could see. She knew that instinctively, but it was proved anyway when another inmate went past them, walking right through the boy and barely veering for the woman.

Alex stiffened when the moving body breached the space where he was standing. After it had passed by, a tremor ran through him. His face twisted into a grimace. He didn't like accidental contact – a fact that made the touch of his hand in Jess's a little more miraculous than it already was.

"I haven't forgotten what I promised," she told him. "And I'm never going to forget."

You're going to find out what happened to me.

"Yes."

You'll find my friend. And the other girl who hurt me.

160

"Yes. I'm going to make a start as soon as I can."

To be with him and to be forgiven. Jess knew that she would do anything in exchange for that. Having already resigned herself once to giving up her life, she found it an easy promise to make, and she meant every word. She came pre-stressed, annealed, ready to do whatever needed to be done.

"Look at her," Hannah Passmore said to Pauline Royal across the width of one of the board game tables. Po followed Hannah's glance and saw Moulson up there on the second floor, her head dangling loosely over her folded arms. "Thinks she owns the place."

Po was peaceable to a fault, but she had to agree. There did seem to be something arrogant about that stance. About how completely Moulson had let her guard down. In a place like Goodall, relaxing was the ultimate show of strength.

"Fucking smirk on her face, look," Passmore went on. "I'm not putting up with this."

"Screws are watching, Hannah," Po warned her. "They know there's going to be trouble. Use your brain and let someone else make it."

Passmore saw the sense of this, but she really didn't like that smile.

There were two more lifers, Doll Paley and Sam Kupperberg, playing draughts at the next table – a strange version they'd made up themselves where each of them alternated black and white moves. Doll looked up from the game. "Why not just leave her alone?" she suggested. "The way I hear it, she didn't even mean to kill that boy. She didn't know what she was doing."

"Only God gets to judge," Kupperberg agreed. "Nobody else has a right to."

Passmore had never had much use for God. She let that pious chatter wash right over her. "You know what we should have around here?" she called out, loud enough for everyone to hear. "A barbecue!"

161

A few women glanced across at her, then saw where she was looking and got the joke. The laughter was thin, but it encouraged Passmore to make a second sally. "Frying tonight!" she shouted. And someone else cried, "Fingerlicking good!"

The screws stepped in quickly, not just down in the ballroom but on the walkways too. They all moved at the same time, which made it pretty obvious that they'd been waiting for anything that looked like trouble. It was the evening shift under Ms Carlisle, so she got to be the voice of authority, telling the hecklers that if they tried to be funny again, they'd be amusing themselves in solitary.

The catcalls subsided into muttering, but the muttering was angry. The women of Goodall had had a lid dropped over them.

Nobody likes that.

34

That first day was indicative of things to come. Jess continued to have problems fitting into the daily life of Goodall wing.

She got beaten up on her second day by some of the other women on her own landing. It wasn't planned or orchestrated particularly. She just walked past a little group of them in a way that rubbed someone or other up the wrong way. One woman threw a punch and then the rest joined in because it was only civil not to leave a friend out on a limb. Jess got a lot of bruises where they wouldn't show, but it was a light beating – which in Goodall meant the kind you could walk away from.

The next day she got it a lot worse. Hannah Passmore led a raiding party into her cell and worked on her for a good five minutes while two other women, Chander and Williams, held her down. Buller didn't intervene, but she told them when enough was enough.

"It's enough when I say it is," Passmore grunted, landing another kick.

"You stop now," Buller said, "or I'm calling a guard."

Passmore did stop then, but only to glare at Buller.

"You'd snitch for scum like this?" Shamone Williams demanded.

163

"If it's that or watch you kill her."

The three women weighed up their options. Sarah Chander started to haul down her trousers and knickers.

"You piss on her, Sachi," Buller said, "and you will clean it up. With your left arm, because I will break the right one."

"Let it go," Passmore decided. "We're finished. For now."

"Thank you," Jess muttered, when the three women had gone.

"You're welcome," Buller told her. "I would have said something earlier, but it's that same principle. It will happen when it happens and the sooner it happens, the sooner it stops. You need a hand up?"

"I think I'll just lie here a while."

"Up to you. You want a chapter of George Eliot?"

And since Jess didn't, Buller went back to her reading.

That was about as bad as it got. There wasn't any sustained vendetta against Jess, which was what Governor Scratchwell had been afraid of. It was only too easy, he knew, for a group of people crowded into an inadequate space and kettled up together for years on end to find themselves all thinking the same thing at the same time, and then all doing it. That was how riots kicked off. One person cracks but everyone else is ready and waiting, right there and totally up for it when the moment comes.

With Moulson, though, there was a collective distaste rather than a collective hatred. It would have been different if she'd abused Alex Beech for fun or profit, but she hadn't. She'd burned him up when she burned her own life up, and that was different. Many of the Goodall women thought she was a piece of shit. A whole lot more of them thought she was a screw-up who deserved their pity, or that losing her face and being banged up in Fellside had gone some way to balancing the scales for what she did. Nobody had warm feelings for her, but nobody had much of an axe to grind.

Well, almost nobody. Hannah Passmore was still taking Moulson personally, and found more than one occasion to slip in a smack or a shove. There were a few other women who followed her lead, although with less venom. And there were a few more who catcalled when they saw Moulson in the commissary or the ballroom.

And one day, ascending one of the stairwells, she met a woman coming down who filled the narrow space and blocked her way completely. The two of them stopped dead, and neither spoke.

The other woman was very tall, with long, rangy limbs and badly mottled skin. Older than Jess, but not by much. The lines on her weathered face seemed to have been carved there by temperament rather than time. She had cut the sleeves off her prison-issue tracksuit top, which was a violation and would have got most women written up. The muscles on her arms moved over one another as she flexed her big hands.

Jess stood aside to let this apparition walk on by. She certainly wasn't going to try to push past her. But the other woman didn't move at all. "You go ahead," Jess said at last. When that got no answer, she made an "after you" gesture. She couldn't even tell if the woman was looking at her. Her eyes seemed weirdly unfocused.

"That's a fucking ugly face," the woman said at last. She forced the words out between her teeth, which stayed clenched together.

"I was . . . burned," Jess faltered. "There was a fire."

"A fire?"

"Yes."

There was a long silence. "I used to like sitting by the fire," the woman said at last. "In the summer."

"In the winter," Jess corrected automatically. The woman's eyes came back from the horizon to fix on her. "Summer," she said. "In the summer. We had a barbecue. Were you there?"

"N-no," Jess stammered. "I don't even know your—"

The woman's face was suddenly an inch away from hers, the eyes boring into her own, slightly sour breath hot against her cheek. "Then don't tell me when it was," she growled. "All right?"

"All right."

"Don't know you're born, do you? Don't know to put yourself out when you're on fire. How fucking stupid is that?"

Jess said nothing. The woman's anger had come from nowhere. It didn't seem to have any object; it had just bumped up against her because she was there. If she was very still, maybe it would roll on by and bump against something else.

The woman breathed out through her mouth: a heavy, world-weary sigh. Then she went on down the stairs, her bony shoulder slamming into Jess's chest as she passed by.

Jess carried on up to her own level and into the cell. Buller was lying on the top bunk, not reading this time but writing a letter. Her tongue sat on her lower lip as she wrote.

"Can I ask you a question?" Jess ventured.

Buller grunted. "If it's a short one."

"A very tall woman who . . . who may have something missing. Dark hair, bad skin, bare arms . . ."

"Liz Earnshaw."

"Does she?"

"Does she what, love?"

"Have something missing?"

Buller put her notepad down.

"Oh," Jess said. "I don't want to disturb you."

"But now that you have," Buller said, "you may as well listen. Stay away from Lizzie. She's a troubled soul, but she's also very dangerous. Has she got something missing? Yes, she has. But probably not in the way you mean."

"What's the story?" Jess asked. "I mean, if it's something you can talk about." She wasn't even sure why she was asking. There was just something about the tall woman that had stayed with her. Something that frightened her but fascinated her at the same time.

"I don't do stories."

"Do you know anybody who does?"

Buller laughed shortly. "Oh yes."

Jess visited Shannon McBride in her cell because she only had the cell number to go on (Buller didn't do descriptions either, or

166

introductions). But as soon as she stepped inside, she knew she'd seen the young woman with the anxious bleached-out features before.

McBride knew Jess too, and was thrilled to receive the visit. "I was the first person in Fellside who even saw you," she said once they were both sitting down – Shannon on the bunk, Jess in the place of honour on the chair. "The first prisoner, I mean. Obviously some of the guards saw you. And some of the nurses. But nobody else. Do you remember that you sang to me?"

Jess didn't. That had gone, along with most of the memories of her first days in Fellside, lost to the meds and the near-coma she'd gone into afterwards. But Shannon didn't mind. In fact she was very happy to fill that gap and told Jess the whole story, repeating some parts of it out of a sincere conviction that once wasn't enough.

"I heard your voice through the pain," she said. "It was so soft, and so gentle. It was like you had a magic power."

"I don't," Jess said quickly. "I don't at all. But I'm glad I was able to help."

"And now you want to know about Lizzie Earnshaw. So you come to me." Shannon's hands were clasped to her knees. She was practically hugging herself. "Of course! Of course I'll tell you! But I can only tell you about Liz if I tell you about Naseem Suresh too. It's like they're two halves of the same story."

Naz had been the youngest woman on the wing, Shannon said, and in many ways the most trouble. She was only there at all because Fellside had landed a contract for dealing with female prisoners who were due to be deported after they'd finished their sentence – mostly trafficked women, but in a few cases asylum seekers who'd blotted their copybooks while their status was still pending. Naz didn't fit either of those categories, but her parents were illegals and her mother had given birth to her in the course of a two-year odyssey from Uttar Pradesh to the British Midlands. She had spent her whole life in the UK, but she was officially stateless. When she was caught in a raid on an East London brothel,

167

she made the mistake of clocking a police officer and running for it. Only an eighteen-month sentence, but she was automatically classed as maximum security because of the flight risk.

"She was cheeky," Shannon said. "Cheeky to everybody. That sounds like a little thing, but in here, respect is very important. Naz didn't have any time for that. She was fearless. If she saw something she didn't like, she just came right out and said it. Which got a lot of people's backs up. The lifers especially." There was envy in McBride's voice. Jess guessed that her own personality tended a lot more towards compromise, and that she wished she could be different.

"So was Earnshaw one of the people Naseem rubbed up the wrong way?" she asked. It seemed to be an obvious inference.

"Oh no! Lizzie was how come Naseem got away with it. Lizzie fell in love with Naz. It happened really quickly, but it took a long time for people to realise. Lizzie had been married. She had kids. She'd been straight her whole life. But one look at Naz and she forgot what straight even meant.

"And because she was older than Naz, and had been inside for longer, and was a lifer and everything, she sort of protected Naz. I don't mean it was . . . you know . . ." Shannon made a vague churning gesture. "What you see in films sometimes, where a young con gets protected by an older one because they're sort of like a toy or a sex slave. It wasn't like that at all. Naz was in charge. Lizzie loved her so much, she did anything that Naz said. It was, you know, first love. First love changes you all the way to the bottom of your heart."

"You said Earnshaw had been married," Jess reminded her.

"Oh, she had," Shannon said, nodding in vigorous agreement. It seemed to be important to her not to disagree with anyone. "But I think you can have first love any time in your life. You can probably even have it more than once, although that doesn't sound like it makes any sense. Lizzie was like a teenager tearing up daisies and saying she-loves-me-she-loves-me-not. You've seen what kind of a temper she's got. But when she was with Naz, she was sugar."

Jess found it hard to imagine the sullen, monolithic Earnshaw in terms of sweeteners. Possibly that scepticism showed on her face, because Shannon hastened to explain.

"It wasn't like she stopped being angry. She's angry all the time, about everything. You know what she came in here for? Aggravated assault. A bar fight with three other women. Her sisters-in-law. Nobody knows why they went for Lizzie, but she left one of them quadriplegic. And it didn't matter that Lizzie had, like, a really low IQ, and her dad used to beat her with a broom handle. They still sent her down for life with eighteen minimum.

"But when she was with Naz, she managed to keep that side of herself locked all the way down. She knew it was in there and she knew when it was starting to come out. She had ways of dealing with it. Just once she hit Naz when they were arguing about something, and Naz cried, and Lizzie swore right then that she would straight-out kill herself if she ever did it again. Just take herself out of the world. And if anyone else hurt Naz, well, it would be the same thing. She'd break them in tiny pieces."

"Jesus!" Jess murmured.

"Everyone on-block knew that. If you dared to touch Naseem, you were going to have Lizzie to deal with. She punched a warder in the face once when he shoved Naz back into line in the canteen. A warder! So you can imagine what she would have done to an inmate who went near her.

"But someone went ahead and did it all the same. Naz had been talking . . . said she had dirt on someone, and a friend who was going to get her in to see the governor. Maybe she thought that with Liz on her side she was safe. But she wasn't.

"One day she turned up dead in the prison showers. Shanked. With toilet paper wrapped around her like a shroud. That's something they do to narks in Fellside — to say they're lower than shit.

"Liz just went crazy. She spent four of the next five months in solitary because she was going straight from one fight to the next. She'd fight you if you said hello to her. Because her girl

169

was gone and she couldn't bring her back. If the world had a throat, I swear she would have ripped it out."

That sounded like the end of the story, but Shannon leaned forward with conspiratorial fervour and put her hand on Jess's arm. As though Jess had been about to jump up and leave and miss the best part.

"It looked like Lizzie was going to end up killing herself. Or just go mad and get transferred to Dietrich. But then Grace picked her up, and that saved her."

"Who is Grace?" Jess asked.

McBride seemed surprised to be asked. "Harriet Grace," she said, as though the name was an explanation in itself. "You know, as in the state of. What they call G block. She runs everything in here. Anyway, Lizzie works for Grace now, and she follows orders. Which means she stays out of trouble because Grace expects her to. If Liz has still got one wheel on the road, it's on account of Grace. It's sort of funny, really. It's like she can't go crazy any more because she hasn't got permission."

"She looked crazy enough to me on the stairs just now," Jess said. She told Shannon about her brief encounter with Earnshaw, which had prompted her to ask for the story in the first place.

Shannon laughed out loud. "That wasn't Lizzie being crazy," she said. "No, really, Jess, it wasn't. Look at you!"

"Look at me?"

"Not a bone broken. You've still got all your teeth. Both eyes. No, what you got there was Lizzie on the leash."

35

Jess had written a letter to Brian Pritchard. She told him she had decided to lodge an appeal against her sentence after all. She couldn't do anything more towards finding answers for Alex's questions until Pritchard replied to her and set those wheels in motion. In the meantime, she endured.

The business of survival in Fellside was complicated and engrossing. For someone who had recently been trying to be done with life, it was also novel. In the first weeks after her transplantation from the shallows of the infirmary into the reefs of Goodall, just getting by seemed to take up the bulk of Jess's days.

Her nights, though, were otherwise occupied. That was when Alex would come and visit her.

Lock-up was the hardest and heaviest time in the prison day. It was also the most regimented. The rules were precise and they were followed to the letter. A buzzer sounded at 9.50 p.m. to tell the cons that free association time was over. That meant they had ten minutes to get back to their cells. To be out after ten o'clock was an infraction punishable by solitary.

Warders checked every level simultaneously. They went round each cell and tallied the occupants on a digital clicker. The numbers

171

fed back to the main board at one end of the ballroom, just inside the main door, where the senior on-block would be standing. The senior had to make sure the numbers added up correctly by cell, corridor and level. All the totals were already in the computer, so it was mostly a case of ticking off OK, OK, OK in a bunch of boxes.

Then the warders called clear and the senior turned the master key, which locked all the cell doors at the same time. There were overrides, obviously, so any level or corridor or cell could be locked or unlocked by tapping in a code. But they almost never were. The drill was close up at 10 p.m. and open again at 8.00 in the morning. When those locks clicked shut, the Fellside women knew they were going to spend the next ten hours of their lives in a box they couldn't get out of. And for nine of those hours, they would be in the dark, because lights went out at eleven.

Alex would usually arrive sometime around lights-out. The stone walls and the closed door, the floor and ceiling were no obstacle to him because he walked along some axis that was at right angles to all of them. He approached Jess through dimensions that she could dimly see because they clung to him for a while after he arrived: the spoor of the night world through which he had once escorted her.

The moment when he came would always fill Jess with an unreasoning fear, a sense that the lid had momentarily opened on a box that was better kept shut. For that moment, the dead boy seemed to be an ambassador from an utterly alien place.

But only until he smiled and spoke her name. Only until he started to talk.

"What was your favourite toy?" she asked him once.

Street Dance MoveMat! he answered with no hesitation at all.

"Which is what, exactly?"

You play the music. And the mat lights up and you have to put your feet and your hands and your bum where the lights are. So you're dancing. And it gets faster and harder.

"I think I would have loved that," Jess said. "But I'd never have

172

got any of the boys I knew to play it with me. They were too macho to dance."

I would have played it with you.

"Yeah, and you would probably have won, too. I danced like a drunken hippo."

Lorraine Buller's rumbling snore was the backdrop to these conversations. She never woke. But then Jess was only forming the words with her lips, not speaking them aloud. Alex could always hear her.

Once the fear wore off, she appreciated the company. She still wasn't all the way back to her normal weight. Her body ached if she lay in any position for too long, and the wafer-thin prison mattress didn't help at all, so she slept shallowly and intermittently. Some nights, her bony hips felt as though they'd been jammed into her torso upside down and sideways, and her shoulders were more like a rack she was tied to than something that belonged to her. She was feeling the tug of her addiction again, too, re-asserting itself as she retreated from death's door. Alex's voice was a thread that drew her through the darkness to the morning bell.

Even by day, though, he would sometimes visit her – although he said the light hurt his eyes and made it hard for him to see. It also made it harder for Jess to see him, but she would feel that slender hand slip into hers as she leaned against the fence in the yard, or sat in the ballroom, and his voice would murmur in her ear – asking her questions about anything that was going on around her, no matter how trivial or dull it was, so her words could fill the gaps in his perceptions.

The gaps were enormous and surprising. Alex was far from blind but his vision was weirdly selective. He could see some things perfectly clearly, possibly in a greater level of detail than Jess herself. He watched Shamone Williams sculpting a horse out of a piece of cedar wood. She did it by rubbing the wood with different grades of sandpaper, because otherwise she could only work on it during the three hours a week she was allowed into the workshop with access to tools, so that horse was coming on slower than arthritis. Alex was fascinated by the work in progress. He talked about the horse's tail — about how it looked like a real tail whisking in the wind, with all the hairs separate and distinct. Another time, he saw a shank Big Carol Loomis was carrying in her pocket, and he pointed to it and asked Jess what it was. *It's like a spike with bandages wrapped around it . . .* And Jess stared at Big Carol for a second too long and almost got herself another beating. She didn't see the shank herself but she knew what it was from Alex's description. She didn't doubt that he could really see it.

Other things it seemed he couldn't make out at all. He had very little sense of the layout of a room or the placement of its walls and furniture. He would stand and talk to her with his phantom body partially bisected by a table or an open door, completely oblivious. He had a much better sense of where people were, and would usually move around them rather than through them. When they walked through him, he stiffened and shuddered as though he'd stepped in a puddle of cold water.

There was nothing wrong with his memory, that was for sure. He was endlessly interested in the minutiae of prison life, and he picked up and hoarded every nugget of information he came across. Within a week, he was referring to all the Goodall inmates — most of them women whose faces Jess couldn't even call to mind — by their given names or nicknames.

It was easier for him, of course. Jess kept herself to herself for very good reasons: if she tried to start a conversation, she was rolling a dice where a lot of the outcomes had her being punched in the mouth. So sitting around quietly and minding her own business was her baseline strategy. Buller was cordial enough, and would talk to her about uncontroversial things. Some of the other women on the corridor would give her a nod. One of them, Sam Kupperberg, had even invited her to come to a meeting of "Moving Forward", the self-help group she ran on alternate Tuesdays. But in the ballroom, Jess still had to keep her head down and her shoulders drawn in.

Invisible and invulnerable, Alex indulged his curiosity without any inhibitions at all. Jess was his epicentre, his tether, but he ran around her in wide circles and drank in as much as he could find.

Actually, that wasn't right. He didn't run, exactly. In fact Jess barely ever saw him move. He was with her when she was still, chatting incessantly in a conspiratorial undertone. When she stood up to leave, he stayed behind, watching her recede. But wherever she was going he would arrive before her, be waiting for her, and would take up the conversation from where he'd left off.

So it was a bit of a mystery to Jess how and when he got to meet the other women and watch what they were up to. She just had to accept that he did – and that he was telling the truth when he talked about all these people whose names meant more or less nothing to her. Yolanda Woods was crying in her cell. Kath Nickell had a picture of a man kissing another man. Amit Liu's bum had broken through the mesh links of her bed-frame and now hung halfway down to the floor when she was asleep.

Right. Fine.

Then Alex got tired of the truth, or outran it, and started to tell her stories of a different flavour. Jess missed the moment when that started. It was probably during one of their lights-out conversations when Buller was impregnably asleep in the upper bunk and Jess was drifting.

The cast was the same – the women of Goodall wing. But instead of detailing the trivia of their days, he made them the inhabitants of a second, secret world that changed according to his whims. Woods was a forester now, improbably dressed in high-heeled boots and a white leather waistcoat as she built tree-houses in a jungle that went on for ever. Maybe that was just Alex riffing on her name, but some of the other connections were more obscure. Nickell wanted windows, more and more windows, but every time she put a new one in, it broke. Liu had cats, but she couldn't get too close to them, because if she did, she started to turn into a cat herself and it scared her.

Where did the dead boy get this nonsense from? Jess didn't know and didn't care. She thought he had a natural gift. She would have read his stuff, back in her Half the Sky days; she would have shelved it flat so people could see the cover and she would have put a "Try this if you like such and such . . ." sticker underneath it.

Alex fed on her interest, making up more and more elaborate fictions. Jess could tell they excited him too. His voice changed when he was making things up, filled with a sudden, nervy energy. And he used his hands, exactly the way someone still alive would do, to draw in the air the things he was describing. At these times, he reminded Jess of Shannon McBride, the other candidate for Goodall's resident storyteller.

He took it too dark, though, especially when you remembered that he was just a kid. A dead kid, yeah, but still.

Hannah meets this man. She thinks she knows him, but she doesn't really know him. Or he's not who she thinks. No, he is. He is who she thinks, but he changes and he starts to get bigger.

And then he grabs her and he's got his hand over her face. He's pulling at it. It's like her face is a sort of a mask on the front of her head, and it hasn't been fixed on properly at the edges, so the big man can get his fingers underneath it.

He's starting to work it loose. And this is the scary bit. Hannah wants to scream. She knows if she screams someone will come and help her. But she can't because her face has almost all come away now, and her mouth is one of the things that was on her face so she can't use it any more. You'd think she'd still have a bit of a mouth left behind and she could use that, a hole or something, but she hasn't. It's just all smooth back there. If the man pulls her face all the way off, she won't be able to talk any more, or see, or hear, and she'll die because she can't breathe.

So she keeps on fighting and trying to make him stop. But he's winning, and she remembers him winning before and that makes her weak. She can't do anything.

The last thing is she tries to cry, but she can't do that either. She hasn't got any eyes. And then the man throws her face down on the floor and a dog comes and eats it.

Jess sat up in the dark. It wasn't perfect dark: there was an orange safety light at one end of the ceiling's strip light that turned the bunk, the table and the seatless toilet bowl into vague, fluid masses with shadows hanging off them like growths. Alex was visible in a different way, and by his own rules. He looked the same by night as he did by day: perfectly clear and distinct. And he didn't cast a shadow.

"Was that story about Passmore?" Jess asked him, fully awake now. "Is she the Hannah you mean? The one who hurt me?" She kept her voice to a whisper, although she'd never known Buller to wake before the bell chivvied her up out of her bunk.

Yes, the boy said. *Her.*

"But . . . Alex, that's horrible."

Yes.

"You shouldn't . . ." Jess groped for words. "You don't have to be angry with her because she hit me. You don't have to hate her."

After all, she thought, when all's said and done, she was putting in a vote for you. With the toe of her boot. Siding with the victim against the woman who burned him.

I don't hate her.

"Then stop."

Stop what?

"Stop telling these stories. Or . . . or give them a happy ending."

I can't.

"Yes, you can, Alex." Jess heard a tremor in her own voice and realised she was shivering. Not from cold, obviously, because this was sweltering summer. It was the sense of his alienness, which she suddenly felt very acutely. That was ridiculous, she knew. She was talking to a ghost and taking that for granted, then getting freaked out because he was telling her scary stories.

But she wanted to protect him. She wanted him to keep his innocence, stuck here among the guilty. He'd brought her back from the abyss, from the mouth of the grave. She owed him everything and he owed her nothing except arguably a life for a life and a tooth for a tooth.

177

So she tried again. "Make up a story about what happens to Passmore after she gets out of here. Where will she go?"

I don't know. And she's not going anywhere. She's a lifer.

"But you can pretend."

Alex considered this in solemn silence.

I'm not very good at pretending, he said eventually.

Jess thought he was being way too hard on himself there. "Stories are like wishes, Alex," she said, aware that she was trying to put something huge into small words. "You should only wish for things that you really want to happen."

Alex nodded to show he understood, but he looked doubtful – and unhappy, as though in attacking his fantasies, she was attacking him. She was quick to reassure him. "Everybody has moments like that, when they want bad things to happen to people they don't like. And I suppose, as long as it's only a story, it does no harm. But it's better to think about people you love, isn't it? Wishing for their lives to be happy and full of good things."

I suppose. Yes.

She still felt she'd hurt him. She opened her mouth to say something else. But right then was when the morning bell sounded. On its first strident yell Buller jumped down in between them, already hawking up mucus from the back of her throat as she headed for the sink. Like a bad wipe in an old movie, she airbrushed Alex Beech out of the room.

36

"I'd say we're in a good place," Grace told Devlin, about a week after he first brought Sally to her.

They were in Grace's cell, and Earnshaw was doing Grace's hair. Earnshaw was surprisingly good at it, her massive hands working the various stylers and straighteners with exquisite care. Grace was the only one she would ever do it for though. Of course, she was also the only one who dared to ask.

"A very good place," Devlin agreed. "Sally's working out great, isn't he?" Grace only grunted. She'd already given the Devil his due where that was concerned – told him that bringing the doctor in was an excellent idea, and given him a finder's fee in addition to his usual cut. She didn't want to spend the rest of her life palpating Devlin's swollen ego.

But her temper stayed sunny for the most part. The hostile takeover of C block was progressing very well. She had hopes that it would be a bloodless coup, apart from the odd drop already spilled here and there.

Dizzy – Ruth Disraeli according to her birth certificate – had been released on 13 May, having served six of the ten years she'd been given for drug offences. Exactly a week before that, there had been an incident in the yard, a fight that got out of hand. Nobody was seriously injured, but two of the women involved, Ajique Hassan and Dominica Weeks, were found to have weapons on them. Hassan had the classic – you could even say stereotypical – shank made from one half of a Wilkinson Sword razor blade stuck in the end of a beheaded toothbrush. Minnie Weeks more imaginatively had a pair of nunchuks made from two sawn-off bits of a chair leg joined together with a length of bedsheet. Both women were given a month's worth of punitive withdrawal, with the possibility of an official deferment of their parole rights.

Goodall wing had its own yard. The other wings, Curie included, shared a bigger space way over on the other side of the prison and up against the outside wall. It hadn't been easy for the Devil to arrange that fight, or those finds, in neutral territory. He'd had to lay off payments to two C wing warders and one prisoner, and make the weapons himself, because sourcing them from inside Fellside would have been seven kinds of impossible. Not that people didn't have them – just that nobody who had one would ever admit it or hand one over to a screw, even a bent screw like Devlin, whatever he promised them. The possible consequences were just too enormous.

But anyway, it had worked. Hassan and Weeks were off the scene, Dizzy was in the wind and Curie's supply of recreational oblivion was hanging by a thread. Enter Dr Salazar, stage left.

It was simple, and it was elegant. Grace was pleased. Not only was Salazar a perfect mule, he was also a known quantity. If he'd ever had it in him to take a stand on a matter of conscience, that time had been long before, and it had ended with his falling back into line completely and unconditionally.

He was very easy to manage now.

The first drop was textbook smooth and went entirely according to plan. Salazar's phone rang at ten o'clock. A voice he didn't know told him what to do. "Wait ten minutes. Then open your door. Don't come out before then. Measure it by your watch."

Sally lived in a narrow cul-de-sac at the shabbier end of Fletchertown. He couldn't quite bring himself to go to the window and keep watch, but he listened for the sound of a car engine. In the still, stagnant night, it would have carried a long distance and been impossible to miss.

Nothing. But at the end of the ten minutes, when he opened the door and poked his head out, the package was there on the mat. It was an open cardboard box with an old issue of *The Watchtower* on top of it, presumably to deter further inspection. Sally picked it up and took it inside, amazed at how light it was.

He kept expecting to come up against something hard and heavy at some point – something solid enough to push off against so he could say no and mean it. But it was just an endless trickle of easy surrenders. Desperately ashamed though he was, and disgusted with himself for going along with Grace and Devlin's schemes, nothing had been troublesome at all so far. Even the threat against Patience DiMarta had made things easier for him because it allowed him to tell himself he was doing this for her. For her husband, who was a bin man for the county council, and for their three kids, who were the apple of Patience's eye and the bulk of the contents of her wallet (far more photos than money in there, most days). This wasn't cowardice, it was selflessness. Philanthropy. Quiet heroism.

Sally set the box down and examined the contents. Inside, under the magazine, he found a smaller container that had once held surgical gloves and looked as though it still could. It didn't. It held what Sally guessed to be heroin, ketamine and cannabis resin, all in their own zip-locked bags and carefully packed so there was no space wasted. It sat on the table next to him as he ate his dinner of scrambled eggs on toast and frozen Birds Eye peas. Knowing what was in the box made the food taste strange to him, as though it was contaminated. He washed it down with most of a bottle of red wine that had no taste at all.

I'm not going to do this, he told himself again. Trying out the words. Knowing they were lies.

The guards at the checkpoint were meant to search all packages entering or leaving the prison, but as Devlin and Salazar were both aware, they were apt to be fairly casual with people they knew. Mostly they waved staff through and kept their powder dry for visitors.

Sally took out the package and showed it at the checkpoint anyway. The guard there, barely out of his teens, didn't even seem to want to touch it, maybe out of fear that germs from infectious prisoners might somehow magically be clinging to it even though it was on its way into Fellside rather than out. The doctor had left an obviously used pair of surgical gloves dangling halfway out of the package to foster this response.

Later that day he took his first back and joint clinic in Curie wing. Being a novelty, the clinic was well attended, mostly by older women who had plenty of aches and pains to report and took a certain relish in talking about them. The two hours went by like treacle running down a rope. When they were done, Dr Salazar went down to the meditation room, unlocked the door with a key that Devlin had given him and stepped quickly inside. He left the package inside a hollow wooden dais that was almost but not quite too heavy to lift. He was in there for less than a minute, then he hurried back out, locked the door behind him and was on his way.

He didn't see anyone waiting or watching, but then he wasn't intended to.

About half an hour later, Devlin brought word to Grace that the drop had gone to plan. Sally had passed his fieldwork test. That was the phrase he used, and they both had a good chuckle at the thought of the doctor doing his cloak-and-dagger routine.

Sally would have been amazed to learn how much of this production had been mounted for his sole benefit. That package ended up in a wastepaper basket right outside the meditation room, where Jazz Sullivan (one of Grace's three designated sales agents in Curie) dumped it in spite of being told to take it apart and leave the pieces in three separate places. The whole thing had been a dry run, with talcum powder and builder's putty in place of actual narcotics, mainly because Grace wanted to see how the doctor handled himself under pressure. He did okay, but then, as the Devil pointed out, he'd had plenty of practice with drug-running on a modest scale back when his wife was dying.

In the normal run of things, Grace's drugs never went anywhere near that checkpoint. It was just unfeasible, given how often the staff rotas changed at short notice and how many people she would need to keep on payroll in order to make it airtight. She had a completely different system in place, and Sally would be inducted into it — the parts that concerned him anyway — soon enough.

But all things in their season. Around midnight, an envelope dropped on to Dr Salazar's doormat. He was still awake, listening to a Deutsche Grammophon recording of *The Threepenny Opera*. In the middle of the "Solomon Song", with Lotte Lenya satirically mourning the uselessness of beauty, courage and wisdom, he heard it arrive.

He went and opened it. Counted thirty well-used ten-pound notes on to the bookcase in the hall. From a framed photo, dead Leah looked down with an incongruous smile, as though she blessed this illegal pay-off and its suspect source.

Sally had a nightmare that night, which drew its imagery from his Jewish religion. Leah's religion, rather, since Sally was never observant until he met her and fell in love with her. For Leah's sake, he went to synagogue on the high holy days, kept milk and meat in their separate corners when he cooked for her and even fasted on Yom Kippur, the Day of Atonement.

Sally's dream that night had a Yom Kippur theme to it. There was a point in the service for that day where the rabbi would read aloud from a medieval document known as the "Unetanneh Tokef". The passage was always the same. It talked about the book up in heaven in which all of God's decisions are recorded. "Who shall die by fire, and who by water. Who by sword, by famine, and by the depredations of beasts . . ." And so on, at great length.

It sounded pretty bleak and fatalistic, but Sally and Leah's rabbi insisted that it really wasn't. The point of the passage was not that God has got your number, but that he keeps an open mind as long as you do. You seal your fate by your actions. If you repent, if you atone, if you try to throw things in the other scale to balance out the bad stuff you've done, then he will keep on giving you the benefit of the doubt. But once you pass the point of no return, once you pile up so many sins that atonement isn't possible any more, then HaShem will wash his hands of you. One day your name will go in that book and then it will be too late. Nothing you do after that time will make a damn bit of difference.

Sally dreamed that his name was being written in the book. He saw an angel take the volume down off a shelf, carry it over to a table, open it up and riffle to the right page. The angel was crying all this time. Bitter, bitter tears. This was another human soul gone to hell, and the angels hate that. They mourn for what you might have been. But in this case, as she dipped her quill in the ink and wrote Sally's name, the angel was crying for another reason too.

The angel was Sally's dead wife, Leah. She was crying because she was never going to see him again.

37

Moulson endured the catcalls and the occasional violence for a little while longer. But then, very suddenly, her situation changed.

For some unexplained reason, across all the wings of Fellside both Friday lunch and Friday dinner were always fish meals. Governor Scratchwell was probably making some kind of religious point – a vague, ecumenical flailing around, because he wasn't Catholic. Anyway, it won him no friends in G block, where the prevailing opinion was that if you liked the taste of fish, you didn't have to walk too far to find it.

One Friday lunchtime, only a week or so after Jess Moulson's arrival on-block, Hannah Passmore pushed her cod fillet aside, stood up and walked the full length of the canteen to the lepers' corner where Jess was sitting.

Jess had her head down. It was a tactic she used a lot in Goodall's common spaces, whenever she had no choice but to be there. For a moment or two she didn't even realise Passmore was there.

When she did, she let her eyes climb up Passmore's solid form an inch at a time. She stopped when she got to Passmore's face – which was twisted into a really alarming expression. Passmore was pushing sixty years old, but she was as tough as a twist of wire. You didn't screw around with her if you had the brains God gave a guinea pig.

"What did you do to me?" she demanded now.

The best Jess could come up with was "I'm sorry?" She didn't want a scene. More than that, she didn't want to be beaten up again.

"What did you fucking do to me?" Passmore repeated. She balled her fists and then flexed them out again. Jess could see that she was shaking. Her eyes were too wide. There was a little blood-red mark on her lower lip where she'd been biting it. She went back to biting it now, and a single bead of blood welled up there, trembling on the brink.

"I didn't do anything," Jess said. She looked down at her tray again, but that gravity-defying drop of blood drew her gaze back. It trickled downwards now like a shed tear, marking a line down the centre of Passmore's chin.

"Then why do I keep . . .?" The older woman shook her head. She couldn't finish the sentence. She grabbed Jess by the throat. The guards moved in quickly when they saw what was going down, but even the nearest of them had a lot of ground to cover in that crowded room.

Jess's eyes met Passmore's eyes across an inch or so of space. Passmore's eyes had little flecks of red in the whites of them from recently burst blood vessels. Her mouth worked as though she was trying to swallow something down.

But she wasn't. She was trying to spit it up. "I'm sorry," she said to Jess, her voice loud and hard. "I'm sorry I hit you. Okay? Just . . . leave me alone!"

And then she turned and walked away, passing the guards, who'd slowed to a dead stop, becalmed by the lack of violence.

She walked all the way back to where she'd been sitting. Her shoulders were hunched and she was crying – shuddering, strangled sobs. Even after she sat down, there wasn't another sound in the big, busy room, so everyone heard her. But some of them had seen her face too, and that was the biggest shock. Passmore wasn't angry, she was scared. And underneath that she was bewildered, as though she didn't know what was happening to her and she didn't know why.

It wasn't as though that was an unusual combination of emotions in Fellside. But it wasn't one anyone had seen Hannah Passmore, or any of the lifers, wear before. It was a "first offence" kind of face – the face of someone who hadn't realised until that moment how bad things could get.

In free association that evening, Shannon McBride regaled a large and varied audience with the story of Passmore's crime and punishment. "She robbed a bank. Robbed a bank with a plastic gun she made up out of a kit and painted to look real. Then when they caught her she chatted to the police while her husband slipped out into the shed and burned all the cash. They only got her because money ash is different from regular ash."

"Is this story going anywhere?" Pauline Royal demanded. As Hannah's former cellmate and good friend, she was standing by to make sure that nothing disrespectful got said.

McBride raised her hands with the palms out to indicate a general openness and obligation to the truth. "You know what Hannah's like, Po," she said. "You all know. You wouldn't think she'd ever been scared of anything in her life. But she was scared today. That's where the story is going, all right?"

Po gave a terse shrug, but she didn't disagree. She had been worried about Hannah after that outburst in the lunch queue and had gone looking for her in free association. She'd found her friend in the library, holding an X-Men comic and pretending to read it. She was still distraught, and Po had done her best to talk her down. But Hannah wouldn't say one word about what Moulson had done to take the wind out of her sails. Actually, she wasn't saying much at all, and what she did say made no sense. She talked about a dog, and a dead baby, and Moulson waiting for her at night. Or someone waiting anyway: the pronoun shifted from he to she and back again pretty freely. "I don't want to see it," Passmore kept saying, her voice hoarse, her eyes wet and wide. "I don't want to see it any more."

That day marked a turning point in terms of the way G block looked on Jess Moulson and interacted with her. There was the odd incident afterwards from time to time. A jostle in the refectory line, or some catcalls on the yard. But Jess didn't catch another beating. Not for a good long while, and not from that direction.

38

When you're getting yourself right with the world, you start by paying off all the old debts you can think of.

Jess wrote to her Aunt Brenda to ask about how she was recovering, but mainly to apologise for not being a better niece. *I was selfish when I tried to kill myself, the same way I've been selfish about everything else that mattered*, she wrote. *I knew it would make you unhappy but I couldn't see past my own guilt and misery. The guilt is still there, but I'm working on it in a different way.*

Brenda, you've always been there when I needed you. After Mum died, you were the only person left who I cared about. Sometimes it felt like you were the only person left who I even knew. And you were so good to me. You did everything you could for me. You always have. Please don't think that the way I turned out is any reflection on you. It was just me. It was always just me. I still don't think you should come up here. It's a long way out across the moors and the journey would half kill you. But more importantly, you're here already – in my heart.

She was going to leave it at that, but she wanted to explain why she had changed her mind. She wanted Brenda to understand that she hadn't been thoughtless or capricious, either when she decided to die or when she veered back at the last moment towards life. *Alex came to me in a dream*, she wrote. *He asked me to help him. I can't really explain, and I know it sounds completely crazy, but I really think I can do it. I think I have to. This is what I'm for, Auntie B. This is why I'm still alive. Don't be afraid for me, and don't be sad for me. I've made you sad enough already. As long as I can, I'll write and tell you how this goes.*

She wrote to John Street too. It wasn't that she felt any weight of guilt about the injuries to his hands. He'd put her through enough pain when they were together to more than offset that. But she had a dim sense of how these things worked. His life must have stopped at around about the same time hers had. When you get caught up in events that loom so big in the world's eye, you're pinned to them for ever. She wrote an equivocal letter to him, saying she hoped they could forgive each other and indicating that she'd made some progress on her side of that equation.

The answer, when it came, wasn't from Street at all. It was from Nicola Saunders, her former work colleague and sometime pusher, who had known Street longer than Jess had and had introduced them in the first place. She and Street were living together now, Nicola said, and she would take it as a favour on Jess's part if she just stayed out of John's life and maybe finished the job she'd started with her hunger strike. *He told me some of what you put him through. And you talk about forgiving him? That's the sickest joke I've ever heard. He won't ever forgive you, Jess. But he survived you. That was a feat in itself.*

There were other letters, but not all that many. If you took Alex Beech out of the mix, Jess wasn't left with many relationships where karmic balance was an issue. Or many relationships at all, for that matter. *First do no harm* isn't a big ask if you don't do anything.

What had she been? She could barely get her head around the question, let alone answer it. What did it say about her life if it had been so empty that a simple addiction filled it to capacity?

It was the other way around, of course. She knew that really. Heroin works the way a cuckoo chick works. It tumbles all the other eggs out of the nest to make sure it gets all your attention all the time.

She had something else to obsess her now, and she was a little bit afraid that that was all she was doing. That she'd taken on this impossible quest on Alex's behalf because her life, that empty nest, needed something else to fill it.

But mostly she only had those doubts when Alex wasn't with her. When he was there, he became the only thing that mattered. Fellside was the illusion and he was the reality, the bedrock. What was the point of worrying about the purity of her own motives? There had never been anything pure about her in the first place.

39

The Devil came into the infirmary right at the end of his shift, looking to talk to Dr Salazar. But Sally wasn't in residence; there was no one in there but Sylvie Stock, tidying up the drug cabinet. She asked if she could help, but Devlin told her no. It was just a sore shoulder that he wanted Salazar to take a look at before he clocked off and headed home.

"I can give you some ibuprofen," Stock offered. This was un-familiar territory for her. Generally she had a strong sense of what was in her job description and what wasn't. Tending the ailments of the staff fell into the *wasn't* category, and normally she would have ignored Devlin until he left. But she was still riding out the waves of emotional turmoil from Moulson's near-death experience and from Sally's having seen what she'd done. Now she was leading a life of virtue in hopes of deflecting the shitstorm she thought had to be coming down on her.

"I'm fine," Devlin said. "I'll just wait."

Which he did. In silence. It played on Sylvie's nerves like a file on a fiddle string, and she got jumpier and jumpier as time went on. What was worse, though, was when Sally finally came back and saw Devlin sitting there. He turned to Stock without a second's pause and told her to go home early. "I'll finish here, Sylvie," he said. "Don't you worry about it. I'll see you Monday."

Stock protested weakly that she didn't mind finishing what she'd started, but she could hardly complain about being let off the last half-hour of her shift. When Sally shooed her out, she had to go, even though she was convinced now that Devlin had come over there specifically to talk about her. She knew, with absolute certainty, that as soon as the door closed behind her, Devlin would turn to the doctor and say something like, "So what do you want to do about this business with Nurse Stock?"

She walked to her car feeling like an axe was falling on her in slow motion and she couldn't move to get out of its way.

The staff car park was on the other side of the road from the prison in a little dip of ground that looked right out over Sharne Fell. There was a footpath going down, but, like most people, Stock just walked on over the verge and down the grassy slope.

This time, though, she kept right on going, through the car park to the much steeper drop on the far side. Four hundred feet below her, a waterfall as thin as a knife fell into a bowl of grey rock that it had made for itself over the space of a hundred thousand years or so. There was a split in the rock so that it really looked – from above, as Stock was seeing it now – like hands cupped to take the water.

She thought for a good long while about letting the cupped hands take her too. She liked to read salacious stuff, from the *Daily Mail* to *True Crime* magazines, so she knew to a nicety how the media treated wicked women, especially nurses. Kristen Gilbert. Genene Anne Jones. Beverley Allitt, the angel of death. Stock hadn't done anything like what those women had done, but that wouldn't stop them. Probably they'd give her a really catchy nickname – something like Allitt's, only more melodramatic.

Her career would be over. She'd only ever wanted to help people but she'd be remembered as a sadistic maniac. All because of Jessica Moulson and her failed hunger strike. If the woman had been so set on dying, what had stopped her? It was as though

193

Moulson had gone to all this trouble just to set a trap, and Stock had walked right into it. It was almost a relief when her despair turned into anger. Then the anger got so hot that it boiled away in its turn, leaving behind a strange calm and clarity.

If she survived this, if God gave her a second chance, she swore to herself that she'd never do anything bad again.

But if the roof fell on her, it would fall on Moulson too. She'd make sure it did.

Once Devlin was alone with Sally, he got right to the point. "Okay," he said. "Grace is happy with how that first one went. You're in. No more drops to your place though. You know Big Carol? Carol Loomis? The way it'll work from now on is like this: she'll bring the stuff to you every Thursday, right before you go over to Curie for your clinic. So make up a reason why she needs to keep coming, and write it up. Some kind of chronic condition. You'll use the same drop-off as before, under the dais in the meditation room. Okay?"

Sally was bemused. "But . . . then . . ." he said. "What – somebody else is bringing the drugs into the prison?"

"You've got a mind like a steel trap, haven't you, Sally?" Devlin sneered. "Yes, we've got someone else bringing the stuff in. All we need you for is to carry it past the guard post into Curie. Half the risk, but the same pay-off, so hooray for you. Now give me my prescription, I'm running late."

Salazar handed over the pethidine and Devlin left without a word. The whole conversation had taken so little time that when he stepped out of the front gate, after signing himself off in the daybook, he could see Stock in the car park across the road, only just now walking to her car. She had her head down and her shoulders hunched, like someone walking through a downpour only she could see.

40

Brian Pritchard still considered himself to be Jessica Moulson's solicitor in defiance of his client's statements to the contrary. But he had stopped expecting any response to his requests for meetings and consultations as the deadline for appeal loomed and then passed. When Moulson finally changed her mind and said she wanted to lodge an appeal after all, and to schedule a meeting, he decided to proceed cautiously.

Moulson didn't like him, and more importantly didn't trust him. Whatever this change of heart meant, it was probably better for someone else to sound her out in the first instance. And he had a particular someone else in mind: his articled clerk, Paul Levine, who had from the first shown a very strong interest in Moulson's case.

Given the arduous journey that would be involved, Pritchard apologised to his junior for the poisoned chalice. Paul said he didn't mind at all. As low man on the corporate totem pole, he was obliged to say that, but it was also the truth. Or if it was a lie, it was only by omission. The full truth was that Paul was overjoyed when Pritchard told him where he was off to. He was hard put to it not to dance.

That crazy excitement stayed with him the whole way from London King's Cross to Leeds City station. It grew, if anything, as he rode (in a taxi which smelled faintly of vomit) across the grandeur of Sharne Fell; as he walked through the gates in the fifty-foot barricade around Fellside prison; as the clanging, echoing doors opened one at a time and ushered him into Moulson's presence. He felt like an ambassador to a foreign court. And he launched himself into the interview like a dam bursting, full of barely suppressed energy and barely comprehensible intensity.

It was just the two of them, in the interview room rather than the main visiting area. Attorney–client privilege guaranteed them absolute privacy, although Levine had a panic button on his side of the table in deference to Moulson's high-security status. Not that she looked like much of a threat right then, only halfway recovered from the beatings that had followed her release into gen pop.

To Paul, she looked magnetic. Beautiful. He had fallen in love with Moulson during her trial, and, although he hadn't seen her since, he still carried that torch. He would have been the first to admit that this was a weird infatuation. Moulson was a convicted murderer, a pariah, and her face, with its asymmetry and its inorganic texture, was about as far from any definition of beauty as you could get.

He was convinced of her innocence, of course. He had seen Pritchard's notes, had helped to prepare them. He knew there were questions that had never been asked at the first trial, let alone answered.

But it was more than that. He found Moulson thrilling to be near and to talk to. He saw her life as a three-act tragedy with opiates in the role of major antagonist. And her face mesmerised him. It had something better than beauty or symmetry. It had transparency. It looked like a mask but it hid nothing. Every emotion that showed there showed huge and clear and eloquent, as the muscles on the bad side struggled to throw up their asynchronous copy of the good side's workings.

It was fair to say that Paul Levine came out of a different corner from most people as far as pain and disfigurement went. He had been a self-harmer in his teens, for more than four years, and that had been the time in his life when he felt most fully and wonderfully alive. He'd stopped cutting when he went to university because he'd become afraid that he would never be able to form a relationship with another human being that was as meaningful as the one he had with his own skin and the blood that flowed underneath it.

A handful of romantic encounters, short but deep, proved that he could make that kind of attachment and left him in a different place mentally. He'd never taken up the cutting habit again, but he remembered those days very vividly. He kept his kit – razor blades and bandages and antiseptic – in a shoebox at the back of his wardrobe where other men might keep porn. He surfed the websites where other cutters put up photographs of their most recent injuries. And he still saw the romance in those injuries, the beauty that was like an offering to a world that was too stupid to understand it.

Beauty was the word that came into his mind when Moulson walked into the interview room. The marks of her beatings mostly didn't show, but the bruises hidden under her clothes caused her to walk with exaggerated care, like a woman twice her age. To Paul, paradoxically, that lent her an air of spectacular grace. He thought she moved like a queen in a medieval pageant.

He pulled himself together, set up his voice recorder and started to tell Moulson – in an over-loud, over-emphatic splurge – what he and his firm had been up to since the trial.

"We've examined all the witness statements for discrepancies, and we've gone over the police interview transcripts for procedural weaknesses. That gave us quite a few small leads to follow up, and one big one. We think we can make something of the fact that Alex Beech was home alone on the night of the fire. His parents said they were at work, but we followed that up and the timing doesn't work. It's possible they were at a pub on Alexandra Park

197

Road. If they were, there's an argument of contributory negligence right there. That ought to play in your favour, and might mean we can ask for a mistrial on the grounds of their perjury.

"Mr Pritchard also thinks we can go for a mistrial based on the emphasis the trial judge gave to your heroin habit in his summing up . . ." And on and on, all this stuff just pouring out as though a million words on other subjects could take the place of the handful he really wanted to say to her and couldn't.

He could see that he was making a bad impression. Moulson didn't say anything, and she didn't move. He wished that he'd started off by asking her if she had any questions. He could have used that as a way of easing her into the discussion.

But he felt he had no choice now but to go on in the way he'd started. He hurried on to his next point, which was mental incapacity. "The conviction is only sound if the psychiatric assessments of you were accurate. If you were of sound mind. We want to open up that question again, and try to make more of the intolerable stress you were under living with an abusive partner. Your extended hunger strike after you were convicted, which came very close to killing you, speaks very strongly – I hope you don't mind me saying this – to a disturbed state of mind. We think we can project that backwards and use it as evidence that you weren't thinking clearly and rationally on the night of the fire."

There was more. He was pretty sure there was more. But he'd got a little lost in his notes through looking at Moulson more than at the page, and he seemed to have reached the end without traversing all the territory on the way.

"I want to ask you something," Moulson said as soon as there was silence for her to speak into. "Sorry, I mean . . . thank you for all this. I can see you're doing a great job for me. I feel safe in your hands. But there are a few things I feel I want to get a better understanding of before the appeal."

"Go ahead," Paul said. He sat back with his eyebrows raised in an expression of attention and interest. He wanted so much for her to like him. He wanted to tell her how well he understood her, although he was astute enough to know that he really didn't – that he was projecting his own fantasies on to her and seeing something that probably wasn't there. He had form, unsurprisingly. Those college love affairs were marked, all of them, by a sudden rush to intimacy and then an equally sudden recoil. Paul was a romantic. That was the vice he succumbed to more than any other.

"Alex's body," Moulson said. "They must have examined it. I mean, there was an autopsy."

"Yes, of course. The findings were submitted into your trial record."

"And what were they? The findings?"

"How do you mean?"

"His injuries. Can you tell me what they were like?"

Paul considered this question. He knew the answer, of course. He knew every inch of her file. But how much detail did she want? "He was burned."

Moulson leaned forward. "Yes, I know he was burned. But was there anything else? Injuries that didn't come from the fire? I'm thinking he might have been attacked earlier. Before the fire started. That he could have been bruised or cut. Was there anything to suggest that? Would there be? Would injuries like that show on a burned-up body?"

Paul made a show of looking through his notes, although he didn't need to. "I don't believe there was anything like that," he said. "Soft tissue injuries wouldn't necessarily show, but cuts . . . yes, cuts would have been visible." He knew a lot about cuts from a different context. He spoke with confidence.

"What I'm getting at," Moulson said, "is that it might not have been the fire that killed Alex."

"It wasn't. Of course it wasn't."

"Then . . ."

"It was the smoke."

Moulson's eyes widened. It was as though this was news to her, although it couldn't possibly be. It had all been covered at the original trial. But then she had been in shock back then. Maybe she hadn't taken it all in.

"The smoke," she repeated.

"Exactly," Paul said. "It's what kills most people in domestic and industrial fires. Twice as many as die from the flames. You were treated yourself, if you remember, for smoke damage to your lungs."

Moulson didn't answer. Paul remembered now what it was that he'd left out of his presentation. He'd meant to say more about John Street. "We also need to revisit your partner's deposition," he said, aware that he was changing the subject. "We want to establish what he did in between the time when he placed the 999 call and the time when the fire engines arrived. He claims not to remember much about that period, but we're pretty certain he didn't go back inside the block . . ."

We know that because of the smoke, Paul thought. That was the connection he'd just made in his mind. Everybody else had breathed in smoke and Street hadn't. That bastard got out clean, when really he was the one who ought to have died. Not a professional opinion, not one he could ever voice, but still . . .

"Even with the burns on his hands," he continued evenly, "there was certainly more he could have done to raise the alarm. The time window before the first fire engine arrived was about thirteen minutes. The fire kept on blazing for almost a quarter of an hour, and Street seems to have let it. With more time, who knows what could have been done?"

Once again, Moulson didn't seem to have listened to a word he said. She was pursuing her own train of thought. Which was still about the boy. "Alex was alone in the flat that night?" she asked Paul. "That's what his parents said, isn't it?"

"Yes. Is that relevant?"

"I don't know. But we're sure? There couldn't have been anyone else?"

Paul shrugged, feeling out of his depth again. "Well, yes. Of course there could have been. But the front door of the block is visible in the CCTV footage. We've accounted for everyone going in or out through that door. And as you know, the back door is only accessible from inside the building. You can't open it from the parking area behind the block unless you've got the key. Which isn't to say that someone couldn't have come in that way. But unless they were a resident themselves, they'd have needed someone inside the building to open the door for them."

Moulson's frown intensified. In some way he didn't understand, he was failing her. "Suppose there was someone else already up there with him. Is there any way we could find out?"

Paul had no idea what to say. The wounds. The mysterious someone. Was there a pattern here that he was meant to see? "We could go back to the witnesses, I suppose. But I'm not sure it would help. The appeal will review points of law; it won't re-hear the case. Why? Do you have any reason to think there was someone else there? Someone the prosecution failed to call?"

"Or someone the family didn't want to mention. A childminder? Might there have been a . . . a relative or a neighbour who was looking after Alex, and who . . ." The words tailed off but Paul could tell from the rapid darting of her eyes that they carried on inside her head where most of this argument seemed to be taking place.

"It might be worth exploring," he said warily. "If there's something you know, or even suspect, I'll be happy to . . ." He was going to say "pass it along" – to the partners, to Mr Pritchard. But that wasn't what he wanted to tell her at all. "I'll be happy to investigate for you." There you go. He'd put it right out there for her. Maybe she saw it, maybe she didn't, but he'd said it.

"I want to see the autopsy report," Moulson told him. "Would that be possible?"

"Of course. But I already gave you all the pertinent—"

"Yes, you did. You gave me a very clear summary. But I'd like to see it please. Actually I'd like to see everything. Photocopies of all the statements, and the trial transcript, and . . . whatever you've got."

Paul made a note. "All right." His hand shook just a little. After all the months of stonewalling, Moulson was engaging with her defence at last. That meant he'd be seeing more of her. More was fine in his opinion. More was excellent. This meeting was going very strangely, and he was sure he was missing a lot, but just being with her was lifting him on to another plane. He knew he would start to feel depressed as soon as he walked out of this room, and be depleted and fretful and dull until he was back here.

"What else are you looking at?" Moulson asked him.

He floundered a little. "Well, the broader . . . technicalities. Formal parameters. Strictly speaking we're outside the limit for filing an appeal. In light of your medical condition over the past few weeks, we're sure we can get around that, but we'll probably have to take it to a hearing so the CPS can state a position too."

Moulson did that thing again, striking off at a tangent so he didn't know if she'd been listening to him at all. "When can you get me those papers?"

"Tomorrow," he promised rashly. "I'll have the copies made when I get back to the office and courier them to you. And then I can . . . I can come up again and go over them with you. In case there are any areas you don't completely understand."

"I'd like that. Thank you."

"You're welcome. I'll put down in my notes that you've made a request to that effect."

Which was stretching the truth more than a little, but Moulson didn't protest the point. *Qui tacet consentire.* If you don't say no, you just said yes.

He had to go. His time had been up half an hour ago and he was amazed that nobody had come. He stood and held out his hand. Moulson took it.

"Thank you," she said again. "I'll see you soon then."

Paul was careful not to hold on to her hand for longer than was appropriate. The contact was electrifying, of course it was, but nothing showed in his face. He walked out briskly, resisting the urge to look back at her.

But all the way through the checkpoints, to the gate, across the fell, down to London and the banal exigencies of his job, he was looking at her beautiful face in his mind's eye and hearing her hoarse, half-broken voice whispering in his ear.

I feel safe.

In your hands.

Paul, I feel so safe in your hands.

41

Jess sat in the interview room after Levine had left, waiting for a guard to come and take her back across the yard to Goodall block.

She felt a little stunned. More than a little. She'd agreed to the meeting so she could start delivering on her promise – to find Alex Beech's friend and Alex Beech's torturer. But she'd gone running into a tripwire before she'd even got into her stride.

It was the smoke that killed him.

Of course it was. And she had known that. She remembered the salient points of the evidence in court, although she'd barely taken them in at the time. Smoke damage in Alex's lungs. Soot deposits in his airway below the level of his vocal cords. Carbon monoxide in his blood. It was cut and dried. If there'd been any doubt at all, it would have come out at the trial, but there wasn't.

Jess, I died because she hurt me!

The vehemence in the words made her wince. She didn't look up. She could feel Alex standing at her side, but she knew he wouldn't be visible in the bright sunlight streaming through the window.

"No, Alex. You died in the fire. Your body was examined by experts. There's no way they could be mistaken."

They could be lying though.

Jess shook her head. "Why would they lie?"

I don't know. Because they're scared of her.

"Scared of . . . You mean the bad girl? The one who cut you?"

Yes. They might be scared she'll cut them too.

"I don't think they're scared of the bad girl." Jess said it as softly as she could, trying to let him down gently. She'd thought he was the best authority on the manner of his own death, but there was no gainsaying this. He had to be mistaken. "There's a person called the coroner, whose job is to—"

If they're not scared, then they're hiding something. That's what the police do. They hide things. They make it look like you did something wrong when you didn't, and they make it look like they're always right.

His grimly matter-of-fact tone surprised her. It sounded as though he was talking from experience, although it couldn't be his own. Was there some history of criminality in the family? Was there a memory there of some clash between his parents and the law where he'd been a piece of collateral damage?

Jess weighed up all the things Levine had just told her and finally, deliberately, set them aside. She wanted to do right by Alex. It was the only thing she wanted right then. Anything she might choose to do with the rest of her life – which she'd only just got back, thanks to him – could go on the back burner and stay there.

She was starting to be afraid that the bad girl was just something he'd dreamed. But she would keep on looking all the same, until he told her to stop.

42

As for the governor, his whole life was like a dream at this point.

Once Jess Moulson had been released into Goodall (the natural habitat of all murderers and monsters) and the world hadn't ended, his confidence in his ability to handle the situation metastasised. He forgot his earlier fears altogether. Requests for interviews from dozens of media outfits were stacking up on his desk; he decided to answer a few of them.

He was selective, or at least he told himself he was. No red-tops. No talk shows. No live interviews. He knew how important it was to stay in control of the message. He favoured one-to-ones with correspondents from broadsheet newspapers, but he would do magazines if they looked to be serious trade publications and radio if it was Radio 4.

In every interview, he stressed the two planks of the Fellside regime: its rigour and its fairness. "These are old-fashioned terms but they're still the bedrock of good prison discipline," he said dozens of times with minor variations. "Prisoners need to know that the same rules apply to everyone, without exception. As long as that's true, nobody objects to the strictness of the regime. Time and again it's when rules are inconsistently applied that you get resentment, unrest, incidents, even riots."

Scratchwell thought he gave a pretty good account of himself in these interviews. He remembered what he'd been told about keeping a low profile, but he convinced himself that discreet briefings of this kind were within the spirit of that advice. If the oversight board had any reservations, they only had to tell him so and he would stop. But no emails came, so clearly he hadn't overstepped the mark. Possibly N-fold were already seeing the advantages of having a celebrity (in a small and decorous way) in their stable.

Scratchwell was well aware that the same media outlets were sniffing around Moulson too. Messages turned up on the prison's website every day which he was obliged to pass on to her, offering her interviews, book contracts, documentaries, even merchandise and licensing deals. Most of this stuff looked like scams and baited hooks of one sort or another, but by the law of averages some of it was probably on the level. It made no difference. Moulson ignored everything even-handedly. She seemed to feel she was already famous enough.

But even without her active participation, she and her crimes were very much in the public eye. There was a series on Channel 4 called *Wicked Women* where they told Moulson's story as part of one episode in spite of the fact that she had an appeal pending. An actress played Moulson, checking that John Street was asleep before she set the fire (Scratchwell was sure that was an invented detail). There was also a charity that was set up for child victims of adult violence, the Angel Trust, that featured Alex Beech's face prominently in its newspaper ads. Fame kept seeking Moulson out whatever she did or didn't do.

The governor congratulated himself that he was navigating these difficult waters much better than she was. By engaging with the media, he ensured that he had a voice. He presented his own case eloquently. Moulson, on the other hand, was being carried along like flotsam in the turbulent tide of public opinion.

He quite liked that metaphor when it first came to him. He

thought he might even use it, or some version of it, in an interview. But on further reflection, he saw it wouldn't do. It suggested that Moulson's concerns and his own amounted to the same thing – the massaging of their reputations.

He needed an analogy that had him disseminating good practice. Sharing his philosophy with the world. Becoming part of a dialogue in which people like Moulson lost their individuality and became examples.

Instances of lasting truths.

43

The documents Levine had promised turned up two days later. Nine boxes of them, making a stack that stretched from floor to ceiling of Jess's cell. Buller was too awed to be indignant, especially when Jess sat down on the edge of her bunk, opened the first box and started reading through the contents.

Once she started, she didn't stop. Levine had sent through the date for her hearing too, and it was only a week away. Jess had the sense that something big and heavy was rolling into motion, and that once it was properly underway, she would have very little power to steer it – might have no choice at all but to hang on tight. But the appeal was also the best chance she would ever get to discover more about what had happened to Alex on the night of the fire. The more she found out now, the better her chances were of using that opportunity when it came.

"She's got some balls on her anyway," Buller told Po and Kaleesha and a half-dozen other women one night in the ballroom. "She's ploughing through that shit, hours on end. Makes you wonder . . ."

"Wonder what?" Po demanded.

Buller shrugged. "Whether she really did it."

"This whole place is full of innocent people," Kaleesha Campbell pointed out cynically. "And her balls weren't on show when she chickened out of that hunger strike. Maybe she just wants the attention."

"Right," Buller agreed. "She wants the attention. That's why she's in here every night, doing the big I am." That got a laugh all round. There was something faintly ridiculous about calling Moulson an attention-seeker. She spent most of her time in her cell. When she was out of it, she folded herself down so small you couldn't see her.

And after the boxes arrived, she became even more of a recluse than before. She lived in those damn things. Thousands of pages of documents, tens of thousands, and after a while most of it was just repeating stuff she'd read before somewhere else. But she read it again anyway, because you never knew.

It became a standing joke on the wing. Then it became something else. The women of Goodall liked a trier, and they liked a story. Moulson was both. As her preliminary hearing got closer, she started to accumulate a capital of goodwill. She was completely unaware of it: out of all the Goodall inmates, she was the only one who had no sense of Goodall as a community. Its webs had started to weave themselves around her as far back as Shannon McBride's first round of confabulation, but those webs were like Alex – so subtle that you couldn't see them in daylight.

What sense of belonging she did have came from two directions: Alex and her aunt Brenda. Alex was close at hand; her aunt far away – and she hadn't responded at all to Jess's letter about her change of heart. That might mean Brenda had finally washed her hands of her, which would be bad enough but hardly surprising. Worse would be if she was ill again and hadn't got the letter. She might think Jess was already dead. Thinking Jess was dead might even be what had *made* her ill.

Jess tried phoning, many times. Paul Levine had topped up her commissary credit for precisely this purpose. She could withdraw up to two pounds a day in coins for the payphone – enough to make contact at least, if not to chat. She stood in line for one of the three phones in G block's prisoner services room. Let it ring as long as she could. Then when Brenda didn't answer, she went to the back of the line and waited all over again.

But even in the line she kept on reading. She didn't have the luxury of standing around doing nothing.

She came back, again and again, to the autopsy report. She thought it had to be the key to everything else, if she could only see it. *Cause of death: inhalation of smoke and carbon monoxide due to fire. Global charring. Significant quantity of carbon deposits in tracheo-bronchial tree. Soft tissues of face are largely absent, with exposure of partially heat-destroyed underlying bony structures. Pulmonary oedema extensive and marked . . .*

She looked in vain for injuries that didn't come down to the simple summary: *he breathed smoke, suffocated and burned.* She didn't find any, but she learned enough along the way to realise they could still have been there. A body that had been incinerated to that extent might still show deep-tissue injury, but cuts to the skin could be confused with damage due to natural drying and cracking of the burned tissue. It wouldn't always be possible to tell what came before from what came after.

Alex Beech stood at her shoulder, showing solidarity every so often by touching the tips of his fingers to her cheek, her neck, the back of her hand. Had he been so patient and uncomplaining when he was alive, or did death do that to you? Either way she was grateful. When she was running on empty, each of those fleeting touches flooded her with a little short-lived energy. Alex was like a car battery, jump-starting her again and again.

At night, though, he had mostly got into the habit of doing his own thing. Jess was sleeping more regularly now and Alex never slept at all, so he got bored and wandered. Sometimes she'd wake and find him missing, always with an ache of dismay.

It scared her how much she would come to need him in so short a time. How much she relied on his being there. She was profoundly alone in Fellside – or felt she was. She might have reached out now and got a very different response from the one

211

she has received a few weeks before, but she didn't know that. And most of the time her isolation didn't trouble her: it was a lot better than the beatings had been. But the more withdrawn she was from the life of the prison, which boiled all around her like soup in a pressure cooker, the more she needed the dead boy as a featherweight counterbalance.

The third night after the documents arrived, with four days still to go before her hearing, she asked Alex to tell her everything he could remember about his friend. Partly she was looking for clues to what might have happened to him on the night of the fire, but mostly, she knew, she was just trying to keep him by her bedside.

She was nice to me. She loved me.

"Was she the same age as you? Older?" She had asked him this question before, but his answer had been vague.

Older. I think.

"What did she look like?"

I don't remember.

"Did she live with you? Or close by? Somewhere else in Orchard Court?"

He thought about this for a long time. *I think she lived with me. Or stayed with me. At least sometimes. I remember falling asleep with her. Her hair smelled nice. We curled around each other. I was on the inside because I was smaller.*

"But you don't remember her name?"

No.

"Or what she looked like?"

No.

"Anything you can tell me might help me find her, Alex. Even a very little thing."

She was clutching at straws, she knew. There hadn't been so much as a whiff of this at her trial. The nice girl. The nasty girl. Alex had been a ten-year-old boy with no sisters or cousins. There weren't that many girls in his life. A girl who was used to staying over, and who shared a bed with their son on the night of his death, ought to have got a mention somewhere. If she didn't, it

212

might be because she was part of a bigger story that the Beeches had decided not to share.

Maybe the psycho with the sharp implements was in that story too.

"Anything," Jess said again, trying to keep the desperation out of her voice. "Anything at all."

She wasn't scared of the nasty girl.

"No?"

No.

"Why not, Alex?"

She was very brave. Always. And she told me to be brave too. She said nothing could ever hurt me because she'd be there watching.

And that had ended well. "So she knew the nasty girl?" Jess pursued.

She . . . yes . . . yes. She did. I think she did. But she always said that, about not worrying. That I had to never be scared because nobody would ever get past her to get to me. She always wanted to give me presents. Making me not be scared was one of them.

"Pretend she's here now," Jess suggested.

Why?

"Because it's nice. It was nice to be with her, wasn't it?"

Yes.

"Then pretend. Close your eyes and think about her."

Alex met her gaze for a moment, looking unhappy and almost suspicious. Had he been tricked once with that kids' joke where you told someone to close their eyes, hold out their hands and make a wish – and then dumped something disgusting into their cupped palms or else just punched them and ran away?

He closed his eyes. He sat there in perfect silence, his lips tightly pursed, his forehead furrowed.

"Is she there?" Jess asked at last. Keeping her voice low, trying to impinge on his thoughts as little as possible.

No.

"Then try to—"

But I remember what it was like. Being with her.

213

What was it like, Alex? This time she didn't speak at all. She just let the words form in her mind. Email for the dead.

It was like being a baby again. She was so much bigger and stronger than me. She could have hurt me, but she never did. She held me as though she was afraid of letting me fall.

This time Jess waited out the silence. It was hard. She was fine with keeping her mouth shut, but she was trying not to think at Alex too – trying to keep her thoughts from hardening into words and distracting him.

People thought she was stupid because she didn't talk. They didn't know her. Nobody knew her except me.

And you loved her.

Of course I did. Better than anyone.

Better than your mum and dad, even?

Much better.

Because she was so kind to you.

Yes.

And it was like being with your mother, when she . . . when she held you?

Alex's eyes opened and he stared at Jess hard.

No. She wasn't like my mum even a little bit.

"But you said—"

No, I didn't. I didn't say she was like my mum. I wouldn't say it because it wasn't true.

"All right."

And you shouldn't say it either.

"I won't," Jess assured him quickly. "I won't say it again, I promise." It was the most emotion he'd shown since the night they talked about Hannah Passmore and the stories he made up, and once again it was anger, anger at her. She'd hurt him somehow with that comparison. She'd walked right through whatever card tower of memories he'd been building, and now it was gone. Blown away.

And a second later, Alex was gone too.

44

The day before Moulson's preliminary hearing, Big Carol and Liz Earnshaw paid her a visit in her cell.

It had been a while since she'd taken a beating, and she'd got out of the habit. She cringed back into the angle of the bunk and the wall, making herself as small a target as she could, covered her face with her hands and braced herself for the storm.

Earnshaw watched all this with her usual poker face, but Big Carol found it highly amusing. "We're not here to hurt you, you daft mare," she chuckled. "Get up out of there."

But Jess stayed where she was so Big Carol had to squat down, with a grunt of effort, to talk to her. "You're off to court tomorrow for your preliminary hearing," she said. "Oxford Row in Leeds. Mr Justice Foulkes. Nod if you're getting this."

Jess nodded.

"Well, while you're there, you can do us a little favour. There's a package needs picking up and bringing back. Stand up. Come on. I want to show you something."

Jess did as she was told, but she was tensing to run or fight if this turned into something worse than a beating. Nobody had tried to kill her yet, but she knew it was a possibility, and these two huge, burly women had something of an executioner's look about them. The story about picking up a parcel could be just that – a story to keep her docile and unsuspecting until the shank went in.

Big Carol lifted up Jess's shirt, and Earnshaw handed over something she'd been holding down at her side – a bulky zip-lock bag about six inches by seven. It had a criss-cross of duct tape across it, the four loose ends sticking out about two inches from the sides. Carol pressed the bag against Jess's stomach. Jess flinched a little: the big woman's hands were unexpectedly cold.

Carol smoothed down the duct tape tabs and stepped back.

"Tuck your shirt in again," she said.

Jess did. She could feel the package hugging her stomach, the tug of the stretched tape, but nobody looking at her would have been able to tell it was there.

"Skinny as a stick," Carol said approvingly. "That's what a hunger strike does for you. Weight Watchers should get onto that. Okay, up again."

Jess raised her shirt. When Carol peeled the tape off, it hurt a little, but less than she was expecting: the slick of sweat on her skin had kept it from adhering tightly.

"And that's all there is to it," Carol told her. "Any questions?"

"No," Jess said.

Carol gave her a smack across the head. Not too hard, but like a teacher disciplining an unsatisfactory pupil. "Have another think, eh?"

"What's going to be in the package?" Jess asked.

Carol shook her head brusquely. "No. Keep going."

"Wh-where do I pick it up from?"

"There you go. It's going to be in the women's toilets behind the courtroom – the one that's just for guards and prisoners. You ask if you can take a piss. Do it right at the end of the day, just before they take you back to the van. In the toilet, go to the middle cubicle. If it's being used, go into the next one and wait until the middle one's free. You'll find the package behind the cistern, taped to the back of it. You'll have to stand on the seat and reach up from underneath. You won't be able to see it, but you'll feel a bit of tape holding it there. You peel the tape off and then just pull it down."

"What's in the package?"

"Then when you get back here, the first thing you do is come over to my cell, which is three-twenty, or Lizzie's, which is four-fourteen, and hand it over. Me or Lizzie here, nobody else. If we're not there, you wait until we are."

"But what's going to be in the—?"

The third time was the charm. Carol looked at Liz, arched an eyebrow and a second later the wall hit Jess hard in the back. Earnshaw's left arm was pinning her in place and in Earnshaw's right hand, an inch or so from Jess's eye, was one of those stereotypical shanks. A wafer of razor blade tucked into the end of – in this case – a paintbrush handle sawn off just below where the metal neck that held the brush would once have gripped.

And behind the blade, Earnshaw's belligerent face. Earnshaw's twisted mouth, her bared teeth. "You stupid?" she demanded. They were the first words she'd spoken. Simple but eloquent.

"No," Jess whispered.

The blade whisked back and forth. Pointed at her left eye, then her right. Earnshaw's gaze went with it, left to right like a metronome. Big Carol sighed and looked at the ground. The expression on her face said, *This is out of my hands now. You went there.*

The blade grazed Jess's cheek just under her left eyelid. The hand that held it shook a little, but somehow the tremor didn't pass itself along the slender shaft to the business end. There was no give or drift in that cold touch.

Something hot filled Jess's body and then drained away again, from the crown of her head down to her stomach.

"Hey," Big Carol said at last. "Lizzie." Her tone was almost gentle.

"Fucking behave," Earnshaw growled, still glaring right into Jess's eyes.

217

Her hand dropped to her side and a second later there was no sign of the shank at all. She stepped back. Jess's legs, suddenly taking her full weight again, buckled under her and she slid down the wall, halfway to collapsing. Her eyes flooded instantly with tears, as though they were trying to flush the wicked little blade away now that it was already gone.

"There isn't much I can add to my learned colleague's remarks," Loomis said laconically. "You did get that, yes? About behaving?"

"Yes," Jess muttered. She wanted to wipe away the tears but she was afraid to reach up and touch her eye in case she found a wound there. In case some of what was trickling down her face was blood.

"You're fine," Big Carol assured her, patting her on the head. "Don't be crying. You're a big girl now. You do as you're told and nobody's going to hurt you. Right, Lizzie?"

Earnshaw just stared at Jess with mute animosity. Her hatred was so vast and so sincere, Jess wondered what had stopped her from using the shank. It was as though she was a trained animal, set on by the other woman's nod and checked again with a word.

"Oh Jesus," Carol said now, looking down at the floor. Jess looked too. The puddle at her feet didn't mean anything for a second. Then she realised what it was, and dismay and shame filled her.

"You'd better clean that up," Carol told her, stepping back from the spreading pool. "And have a word with yourself. If you take a piss in the courtroom, no one's going to believe you need to go again later, are they? Come on, Lizzie."

The two women left, taking the dummy package with them. Jess closed the door with shaking hands and did what she could to clean up the puddle with paper towels. The towels filled the wastepaper basket before she'd finished. She took it along to the shower room and emptied it, grateful for once that nobody was going to step up and ask her what she was doing.

While she was there, she stripped off and showered. At that time of the day it was against the rules, but she didn't care. Punitive

218

withdrawal didn't mean much to someone who was already living like a nun in a closed order. She rinsed off her tracksuit bottoms too and hung them over the cubicle door to air a little.

Alex appeared while she was drying herself and asked her what was wrong. Flustered, she turned away from him and wrapped the towel around her body. She knew by then that he didn't really see the things that were in front of him. If anything, he seemed to see what other people saw, or what they thought about, as though their attention was a searchlight that guided his eyes. Still, she was ashamed right then to be naked in front of him. The emotions sloshing around her insides felt like nakedness enough.

"Go away, Alex," she muttered. "Come back later."

What's the matter?

"Nothing."

Yes, there is. You're crying.

"I'm not crying."

But you were just before. You're thinking about it.

"I'll think about something else."

Did somebody hurt you? If somebody hurt you, I'll hurt them back!

"No. They didn't." And that was the truth, more or less. They'd only threatened her. It had been a performance, even when Liz Earnshaw had put the knife to her face. A performance intended to make her obey.

The ghost boy's presence calmed her. His willingness to be indignant on her behalf. She had to reassure him, and in doing that she reassured herself. "Nobody hurt me," she said. "It was just an argument and it made me upset. I'm fine now."

Are you?

"Yes. Look." She gave him a smile that was halfway convincing. "Someone wanted me to do something I didn't want to do, that was all. We got into an argument about it."

Something bad?

"I suppose so. Yes. Something bad."

You should tell them no.

"I will," Jess assured him.

It was meant to be a lie, but once the words were out, they were suddenly the truth. Pastor Afanasy's words came back to her.

You can't make up for something bad you've done by killing yourself. You've got to try to do good things going forward.

45

Dr Salazar fell into his new routine. Self-hatred and despair were a big part of it, but they were invisible. On the surface, things were going fine.

Every Thursday morning, Carol Loomis would stroll into the infirmary and announce in a bored voice that she had a touch of the usual problem. Salazar would put the screens up so she could undress, and behind that cover she'd slip the regular package (picked up earlier in the week by one of Grace's busy little bees) into the drawer underneath the medicine cabinet that was mainly used for dressings and sticking plasters.

Then Salazar would make a show of listening to her heartbeat and her breathing before telling her she should keep up the exercises. Big Carol would say, "Thanks, doc," put her kit back on and hit the road. All of this was for the benefit of whichever nurses were on duty, and if any of them suspected there was more going on, they didn't say anything. Possibly they thought Salazar might be banging Big Carol, which few of them would have begrudged him.

The bottom line was that Grace's system worked. It was fit for purpose. Carol would make the drop. Salazar would get the package out of the drawer as soon as he could do so unobserved, and transfer it to his doctor's bag. Then at three o'clock in the afternoon he'd trot over to Curie and deliver it to the meditation room.

The circle of life went on.

As for Salazar's guilt and horror at what he had become, it turned out that he could live with them. That was astonishing to him, but it was demonstrably true because he was still alive. Corruption – preying on the people he was meant to be helping – was the worst sin he could name. But he'd immersed himself in that sin so deeply that he couldn't see the surface any more. And he'd done it for the simplest and basest reason: because he was afraid.

Not of losing his job. He felt he could cope quite well with public humiliation, arrest, imprisonment. But physically he was a complete and utter coward. He knew too much about how human bodies worked, or failed to work. Even death was a bearable thought, but the pain you might have to encounter on the way was another matter.

So he became the thing he most despised, and told himself that the threat of death (other people's, not just his own) absolved him. He focused in on logistical decisions, on the short-term and immediate, and abandoned any train of thought that might lead him to more dangerous perspectives. He did what he was told.

But any system is only as good as its moving parts. And the Thursday after the day when Loomis and Earnshaw visited Jess Moulson in her cell, one of the moving parts failed to move.

It was Moulson of course, but Salazar had no way of knowing that. Neither Grace nor Devlin had any intention of letting him in on that side of the operation. Moulson had had her preliminary hearing, which had lasted all of twenty minutes. Mr Justice Foulkes – in his chambers, as informal as the criminal justice system ever got – listened to the tragic story of her hunger strike and said he was minded to waive the submission deadline in this instance. The Crown Prosecution Service, represented by a thin-lipped man who looked as though his grey suit was welded on to him like roofing felt, raised no objection. Moulson had leave to appeal.

After the hearing, she came straight home. She didn't visit the toilets. Grace's package stayed where it was.

That had all been on the Wednesday. So now Thursday morning came and went, and Big Carol didn't make her scheduled visit to the infirmary – the first time she'd ever defaulted. Sally waited as long as he could, but he was scared to go off-schedule in case someone was watching. He walked over to Curie, did the clinic and walked back again without making the drop-off.

Then, because he didn't have any idea what else to do, he went and found Dennis Devlin in the guardroom. Behind the guardroom actually, on a cigarette break. Half a dozen other screws were there along with the Devil, talking the sort of shit men usually talk when they get together. They didn't pay much attention to Sally, who didn't count as a man for these purposes, but Devlin saw him there and signalled for him to wait – a discreet gesture where his hand didn't leave his side.

He finished his cigarette and stamped out the butt before coming over.

"What?" was all he said.

"There wasn't a package."

The Devil stared Salazar down, unamused. "All right. What did Big Carol say?"

"Big Carol didn't come."

Which told Devlin that something had gone wrong further up the food chain and he'd better get together with Grace as soon as possible. "Go back to the infirmary," he told Sally.

"I'm meant to be—"

"Hey. Shut up. Wait for me in the infirmary. I'll be back to tell you what's what."

He left the doctor standing there and hastened to his lover's side. Big Carol stood alone at the door to Grace's cell, arms folded and face full of a sort of brooding calm.

"She in there?" Devlin demanded.

"Yeah, but she's got company," Loomis said. "Let me tell her you're here."

"I'll tell her myself," Devlin said, and walked on past her.

He knew that was reckless – stupid, really – but he was always on his spiky dignity with Grace and her people. He felt it harmed his status to stand around and wait for her. He opened the door and walked inside, and right away he was sorry he had. The company was the kiddie cooker, Jess Moulson, one of the designated mules, who had clearly been summoned there because she had failed to perform according to instructions.

It was a harmless enough little tableau – Grace and Moulson sitting opposite each other in the two ladder-back chairs Grace's cell boasted (real canvas backs and seats, and wooden frames, not ply and plastic). The only sinister touch was the music coming out of the speaker dock. It was classical, which meant that Grace was pissed off and needed her spirits soothed. Oh, and there was Liz Earnshaw, standing right beside Moulson and watching Grace's face in case some hurting was needed.

In Grace's cell, of course, hurting would be limited and bloodless. All the really life-changing violence happened at a safe distance. But this was a serious interview with serious things depending on it. Devlin knew at once that it had been a mistake to charge in here. He stood there for a second with his hand still on the doorknob, weighing up the possibility of backing out again without being seen. But Grace had already seen him and she beckoned to him.

Which of course made Moulson turn and see him too.

Her eyes got a little wider. He could sympathise, as far as that went. Him standing there was the visible sign that there was no cavalry coming.

"You're talking to me," Grace reminded her.

Moulson took her skittish gaze from Devlin's face and gave it back to Grace. "Well, I think . . . I think it's possible I looked in the wrong cubicle," she said, sounding about as convincing as a schoolgirl explaining that the dog ate her homework.

"That doesn't make any sense to me," Grace said. "There are only three cubicles in that toilet. Which means there's only one you can say is in the middle. I don't see where the possibility of confusion comes in. Frankly, I'm disappointed."

Devlin knew what it meant when Grace said something like that. Never anything good, often something sickening. The stupid bitch who'd blown her own hunger strike might get to be dead after all, he thought – which made him wish all over again that he'd been a bit slower in coming over here. He liked to keep up an arm's-length sort of relationship with the bloodier side of Grace's operations. Fingering Shannon McBride and then stepping out of the way so Grace could do what needed to be done was absolutely fine. Anything more than that made him sweat, not from squeamishness but from a healthy sense of self-preservation.

"People were in there with me," Moulson pleaded. "The right-hand cubicle was locked and there was someone washing their hands at the sink. I think I just panicked."

"And missed your aim when you were going for one of three doors right in front of you?" Grace shook her head. "I'm trying to see it, Moulson, but it's not coming clear. Not at all."

"I'm sorry," Moulson said.

"Well, that's fine as far as it goes. I would want you to be sorry. But sorry as you are, I've still got to deal with the mess you've made."

She sighed loudly. Liz Earnshaw shifted her stance, sort of standing to attention, alerted by that sigh. It seemed likely that the verbal part of the interview was over and that something else was about to happen. But Grace shook her head and Earnshaw relaxed again.

"I'm assuming you took a lot of beatings when you got out of the infirmary," Grace said. "I know Hannah Passmore had a smack at you. But she wasn't the only one, was she?"

"No," Moulson muttered.

"And before that, you were trying to starve yourself. And before that, you almost baked yourself alive. So a few more bruises here and there, probably you think they won't be so much to worry about. And probably you're right. They won't be." Grace smiled, but only for a fraction of a second, waving goodbye to that cheery perspective. "But we'll do it, so we can say we did, and then we'll move on. Carol and Lizzie will take you back to your cell in a minute or two, and they'll lay into you very seriously. They'll leave marks. Visible ones, because this is about making a point. Then you'll curl up under the blankets and put yourself together again and everything will get back to being much the same as it was. For the most part."

Grace leaned forward and stared into Moulson's eyes – a hard, appraising stare. "That hunger strike," she said. "You went all the way to the edge and you looked down, but you didn't jump. That's a hopeful sign."

She brushed a stray hair away from Moulson's face. It would have been a gentle gesture anywhere else, but here and now it implied one thing and one thing only: ownership. "What happened at the court today?" she asked. "You got leave to appeal?"

Moulson nodded.

"Good for you," Grace said. "Well then, here's what I'm going to do. I'm going to put you back in the mix when your appeal date comes up. Mr Devlin over there will tell me when that is. And if you ever let me down again, Moulson, I'm going to kill you. There won't be any warnings, or any more second chances. I'll make arrangements, things will happen, you'll pop your little clogs. Please notice that I'm not telling Liz to twist your arm or pull your hair back while I'm saying this. I don't want you to be distracted. I want you to take these words away and think about them. Will you do that for me?"

Moulson was still staring into Grace's placid, motherly eyes. She didn't seem to realise she'd been asked a question. Until Liz Earnshaw nudged her shoulder, and she blurted out a "Yes!"

"Off you go then," Grace said.

Moulson got up to leave. Her gaze shifted to Devlin again. As a signifier of Grace's power and reach, he couldn't have been better placed.

"What are you looking at?" he asked her belligerently. Moulson looked away.

She was shaking visibly as she walked past him, eyes on the ground. Liz Earnshaw followed her, and Big Carol fell in behind the two of them.

"You need me for anything?" Devlin asked Grace.

She looked at him like he'd just asked her what two and two made.

46

After Moulson left, Grace turned her mind to damage limitation. There were steps that needed to be taken to prevent this from getting any worse, and unfortunately some of them seemed to require a redrawing of her contract with Devlin. "You'll have to go to the courthouse," she told him, "and pick up that package."

"Tonight?" Devlin was appalled.

"Yes, Dennis, tonight. We're still building up our business in Curie, and that fucker Kenny Treacher has been sniffing around. The first thing that happens after Weeks and Hassan get out of solitary is he'll reach out to them and try to get a shop-front up again. If we're solid, we can keep him out, no trouble. But we need brand loyalty. If we let the tap run dry, we're just inviting him in."

Devlin went over to the door, closed it and set his back to it. His expression was strained and unhappy. "I don't handle the drugs," he reminded Grace, lowering his voice. "I don't go near them."

"In the normal run of things, no. This is an emergency."

"I can pay one of the drivers to—"

"No."

"Why the fuck not?"

"For two reasons," Grace said. "Think, Dennis." She took his hand and pulled him away from the door. He came docilely enough, but there was still tension in his rigid stance. She pushed him down on to the chair Moulson had vacated and stood over him with her hands on his shoulders, holding his gaze. And she spoke in her warm, persuasive voice rather than her robot drone. "There's no run scheduled, so a driver doesn't have a reason to be there."

"Neither do I!"

"And the way we've divided it up, the drivers don't see the packages. Only the cons do, and the cons do what they're told because they know which way the wind blows. This particular package is full of every good thing schedules one and two have to offer. If your driver takes a look inside, he'll shit bricks and broken hearts. We've got to keep this between the two of us."

Devlin still wasn't happy. He kept on blathering about how this went against the way they worked together, and what it would mean if he were caught with all those drugs in his hands.

Grace knew she could convince him, but there wasn't much time to waste. She could see two quick ways of getting him over the finishing line. Either she could elevate him to full partner (which he probably already thought he was) by giving him the numbers of some of those bank accounts, or else she could give him a sexual favour she'd held back until now.

She mulled that little riddle over for a full two or three seconds, which for Grace counted as serious indecision. Then she knelt down and unzipped Devlin's flies. Either of these courses was going to shift the balance of power between them, but she could easily rinse away the taste of his cock: telling him where the money was meant giving hostages to fortune forever.

"I know it goes past what we agreed, Dennis," she murmured, sighting past his crotch at his guarded, uncertain eyes. "But sometimes it's good to go outside your comfort zone. Let me show you, baby."

It didn't trouble her. It would only have troubled her if her marriage of convenience with Devlin had grown into something more. Since it hadn't, one lever was as good as the next.

Something was sticking in her mind, though. After she'd brought Devlin to his climax, done a little hugging and murmuring and pushed him out through the door, she meditated for ten minutes to try and get her head straight. It didn't work. She kept seeing Moulson's face.

The trouble with Moulson's face was that it reminded Grace of her own. Not the one she had now, but the one she'd been born with, disfigured by the facial cleft that had turned her childhood into a perpetual hell. Grace had fought hard to distance herself from the false start heredity had given her. Moulson was like the ghost of that false start come back to haunt her. She told herself that the resemblance was superficial. She had been born with her disfigurements and triumphed over them. Moulson had come by hers through weakness and self-destructive stupidity. The two of them were poles apart.

She pushed away the treacherous temptation to be merciful by rethinking it. Rough edges were what you needed because they were what you sharpened yourself against. Nobody ever got sharp from lying in a feather bed.

47

Jess lay as still as she could under the beating. Afterwards, lying still was easy because it hurt to move.

"A few more bruises here and there . . ." Grace had said. But there would be more than a few. Earnshaw and Loomis rolled over her like articulated trucks. Earnshaw in particular went at her with a wild, joyless enthusiasm that was like nothing Jess had ever seen.

She'd read somewhere about flagellants, religious zealots who mortified their own flesh by whipping or torturing themselves. Earnshaw was like that, except that she chose other people's flesh to work on. It wasn't sadism, or at least the look in her reddened face didn't suggest any kind of fetishistic pleasure: it was as though she took the lid off some internal pain and it came out of her in a torrent, her flailing fists and boots just conduits for something that was ripping a hole in her as it came.

Once again Carol Loomis called Earnshaw off, with a gentle, indulgent "Hey, Lizzie. Fuck it, come on." Earnshaw stood back, panting and sweating like a boxer, blowing air past her bared teeth. Jess looked up at her through eyes that were swelling shut. She didn't move or speak or even cry. It was impossible to tell what might start the process off again, and she didn't think she'd survive round two.

Big Carol took charge of the situation, lifting Jess up by her shoulders and dragging her over to the bunk. "Congratulations, by the way," she said as she wedged Jess into a more or less stable position – one where she wouldn't just fall back out on to the floor. "On the appeal, I mean. You might get away with killing that kid yet, Moulson."

Their footsteps receded, but there was no sound of the door closing. Of course they wanted her to be seen since she was an exhibit illustrating an important principle. You didn't fuck with Harriet Grace, or else this would happen to you too.

For a long while she lay alone. Then Buller came in very quietly, inspected the damage and got to work. She wadded up handfuls of toilet paper to dab at the places where Jess was bleeding. For the bruises, there wasn't anything much to do.

"You're a mess, love," she muttered as she worked. "But it's not broken bones or anything. And that eye will probably be fine when the swelling goes down. You've just got a bit of a burst blood vessel there, I think. Here, press this on your cheek."

Jess did as she was told. Buller left the cell briefly and came back with a couple of plasters. The antiseptic she already had to hand from when she'd used it to wash Shannon McBride's wounded hands all those weeks ago. She didn't suggest going to the infirmary and Jess didn't bring up the possibility either. As with the earlier beatings, this was something that hadn't officially happened.

"Lizzie gets carried away once she gets going," Buller said, dabbing carefully at Jess's cuts. "I did tell you to stay away from her."

Jess didn't bother to say that she hadn't been given any choice. Her lip was shredded where it had impacted against her teeth: it was easier not to say anything at all.

When lock-up sounded, Buller helped her stand up long enough to shuffle to the door and be counted. If the warder with the click counter noticed the condition she was in, he didn't feel it was worth commenting on.

232

48

Devlin went and fetched Grace's package from the courthouse, using up a favour or two by getting one of the clerks there to let him in through the side door. He would have preferred not to be seen by anyone at all, but you couldn't get into the back of the building, where the prisoner toilets were, unless you passed through security. So now he was on record as being somewhere he had no business to be, with no more of a cover story than that some other guard had left his cap behind. He hated everything about this.

But what choice did he have after Grace went down on him? If he'd said no, it would have felt like he was throwing that intimacy, that gift right back in her face.

He knew he was being played, of course. He wasn't stupid. But the relationship he had with Grace still seemed to Devlin to be something special, something unique. They might have come together in the first place purely for mutual profit, but after that they'd found each other, found a kinship that wasn't just about the money or the convenience. They worked well together. So it was okay, he told himself, if once in a while she manipulated him. She would still respect him in the morning. She knew what they had as well as he did, and needed it more. And it had been her down on her knees, not him.

And much more in the same vein.

It was past nine when he got back to Fellside, and his shift had finished at eight. That made things more than a little awkward. The Fellside regime, a leaky ship in a lot of ways, was incredibly strict and exacting about logging staff movement. Signing in and signing out was mandatory, and was meant to occur within fifteen minutes of the start and end of your shift. Devlin had slipped out without signing the daybook, courtesy of a stiff bribe to Donaldson, the officer on duty. Now he had to go back on-block when he had no fucking business being there, and pay Donaldson for his trouble all over again. Fortunately, one of Devlin's duties was to maintain the shift register. The first thing he did was to write himself in for two hours' overtime.

With his arse covered, he went to the infirmary. He found it locked up. Fucking Sally, reliably unreliable. But as he turned away the door was unlocked from inside. It opened about an inch, Sally peering through the gap like a rabbit looking out of his hole.

Devlin pushed the door wide and shouldered past the doctor into the room. He threw the package down on the table. "Is there some fucking reason you're playing hide-and-seek?" he grunted.

"The room's meant to be locked when nobody's in here. Patience is still on-shift but she's over in Blackwell, and I didn't know when you were going to—"

"Sally, I asked but I don't care. There's your stuff."

Salazar stared at the package with open disgust. "Well, it can't stay here," he said. "Not until next week."

That struck Devlin as a really stupid thing to say. The place was full of drugs, wasn't it? But it didn't matter in any case. "Find somewhere to stash it overnight," he said. "Tomorrow you do the clinic again and make the drop-off. We need to keep this moving."

Sally had an objection to this too, inevitably. Lots of objections. It made no sense to run the clinic twice. He didn't have a room booked for a Friday session, he didn't have appointments. He didn't have a bastard clue, was what he meant.

Devlin was suddenly sick of humouring him. It had been a shitty, stressful day even in spite of the blowjob. He'd been made to do something he'd promised himself he wouldn't ever do. He wasn't harbouring any resentment against Grace: he didn't allow himself to go too far along that road. But he was full of a sort of unfocused indignation about how the world worked. Right then, having to stomach a big sloppy dose of Salazar on top of everything else felt like God taking unnecessary liberties.

The table was covered in all kinds of medical bullshit: Devlin pushed it to one side and off on to the floor. Tearing open the zip-lock, he spilled the contents on to the table. It was what he'd expected to see. A cling-film-wrapped block of cannabis, a smaller zip-locked bag of heroin and another of crack. Some pastel-coloured pills, looking as innocuous as the Swizzels sweets Devlin used to gorge on as a kid, were probably MDMA.

He broke open this last bag before he'd even thought about what he was about to do, his hands running ahead of his furious mood. Sally's passive-aggressive bleating was feeding that mood somehow. Devlin had come in here more or less on an even keel, just a little bit frustrated by the locked door, but the longer he had to look at that sad, kick-me face, the more he wanted to take a poke at it.

In the old days, of course, he might have taken a poke at Sally's wife Leah instead. He'd had an understanding with her for many years, and it had even lasted some way into her terminal illness. But alas, that well-travelled avenue was now closed.

He shook out a single pill, a yellow one, and pushed it across the table with his thumb. "Here you go, Sally," he said. "Free sample. Don't say I never give you anything."

Salazar stared at him in silence for a moment, then turned and headed for the door.

The Devil got there before him and headed him off. "What,

you're not going to break bread with me?" he said. He smiled widely, knowing what kind of effect that would create. He wasn't really out of control, but it amused him to let the mewling little prick think he was. "Yeah, you are. You swallow that down or I'm going to take it personally."

"I'd prefer not to," Salazar said.

Their faces were about an inch away from each other. Salazar was trying his best to hide it, but he was just about ready to shit himself. Devlin pushed him back into the room, nodded down at the table. At the little yellow pill.

"You're going to eat that," he said. "The question is whether you're going to eat any of your teeth first."

Sally shook his head. "You're drunk, Dennis," he said. "Or something worse. You should go home and sleep it off. Okay, fine, I'll take the stuff over to Curie tomorrow morning, but I'm not going to—"

Devlin had changed into civvies to go to the courthouse but he'd put his blacks on again as protective camouflage when he came back into the prison. So he had his nightstick sheathed at his belt. It made a blade-on-silk stropping sound as he brought it out of the holster and lifted it up.

The nightstick was a twenty-inch sidewinder made in McKinney, Texas, the home of take-it-or-fucking-leave-it law enforcement – injection-moulded in impact-resistant polycarbonate, with a lustrous midnight shine to it. It weighed less than two pounds, but that was by the by: you could tell just by looking at it what it could do. You could beat a man to paste with it and it wouldn't look any different, wouldn't have a dent or a nick or a splinter.

Sally's jaw gaped when he saw the baton. He backed away from Devlin, but there wasn't much space to back into. He came up against the front of a cabinet after the second step. Devlin whipped the nightstick backwards a half-turn, bringing it into strike position against his shoulder.

"Take your pill, Sally," he suggested. "I'm all over being reasonable with you."

236

"It's Ecstasy!" Sally yelled. "How am I supposed to drive home if I'm off my head?"

Devlin laughed. "Shit, that is a bit of a poser, no denying. Then again, how are you going to drive home if your arms and legs are broken?"

"Dennis, you've made your point."

"Have I? What point is that?"

"I am not taking the—"

Devlin swung the baton, slamming it into the front of the cabinet a couple of inches above Sally's head. Sally flinched and ducked, but only after it had hit: he would have left his brains all over the door if Devlin's aim had been off.

At the same time, Devlin let out a bellow from deep in his lungs – not just at Sally, but at everyone who'd ever wasted his time or said no to him or looked at him with a sneer on their mouth because of his thick accent and his bald patch and his spreading gut. It came out of nowhere but it seemed to have been building for a while. It felt good to let it out.

Whatever Salazar read into that scream or saw in Devlin's eyes, it did the trick. He grabbed up the pill and shoved it in his mouth. His throat bobbed as he swallowed it down. Then he just stood there, staring at Devlin, his chest heaving as though he'd run a mile.

"Good," Devlin grunted. He slipped the nightstick back into its holster. It had left a deep dent in the cabinet door where it had hit – a ridged groove about six inches long, right up against one edge and close enough to where Salazar's head had been to raise a doubt.

"If you've got any Vicks, you should rub it under your nose," Devlin said. "Cool you down when the hit comes." He scooped the bags back into the zip-lock and shoved the zip-lock into Sally's hands. "Stow these first though, and then fuck off out of it. Stock has got big eyes and an even bigger mouth. The less she sees of you right now, the better."

The doctor hadn't moved since he'd swallowed the pill. He was

237

tensed and braced, his shoulders against the cabinet and his knees half bent. He looked like a rugby forward about to block a tackle – as though he thought the drug was going to slam into him with physical force. Devlin had to laugh. Maybe this would even do Sally some good. Make him cheer up a little for once in his life.

"Don't forget the lights," he said, and left the way he'd come.

Dr Salazar knew a lot in theory about the way phenethylamines worked. Enough to be aware that he had some lead time, which he put to good use. First, he hid the package underneath the dead files in the bottom drawer of his filing cabinet, where nobody ever had cause to go. Then he tidied the room a little, making good some of the mess that Devlin had made. He stuck up an AIDS awareness poster on the dented cupboard door, hiding the damage as far as he could.

He clocked out, taking care to bid a courteous and level good night to John Donaldson, the guard on gate duty.

Then he got into his car, drove it carefully down to the bottom end of the car park, which was empty at this hour, and waited for the rush to come. It might not be very strong at all. It depended on how much of the active ingredient the little pill had harboured. But it would be stronger for Sally than for a regular user, whose dopamine and norepinephrine receptors would be better used to unusual traffic. Outside of the neurochemistry, he had no idea how it would feel.

The answer was it felt good. Very good. Really quite surprisingly wonderful and uplifting. Sally became purely, uncomplicatedly happy and euphoric for the first time in what felt like years. He sprawled in his seat with his head tilted back against the knobbly beaded top of his orthopaedic backrest, while the beauty and perfection of everything that lived filled him from his toes on up like a thick, sweet liquid.

He was in love with the world. In love with everyone he knew. He summoned their faces one after another so he could tell them how very much he cared for them.

238

But even in that euphoric haze, when he got to Dennis Devlin's face, he felt the undercurrent of a different emotion.

"I'm going to kill you," he murmured, with the tides of hyper-active neurotransmitters drowning his brain and a big lopsided smile slapped across his face. "Oh, I am I am I really am. I'm going to kill you, you bastard."

49

Jess lay in her bunk, the still centre of a world of hurt.

Loomis and Earnshaw had left her ribs, sides and back monumentally bruised and battered. She couldn't find a way to lie that didn't leave her in agony after ten or fifteen minutes – but shifting her position hurt too, sometimes even worse. Every move she made was a desperate sprint across no-man's-land, looking for cover that wasn't there.

Sheer exhaustion was pulling her down into sleep, but she couldn't stay there. She was like one of those drinking bird toys that keeps on dipping and raising its head as the liquid inside it expands and contracts. Every time she dozed off, her muscles relaxed a little. Then some part of her body moved and she woke in a brimming rush of agony.

Sweat cooled on her skin as the night went on, but nothing else seemed to change.

Until it did. Until he came.

You should have called me, Alex Beech said.

Didn't know how.

Yes, you do. You just think about me and I'm here.

But Jess hadn't been able to think at all after the beating. Her brain's higher functions had gone AWOL. What was left had no plan and no horizon, no future or past.

You can get away from it. Look, it's easy. Take my hand, like this, and . . . no . . . No, hold on to me. Step sideways.

His hand was pulling on hers insistently, but she was afraid of what would happen when she moved.

Alex, don't!

Yes. Come on, Jess.

It was her name that did it. She surrendered to him, and to her instinctive trust in his benevolence. She let him pull her up off the bunk, first by one hand and then by both. He stepped back and she came forward in lockstep, flinching from the recoil of her outraged muscles.

But the pain didn't come. She looked into the boy's solemn eyes. Then back over her shoulder at her own body lying there like an abandoned car, eyes closed and mouth slack. The sudden absence of pain was so overwhelming, she wasn't even scared about what it meant. All she felt was a fizzing sensation of surprise, and then a dead weight of realisation.

I'm dead, then?

No! Alex's tone was amused. *You can go back any time you want.*

Jess looked down at her hands. Her torso. Her legs. She was wearing the rudimentary body that she'd made for herself down in the abyss. It felt a lot more comfortable this time – which maybe wasn't surprising considering what a desperate wreck her real body was right then. But it had gone back to the way it had been when she first made it, rather than the way it was after she hauled herself up over the pit's rim. It was no more than a sketch waiting to be filled in.

Is this my soul? she wondered. *But why should my soul look like a badly drawn stick figure?*

Because that's how you're thinking about it, Alex told her.

Jess wasn't religious. Not even a little bit. She thought all gods were basically big bully-boy cops dreamed up by people who wanted the laws they liked on Earth to be true everywhere else.

So she didn't want to think of this pathetic drinking-straw doll as her soul. *This is the ghost part of me,* she thought. *The part that stays when everything else falls away. It's just . . . coming out early.*

She knew now that she could improve it by concentrating on it. She stared hard at her withered, wilting arm, willing it to fill out into something more nearly human. Almost immediately it began to respond. As she watched, her silly-string fingers thickened, and at their tips an area became faintly shinier and smoother: the beginnings of nails.

Shall we go for a walk? Alex asked. *I can show you where I live.*

Jess raised her head again. And immediately she realised what was missing from the scene. "Oh my God!" she whispered.

Everything. What was missing was everything.

When she'd first stepped out of her flesh, she was still in the cell. Now she was . . . somewhere else. There were no walls, or floor, or ceiling. No bunk or table. Or rather, she could still make out those things, just about, but they were tiny and faint. All around them, above and below and woven through them was something else that was much harder to define – a churning, changing mass like a stormy sea somehow tilted so that it stood upright. Colours and shapes moved there, abstract but teasingly familiar, as though they were only out of focus and might resolve at any moment into things she knew. And what was truly terrifying was that it was two things at once: vast and measureless, and yet right there in front of her and close enough to touch.

She didn't touch it. She backed away quickly and raised her arm as though to ward it off. "Alex!" she blurted. "What is this?"

The boy looked where she was looking. He hadn't been paying the churning mass any particular attention until then. *The other one,* he said. *You know. The woman who sleeps up on top of you.*

"That's Lorraine Buller?"

Yes.

"Then . . . why don't I look like that?"

The boy gave her a puzzled, pitying look. *You do when you're asleep.*

242

"What? But—"

Everybody does, Jess. You saw what it was like down in the hole. You weren't anything until you thought about it. And then you got to be a bit more like a person. But when you're asleep, you're all kinds of things at once. You're everything you ever thought about. And there are hundreds and hundreds of people here all asleep and dreaming at the same time. Everything inside them is just all mixed up.

"And this is where you live?" Her voice was strained. If she was seeing the world the way he saw it – seeing with ghost eyes rather than eyes made out of flesh – then how did he even manage to find her each night? Fellside had thousands of inmates. Wasn't his world just . . . oceans made out of other oceans, more and more of this chaos, going on for ever?

It is to start with. But you get used to it. And it starts to be different when you get closer.

"Different how?"

I'll show you, he said, and took her hand again.

And he led her through the chaos and the silence, along roads she couldn't see, through territories she didn't understand.

Fellside at night, through the eyes of the dead, was like the first day of creation. The waters had been divided but darkness still lay on them. Some were puddles you could skirt around or splash through, but some were oceans that took you whole.

After a little while, it was impossible to say what was wet and what was dry. There was no shore, and one stream let into another stream, a river poured out of another river.

But this wasn't water she was walking through. It was lives. And Alex was right when he said that distance mattered. From far away, the waves were made of millions of scattered droplets. Close up, each droplet was another wave, each wave another world that you could step right into and then right on through.

She was circumnavigating the dreams of the women of Goodall wing. She saw what they saw on the inside of their closed eyelids, except that each of them only saw their own dreams, while Jess saw them all, was drenched and deluged by them. One moment she was crossing a busy street, crowds pressing in on her from all sides. Then the wave collapsed and she was somewhere else, standing in a narrow room that smelled of sweat and cinnamon, watching a naked man bowing over a basin as he shaved himself with a straight razor.

You see?

Yes, Alex. I see. And she did.

She saw too much. Fellside's inmates were a skewed sample. Every single one of them had a life that ended in the utter disaster of prison. Relationships sheared off. Jobs and reputations lost. Kids left with overburdened partners, thrown on the winds to relatives who didn't really want them or (dear Christ Jesus!) taken into care. She saw the women of Goodall from the inside, and from the inside they were all of them bowed down by the weight of what had befallen them. They were all on a catastrophe curve, sailing frictionlessly towards this precipice or that. It was little wonder that they were capable of brutality. What was amazing was that they ever managed to be kind to one another.

Jess was overwhelmed by these visions, and she struggled to understand them. The last time she'd walked here with Alex, she'd kept her eyes shut and gone where he had led her. All the same, she felt she knew this place from somewhere. Its contours were terrifying and alien but they were also familiar. That dissonance was the scariest thing of all.

These were other people's memories and dreams she was walking through, that much was clear. But what did her being here mean? She remembered a story she'd read in school when she was about fourteen, where a man stepping on a butterfly had changed the whole history of the world. What damage could a careless footfall do in this place, where the butterflies were pieces of people's minds?

Suddenly and deeply afraid, she turned to the boy. *Take me back,* she told him.

It will still hurt, Jess.

I know, but I don't like it here. It's too big. Too . . . shapeless.

You can make it be any shape you want, Alex said with sublime unconcern. And that struck Jess as the scariest thought of all. That without even knowing what this stuff was, she could run through it and kick it into spray.

Take me back, she begged. And Alex did. He led her through the endless, unspeakable chaos to her own small self, and helped her back inside.

Her battered body creaked and yawed like a house in a hurricane, but it didn't fall down. And the pain held her close until the morning came.

In the still, pregnant minutes before the rising bell, the blocked memory finally came free. She knew Alex's night world because it had once been her own. She'd called it the Other Place. She'd told her mother it was like the seaside except that it was all on fire. And as a six-year-old, she'd gone there every night until Dr Carter, with her well-intentioned rummaging, had forced her to beat a tactical retreat.

It was a world of dreams. Dreams with windows that let you look inside. Six-year-old Jess had mistaken the sleeping men and women she encountered for angels. By the time she might have been old enough to recognise them for what they really were, she'd had her passport to the night world revoked.

All of which led her to another disconcerting conclusion. Everything Alex had ever told her about the nocturnal adventures of the G block inmates was true. Not random invention but meticulous reportage. He was seeing – and walking – into the women's dreams.

No wonder he'd lost so many of his own memories. He'd left them behind in everybody else's.

50

"I had a weird dream," Kaleesha Campbell muttered. Her face was buried between Po Royal's breasts, but Po pushed her back so she could look right at her.

"What dream?"

"Well, first I was watching my dad shave in the bathroom at home with his old cut-throat razor. I used to hate him doing that. But then that kiddie-killer, Moulson, came walking right through the room. With a little blond boy. They were hand in hand. They didn't say anything to me or my dad; they just went on through and out into the street. It was like she was taking him for a walk or something."

"I dreamed that too," Po told her.

"Fuck you did!" But Kaleesha could see from Po's face that she wasn't lying. She listened while Po told her her own dream. Not quite the same as Kaleesha's, because Kaleesha's dad didn't show. And besides that, Po knew who the little kid was. She recognised Alex Beech from seeing his photo on the TV news. So she knew this wasn't Jess Moulson out for a random walk. It was Jess Moulson replaying the crime that got her thrown into prison in the first place. Or else it was Moulson doing a Dante, with the boy she killed acting as her spirit guide (there was a *Divine Comedy* in the prison library, and Kaleesha had given it to Po to read once when there were no fantasy or horror novels in).

This business was creepy as shit, any way you looked at it. Po and Kaleesha did everything together so they could have written off that weird echo as the two of them being soulmates. In fact that was pretty much what Kaleesha did: she pushed the knowledge away and refused to talk about it. But Po went around the whole of that day asking people what they'd dreamed about the night before.

Mimi Acosta, Todd, Sharpe, O'Hanlan, Sam Kupperberg . . . The Moulson sightings kept piling up. She was in my bathroom at home, in the corner of the exercise yard, onstage at the Lexie, wherever.

Po tried to rationalise it. Why shouldn't the whole of Goodall dream about Moulson? There were lots of reasons why she should be in their thoughts, starting with the massive media coverage of her crime and going right on through her botched hunger strike to her turbulent adventures in gen pop. The roots of coincidence were right there in plain sight. You didn't need to invoke magic to explain it.

And if this was some supernatural harbinger, it didn't harbinge anything very much. Moulson didn't rise like thunder that day, or speak in tongues. She went creeping around like her usual quiet self, only with a split lip and maybe a tooth missing and definitely a limp.

"Who's Moulson been playing bumper cars with?" Po asked Lorraine Buller. Buller had to know but she didn't answer. She just told Po to mind her own business.

Po gave it up. It was some weird coincidence after all. Even so, she was bracing herself the next night as she lay down next to Kaleesha and closed her eyes. She was scared she'd meet Moulson in the dark, and that this time Moulson would talk to her. Say something prophetic that she couldn't ignore.

But nothing happened. When she finally drifted off, it was into black nothingness. Moulson didn't show. The kid did briefly, but he was a little blond scrap at the outer limits of her mind's eye. An echo of the dream of the night before that barely registered and didn't merit any special attention.

So there. Reason had triumphed, and it was all good. Po forgot about the Dante hypothesis and had a good laugh at herself.

The truth was Moulson was running scared. The discovery that the chaos realm Alex now inhabited was the Other Place of her childhood had shaken her badly. The boy was dead, not dreaming, but dreams were a gateway to that place. That was how she came and went, and presumably how she'd been able to sense Alex's presence on her first day at Fellside. She was attuned to that weird night world from which he watched and listened to the living.

But then why hadn't she met Alex before Fellside at the hospital or in the remand wing at Winstanley? If she'd had the talent even as a child, why had it taken so long for it to wake up again? Was it the drugs she'd been given, or just being so close to death herself?

Even more than Po Royal, she didn't want to think about what all this meant. When she did finally go back into the dreamscape, it was because she had to.

51

After the court granted Moulson leave to appeal, Paul Levine visited her two or three times in successive weeks to talk strategy. But Moulson mostly wanted to talk about Alex Beech.

She'd been trawling through all those trial documents and depositions, looking for any clue as to who the nice girl and the nasty girl might be. There weren't many quality candidates, but she'd kept at it and now she had a shortlist of sorts. There were quite a few teenage girls who'd lived in the same low-rise block or in one of its near neighbours and who had had a witness statement taken at the time of the initial investigation. They weren't called at the trial because none of them knew Moulson or had anything particular to say about her, good or bad. But any one of them could have known Alex Beech.

She asked Levine to do some cross-checking. "Maybe some of them babysat him, or went to school with him. But it wouldn't have to be that. Any history he had with girls who were older than him. Cousins, neighbours, anyone."

It was easy to see that Paul was baffled. He'd already told her that the main thrust for the appeal was going to be attacking the conviction on the grounds of mental incapacity and poking at

Street's testimony to show that he could have done more to mitigate the damage. If they were very lucky, they might get the conviction overturned, but that was an outside chance. What they were really hoping for was to get a reduction of Moulson's sentence by arguing that (a) there was a lack of intent and (b) she wasn't solely to blame. But none of this required investigating the dead boy's friends and enemies.

"I mean, don't get me wrong, I want to help," he said. And she knew he meant it. He'd been really alarmed by her fresh injuries, had insisted on taking photos of them. He wanted to put pressure on the governor to get her put into solitary for her own protection, but Moulson told him to leave it alone. He kept reassuring her of his good intentions, but she knew he was also trying very hard to shift her thoughts on to another track. "It's just . . . we've only got a limited amount of time. Anything I do to chase up this stuff you're talking about will take away from the time I give to . . . to the central planks of our argument."

"You mean to the things that actually matter."

"I mean that I need to do the things that will help you. That's my job."

"This will help me," Moulson told him. "I can't explain how, but it's relevant. Please, Paul."

She used his name consciously, tactically, remembering how it had felt when Alex used hers. She put her hand on his and stared into his eyes. She needed this. If leaning on Levine's emotions a little would make a difference, she would do it, however shitty she felt about it afterwards.

"Can you give me a clue?" he begged. "What am I looking for?"

Jess hesitated. How to explain the two parts of this, the friend and the torturer? She couldn't. So she went for the simpler part of the explanation, the one where there might be some actual physical evidence. "If Alex was being abused . . . I don't mean sexually, but if he was being hurt by someone close to him, someone who knew him . . ."

250

No. It still made no sense. Paul's expression stayed the same, pained and puzzled. "I think there was another witness," Jess said, trying another tack. "Someone who was there when Alex died and didn't come forward because she was afraid."

"Afraid of what?"

"That this other stuff would come out. That she'd be caught and get into trouble."

"Okay," Paul said. "But what would that mean for us? I mean, unless you're saying she incapacitated him so he couldn't get out when the fire started . . ."

"Yes." Jess jumped on this suggestion eagerly. "Maybe that's what happened. And then in the end Alex would still have died from the smoke, not from the other injuries. The forensic evidence would still make sense."

"But you know we don't have a shred of evidence for this?"

Jess nodded. "Yes. Of course I know that. I'm asking you to find some."

Paul looked almost despairing. "Jess, I don't want to dismiss any possible avenues, but Mr Pritchard will be looking over my shoulder, and he has to sign off on my time sheets. I don't see any way I can put serious effort into this if I can't explain to him why I'm doing it. And he won't take a simple maybe as an explanation. He'll be looking for something more solid than that."

"Just do what you can," Jess begged him. Begging was all she could do. It wasn't as if she was paying him.

"I'll ask around," Paul told her. "But would you please just tell me one thing: what makes you think this girl exists?"

For a wild moment she considered telling him the truth — that she was keeping a promise she'd made to the boy she killed. But if Levine thought she was mad, he'd be much less likely to help her. Then she thought about lying, but she couldn't come up with a lie that would serve. "I can't explain," she said.

Paul smiled weakly. "Just 'sources close to Jess Moulson', then? All right, I'll do what I can. But it might not be much. We've got three weeks before the appeal comes up, Jess, and vast amounts

251

to cover if we're going to have any kind of a chance. You know that's got to come first, right?"

"Yes," Jess said. "Of course. Of course it does. Whatever you can manage then. Thank you. Thank you, Paul."

"Is there anything else I can do for you?"

He said it in an almost ironic tone, but there was. "My Aunt Brenda. My mother's sister."

"What about her?"

"I can't get through to her. All I've got is the phone and letters and she's not answering either one. She's . . . she was sick recently. She had an operation. I want to know she's all right."

"Where does she live?" Paul asked. He'd already put his notebook away in preparation for leaving, but he took it out again. Jess gave him the address and he wrote it down. "Okay," he said. "That's not too far. I'll go round there."

Paul knocked on the door for the guards to let him out. While he waited, he turned back to say goodbye to her. Moulson, still sitting at the table, was looking up at him, the swelling of her bruised cheek changing the topography of her features so that one of her eyes was thrown into shadow. Her face had become a kabuki mask, painted black and white.

There was an urgency in her lopsided stare, as though she was waiting for him to get out there and do his stuff and she would keep on waiting in exactly that place, exactly that pose, until he came back.

Their relationship was just as lopsided. It was even exploitative in a way. Well, it was if she knew how he felt about her. Mr Pritchard had warned him about that possibility. "Everybody works the resources they've got to hand, Paul. Prisoners have very limited resources so they work them very hard. If you're going to become a resource to Ms Moulson, go in with your eyes open."

Paul's eyes were wide open and he knew exactly what he was doing. He wouldn't fail her.

52

The word got out over breakfast, a day or two later, that Hannah Passmore had tried to kill herself by chewing through her own wrists. It got out through Debbie Ochs, Passmore's cellmate.

"I woke up in the night, yeah? There was something dripping on my face. I thought Hannah had pissed the bloody bed, but it got on my lips and it wasn't piss. It was blood. I shouted until the warders came. It was lights-out, wasn't it, so I couldn't tell what she'd done to herself. But when they put the lights on for the warders, I could see it all. She'd opened her frigging wrists up and everything. Christ, she was a mess. It was all over me, all over the bed, on the floor . . . Couldn't have been much left inside her, I'll tell you that much."

Now Hannah was in the infirmary and nobody knew if she was going to live or die. Debbie wanted to be in the infirmary too. She was shit-scared she might have caught something from drinking Passmore's blood – AIDS maybe, or hepatitis. And she didn't think it was the slightest bit funny that everyone on the corridor was calling her Vampirella.

Debbie hadn't exaggerated though: Passmore had lost enough blood to leave her as white as the sheets she was lying on. As failed suicide attempts go, she had come close to sealing the deal. Dr Salazar gave her three pints of full and one of serum. The only reason she stayed in the infirmary rather than being transferred directly to the intensive care unit over at Leeds General was that she was too weak to be moved.

And it was no secret who was behind this. Every woman in Goodall had heard by now about what Passmore had said to Moulson in the refectory a few weeks before. *What did you do to me?* And they remembered what Passmore had looked like when she'd said it. Or if they didn't remember, they heard it all over again from Shannon McBride, who was only too delighted to have a new verse or two to add to the ballad of Jess Moulson.

Passmore had been very quiet since that outburst at breakfast. Not peaceful quiet but ominous quiet. Mostly if you spoke to her, you'd get a wild stare and no answer, and then she'd take herself away to somewhere else where she didn't have to deal with you. There had been something not right with her, that was for certain.

A crowd of people were talking this over in the ballroom when Moulson herself came over. She'd heard Passmore's name and she wanted to know what was going on. She looked anxious, strain showing in her face like she was asking the radiologist what that shadow on her lung was.

"Piss off out of it," Marge Todd suggested.

"Has something happened to Passmore?" Moulson asked again. "Please just tell me and I'll go away."

She turned from Todd to Shannon McBride and said it again. "Just tell me!" Shannon stared back at her, blank-faced. She was smack in the middle of a great Moulson story, but for once it was a story that had Moulson as the villain of the piece. Moulson appearing in person made the words dry up in her mouth.

"I—" she said. And got stuck there.

"Hannah tried to kill herself," Po Royal said. "Bit her wrists and bled out. But Ochs raised the alarm and they took her to the infirmary."

254

"Does anybody know why Passmore would do a thing like that?" Moulson asked, looking from one of them to the other. "Was something bothering her? Did she get bad news?"

"Nobody knows anything," Todd said. "What's it to you anyway? Hannah smacked you up and down the corridor your first night out of solitary. If you want to have a nice gloat, Moulson, go and do it somewhere else."

But whatever Moulson was doing, it wasn't gloating. She looked scared.

Sam Kupperberg, founder member of the "Moving Forward group", looked across at them from the next table. "Hannah had her troubles," she observed to the room at large. "Had them long before now. It's not like this is her first time."

"That's right," McBride confirmed, recovering some of her lost traction. "It was her kid. The baby. The one that had something wrong with his brain. He had a fit or something, and they thought he was going to die. The governor turned Hannah down for compassionate. And then the kid did die. That was when she tried to kill herself. She made a rope out of her sheets, like a lot of people do, but then—"

"I was there, Shan," Po said quietly. "Not really keen to go there again."

Moulson muttered, "Thanks," and walked away fast. All the women there could see that something about the conversation had really got to her. "Almost like she's mixed up in this in some way," Po suggested darkly.

No takers. Not even McBride.

53

Jess went out into the exercise yard. She found herself a bench where nobody else was sitting, mostly because of the waist-high nettles growing through the fence behind it. She sat down in the blinding sunshine and waited.

For Alex.

But Alex didn't show.

Please, Jess said inside her mind. *You said I just had to think about you. I'm thinking about you now, so please come.*

Nothing for a long time, but she waited him out. Eventually the ghost boy came trudging through the fence and through the nettles, which didn't move at his passing, to stand beside her.

What? he asked. His tone was guarded – picking up, Jess thought, on the thoughts she was trying to keep out of her mind. Hannah Passmore with her twisted bedsheet. Hannah Passmore with her wrists bitten through. *I didn't bite her.*

"I know that," Jess murmured, glancing at him once and then looking down at her hands – trying to give the impression, if anyone was looking, that she was lost in her own thoughts. "But did you do something else to her, Alex?"

Like what? What can I do?

"I don't know. But she was afraid of me. She looked at me like I was a monster. And she said she was sorry for hurting me."

Good. It was mean of her to do that.

"Alex, didn't you ever say sorry for something just because you'd been made to? Because someone told you you'd be punished if you didn't?"

No.

"Really? Never?"

Maybe once.

"Well, that's what it felt like when Hannah said sorry to me. She didn't mean she was really sorry; she meant 'if I say I'm sorry, will you please not do anything bad to me?' Only I didn't. I didn't touch her. So did you?"

Alex put his hand on Moulson's and then through it, making her shiver a little despite the sweltering heat. She felt the contact much more vividly than she would have expected, like ice water splashing on her skin.

"I know, I get it," she said, shooting the boy a reproachful glance. "You can't touch her in that way. But did you go into her mind, Alex? Did you touch her from the inside?" He said nothing but there was enough of an acknowledgement in his face to make her press on. "That night when you . . . when we walked together, what we were walking through was other people's dreams. I said I was scared because it was all so shapeless. And you said you could make it be any shape you wanted. What did you mean?"

Nothing.

"It wasn't nothing, Alex. Tell me the truth!"

Across the yard, Harriet Grace was sunning herself in one of her favoured spots, behind the refectory, where cooking smells sweetened the air and the projecting wall of the admin block created a windbreak. She had her usual entourage with her. For some reason, Moulson caught her attention. Maybe it was because Moulson's face still bore the marks of the smacks and punches she'd got from Liz and Carol, and this in turn reminded her of

257

Moulson's misbehaviour. For whatever reason, she watched for long enough to be certain that Moulson's lips were moving.

"That crazy little bitch is talking to herself," she remarked.

Loomis and Earnshaw both looked across at Moulson. Big Carol shrugged and glanced away again, but Liz kept on looking.

"No good her praying," Big Carol said. "God's a bit more choosy than that."

"God's blind, deaf and dumb," Grace scoffed. "Or else he's worse than we are. Liz, what's the matter?"

Liz was still staring, her eyes narrowed against the slanting autumn sunlight. She looked like someone trying to add up a long column of figures and not quite making it.

"Nothing," she said, slumping back against the wall and folding her arms. "I thought I saw something."

Moulson was definitely remonstrating with the empty air now, her hands moving as she talked to the vacancy beside her.

In fact she was still pushing, asking Alex to tell her the truth. But the dead child had fallen into a sulky silence, and finally he faded from her sight. She felt he was still there though. Still within range of her voice.

"Please, Alex," she said. "I don't think Passmore deserves to die because she hit me in the face a few times. But what really matters is that you shouldn't be the one who kills her. Don't you see that? You're just a little boy. If you start hurting people just because you can, then . . ."

Then what? He was dead. The worst had already happened. But Moulson's mind recoiled from the thought of him being at Fellside for eternity, corrupted and degraded more and more by the things he had to see here.

Because of her. Because she'd killed him, even if she hadn't meant to. Even if the mean girl had got her digs in first, she'd killed him. And then she'd gone like a pearl diver through the land of dreams to the land of the dead, and brought him right back again.

54

It was the second anniversary of Naseem's death.

Two years without her.

Grace had told Earnshaw, right afterwards, that the pain would fade in time. "That's the way it works, pet. You won't stop remembering her, but you'll remember the good times and you'll smile. What you're feeling now . . . that will go. It's the love that will stay."

And the love had stayed. It still humbled Lizzie, brought her almost to her knees, that Naseem had even looked at her. They'd been together for no time at all but really it was all the time there was. Her whole life, squeezed into eleven months. Since then: nothing.

On Valentine's Day, the only one they'd had together, Naz had given her a card. A red heart, made out of crêpe paper, glued into a folded order of service from the prison chapel. Lizzie had turned it upside down, then the right way up again, looking for a message. The only words she could read were "HYMN: O GOD OUR HELP IN AGES PAST. SERMON FROM PASTOR SARAH AFANASY. GUIDED PRAYER AND MEDIT".

"What's this?"

"You're my heart," Naz told her. "And my religion."

Love like that couldn't be earned. It was a miracle that fell on you out of nowhere. It would be with her for ever. But the pain had stayed too. It hadn't moved. It hadn't lessened.

On a day like this, death was uppermost in Lizzie's mind. Perhaps that was why she'd seen, or thought she'd seen, at Moulson's right hand, a shifting and contradictory shape. Just for a second, dazzling in the sunlight, so tall and attenuated it was like a shaft of sunlight itself.

Why would Moulson of all people have a guardian angel?

55

Alex came to Jess in her cell that night, while Buller snored peacefully away in the bunk above.

All right, he said.

All right what, Alex?

I scared her. I didn't hurt her, I just scared her. I did it so she'd think it was you that was scary and stay away from you.

How? How did you scare her?

I showed her some things. It was because of what you said, Jess, about stories being like wishes. I was wishing for her to leave you alone. You said it was all right to wish for things that I really wanted to happen.

Jess sat up in bed, wincing as her bruised limbs protested at being made to move. "What things did you show her?" she whispered.

There was a dog that bit her once. A long time ago. It's really stupid. When she thinks of the dog, she makes it all big like a lion, with millions of teeth. And there was a man who she used to live with, who hit her sometimes. Lots of times.

"And you . . . you showed her . . .?"

The dog, and then the man, and then you. Again and again. And sometimes I gave you the dog's teeth, or the man's hands and arms, so the scaredness would get mixed up and she'd be scared of you too.

Like conditioning someone not to smoke by zapping them with an electric shock every time they light up, Jess thought. This was awful. Unbearable.

You have to take me with you, she told him. *You have to, Alex. Right now.*

Where?

Where do you think? Where you were when you did this. Inside Hannah. Inside the thoughts she has about the man and the dog and me.

The ghost scowled – really looking his age for the first time since she'd met him. *I don't want to go back there.*

But you've got to. You made Hannah unhappy. You made her so unhappy that she tried to kill herself. You can see that's wrong, can't you?

Alex grimaced, but he nodded.

So you'll take me?

Yes. He held out his hand and she took hold of it. Just like before, he tugged gently to release the ghostly part of her from the grip of her body. That grip felt a lot weaker now: she was learning the trick of it. They walked together out of the cell and out of the world, into the maelstrom that was made of other people.

It was different this time. The formless, foaming oceans of dream imagery were still there. But in among them there were glowing spires like lighthouses, irregularly shaped but for the most part solid and stable.

Alex felt the question in her mind. *It's earlier than last time*, he said. *Some of them are still awake.*

The towers were a little frightening to look at. They were impossibly tall, without doors or windows. Did all waking minds look like prisons? Was every human soul a Fellside, self-enclosed and blind?

Every human soul except herself and this dead boy beside her, apparently. Their lives had become tangled together back when he was alive, but it was this that had let them come together again and stay together. This shared ability, or shared citizenship.

Over here.

Alex pointed towards a seething space close at hand that was like nothing Jess had seen in the night world. It was more like the oceans than the towers – changing rather than constant, breaking up and re-forming itself with each moment – but there was something terrible about it that marked it out as different and made her instinctively want to avoid it.

After a minute or so of staring, she realised what it was that was so unsettling. The movements of this piece of dream space made up a sequence, each expansion and contraction precisely echoing the one before it. It was stuck in a loop, repeating itself endlessly. There was less variation in colour too. A sludgy grey-brown dominated, and where other tones appeared, they didn't last for long. The mass swallowed them back into itself, like sugar sinking into hot coffee and taking the colour of the coffee as it sank.

That's her? Passmore?

Yes, Alex confirmed.

Then we have to go in.

She took a step towards the dark, shapeless mass. Alex didn't move. She turned back to look at him. *I don't want to,* he said. *It's not nice in there.*

But that's your fault, Alex. You did this.

It wasn't nice before either.

We'll be together. I won't let anything hurt you.

The dead boy didn't say anything. His unblinking stare told her how ridiculous that statement was. This was his element, awake or asleep, now and for ever. Being dead, he ranked her. If anyone needed protecting here, it wasn't him.

Please, Jess said.

But it's stupid. She doesn't even like you.

Are we only nice to the people who are nice to us?

Alex laughed incredulously. *That depends! Are we clever or are we stupid?*

Jess was shocked, as she had been when he'd said that thing about the police deliberately fitting people up for crimes. It was this place, changing him. It had to be. Sometimes he talked like the Fellside women rather than how she'd expect an innocent child to talk.

She wanted to say that she was doing this for his sake, not Hannah Passmore's. That they had to fix this so it wouldn't be on his conscience. And that was a part of the truth. But it was true too that she was clinging hard to a sense of mission. If she wasn't there to save him, then what was all this for? And since he was dead already, what could she save him from except himself?

I don't need to be saved from anything, Alex said sourly. But he came to join her at the threshold of Hannah Passmore's sleeping mind, its mud-coloured wings beating spastically over their heads. *I'll come, but I don't want to stay long. It was horrible last time.*

Jess took his hand again and they stepped inside together. It was a strange transition. They were in the same place but the perspective lurched and juddered sickeningly. Things that had been far away became close, and vice versa. Mostly what changed was the weather, both inside their minds and outside: the feel and sense and smell of it. Hannah Passmore had become, for the time being, their world.

One look was enough to tell Jess that Hannah was in a bad way. The repeating cycles, like the stammering of a broken record, played and replayed on all sides of them. Tight loops of colour, shape, sound, movement, blending into each other at times but always re-forming as themselves. These patterns didn't resolve into coherent memories now that Jess and Alex were seeing them close up: they stayed abstract, and something about them made Jess certain that their touch would be toxic.

Where is she? she asked Alex. Everywhere, obviously, but also somewhere. She knew there was a centre to this maze and that Hannah would be there.

The boy looked around, getting his bearings. The sound of a siren from a police car or an ambulance came to them suddenly and clearly, but then it faded away into random squeaks and caws like discordant birdsong.

264

She's here, Alex said. It was more like, *She's* down *here*, except that the word he used didn't really mean that Passmore was below them, and the direction that he took and Jess followed wasn't really down at all. Or perhaps it started out as down and then became something else. In the process, all the other directions shifted in Jess's head like an optical illusion where a hollow cube becomes a solid one or the space between two faces becomes a vase. It was scary, but it was a revelation too. As with the body she wore, this place was no place at all.

She remembered, out of nowhere, a moment from her childhood: not a dream this time, but a real memory, if that distinction still meant anything. A swimming lesson. She saw herself clinging to the brass rail at the side of the pool, her legs curled up under her, paralysed by the knowledge that if she straightened them and tried to put them down on the floor of the pool, it would be beyond her reach. Everything in the dream world was like that.

But once you let go of the bar, you could use your legs to kick off from the side. Where you couldn't walk, you could tread water. And maybe, eventually, learn to swim.

More sights and sounds assailed them as they walked. And they must be walking in the right direction, because some of the sights and sounds now belonged to the group of images Alex had described to her in her cell. Jess flinched away from a dog's muzzle that coalesced in front of her, snapping and drooling. A second mouth gaped behind and around the first, closed on it and swallowed it down. Then both were gone. The rumbling snarl came a few seconds later, sounding like distant thunder.

Alex slowed and stopped, looking around into the visual soup that surrounded them.

Are we close? Jess asked.

I don't know.

But you said . . .

I said this was the right way. It was. But she's hiding. Just wait.

They waited. Things came and went in the chaos – the same things again and again, although the scale changed radically. A

265

man's fist filled the sky, his dark eyes floating above it. It descended towards them but was gone before it hit. Then it was right in front of Jess's face, shrunk to its proper size. At that point-blank range, she could see that the knuckles were streaked with blood, red-raw from recent impacts. The dog's jaws gaped repeatedly, and the smell of its breath hit them like a wave. Jess could feel its teeth closing on her arm, could feel herself dragged off her feet, as helpless as a puppet, but it wasn't happening. She was still standing there, with Alex at her side. She hadn't moved at all.

Worst of all was her own face, regurgitated out of the random swirl of shapes and colours at least as often as the man and the dog. Her eye was bruised, her lip swollen – but her features were twisted into a predatory leer, as though she wore the damage deliberately, like a threat or a warning.

Through it all a baby cried, and the sound of the siren came and went until that sounded like crying too.

This is terrible.

I told you, Alex said. *But we can use it to find her. Listen.*

And again, *listen* wasn't the word he used or the thing he meant. He meant that Jess had to pay attention with a different sense – one that she didn't think she had. But as soon as he said it, she began to feel it. A sort of tension, not sound but just beyond sound, like a million split and broken fingernails drawn down a million blackboards.

It was Passmore's pain they were hearing. Her emotion, trans-muted into white noise. And Alex was right: it gave them a trail to follow. She took a few tentative steps, then stopped because almost at once there was something at her feet that she nearly tripped over.

She knelt to look at it, a sick fascination creeping over her as she realised what it was.

A cat. Not a real one, but a child's toy. It looked as though it had been loved to death, the body squeezed out of shape and the head narrowed to a bullet like the head of a baby just coming through the birth canal. Its black and ginger fur stuck up in tufts

266

where it was there at all: there were big bald patches on its tummy and on one of its front legs.

Its name was Cassie. It had sustained most of this damage not through years of being cuddled but in a single traumatic night when it had gone into the washing machine in the Majestic Hotel in Eastbourne, accidentally taken off the bed along with the sheets. Cassie had had a purr up to that point, which was activated by tilting her from side to side. Something had happened to the mechanism when it got flooded with water: after that, Cassie's purr sounded like a death rattle.

Jess wasn't sure how she knew all this, but she knew it in a way that didn't leave any room for doubt.

A lot of other knowledge came along with that rush of second-hand recognition. This was more than just a toy: it was a shield – the last rampart Passmore had thrown up in the face of thoughts too terrible for her to bear any more.

Passmore was right here. Inside the cat, or behind the cat, or peering out from somewhere really close – watching Jess as she knelt beside the battered little toy like a paramedic beside a body after a car crash.

"I'm not going to hurt you, Hannah," Jess murmured. It seemed to be a reasonable place to start. She said some more things after that. A lot more things. About the dog, and the man with the heavy fists, and about the baby, although she hadn't ever seen the baby, only heard it crying. The story Shannon McBride had told about Hannah's last suicide attempt made it clear enough how the baby had come to be a strand in all this hurt and horror.

The one-sided conversation started slow and got slower. Jess had no idea how to do this. She was trying to change the way Hannah Passmore felt about very fundamental things, including herself. She was probably doing more harm just by being here than any number of words could balance out.

And it wasn't words that did it in the end. It was the baby. As she talked about it, as she asked Passmore what its name was and why it was crying, Jess found herself describing the shape of a baby with her hands in the air in front of her. And slowly, in stop-start increments, like water dribbling into a bowl, the baby came to inhabit that space until Jess to her astonishment was holding him in her arms.

She knew this wasn't a real child, any more than the dog or the man or the toy cat were real. Any more than her own battered face looming out of the dark was really her. It was an image conjured up at the point where her words touched Passmore's memories.

But it was an image with power.

The colours in the churning mass around her shifted. They didn't lighten, but the drab greys and browns began to be broken up by other colours, and the siren sound lost its distinctness, became some other sound that Jess couldn't make out: someone singing a lullaby maybe, or children chanting multiplication tables in shrill, clamouring voices.

Passmore was standing in front of her. Showing up at last in her own dream.

Jess stood. The legs she didn't really have felt shaky. She held out the baby and Passmore took it. For a moment, the two women were looking right into each other's eyes. Moulson could read nothing into that stare, intense though it was. She wasn't even sure if it meant that Passmore knew she was there.

I'm not, she thought. *I'm not here. I'm a dream. Inside another dream.*

"He needs changing," Passmore said. She was still looking right at Jess, not down at the baby. She spoke with slow, massive emphasis.

"That's probably why he's crying," Jess agreed.

Passmore didn't seem to hear. She walked away, singing to the baby in a throaty undertone they could barely hear.

The ghost of Alex Beech watched her go with a troubled, disapproving look on his face.

She still doesn't like you, he said after a few moments' silence.

"I don't need her to like me. Where's the door, Alex?"

Everywhere, he told her curtly, already turning his back and walking away. Jess ran to keep up with him. She thought he was probably right — that you could walk in any direction here and get to where you wanted to be, as long as you knew what you were doing. But she still didn't, and the thought of being trapped in Hannah Passmore's nightmares terrified her.

As they walked back together through the endless dark, she tried to placate Alex. "I know you thought you were helping me when you scared Hannah," she said. "And it's wonderful that you would want to protect me, Alex, it really is. You're my only friend in Fellside. I don't know what I'd do without you." When he still didn't talk, she tried to break down his sullen silence by another route. "How did you learn to do all these things? To find your way around in this place? It must have taken you ages."

It's not hard.

"It's hard for me. It seems to go on for ever."

The ghost shook his head emphatically. *Nothing goes on for ever. If it did, there wouldn't be anything else, would there?*

56

That night also, Sylvie Stock fell asleep at her desk in the infirmary and had her very own Moulson dream – joining that party a little late, all things considered.

She dreamed she saw Moulson walking down a street in Walton, Liverpool, which was where Stock was born and where she lived until she was nineteen years old. They were on Breeze Hill, the street that led from the ring road down to Walton Hospital. Stock was walking behind Moulson, hurrying on her way to somewhere, but she had to slow down because Moulson was right in her way. Moulson didn't seem to notice her – didn't speed up her pace or step aside or even look around.

"It's hard for me," she said. It wasn't said to her but it was loud enough for Stock to hear. "It seems to go on for ever."

There was someone walking next to Moulson, and that was who she was talking to. This second person wasn't there until Stock turned to look at him, but then it felt as though he'd been there all along. She thought at first it was the boy Moulson had killed, but it wasn't. It was someone else entirely. Someone who kept his face turned away, either out of anger or because he didn't want to be recognised. The other person answered, but all Stock heard was a mumble.

Still, that's how close Moulson came to her. How close they both came.

In the dream, Stock didn't hate Moulson, and she wasn't afraid of her. They just passed each other by. Close enough to talk, but neither of them said anything, and it didn't even seem to Stock that Moulson noticed she was there.

It was a missed opportunity, she thought as she woke up. Not a real one, obviously, but the melancholy of that thought stayed with her for hours afterwards as the atmosphere of a dream sometimes can.

57

Grace was a victim of her own success.

Her expansion into Curie wing went almost unchallenged, and it turned out there were more customers there than she'd ever imagined. She'd always thought that people on longer sentences, and especially lifers, would be more likely to turn to chemical consolations. The opposite seemed to be the case. The Curie women, so much closer on average to getting back out into the big wide world, seemed to have stronger links to it, along with more disposable income and more ingrained habits.

Habits which it was now Grace's job to service. And that meant higher turnover, which meant more product coming through.

"Well, it goes one of two ways," Devlin told her in the course of another après-sex summit conference in her cell. "Either the couriers have got to carry more each time, or there've got to be more pickups."

Grace didn't waste a lot of thought on that conundrum. "Maybe we could slip a little more into the packages, but we'd be talking a gram here and a pill there. There just isn't any leeway, Dennis. You know what will happen if any of those women shows a bulge where they shouldn't."

"Who's going to look? If they've been under supervision the whole time they were out . . ." But Devlin ran out of steam mid-sentence, thinking about all the checkpoints the women had to walk through when they came back on-block. Not even Grace could bribe every guard along the way.

"So we need more couriers," Grace summarised, as though the Devil hadn't spoken at all. She stroked his chest to soften the blow. "Get me a list. Anyone who's got an appeal pending or any kind of a medical condition. Get Sally to authorise more trips to Leeds. X-rays. Consultations. Whatever the fuck. He can make up the paperwork as he goes along."

"There's something else," Devlin said, looking hangdog.

"What? Don't tell me Scratchwell is going back to random searches."

"No, it's not that. It's Kenny Treacher."

Treacher had slipped to the back of Grace's mind, but Devlin assured her that it wasn't mutual. "We knew he wasn't going to like being pushed out of the picture. He's still mixing it with Dizzy, and he's still talking to Hassan and Weeks."

"Talking?" Grace's tone had a dangerous edge to it.

"I think maybe supplying."

"Fuck!" Grace threw off the blanket and got out of bed. Devlin watched her pace for a while. His frank admiration for her well-toned body was tempered by his unease at how tense and edgy she was. These were dangerous waters. "We can't let that go by," she said at last. "They're dealing again? Seriously?"

"A little bit, yeah. You want to come back in here? I can warm your—"

"Dennis. We've got to do something."

She stared at him, waiting for him to do his usual thing. Raise half-arsed objections, be argued down, finally accept the obvious.

"Yeah," Devlin agreed wearily. "I know we have. Look, the warders I bought off when we arranged that fight, they're still onside. This will cost more because . . . well, because of what it is. But I can do it. You just say the word, I'll make it happen. Pay them to pay someone else to pay someone else, et cetera, et cetera. Long distance, no bounceback to us."

That was the crucial factor, of course. He was okay with this, more or less, because it wouldn't be him taking any of the risks. Grace got back in beside him, took his head in her two hands and kissed him, long and hard. "I knew I could count on you, Dennis," she said. "Nobody gets me the way you do. Make it good, yeah?"

And it was. The price was steep, but Devlin made sure that Grace got plenty of bang for her buck. Two days after that conversation, Hassan and Weeks slipped in the shower, and kept on slipping every time they got up again. Hassan was hospitalised with a broken collar-bone. Dominica Weeks wasn't so lucky. That was one very slippery shower.

The news of her death took the wind right out of Devlin's sails. He'd thought he was buying a beating, hadn't counted on a murder. "What does it matter?" Grace asked him. "It got the job done, didn't it? It's not like it's your first, Dennis."

Devlin knew what she was referring to, and shook his head. "Suresh was different. All I did was clear the way that time, I didn't hand over any money. Jesus, Grace, Weeks is dead. There's going to be an investigation. There'll have to be."

"It won't come anywhere near you," Grace promised. "It will die on Curie."

Which it did, eventually. There were detectives and uniformed cops on-block for a few days, going over the crime scene and taking statements. But part of Grace's outlay had been to a lifer named Stephie Monk, whose terms – five thousand in used bills to her daughter Agnes in exchange for a full and circumstantial confession – were very reasonable. The investigation was a three-day wonder.

That wasn't the end of it, though. Not entirely. A few weeks after that, Devlin started to hear stories about suspicious strangers showing up at the Pot of Gold, the pub at the bottom of the long road that led across the fell to the village of Ireby. A lot of the warders drank there at the end of their shifts, especially the ordinary turnkeys. Supervisors and above favoured the Mason Arms in Wigton or the Sun Inn in Keswick.

The strangers were cheerful in their manner and open-handed to a fault. They were happy to get rounds in for the Fellside screws, and to listen to their stories about the rigours of their shitty job. Moreover, they were willing to pay big money for a name: the name of Harriet Grace's mule.

When he heard about this, Devlin immediately took it to Grace. But Grace wasn't concerned at all. "It's Treacher," the Devil told her. "These are Treacher's people. He's still after us."

"Of course it's Treacher," Grace agreed. "He had a hard-on for Dominica Weeks and he's taking it personally that she died. But he's got no foothold here now. Hassan and Weeks are out of the picture and nobody else is going to deal for him after what happened. He wants to hit back at us, but he doesn't even know what he's looking for. He thinks we've just got the one courier bringing our shipments in. Let him go piss in the wind for as long as he likes."

Devlin was less sanguine. He got Grace's point about her massively decentralised network. It was very clever. But to his mind, the problem with a system where everyone knows a little bit about a big thing is that there are an awful lot of people holding clues as to how that big thing works. Treacher was groping in the dark right now, but it wouldn't take very many loose words to bring him illumination.

"And then what?" Grace scoffed. "It's not like we've got fixed times or fixed drop points, Dennis. Well, we do in here. Outside, we rotate – and our schedule depends on who's going out when. Even if Treacher knew how we were working it, he couldn't block us. Not unless he sends his people to squat in the courthouse, Leeds General and the bloody probation office."

Which was true as far as it went. But Devlin really missed the good old days when everything was contained in G block. In G block, he was like God, and Grace was like the archangel Grabriel.

275

He could see trouble coming and he knew he couldn't stop it. There was nothing to duck or dodge, just a sense of a big shit-storm impending. An argument could be made for battening down the hatches and waiting until it had passed, but Grace wouldn't entertain that idea for a moment. "We're still setting up," she said. "Still building the architecture. If we close the shop now, we'll never get it open again."

So much for the voice of reason. Devlin wondered if he should put his foot down, tell her that this was just how it was going to be, but he couldn't make himself commit to such a reckless course of action. A part of him knew that he would only have the whip hand over Grace as long as he never, ever made any sudden movements in the direction of the whip.

So he did nothing, and tried not to think about what might be building under the horizon.

58

Paul Levine played detective with no success at all.

He started by re-reading the files on Jess Moulson's original trial from cover to cover. They included a fairly detailed set of background notes on Alex Beech which explicitly stated a complete absence of siblings, half-siblings and cousins of any degree of consanguinity.

Then he went through all the witness statements that had been assembled by the defence but not used in Moulson's trial – two boxes full of them. He was just duplicating Moulson's own efforts there, but it was a place to start. There was no mention in any of those documents or in Brian Pritchard's notes of any female friend or relative who had a particularly intense relationship with Alex Beech, either positive or negative.

It was a waste of half a day – although admittedly not all of that time was spent reading the statements. Somewhere along the way, Paul turned up the folder containing the photographic evidence, much of which concerned Moulson's and Street's burn injuries. He wasn't being prurient, or he told himself he wasn't, but he found his mind drawn to those images. He couldn't help himself. The photographs of Moulson's face before and then during its surgical reconstruction fascinated and moved him. The photos of Street not only left him cold but actually repulsed him. He wasn't sure why. Because Street wasn't Moulson, probably.

But there was something else in his mind besides those purely personal responses. Something about the images was affecting him, touching his perceptions on a different level. He kept on looking, turning the entire stack over at least three or four times. When he glanced at his watch, he saw with shock and dismay that an hour had passed. He put the photos away and got back to work. Whatever was in the pictures, it had nothing to do with what Jess Moulson had asked of him. Or if it did, his subconscious would work on it and at some point the toast would pop up of its own accord.

The next thing he did was to tackle the media eulogies on Alex Beech, which were daunting. There were more than a thousand. Most of them rehashed the same few facts, the same handful of juicy quotes, so Paul's read-throughs got quicker as he went along, but it was still a mountain of windy prose, and after he'd scaled it, he was left nauseous and numbed.

There was nothing in there. The dead boy was described in relation to his parents, whose marriage had since broken up, or else in terms of his hobbies and interests: his favourite book or movie franchise (*How to Train Your Dragon*), his first pet (goldfish), a brief flirtation with Shotokan karate that left him with an orange belt, the lowest after white.

Paul could read between the lines, at least a little. Where were the tearful encomiums from Alex's school friends? The accolades from his teachers? One or two of the articles had photos of crying kids at a school memorial service, but there were no pull quotes. There ought to be dozens.

He called the school that Alex had attended, Planter's Lane, and managed to get through to Alice Munroe, his last teacher there. He told her he was trying to build up a profile of Alex to get a better understanding of him. He was upfront about the context, which was Jessica Moulson's appeal, and even over the phone he could feel the frost settling in.

"I don't see where getting a fuller picture of Alex helps her at all," Ms Munroe said. "Unless you're going to try to blacken his character in some way."

"He was just a child," Paul pointed out.

"My point exactly."

"We would never dream of attacking a child in court."

"No? Not even if it would help your client?"

"Well, I'm not saying it hasn't been done. But please believe we're not thinking of taking that approach. We're just trying to establish beyond a doubt what happened on the night of the fire."

"So you think it hasn't been established?"

"I'm wondering if it's possible that someone else was there that night who hasn't given evidence yet. A friend of Alex, or . . ."

"Or what?"

Paul decided to go for broke. It wasn't like he had to worry about forfeiting Ms Munroe's good opinion. "Possibly not a friend. Possibly something else. Somebody who didn't like him much at all."

"I don't think I get your meaning."

"Well, was Alex ever bullied at all? Perhaps when he first came to the school? Some kids find it hard to settle in, and then . . . well, you know. Other kids might target them."

"Alex settled in just fine, Mr Levine. And we don't have a problem with bullying here." The teacher's tone had become even harder and more brittle, from a hard and brittle baseline.

"No, I wasn't suggesting that you do. I'm just . . ."

"Building a picture."

"Trying to, yes."

He heard the white noise of a sigh, and waited. People don't usually sigh before hanging up.

"He didn't have any friends or any enemies." She said it flatly, with resignation – confessing her own sins, at least in part. "The truth is Alex kept himself to himself. I tried to coax him out, but he barely ever spoke in class. To me or to anyone else."

"He was a loner?"

279

"Yes. Wonderful. Why not? If you want to sum up a dead human being in one word, he was a loner."

"I'm sorry," Paul said. "And I don't. I don't want to do that. I'd really like to get a sense of what made Alex tick. I just . . . it doesn't seem to be there, in any of the testimony."

"No. Well, I'm not surprised. I taught him for most of a year and I never felt like I knew him. I'm sorry."

"Not at all," Paul said. "I appreciate you agreeing to talk to me. And I assure you, nothing you've said is going to make it into any report or statement or submission. If there's anything else you could give me, or anyone else you could point me towards . . ."

"Well, there are his school reports." Ms Munroe sounded doubtful. "I could send you those. It's just . . ."

"Yes?"

"Well, they're written in a sort of tick-boxy way these days. There are a set of sentences in each skill area, and you choose the one that's closest to a given student's performance. They're not likely to yield any startling insights."

"But you could copy them for me?"

"They're all stored as files on the system. I could send them to you. For what they're worth. It will take me a while to dig them out though."

"That would be great," Paul said. "Thank you."

"I really doubt they'll be much use."

Paul doubted it too. A school report might speak to Alex's personality, but not to his friendships or enmities. He was just clutching at straws, and probably wasting his own time and hers. But Jess was relying on him. In the absence of anything useful to do, he was prepared to do futile things and take them to her as an offering.

But there was one other thing he'd promised to do, and he remembered it now. He'd said he would try to contact Brenda Hemington, Jess's aunt. He'd called her once or twice but got no answer, which was no surprise since Jess had been doing the same thing with the same result. Maybe she was screening her calls. He decided to call round to her house after work and see if he could catch her in.

The house was in Effra Road in Brixton, only two or three miles from Paul's flat in Clapham. He switched lines at Stockwell and made his way there. The light was starting to fade out of the sky when he arrived, but there were no lights on in the unremarkable Georgian semi. Paul stood on the doorstep and rang the bell about twelve times, noting how the paint was starting to peel on the lower panels of the door. A thick wodge of circulars was jammed into the letterbox. A glass panel to the right of the door showed him more junk mail piling up inside.

Screwing up his courage, he knocked on the door of the house to the left. Then, when nobody answered there, he went to the house on the right. An elderly man opened up on the third knock. His wispy hair was in wild disarray, so it was possible that Paul had woken him from a sleep.

"I'm really sorry to disturb you," Paul said. "But I'm trying to get in touch with your neighbour, Mrs Hemington."

"Miss," the old man said with fragile dignity. "Miss Hemington. You won't find her here, I'm afraid. They took her back in again."

Paul's thoughts were so Moulson-centric that he mistook the old man's meaning. He was about to ask what the charges were when he realised that Moulson's aunt had been taken into hospital rather than custody.

He'd come far enough now that he didn't want to give up halfway. Jess would want to know how her aunt was doing. He followed the trail to ward 22 in Lambeth Hospital, where Brenda Hemington was currently recovering from a third round of spinal fusion surgery.

She looked like the wreck of a noble vessel: tall and solidly built, but with a waxy pallor to her skin and black rims around her eye sockets like make-up that she hadn't managed to wipe away. She was weak and in a lot of pain, but conscious. Paul was impressed by her willpower. She was self-medicating via a morphine drip but she didn't touch the clicker the whole time he was there:

281

once he told her he was Jess's emissary, she clearly wanted to stay awake and relatively sharp.

She'd received Jess's letter on the day she was taken into hospital, and had been writing a reply when her back gave out. She'd had to crawl across the floor to the phone so she could call 999, and then she'd stayed there on her hands and knees for the thirty-odd minutes it took for the ambulance to arrive. She was scared to move because the pain was so great.

"I want . . ." she whispered to Paul. "I need to talk to her. Can I talk to her?"

"Do you have a mobile phone?" Paul asked. "If not, I can get you a disposable. She'll have to call you, obviously. There's no way for her to receive calls. In fact, she's got to stand in line for—"

"I meant face to face," Brenda muttered. "Can she come here? Compassionate leave, or something like that? Because I'm sick?"

"To be honest, I doubt it," Paul admitted. "But we can ask."

Brenda grimaced. "How long will it take?"

"Days. Weeks. It's hard to tell."

She nodded. "All right. The mobile, then. Thank you, Mr Levine. You're very kind."

"Only what I'd do for any client," Paul said. Which was close enough to a flat lie that it made him blush.

Alice Munroe's email was waiting in his inbox the next morning. He opened up the files and read through them with increasingly glazed eyes. They were as vapid as she'd hinted, full of generalised statements about core competences and personal targets. The kind of net that's mostly made out of holes.

Paul read every last word of those reports and found nothing relevant or helpful there. Like all of the paper evidence, it was just a hydra-headed dead end. So what did that leave?

It left the CCTV footage, which might possibly show someone entering or leaving the block earlier in the day.

The film came from a council-owned camera about fifty yards down from Orchard Court, where Moulson had lived, set up to monitor a bus lane. The prosecution had entered the footage into evidence because it corroborated Street's account of his and Moulson's movements on the night of the fire. His leaving the flat at 6 p.m. His returning two hours later with the drugs he'd just scored from an acquaintance at the Hay Wain public house. The fire starting. The 999 call, which he made from the pavement outside the block. It was all there, and it told a simple enough story.

Paul watched the footage in a tiny window on his PC. Grainy black and white with a running time stamp at lower right. The resolution was terrible, but enlarging it just made the image break up into a jungle of edge noise. The first time signature that was relevant was 22:54:33, when the fire became visible in the window corresponding with Jess Moulson's living room. Paul started there, but skipped backwards and forwards between the high points. The spectacular plume of flame that rose into the sky from the rear of the block when the bedroom windows blew out. John Street running out of the front door of the block (at 23:00:58), his upper arms pressed tight to the sides of his body but his forearms horizontal, pointing forward, chargrilled hands spread wide. Street trying to place an emergency call with his phone balanced in the crook of his elbow, stabbing at key after key in staccato desperation.

It was hypnotic. The fire in the windows above the injured man was such a bright white that dropouts of black appeared within it where the camera's CCD had given up trying. It almost looked like faces pressed against the glass.

Paul watched the sequence four times, fascinated. But nobody apart from Street himself went into or out of the building in that time frame, so he started working backwards and forwards from it.

Still no arrivals or departures, but at some point as he was scrolling through the sequence almost at random, his attention was caught by a flare of light that seemed to come out of nowhere. The time signature was 22:47:13, and the duration was very short – less than half a second. It was in one of the windows on

Moulson's floor of the building, but not her living room. And both the kitchen and the bedroom windows were at the rear of the property. Paul measured by eye and realised that the window was directly above the building's front door. It must open on to the stairwell.

So what was the flare? It was too early to be John Street running out of the flat. By his own evidence, he wasn't even awake yet. Paul pondered for a moment or two. It was easy to magnify the image, but it was so grainy and pixelated that the closer in you got, the less you saw.

He tried it anyway, and saw . . . something. Something that confused the issue further. The anomalous flash of light wasn't from Moulson's side of the stairwell at all: it was from the other side. The flat there had been empty, according to the notes from the first trial. There was no reason for anyone to be there.

Paul went back to the box that held the photos. There were dozens of internal and external shots of the building in the wake of the fire, and a few from before obtained with more difficulty for purposes of comparison. One of the "before" shots of the landing outside Moulson's flat explained what he was seeing. But it didn't answer the wider question of why he was seeing it.

The envelope that held the injury photos was sitting right in front of him again. And now he was thinking about oddities, anomalies, things that sat in the wrong place or at the wrong time. This time he gave himself full permission: took his old fetish off the leash. He spread the pictures out in front of him and stared at them hard for several minutes, interrogating them rather than just drinking them in. A feeling for wounds isn't like a feeling for snow. There was no mystic communion going on here. But Paul was something of an expert in the things you could do to flesh and the results you could expect to get.

This time he saw it.

"Oh my God," he whispered.

He went back to the CCTV footage and watched it in sequence from about 10.50 p.m. through to just after eleven, with lots of stops and starts and rewinds. He was so absorbed that he didn't see the intern, Susannah Sackville-West, until she reached past him and turned off the monitor.

"Hey!" Paul protested.

"Sorry," Susannah said indifferently. "But you weren't listening. Pritchard wants to see you."

"I'm working!"

"No, you're not, Paul. That's why he wants to see you. He says you should be doing trial docs on Bowker and he hasn't seen hide or hair of you." She was smirking just a little. He was the one on contract; she was the one working for free in order – gradually, painfully, evitably – to pick up enough experience to someday slide sideways into a salaried position. She had nothing against Levine besides finding him a little creepy, but if he fell down badly enough, she might be able (with no hard feelings) to walk over his prostrate body into his job.

Paul was almost certain that wasn't going to happen. All the same, in dread of a severe and embarrassing shit-canning, he went to find his boss and tell him by way of mitigation that he'd broken open the Inferno Killer case.

Pritchard wasn't in his office. He was in one of the boardrooms, walking around and around the table where stacks of paperwork relating to a completely different case (the Crown versus Liam Bowker) were being assembled into a three-dimensional labyrinth of truth and lies. Or four-dimensional really, since Pritchard's path through them as he walked back and forth was a sequential one, adding the element of time as he decided on the best running order for the defence. He looked like a monk in a cloister, endlessly circling the same space and finding different things to meditate on every time he went around.

"You're working Moulson," he said without looking up at Paul as he entered.

"I am, sir," Paul admitted.

"Bowker first. Then Attalie-Ziscou. Then Moulson. Is your calendar broken, Paul?"

285

"No, sir, but I . . . I think I may have found something."

Best foot forward – offer the outcome as though the outcome justified the process. Because in this case it just might.

"Found something?" Pritchard's tone was absent, his gaze wandering over the various piles of papers ranged before him. The facts in the case of Crown versus Bowker, insofar as there were such things as facts. "Such as what exactly?"

"Such as a suspect," Paul said.

Which did the trick. The Crown and Bowker were left to talk among themselves for a while.

There was a big, glaring anomaly in the evidence, Paul told his boss with nervy, hectic eloquence. A wrecking ball for the prosecution case. Jess Moulson's chances had just gone from snowball in hell to pig in clover. No, in shit. She was still in shit. But with a genuine shot at being hauled out of it.

He talked Pritchard through the CCTV footage – pausing when he got to the big clue that everyone had missed, even though it was so obvious it might as well have had BIG FUCK-OFF CLUE painted on it in neon yellow.

Then he spread out the injury photos and pointed to the odd one out.

"That was nicely done, Paul," Pritchard allowed when Paul finally wound down. "You've given me something to work with. A great deal of something, in fact. Possibly even enough. But still, Bowker first. This will keep."

He waved Paul back to his desk with a gesture that might have been considered dismissive. But Paul's heart was singing. Pritchard's faint praise spoke volumes. More importantly, Jess had put her trust in him and he hadn't let her down.

When the fire that had destroyed her face had at last decided to speak, it had spoken to him.

59

The Devil was a little wary around Dr Salazar for a while after the Ecstasy incident. He was aware that he'd been coming off the spool that night, and he didn't feel quite so good about it as he had at the time. He didn't want to apologise to Sally, obviously. He just wanted the whole thing to pass off without comment.

By way of a peace offering, when he warned Sally about Treacher, he put a little tact into it. He made it seem like he was concerned for Sally's safety rather than just not wanting him to get out of his depth and fuck up. But the underlying message was still clear. "Anyone asks you anything about Grace or drugs or Curie, you play really stupid and you get out of there fast. Don't even bother to lie. Just move to higher ground and stay there."

Dr Salazar pointed out that since technically it was him who was bringing the drugs into Curie, at least for the last leg of the way, he wasn't likely to be tempted to answer any of those questions. But in any case, nobody had asked him. "Who'd be asking anyway? There's nobody in Fellside who—"

"Shit!" Devlin exclaimed. "I already told you. These aren't inmates. They're the people who used to supply over in Curie before we did. They're hanging around the Pot of Gold trying to get a sniff of Grace's operation."

Sally drank at home. Red wines from the cheaper end of the Waitrose spectrum, one bottle lasting two nights. It was no surprise that all of this had passed him by.

"And they're just walking up to people . . .?"

"Sally, you'll know them if you fucking see them," Devlin said. "They'll offer to buy you a drink. Then they'll get talking about something that's a million miles away from drugs and prisons, and they'll work you around to it so cute and slow you'll think it was your idea. I'm telling you not to get into that conversation. Nod to show me you understand."

Salazar nodded.

His mind was elsewhere, as Devlin had noticed. He wasn't thinking about drug muling at all: he was thinking about murder. He'd begun to lay his plans for killing Devlin as soon as he came down from his involuntary Ecstasy high. By the end of the first day, he'd identified the simplest method, done a risk analysis, costed it and given it up as impossible. And he'd done the same thing every day since: he just couldn't get his mind off it.

The obvious way to do the deed was with poison. Devlin's pethidine addiction provided a perfect delivery system, and the doctor had access to plenty of things that were lethal in the right dosages. It would be almost too easy.

Looking at the risks, there really weren't any that he couldn't get around. The only people who knew that he was supplying Devlin's habit were him and Devlin. And Devlin wasn't going to offer that information up, even as he was dying, unless he guessed what was happening to him. The important thing was to choose a poison that took effect very quickly, to shrink the window for deathbed soliloquies.

Sally could use his own stock so long as he didn't use his own packaging – the box would have a batch code that would lead right back to him. But that wasn't a problem, since Devlin invariably threw away the box before he left the infirmary, leaving the tiny white pills safely anonymous to a casual glance.

Three easy stages would do it. One: peel back the foil on the container, take out the pethidine tablets, replace them with a doctored alternative. Potassium cyanide would be quickest, but would also be quite hard for Sally to source without leaving a trace. Much better was *Conium maculatum*. Hemlock. There was a clump of it growing in full view in the horticultural gardens at Cholt Hey. A dozen leaves, mashed and boiled and dried and powdered, would be more than enough. Complete respiratory collapse in a couple of minutes at most if he got the concentration right. Devlin would think he'd got something caught in his throat right up until the paralysis set in.

Two: replace the foil. And then three, remove his fingerprints from every last centimetre of the foil strip and the plastic blister pack. He would need to do a few dry runs to get his hand in, but he had interned in a pharmacy and he was sure he could make it work.

He was equally sure that he never would. This pleasant stroll through the logistics had made him aware of the one piece of equipment he was lacking. He just didn't have a killer instinct. Even playing the murder out as a fantasy left him queasy. There was no way he could bring himself to do any of this in real life.

He tested himself, just to be sure. He imagined killing Devlin face to face, using every method he could think of. Gun. Knife. Blunt instrument. Strangling cord. Hand grenade. Even in the ideal theatre of the mind, he couldn't close the deal. Just couldn't. There was a hole where his bloodlust should be. He hated Devlin enough to kill him a hundred times over, but it seemed the first step was always going to be too steep for him.

So what did that leave?

He could go to the governor with what he knew. But he had put his eggs in that basket once before and the bottom had fallen right out of it. There was nothing to hope for from the governor except disaster.

Go to the papers? *Panorama*? The World Wide Web? But with

what? All he had was his bare word. And he wouldn't even have that for very long because Devlin or Harriet Grace would kill him for certain as soon as he opened his mouth.

The doctor raced around this little rat-run in his mind until he thought he was going crazy with it. All his hatred was focused on the Devil. He didn't resent Grace much at all. Criminals doing criminal things? That didn't count as news. Devlin was different. Devlin was meant to keep order in Fellside, and instead he was a vector for evil and chaos. Devlin controlled him and humiliated him and terrorised him on a daily basis. Sally couldn't live with it any more.

But there didn't seem to be any way to take Devlin down that didn't lead to self-immolation. And Sally wasn't under any illusions about his courage or his moral fibre. Not any more. He'd proved time and time again that he wasn't built to be a fighter or a martyr. So what he needed was a way to strike at Devlin from cover and never be caught.

One thing he did have was money. Every drop he made brought another envelope full of grubby, crumpled, non-sequential bank-notes, which Devlin had warned him not to even think about taking to the bank. Sally's vices were cheap ones – Indian take-aways and DVD box sets – so the money was just piling up in a kitchen drawer, which was getting a little hard to open.

Sally invested some of it in a very expensive, very high-spec gadget that called itself a Spycam Super-Pro. It was about the size of his thumbnail, but was miraculously capable of recording video with full sound. The receiver was a lot bigger but looked innocuous, a flat black box that might hold a socket wrench kit or a set of steak knives. It had sufficient range to be left in Sally's car, drawing power off the 12-volt socket, while the camera sat in the infirmary underneath a framed photo of Sharne Fell, safely hidden in the flame's shadow. A day's footage took up about five per cent of the receiver's hard disk space.

Once Sally had installed the camera, he took pleasure in coaxing Devlin to say incriminating things about their joint enterprise in front of it. He would ask leading questions about Grace, their expanding client base in Curie wing, the timing of the drops. Devlin usually told him to mind his own business, but even these equivocal responses made it clear what the two of them were doing. And every once in a while, the Devil would make a slightly longer speech, mostly out of a desire to put Sally in his place: there were lots of circumstantial details in those.

Each night Sally would review the day's footage, meticulously extract, label and save the files he wanted to keep, transfer them to his home computer and trash the rest. He was building up a pretty impressive archive. But he could never get Devlin to tell him anything about the other side of Grace's operation – how the drugs got into the prison and who carried them. He tried to lay out bait in the form of general statements, thinking aloud about the logistics of the drops and pickups, but Devlin just ignored him.

It was all sky-pie, in any case. Sally didn't have a clue what he was going to do with any of this stuff. Leave it to someone in his will, maybe. Even a revenge he wouldn't be around to see would be some comfort. But in the meantime, he drew a little strength from the knowledge that he had something in his back pocket that the Devil knew nothing about.

Two things actually.

"I'm going back home to Portugal," DiMarta told him one evening when they were clocking off together. "I'm giving in my notice tomorrow. But I wanted you to know first."

"Your mother?" Sally guessed.

Patience nodded. "She's finding it much harder to move about. And there's a vacancy at Dona Estefania. Shift work, just like here. I think I could make a go of it."

"I'll miss you," Sally said, meaning it. "But you should be with her. No doubt about it."

60

Jess was distressed to hear about her Aunt Brenda's relapse. Then delighted when Paul handed over her new number. Then distressed all over again when he told her that he couldn't help her any more. "Directly, I mean. With your own . . . investigations."

He knew he sounded evasive. He couldn't help that: he was evading her. Hoping to forestall questions, he lifted the cardboard box from his lap and pushed it across the table. Seven thousand pages of documents, exempted from quarantine by the magic of lawyer–client privilege.

"I want you to have this," he told her. "It's everything I could find on the case that wasn't in the evidence boxes. There's newspaper articles, our own internal notes, a few other bits and pieces that I picked up along the way. I went through all of it at least once, but maybe you'll see something I missed."

Jess was dismayed. "But I need you to keep working on this," she said. "It's relevant to my appeal. I already told you—"

"We're taking a different tack with the appeal, Jess."

"What tack? Tell me."

Yeah, well, I would if I could, Paul thought glumly. It was less than twenty-four hours since he'd sat in front of the partners in one of the boardrooms and tried to make a case for letting her in on the secret. He'd been a lone voice.

"I'd prefer not to at this stage," Brian Pritchard had told him. "We're still researching your find, and we need to be absolutely sure of our facts before we finalise our strategy."

What he meant was: leave her out of the loop. Paul knew that, and he knew why. Most of the evidence that had condemned Jess had come from her own mouth – and at the end of the trial she'd wanted to change her plea to guilty, against the advice of her counsel. Then after that there'd been the hunger strike. "Martyr syndrome," Pritchard called it. He saw Jess as a loose cannon who could easily sabotage her own appeal, either intentionally or by accident. And while it was her legal right to do just that, the partners on the whole preferred to win their cases when they were susceptible to being won.

So Paul was here to review one or two relevant portions of Jess's testimony, and to give her the box as a consolation prize. But his timing was off, and the second part of that agenda torpedoed the first. He was too anxious, as always, to show her he was on her side. Jess opened the box and started to sort through the contents, seeming much more interested in Alex Beech's past than in her own future.

Which, when you thought about it, pretty much proved Pritchard's point.

"Can I just ask you to re-read this?" Paul said, thrusting a document out towards her and holding it in front of her face until she looked at it.

"What is it?" Moulson asked.

"Part of the transcript from your first trial. John Street's testimony about the night of the fire. Could you read it over and tell me if there's anything there you disagree with?"

Moulson read quickly and distractedly. "No," she said. "It's all correct."

"The times? The sequence of events? Everything is accurate?"

"I think so, yes. Didn't I already say that?"

"Yeah, you did. But we want to make sure nothing slipped through the gaps. Please, Jess, read it carefully."

She did her best, her eyes flicking over the lines, most of her mind somewhere else entirely. "It all looks fine," she told him.

"Okay. One more." He handed her a second sheaf of papers: more transcripts, this time of her own testimony.

Moulson gave him a sour look when she realised what it was. "I'm not going to remember better now than I did at the time, Paul. If I disagree with anything I said back then, the clever money would be on the original version."

Paul shrugged. "I'm just asking you to read it and tell me if that's still how you remember it."

He thought for a moment she was going to rebel even at that. Her mouth opened, then closed again. Scowling, she read the document. She gave it a lot more attention than she'd given to Street's account. She read every line.

Then handed it back to him. "Yes," was all she said.

"The timing. The sequence."

"Yes. That's how it is in my mind."

"You both shot up at eight o'clock? You and John Street?"

"Yes. Or a little later, maybe. John went out and bought the stuff. We shot up as soon as he got back."

"You don't mention whether he went first or second."

Moulson thought for a moment before she answered. "I went first."

"Because you asked to, or just because?"

Another pause. "Because John was in charge of the needle."

"That was something that was agreed between you?"

"It wasn't something we ever . . ."

"Okay, so it was just assumed? Taken for granted?"

Jess nodded.

Paul asked her a few more questions about her memories of the fire, but didn't go anywhere near Alex Beech. He was afraid to set her off again now when he needed to leave.

He kept a disciplined silence as he gathered his notes, shut down his laptop, stowed everything back in his briefcase. He made it all the way to the door, but as he reached for the handle, the temptation just got too strong to resist. He turned on the threshold and looked back at her.

"What would you do," he asked her, "if you won the appeal? Where would you go?"

Moulson only stared. "Decisions, decisions," she said after a few moments, trying to make it into a joke.

"Seriously, Jess, do you have a place to stay?"

"Seriously?" The good half of her mouth quirked and trembled a few times. For once he couldn't tell what emotion it was trying to convey. "I think I'd have to check into a hotel somewhere. And then get thrown back in here again for bad debt. I suppose I'll cross that bridge when I come to it."

"When you come to it," Paul said, "you can stay with me. If you want to."

He put the door between them before she could reply.

As he left the prison, Paul had so many contradictory emotions churning inside him that he thought he might be sick. He was still jubilant about what he'd found in the CCTV evidence. That had given him the confidence to say what he'd just said to her. But saying it left him terrified. He had exposed himself so blatantly! And then there was the guilt. He'd promised her that he'd try to find out about Alex Beech's friends, and he'd been doing his best, but then – because of what he'd found – he'd had to leave her stranded. He was going to save her, but failing her still hurt.

61

Jess went from the interview suite to the phone queue, where she stood her vigil with the box of documents in her hands. There was no answer from Aunt Brenda's mobile, and when it went to voicemail, the payphone pocketed her 60p. She queued again, struck out again and lost another chunk of her diminishing change. After that, she gave it up, deciding that she might have better luck if she tried again later. At 60p a shot, she would only get three tries each day.

She took the box back to her cell, which was already full of boxes. "Oh, fucking wonderful," Lorraine Buller muttered when she saw it.

"Sorry."

"No, it's fine. There's still a land route to the sink."

Jess was still thinking about what Levine had said as he left. She'd realised by this time that he had a sort of infatuation with her. Those heavy-handed hints that she was going to win her appeal were probably just wishful thinking – part of a romantic fantasy that ended with her falling into his lawyerly arms. That might have been a pleasant fantasy for her too, back before her face got ruined. Now – quite apart from her being damaged goods, bad news and hard work – her fantasies mostly centred on being in a place without any mirrors in it.

It was free association time, so she broke the box open right away. The lid was tight, and she had to tug a little harder than she'd expected. The box slipped out of her hands and the contents spilled across the floor. Lorraine Buller, who once again was reading on her bunk, complained about the mess but without much animation. It was too hot to get angry, and anyway it didn't take more than a few seconds for Jess to scoop up the fallen papers, handful after handful, and stack them on the table.

She sat down and read. She started with the newspaper articles. They were written in a racier style than the notes and depositions, and they had pictures, so they leapt to the eye. But as she read, a different image kept catching the ragged edge of her attention. It recurred in a lot of documents, always in the same place – right at the top, dead centre.

Jess fished one of these documents out and flicked her eye down the rows and rows of little boxes filled with neatly typed platitudes. It was one of Alex Beech's old school reports. C for English, B for Maths and Science, B for Art. Bland generalisations about skills attained or not attained. There were no insights here. Only, at the bottom, like a little white flag of surrender, his form teacher's summary that "Alex is a quiet boy who pays attention in class but could be encouraged to participate more".

This man or woman (the signature was a squiggle, something-something-Munroe) hadn't known Alex Beech. Not at all. Or maybe the assessment had been an accurate one until the fire. Maybe it was death that had changed Alex from a cipher into an avenging angel who could walk into Hannah Passmore's dreams and slap her senseless.

Jess put the sparse, unconvincing document aside and went back to the newspaper articles.

But something was nibbling away in a corner of her mind, and after a minute or so she went back to the school report. She'd already noticed what was weird about it. Now she had to wait while that knowledge made its way from subliminal alleyways to the forefront of her mind. Her scalp prickled a little when the full realisation hit her. She sorted through the box's contents looking for the rest of Alex's reports. They were all the same.

It was probably nothing, she told herself. The dead boy had forgotten a lot of things about his past life. He'd even been a little vague about his name the first time they'd met. But this wasn't forgetting exactly. And it didn't feel like nothing to her.

Alex? she called inside her mind.

He didn't come. He still didn't like the daylight hours much, and as they got closer to midsummer, the hour of his arrival had slipped a little later each day. When the sun hit the top of Fellside's outer wall, chasing the thin sliver of remaining sunlight across the exercise yard to the back of the refectory, that was when he would make his entrance, walking through the wall of the cell as though it wasn't there at all – which for him, of course, it wasn't.

"Walk," a gruff voice said.

Jess turned at the sound to find the cell suddenly a lot more crowded. Carol Loomis and Liz Earnshaw had walked in together, but now they separated to stand on either side of the door, very much the way the warders did when they picked a cell for a random search. Carol was the one who'd spoken – to Lorraine Buller, not to Jess. She hooked a thumb over her shoulder to indicate in which direction Buller's walk should take her. Out.

Buller climbed down from her bunk slowly, reluctance written on her face. "You going to hit her some more?" she asked.

"None of your fucking business," Earnshaw rumbled. "Off you go."

Lorraine headed for the door. But she stopped on the threshold. "You know she's got her appeal coming up? If she goes into court looking like raw meat, the governor will come after you. He'll have to."

Carol Loomis gripped Lorraine's shoulder and pushed her out. "We just want a word," she said. "Don't you worry about it."

She shut the door, and the three of them were alone. Jess's

mind fizzed with terror. Her memories of Earnshaw's unfettered violence were still very fresh. She backed away, even though neither of the women had made a move towards her.

Big Carol grinned and shook her head. "You know what your trouble is?" she said. "You always pick the wrong moments to piss yourself. We're not here to hurt you. Just to pass on a message."

Jess waited. She didn't trust herself to speak. Losing control of her bladder again seemed like a very real possibility.

"You're still employed, remember?" Big Carol said. "Grace covered this with you way back, so you must have known it was coming. Your appeal's on Wednesday. Same arrangement as before. Middle cubicle, end of the day. You're not going to fuck up this time, are you?"

Jess still didn't say anything. Earnshaw tutted deep in her throat and took a step forward, but Loomis raised a hand. *Wait for it.* "You're not going to fuck up, because if you do, you won't live past dinner-time. You'll peg out in the showers, after some high jinks that will make you glad to go. You know that, don't you?"

"Yes," Jess whispered.

"Of course you do. So there's no need for any unpleasantness. You'll do as you're told and we'll all be friends."

She clapped a hand down on Jess's shoulder and shook her affectionately. "You see? This is how it's meant to be. All on the same side, all pulling together. We're a team, Moulson. And being on the team is like being in love. It means never having to say you're sorry. Not that being sorry would help you this time. Okay?"

The two women left, Loomis giving Jess a cheery wave. Jess sat down again, weak with self-disgust, with relief.

Buller didn't return. Possibly she felt like she'd stuck her neck out far enough for one day. Jess sat in silence, her thoughts too scattered to go back to her reading.

If only the appeal was a bit further off. If only she had a little more time to keep working through the files with Paul Levine while the world stood off and waited. Instead she was being pushed towards a reckoning, or maybe more than one. She thought she would be strong enough to see this through – to stand up to Grace's threats and to get Alex the answers he needed – but she wished that everything wasn't happening at once.

Jess touched her ribs where they still ached from Earnshaw's kicks. But whatever Grace said, whatever Loomis threatened, they surely wouldn't kill her? Even in a place as corrupt as Fellside, there would have to be an investigation. Something would come out.

So it would just be another beating. A bad one, but not a fatal one. Unless Loomis didn't manage to pull Earnshaw off her in time.

Jess told herself these things in a tentative way, to see if she actually believed them. It was difficult to reach any absolute conclusions. When Alex arrived, he found her lying on her bunk facing the wall, eyes open.

What's the matter, Jess? he asked her anxiously. *Did somebody hurt you?*

There was no point in trying to hide her troubled mood. Her emotions were at least as loud to him as anything she actually said. "I'm worried because I have to go back into court," she told him. "That's all." She sat up quickly, turned to face him. It was still too bright in the cell, even with its one little window, for her to see him clearly. He was a sort of vaguely boy-shaped movement. God, it would be so easy to set Alex loose on Earnshaw and Loomis. And so unforgivable. She had to steer him away from this dangerous subject – from the possibility of another Hannah Passmore.

"I want to show you something," she said. Fortunately it was true, so she was able to sell him the non sequitur with some real conviction. She spread some of the documents she'd been reading across the table. The dead boy's gaze ranged across them, impassive.

"You remember these? Your school reports?"

I remember being at school.

"Right. You told me a little bit about your school just after we met. But look at this, Alex."

She tapped the top of the sheet. The school's logo stood out there front and centre, darker and more clearly defined than the text underneath. It was penny plain and indefinably ugly. The letters PLS, in a spindly serifed font, running diagonally down and across an unadorned shield.

What's PLS?

"Planter's Lane School."

She waited for Alex to say something. He looked at the report with his head slightly tilted, trying to see what she was getting at but clearly not very interested.

"What does *dum spiro spero* mean?" Jess prompted him.

"While there's life there's hope." But it doesn't say that.

"No. I know it doesn't. That's my point. You remember telling me about your blazer? Black with a red badge is what you said. And there was a goat and a flag. And the motto was *dum spiro spero*. Do you still remember those things?"

Alex glanced from the report to Jess and back again. His expression was guarded, as though he felt he was being lured into a trap of some kind.

"Do you, Alex?"

Yes.

"And it was definitely your blazer? Your badge? You've forgotten a lot of things about . . . before."

You mean about when I was alive. He stared at her with something like reproach. *You've been there, Jess.* In the night world, he meant. In the flood of lives, the nakedness and fury of a thousand overlapping minds. *I remembered everything at first. Then I forgot everything and I wasn't anywhere at all. I was like a nothing that sort of knew it was a nothing. Then you came and I started to wake up again.*

Jess's mind shied away from this bleak vision, but she forced herself to interrogate it. Alex had found her in the abyss, falling, and brought her back here. He knew his way through the night world, and how to walk there. How to find her body where it lay in the infirmary. So had he come here before her? That made no sense. Surely his link was to her, not to Fellside.

301

Was it possible that the night world's geography was just different? That all spaces came together there? Perhaps she'd always been his focus, his tether, and didn't even know it until her coming so close to death herself permitted them to see each other. But even that begged so many questions. Were killers and their victims always psychically joined at the hip? If so, Fellside ought to be teeming with unquiet ghosts.

In any case, she didn't find it strange at all that rubbing up against all those minds, all those memories, had abraded the boy's sense of himself. She'd seen first-hand how much he'd forgotten. But the description of the blazer and the badge had been so specific, so circumstantial, she thought it must mean something.

"So was there another school you went to before this one? Before Planter's Lane?" she asked him. Alex didn't answer, so she pushed again. "Did your parents transfer you for some reason? Because you were being bullied there? Is that maybe where you met the mean girl?"

Just more silence.

"I'm trying to help you," Jess said. She could feel a little stridency creeping into her voice but she fought against it, tried to speak more softly. "Concentrate, Alex," she coaxed him. "Think about it."

He stared solemnly into her eyes. *It's hard. It was a long time ago.*

"But you're sure about the badge?"

Alex nodded emphatically. *My badge had a goat and a flag. I don't remember this badge at all.*

Jess considered. It was still six days before her hearing. Paul had said he couldn't help her any more, but this was a tiny thing. If she presented it as a personal favour, he wouldn't refuse her.

She had to use up the last of her phone credit for the day, but she made the call. It went to voicemail and she left a message.

She would wait until the next day to call Brenda again. She didn't have any choice.

62

Sally was leading a double life, and he wasn't enjoying either of them.

His normal working week at the prison was comprehensively overshadowed by his hatred and fear of Dennis Devlin to the point where it was hard for him to see anything else. He was distracted and forgetful, allowing prescription drugs to run out, failing to submit reports, even missing clinic sessions.

Except for the Thursday clinic in Curie. That one ran like clockwork. And afterwards, like clockwork, Sally would go down to the meditation room, where he would drop off Grace's basket of goodies. The weight of unhappiness that settled on him as he did this stayed with him for hours afterwards, cutting the fear and loathing with something even darker.

Sylvie Stock was very much aware of Sally's perturbed state of mind since she'd switched to days now and was therefore the one who was mostly picking up after him. She had no idea what it was that was getting to him, so she made the same mistake as before and assumed it had to be her. She wound herself up into a tighter and tighter coil, convinced that her guilt was the one thing everyone was focused on. That preoccupation made her as negligent in her duties as Sally was in his. DiMarta kept the surgery together through that weird time, changing Passmore's dressings three times a day and reporting on her progress to Dr Salazar's more or less deaf ears.

Passmore was doing remarkably well all of a sudden. She'd hit the bottom and done a spectacular bounce, the same way Moulson had done a few weeks before. Miracle recoveries were becoming the regular backdrop to Salazar's life, and to Stock's – their patients rallying as they themselves fell apart.

Stock decided that the only way she would stay sane was if she could put the business with Moulson out of her mind altogether. Just forget it. Not think about it. Let the whole thing fall where it wanted to fall. The first day she tried this strategy out, she was called over to Dietrich block to sedate a patient who'd had a religious vision and responded to it with a hysterical fit. That was what she was told anyway, although the inmate, Waites, had calmed down by the time she got there. "He was an angel," she whispered to Stock confidentially as Stock prepped the hypo.

"Was he now?" Stock murmured.

"And she was with him. That murderess with the ugly face. I think they're friends now."

"That's nice." Sylvie pushed the needle in and gave her the dose. Waites sighed, closed her eyes and settled back on her bunk, already half asleep. Sylvie only realised then what she'd been saying.

"Hey," she said, giving Waites a hard nudge in the ribs. "Who? What murderess? Who are you talking about?"

Waites's lips formed the shape of a name. Stock's wide eyes took it in.

63

The night before her appeal hearing started, Jess finally got through
to her Aunt Brenda.

It wasn't for want of trying. She had stood in the phone line
every day since Paul Levine gave her the number, using up her
daily cash allowance each time in three vain attempts.

"Hello?"

Jess had given up expecting an answer, so the single halting
word from the other end of the line startled her and scattered
her thoughts. "Brenda!" she yelped. "Brenda, hey! It's me. It's Jess."

"Jess!" Her aunt's voice was slow and slightly slurred. She sounded
like she'd had a few too many, but then the effects of a morphine
drip were very like a mellow drunk. Her joy and relief came
through in any case. "Oh Jess, it's so good to hear your voice!"

"It's great to hear yours," Jess said, choking up a little. "How
are you?"

"Let's not go there, sweetheart. Not unless you've got an hour
or two to spare."

"I've got maybe seven minutes," Jess said. It wasn't a guess: the
payphone had a digital timer, which was counting down relentlessly.
"But seriously, how's your back? How did the operation go?"

"Operations. Every time they fix one thing, they find something else that's wrong. My back is made of Lego bricks, and they're not load-bearing."

"But do they think they've fixed—?"

"Jess, listen. Listen to me, please, just listen listen listen." Brenda's voice was still fuzzy and soft, but she won that tussle by speaking right alongside her niece until she shut up.

"All right. Listening."

"Good. I wanted to tell you something about when you were little."

"Still listening."

"Actually it's about Tish."

"Tish?" Jess repeated blankly. "Made-up Tish? Imaginary friend Tish?"

Brenda sighed. It was a brittle, hollow sound fizzing with static from the bad connection. "The little boy," she said. "You said you saw him in a dream. It made me think of something I hadn't thought about in a long time. Was he in the Other Place, Jess? The place you used to go to at night?"

"I . . . " Jess hesitated. There were a lot of possible answers to that question, but she went with the simplest. "Yes. He was."

"And that was where you saw Tish too."

"Auntie B, I didn't make this up. Alex is more than just a dream."

Silence on the line. Then: "So was Tish, sweetheart."

"What?"

"Her name was Patricia Mackie. She lived opposite you in Paley Close. And she was in your class at Heathcote Road. At least, she was for a little while."

"But . . ." Jess tried to make sense of this absurd contradiction. "I made Tish up. She had wings. And a magic necklace that sang songs and shot fire."

"In your dreams she did. In real life she was an unlucky little girl with a rare illness. Farber disease. I don't remember all the details but it made her joints swell up so she couldn't walk, and

306

it affected her heart. That was why she stopped going to school. She was too sick."

"I don't remember any of this," Jess protested, but already that was a lie. Memories were starting to stir at the back of her mind, to bubble up and burst in quick flashes of random association. Pink plastic beads threaded on elastic. A school satchel with the initials P.M. embossed in flaking gold. Her own name, Jessica, pronounced with a long "a" at the end: *Jessicay*.

"She was your best friend in Year One, and then she was gone. You weren't even allowed to see her because she had to be kept in a germ-free environment. Except that you did see her, of course. You saw her in the Other Place."

As Tish. A composite figure assembled from half a dozen books Jess had read to her, with wings and pirate boots and a sword and many magical accessories. That necklace . . . it . . . It had been pink. Pink gems all in a line, all identical. It was a magnificent thing but Jess knew that the cheap little toy she'd just remembered had been the source material for it.

"You didn't want to let her go," Aunt Brenda was saying. "Of course you didn't. So you made her into a hero in your stories. But then you said that she was *happier* in the Other Place. She was stronger there, and she could do all sorts of things she couldn't do in real life. You said . . . she'd decided not to come back.

"And that was the night she died."

Jess's stomach clenched. The room turned a circuit around her.

"Jess? Jess, are you there?"

It was true. All of it.

She remembered now all the things she'd worked so hard to forget.

She'd cauterised her mind after Dr Carter. Tish was one of the things she just made herself not think about. But Tish wasn't a casualty of Dr Carter; she was already gone.

I'm going on a long sea voyage, Jessicay. To a million places.

"I'm here," she said. "Auntie B, was that . . .?" But she didn't know how to get the question out.

"That was why your mum took you to a psychologist, yes. Because you didn't seem to be coping with Patricia's death. And because what you said was so upsetting. That she actually wanted to be dead."

No, not that. I never said that. I said she wanted to be in a place where she could run and fly and fight and explore and do magic. Being dead was just the price of admission.

"Jess?"

"I'm still here."

"I hope you're not upset. But what you were saying about . . . the boy. It sounded so much like what you said back then, when you were just a child . . ."

Jess bowed her head until it pressed against the top of the payphone cabinet. The touch of the cool metal was soothing. "I get it," she said. "The old crazy stuff coming back."

"Not that. Not crazy, Jess. But we all have our own ways of dealing with stress. With grief. Like Dr Carter said, we make the things we need. I wanted you to remember because it might make you stronger if you know that you've been here before, and survived it."

"Thank you. Thank you, Auntie B. I won't forget that."

"And Jess . . . I'm so glad. I'm so glad you're back. That you didn't decide to—"

The counter hit zero and the line went dead, but Jess could finish that sentence off for herself. And she knew why poor Patricia had come into Brenda's mind so vividly. It must have seemed to her that her niece was making the same choice. To go off on that long sea voyage and never come home.

After lights-out, she lay in her bunk and counted the hours. She didn't even try to sleep because she knew she wasn't going to get there.

Alex came and sat with her, but for a long time they didn't talk. Jess was thinking about a lot of things. Paul Levine's offer of a place to stay. The memories her talk with Brenda had stirred

308

up. And looming over everything else, the orders she'd received from Big Carol.

Paul had implied that she had a good chance in her appeal, but that almost seemed like a side issue right then. Whatever happened, she was going to reach the crunch point with Harriet Grace long before any verdict came in. If she refused to make the pick-up, Grace would have her beaten and perhaps killed. But if she said yes, she might lose something even more fundamental. Because whatever power had sent her Alex and offered her this second chance to help him, it had to have a working definition of failure.

Unless the power was hers. Perhaps it was just a knack she had, to talk to the dead, and the dreamers, and the dreaming dead. To gather them around her.

Grace. She had to decide what to do about Grace – and the package. She could go to the prison authorities, of course. But from what she'd seen, it seemed that Grace owned the authorities. And she had no evidence at all. Nothing but bare assertion to set against the weight and mass of an entire institution.

The dead boy interrupted her fretful thoughts. *You're going away tomorrow.*

Yes.

She'd told Alex about the appeal more than once. He'd seemed to listen, but then treated it as new and unwelcome information every time she brought it up. Now that he'd finally got his head around the idea, she moved quickly to reassure him.

But I'll be back in the afternoon. It's just a few hours.

And the next day?

The same. And the day after that, probably.

The original trial had taken two weeks. The appeal would run for at least three days, with the first day and part of the second devoted to procedural submissions and arguments that were technical, abstract and complex. Any one of those quibbles could get the original conviction declared unsafe and turn the appeal into a retrial, so they had to come first. That was just how lawyers

309

rolled, according to Levine. But it was all foreplay. The main event, barring a miracle, would start on day two, after the judge had worked through all the summary rulings.

Jess hadn't thought about freedom for a long time. She was still getting used to being alive again. But freedom would have two big advantages: it would cut her loose from Harriet Grace, and it would mean she could go looking for Alex's friend and his tormentor – the nice girl and the nasty girl – herself instead of having to cajole Levine into doing it for her. She'd be a better agent for Alex as a free woman than she could ever hope to be cooped up in Fellside.

So you want to leave? Alex's tone was uncertain, almost accusing.

Yes. I think so. And you'd go with me, right? You must have come here with me in the first place. We'd still be together.

I suppose. He sounded as though he didn't suppose at all.

Jess sat up and looked across the cell at him. He was sitting on the floor – or close enough – with his knees drawn up to his chest. Just a little kid at first glance, then on the double-take a scary optical illusion, lit up by remembered sunlight, clearly visible despite the full dark.

I wouldn't leave you, she told him.

Alex looked at his shoes, his face studiously blank. She could see that he wasn't convinced, but she couldn't think of anything she could say that would reassure him. Out of ideas, she settled for a diversion.

Alex?

He looked up at her. *Yes?*

She held out her hand. *Let's go for a walk. I want to see the other world again. Your world.*

This time leaving her body was almost effortless. Walking was easier too: she ballasted herself against the storm of thoughts by thickening the stringy limbs of her imaginary body, giving them muscle and bulk and sinew, thinking of herself as solid and weighted down. She could feel it working at once, much more quickly than the other times. She was able to hold to more of a straight line

310

as they threaded their way through the chaos. That in itself made it less frightening.

She threw out a froth of chatter. How long had it taken him to learn to navigate the dream space? Did it scare him at first, or had he always taken it for granted? How had he found the pit?

I woke up there, he said to this last question. *After they hurt me.*

"They?" Jess picked up on the plural pronoun at once.

She. When I opened my eyes, I was just there, on a ledge a long way down. It took me a long time to climb out.

"And then?"

And then I was here. I was here for ages, by myself. It wasn't too bad at first. Some of the dreams were like TV shows that I could be in. It was exciting. I'd live in one for a while, then go and find another one I liked. But I started to forget. A little bit at a time, until most of me was gone. That was when you came. Jess, you have to stop thinking so hard.

She started to ask him why, but she saw what he meant before she got a single word out. She had tried to push down her thoughts of Harriet Grace and the drug package, of Liz Earnshaw and Carol Loomis. All she'd done was suppress the words. The images were still bubbling at the bottom of her conscious thoughts.

And they were being echoed on all sides. Wherever they walked, Grace's face loomed out of the dark in a thousand fractured reflections. Duct-taped packages crunched under their feet. The dreams they walked through had taken on the tenor and pattern of her fears.

"Are they . . . Is everyone dreaming this?"

I think so. But they won't all remember. At least if we think something else, or go away. The longer we stay here, the more they'll remember when they wake up.

They kept moving, but the desultory conversation petered out. Jess tried to make her thoughts range over a lot of different things, to keep them from coming back to the one thing that haunted her. Finally she gave up the unequal struggle. The two of them made their way back through the night world to the place where her body lay. They lingered there a while, on the doorstep of Jess's physical self.

"Are you still worried about me going away tomorrow?" she asked Alex.

Yes. But so are you.

"Actually, I'm more worried about what happens when I come back. But you can come with me if you want to. Then you'd know I wasn't going far and you'd know we were still going to be together."

But I don't know the way.

"Okay, but if we leave at the same time . . . if you follow me . . ."

She didn't finish the thought. She was going to be taken in a van across the moors. Was it even possible for him to ride with her? Was that something ghosts could do? And if he lost his way, how would he ever find it again? There were no road signs where he lived, no maps. She realised for the first time that the entire geography of Alex's world was made out of people. The only way he could see walls or ceilings, or trees or rivers or mountains, was if somebody else dreamed about them or remembered them.

If Jess took him away from the prison, out on to the moors, and lost him there – in a place where people mostly didn't come – he'd be alone and functionally blind. He could be lost for ever.

"No, you're right," she said quickly. "Much better if you wait for me here. I'll be back very soon."

You promise?

"I promise, Alex."

And will you always come back?

That gave her pause. "I don't know," she admitted. "If they set me free, I won't really have any choice. But if I do get out – if I ever really get to go away from here – I promise I'll find a way to take you with me. I won't leave you alone again."

The ghost stared at her wordlessly for a moment or two.

I know you won't, he said at last. *You're my friend, Jess.*

"I'll always be your friend."

Another silence.

I don't think you killed me, he ventured at last, *but if you did* . . .

"If I did?"

Then I'm glad.

Jess was appalled. "Glad? Alex, why would you say that?"

Because otherwise we might not ever have met.

64

The first day of the appeal hearing was exactly what Levine had promised. Long, baffling and deadeningly dull.

There was excitement enough in getting there though. Even before they reached the outskirts of Leeds, the driver was talking on the radio and passing nuggets of news on to the two guards, Ratner and Corcoran, who were with Jess in the back of the van. "There's protesters," he said. "All the way along the street. They said to bring her through to the back bit. There'll be someone waiting to open the gates for us."

"There'd bloody better be," Corcoran said.

When they turned on to Oxford Row, they were forced to slow to a crawl, inching their way through a dense crowd of people who hammered on the van's armoured sides as it passed. Jess thought she recognised a few faces from her first trial. Certainly she recognised the slogans on their placards. YOU'LL BURN LATER, accompanied by a cartoon graphic of hellfire; WHAT THOU HAST DONE UNTO THE SMALLEST OF MY CHILDREN, THAT THOU HAST DONE UNTO ME; and everywhere the same photo of Alex Beech, smiling at the camera, with the bend sinister of a Christmas tree branch bisecting the background.

The van nudged its way through the throng in painful slow motion. Jess knew that the security windows shut out any view of the van's inside, but the flushed, angry faces still seemed to be shouting directly into hers. She flinched back from them: she couldn't help herself.

"Idiots everywhere," Corcoran told her, seeing the look on her face. "Just got too much time on their hands, that's all." *But it's not that*, Jess thought bleakly. They were angry because a child had died and the engine of justice was still spinning its wheels. She couldn't blame them.

They turned off on to a side street but the crowd knew who was in the van and they came along too, still shouting and banging on the windows. Fifty yards down, there was a gate which led through to an enclosed area behind the courthouse. Two small wedges of uniformed policemen pushed the crowd away from the gate as it opened to admit the van and then closed again behind it. A roar of frustration and protest followed them.

In a courtyard roofed in by anti-suicide netting and razor wire, Paul Levine stood in a small patch of sunlight waiting to take her inside. In his black suit, he looked for a moment like a shadow that had lost its owner.

Jess stepped out of the van and walked straight over to him. He had his mouth open to say something – a greeting, most likely, or something about the appeal. She didn't have time for that.

"Did you get my letter?" she asked him quickly. She hoped that the answer would just be a yes or a no, but Paul responded with a non-committal gesture. "We'll talk inside," he said.

Corcoran and Ratner took an arm each and hurried her away through a door marked COURT OFFICERS ONLY. They led her along echoing institutional corridors to a bare waiting room, where they sat her down. Ratner told her sternly to stay put. She unhooked a clipboard from the wall and scribbled in it, then took it away somewhere.

"Are you all right here?" Corcoran asked Jess. "Do you want a glass of water or anything? Cup of tea?"

315

Jess shook her head. "I'm fine," she lied.

Footsteps sounded in the corridor. Jess turned, expectant. But it wasn't Paul Levine; it was Brian Pritchard. He greeted Jess with a polite handshake and then turned to Corcoran.

"Can I have a word in private with my client?" he asked her.

"Have several," Corcoran said equably. "My colleague has sneaked off for a gasp. I'll go and breathe in her second-hand smoke for a bit. Remind myself why I quit." She gave Jess a nod as she walked away.

"Has Paul explained what's going to be happening today?" Pritchard asked her when they were alone. He'd sat down on the bench that ran the length of the waiting room, but Jess was too nervous and too wired to sit next to him. This was the first time they'd spoken since her original trial.

"Yes," she said. "Today is procedural submissions."

"Chief among which is that we don't believe a charge of murder is applicable to a death that was never intended. There's a chance we might make that one stick, but it's not a very good chance." He gave her an austere smile. "Are you sure you don't want to sit down?"

"I'm fine as I am," Jess said. "Thank you."

And that was another first, she realised. She'd never used those two words to him before about anything.

"Anyway," he went on, "assuming these wider arguments fail, which I am very much assuming – not because they have no merit but because I can see which way the land lies – then the appeal proper will start tomorrow. With that in mind, I'm going to be having a lot to say today about evidence, and the disclosure of evidence. Re-examining evidence isn't normally part of what the appeal court does. It's meant to restrict itself to matters of legal interpretation. But we're going to try very hard to break that rule because we'd like – very much indeed – to call John Street back to the stand. And we believe we have a chance. So some of what I'll be doing today will be laying down ground rules that we can use to our advantage later. I'd like to say more, but I'm frankly afraid to."

316

"Afraid?" Jess echoed. "Afraid of what?"

Pritchard made an equivocal gesture, perhaps trying to take some of the sting out of the words. "Of you, Ms Moulson. The last time we spoke, you were a hostile witness, even though I was defending you."

"That's not true."

"Yes, it is. You cared more about paying for your sins than about establishing what those sins actually were. My priorities ran very much the other way. But I suppose that by telling you this I'm giving you the right to choose. If you insist, I'll unpack our whole strategy to you. I'm obliged by law and by the ethics of my profession to do so."

Jess thought about this. "But you'd rather I didn't know? You think that me knowing would make things worse rather than better."

"Yes. I do think that."

Jess shrugged. "Then I don't insist."

"Very good," Pritchard said. "Excellent."

"But . . . there's one favour I'd like to ask you. Can I talk to Paul? Please?"

Pritchard pursed his lips. "Would what you have to say to him concern the appeal?"

Jess could see that there was no right answer to that question. If she said yes, Pritchard would tell her she should say what she had to say to him. If no, he'd refuse and tell her to focus on what was relevant.

So she said nothing at all, and finally he stood. "Later," he said. "Before the end of the day. For now, let him focus on his job."

"But I thought you were going to be the one presenting the case."

"Oh yes, I'm the big gun." Pritchard said this with neither arrogance nor false modesty. "Mr Levine and Ms Sackville-West are my spotter and my . . ." – he made a vague gesture – " . . . the, um, person who loads the shells, or feeds the bullets through the magazine. I'm afraid I lack the technical vocabulary. In any

317

event, I need them to be focused. I believe you have a defocusing effect on Mr Levine. Tell me if I'm mistaken in that."

Jess said nothing. Pritchard acknowledged her tacit admission with a nod. "I don't judge," he said. "Someone in your position has to use every small advantage she has. Someone in his needs to learn the exacting habit of objectivity. Good day to you, Ms Moulson, and . . . good luck." He took his leave. No handshakes this time.

As soon as he was gone, Ratner and Corcoran emerged from wherever they'd been hiding and laid claim to Jess again. They led her along the corridor and through a wood-panelled door into the courtroom.

Jess's first trial had been at the Old Bailey, which had had a cold grandeur to it. This room, by contrast, was just a box. It reminded Jess of the classrooms in her secondary school: places you inhabited temporarily but never owned or felt at home in, their divisions and the rules that applied to them worked out by other people to whom you were always beholden. Now that she thought about it, most of the rooms she'd known since she left her mother's house had been like that.

There were three judges. Mr Justice Foulkes, whom Jess had met at her hearing, was there along with two strangers, a man and a woman. There was no jury. On a bench to her right sat two lawyers from the Crown Prosecution Service. In the corresponding position on her left, Brian Pritchard sat between Paul Levine and a very young, very attractive woman in a pinstriped dress. Ms Sackville-West, Jess presumed. Paul gave her a smile of encouragement but there was no way he could speak to her. The woman appraised her with cool interest, then looked away. Pritchard didn't acknowledge her at all.

The public seats were more sparsely populated than Jess had expected. Only a handful of reporters with notebooks and sketch pads sat there, looking bored. Presumably the public was excluded from these preliminary submissions. At least that meant there'd be a little peace and quiet.

318

For the first few minutes, the three judges just talked in low voices among themselves, while everyone waited. Then one of the three – the woman – signalled to the clerk of the court. The clerk stood up and declaimed. "In the case of the Crown versus Jessica Laurel Moulson, this court of appeal is now in session. His Honour Mr Justice Foulkes, Her Honour Ms Justice LePlastrier and His Honour Mr Justice Macclehurst will jointly preside. The court will hear an appeal against conviction and an annexed appeal against sentencing. Prior to proceeding, counsel has requested summary review and judgement on several heads, as submitted to Your Honours in affidavits."

"Very well, Mr Pritchard," LePlastrier said. "Let's speak to that."

Brian Pritchard stood up. "Your Honours, thank you," he said. "I believe there are a number of outstanding procedural issues relating to the handling and presentation of the prosecution's case in my client's trial." He picked up a document from the desk in front of him – the top one in a sizeable pile – and held it up. "I refer you, in the first instance, to our prepared brief 1(a)."

He read aloud from the document, which soon branched into subheadings and sub-subheadings. Some clauses called on other clauses. Statutes were referred to by number and date, precedents by the names of principals in cases Jess didn't know. The overall topic was the legal distinction between murder and manslaughter, but the arguments were so abstract and involved that it was easy to forget what murder meant. The blood had been drained out of the word.

The judges interrogated every sentence, sometimes asking Pritchard to go back three or four times to a point already covered. Jess tried to follow the arguments at first, but soon gave up. She didn't speak this language.

After more than two hours of discussion, the judges conferred again. "Well," LePlastrier said, "there's a great deal of food for thought there, certainly." She turned to the CPS lawyers. "Mr Anson, Mr Carlisle, do you have anything to add?"

The two men shook their heads, not quite in unison. "Not at

this time, Your Honours," one of them said. "We disagree, obviously, with counsel's substantive point about motive. However, we feel that this was adequately addressed at the original trial. You have our submission. We won't rehearse those arguments again in this courtroom unless Your Honours are minded to reopen the wider discussion of *mens rea*." The judges went into a brief huddle, then declared a recess for lunch.

Jess ate in a side room in the restricted area behind the court, underneath a fly-speckled print of the William Yeames painting "And When Did You Last See Your Father?" with just the two Fellside guards for company. The guards traded gossip and operational minutiae and mostly left Jess to her own devices. She chewed her chicken salad sandwich without tasting it, then sat in silence waiting for proceedings to resume. She hoped Levine might come by to see her, but he didn't. *Let him do his job*, Pritchard had said. But she and Pritchard probably didn't altogether agree on what Paul Levine's job was.

Through the window, faintly, she heard the protesters chanting something that had her name in it. She couldn't make out the whole of the rhyming couplet, but the rhyme words were "dead" and "instead". She got the gist.

The afternoon session began with the judges' decision on the issue Pritchard had raised – the question of whether it had been right to try Jessica Moulson for murder when the death of Alex Beech had never been a project she entertained. They decided that it had, notwithstanding the apparent contradiction. A plot to kill, they said, was in itself *mens rea*, the intent that was needed in law to distinguish murder from mere manslaughter. The fact that the plot had killed the wrong person should not and could not be offered in mitigation.

Brian Pritchard took the bullet with the very slightest of bows and moved on to the next matter on his extensive list, which was the presentation of the prosecution evidence in the original trial.

Once again the ins and outs of what was being said were hard to follow and, for the most part grindingly dull; until out of nowhere the debate suddenly became a little more intense. Pritchard was talking about the duty of disclosure and questioning whether – for example – a continuous CCTV feed (such as the one from the street in front of the block where Jess and Alex Beech used to live) counted as a single piece of evidence. He seemed to be suggesting that the prosecution should have identified specific segments of video to be entered into the proceedings. The judges, at considerable length, disagreed.

"The presumption then, Your Honours," Pritchard said, "is that the entirety of this video feed, from the creation of the world until the present day, can now be considered as having been entered into evidence for an act which occurred at a very precisely defined moment."

"Mr Pritchard, please don't belabour the point," Judge Macclehurst told him sharply. "Remember that time is infinitely divisible. If you want to open this particular can of worms, it might be difficult to close it again."

"I'm merely establishing, Your Honour, whether a body of evidence that is potentially of infinite size can be considered to have been adequately disclosed."

"Then I believe you may take that as a yes." Pronounced in a dry tone, this got a small chuckle from some of the reporters and a half-hidden smile from the clerk of the court. Pritchard didn't join in the laughter but he seemed pleased rather than put out. He glanced across at Paul Levine – a look that Jess caught but didn't really understand. "I am grateful for the clarification, Your Honours," he said mildly.

And on and on. Pritchard held forth on one technicality after another. Jess tried for a while to stay abreast of what was being said – it was her life that was in the balance, after all – but in the end it defeated her. She defocused her eyes and her mind and wandered away from it.

Her body stayed where it was. The other part of her, the part that walked at night with the ghost of Alex Beech, climbed cautiously out and stretched itself. All the noises in the courtroom died at once – not just Pritchard's booming voice, but the sounds of breathing, the rustling of paper, the million-fold noises of bodies just being bodies and never quite being still.

She felt an immediate and dizzying sense of relief. Nobody could pursue her here and bring her back. Nobody would even realise she was gone. It was like the scene you saw in old movies sometimes where someone left a pillow or a wadded coat stuffed down under their blankets so it looked like they were in bed asleep while they slipped away unsuspected for some crazy adventure.

Jess circled the court, staying out of the shafts of sunshine that came in through the skylights above. Alex had said that light hurt him. Jess felt it not as pain but as pressure, the bright beams beating against her insubstantial body like a tide, so that she had to push against them just to stay where she was.

She studied the sketches some of the journalists were making of her. They were mostly very good, although some of them turned her bored, blank look into something belligerent and sinister. She read the notes the reporters were taking too, where they weren't written in shorthand. Most of them were descriptions of her, or rather fragments, impressions, odd words and phrases to be slotted into descriptions later. *Glassy-eyed, cold-eyed, flint-eyed*, one had written. Another one had *unnatural stillness*, underlined twice. Well, that was probably fair. Some hadn't written anything at all yet – presumably keeping their powder dry for when things got interesting, if they ever did.

Jess was tempted to go further afield, but that was probably a bad idea. It was always possible that Pritchard or one of the judges would speak to her, ask her a question, and she didn't want her catatonic state to be discovered.

Could she still move her body when she was outside it? She tried, flexing the fingers of her ghost hand and willing her real fingers to move. Nothing at all happened. That didn't surprise her, but it frightened her a little to realise how helpless her body was when she abandoned it like this. She crept back and climbed inside her own flesh with a prickling sense of relief.

The experience left her exhausted, but glancing up at the courtroom clock she realised that much less time had passed than she'd thought. Her out-of-body experience, which had felt like an odyssey, had taken up no more than a couple of minutes.

She was emotionally drained too. Ghost-walking had given her a feeling of freedom, and re-entry made her painfully aware that this feeling was totally illusory. However far she let her mind roam, it would always be tethered to her body.

She was tied to other things too. In the toilet next to the room where she'd eaten her lunch, taped behind the cistern of the middle cubicle, Grace's package waited for her. Jess could take it or leave it, but she couldn't escape the consequences either way.

Pritchard sat down at last, and the judges once again asked the CPS lawyers if they had anything to say for themselves. This time they did, and another hour or so passed while they rebutted Pritchard point for point. And on each point the judges finally agreed with them.

Pritchard had made more than a dozen separate submissions in the course of the day, and every single judgement had gone against him. He seemed completely at ease with that. Presumably getting a mistrial declared had always been a long shot.

But the last time he stood up, his manner seemed different. Jess thought she saw him gather himself. He stood more erect, his posture and his tone more combative. "Your Honours," he said, "there remains the question of witness evidence."

"We're not minded to allow it," LePlastrier said. "We've read your submission, Mr Pritchard, but it would be an enormous departure from the structures in which we work. The courts of appeal concern themselves with substantive points of law, not with matters of evidence, however hotly contested."

"Yes, Your Honour," Pritchard agreed. "But I'm not talking about contested evidence, I'm talking about evidence that was never heard. On the twelfth day of my client's trial, her boyfriend John Street – the only eyewitness to any part of the relevant events – was called to give evidence. Towards the end of that day, I began my cross-examination. But I was never able to complete it, because Mr Street went in for surgery the next day. Complications relating to the skin grafts on his hands, I believe. It was not possible to recall him to the stand during the remainder of the trial."

The judges looked grave. So did the CPS lawyers. Jess had the sense of the same penny dropping in many minds.

"So," Pritchard resumed after a slight pause, "it seems to me that the defence should be allowed to question Mr Street again. The only alternative would be to declare a mistrial and begin again from the opening chorus."

The judges conferred once more. Pritchard waited with an impassive face, but his posture was tense. Paul Levine had his chin on his fist, the knuckles pressed up against his mouth.

"And is your thought, Mr Pritchard," Judge Foulkes asked, "that if anything arises from Mr Street's testimony that materially affects the safety of your client's conviction, a mistrial would be declared at that point?"

"And the conviction therefore overturned. Exactly, Your Honours."

"Do you consider that a likely outcome?" Judge Macclehurst asked.

Pritchard shrugged. "Evidence is evidence, Your Honour. Like water, it finds its level."

The judges went into another huddle, but only for a few seconds.

"Yes," Foulkes said at last. "It's unorthodox at the very least, but this is a highly unusual situation and there's little likelihood of establishing a wider precedent. We'll allow it."

"Thank you, Your Honours," Pritchard said. "Then I've nothing more to add. If my learned colleagues have no issues to raise . . ."

They didn't. The judges stood, the clerk called, "All rise!" and the day's proceedings were over.

Jess was led out of the courtroom through the same door by which she'd entered, and back into the short corridor behind it. It smelled strongly of disinfectant now, where before it had smelled of dust and floor wax. She wondered if someone had scoured and disinfected the place where she'd sat to eat her lunch.

She could just walk away. She should. But another day or two . . . It might be enough. Paul Levine might already have the answers that she needed. And she could buy that time just by doing what she was told.

"I have to go to the bathroom," she said. Her voice shook a little.

"Go on, then," Ratner said. "Make it quick."

"I might as well pay a visit too," Corcoran decided. She pushed the door open ahead of Jess and went into the bathroom. By the time Jess followed, Corcoran was already heading for the middle cubicle.

Jess took the left-hand one and waited in silence with her back pressed against the door. After a long interval, she heard the sound of Corcoran running the tap, and then the rumbling blast of the drier. She waited for the bathroom door to slam shut again so she could come out and go into the middle cubicle. But it seemed that Corcoran was waiting too.

"When you're ready, Moulson," she said from just outside the door.

"I might be a while yet," Jess said. "I think I'm a bit constipated."

"Oh please, spare me the details!" The door creaked as it opened, boomed as it closed.

Jess quickly swapped cubicles, locking the door behind her.

She reached up and groped behind the cistern. The bag was right there, but for a moment as she tugged at its bottom corner, it refused to give. Then it came free all at once and she almost dropped it into the toilet bowl, saving it with a frantic fumble.

She turned the bag in her hands and examined it. It was fairly bulky, but lighter than she would have expected given its size.

The disinfectant smell was fresh and strong, almost overpowering. Someone had been through this place while the court was in session. A caretaker or cleaner with a cart full of brushes and bags and cleaning products and total freedom to come and go between the restricted area and the rest of the building. Jess would have bet good money that that was how the bag had got there.

Now what? It came down to three choices. Tape the bag to her stomach as she was meant to do, and rejoin the guards outside. Put it back where she'd found it. Or rip it open and flush the contents down the toilet.

"Prisoner, get a bloody move on. Now!" Jess started violently. Ratner's voice was so loud that for a second she thought the guard was right in there with her.

"I'm just coming," she called. There was no time to think. Certainly no time to get rid of the package's contents. And if she tried to tape it back up behind the cistern, she'd probably make a fair bit of noise. The training she'd been given by Loomis and Earnshaw kicked in. She slid the package inside her tracksuit top and smoothed the loose ends of the tape down on either side of her abdomen.

She remembered to flush the chain before unlocking the door.

Ratner was standing right outside with her arms folded and her face set. "I don't get any overtime for this," she said.

"Sorry," Jess mumbled.

The guard herded her back outside with shooing motions of her hand. Corcoran ambled along behind, raising an eyebrow to show that she didn't see any need for all this haste. In convoy they walked down the corridor and out into the little yard, where the van was already waiting.

Paul Levine was waiting too. "Could I please have a word with my client?" he asked Ratner.

"We're on a tight schedule," she told him coldly. "You'll have to do it through channels, during proper visiting hours."

"Oh, a few minutes won't make any difference," Corcoran said. "Just keep it short, okay?"

Ratner gave her a disapproving look, but she didn't argue. The two of them withdrew to the rear of the van.

Paul turned his back on them, speaking too softly to be overheard even though they were only a few feet away. "How did you find today?" he asked.

"It was fine," Jess said. She shrugged. "It didn't feel like anything very much happened."

"You'd be surprised," Paul told her. "Anyway, tomorrow will be different. And I'm afraid that parts of it might be hard for you. But there's no getting around it."

She read concern in his face. It crossed her mind to tell him about Grace, but how could she? Willing or not, she was part of a drug ring. She had drugs taped to her belly right then. Bringing the roof down on Grace would bring the roof down on herself too, probably blowing her appeal sky-high in the process. And a lot of other things with it, since most of the Goodall inmates who'd been roped into Grace's shifting, non-consensual workforce were women with appeals or retrials pending. No. Definitely not. If there was a way out of this trap, Paul wasn't it.

He was still talking – explaining what he'd meant when he said the next day would be hard. "We want to go over everything you and John Street said in your original depositions. The sequence of events on the night of the fire. We're going to put it under the microscope. I imagine some of that stuff will still be painful to you."

"I'll be fine," Jess assured him. That was almost certainly a lie, but she thought she could stand it. Her relationship with Alex Beech wasn't a one-off atrocity any more. It was ongoing. She was working out the terms of her atonement.

With some backsliding. The drug package clung to her flesh like some ghastly parasite. She could feel it moving, could almost imagine that it was burrowing into her.

She pulled her thoughts away with an effort. Alex. Alex was what mattered now. "The letter," she said to Paul. "Did you manage to . . .?"

He breathed out hard. Almost sighed. It wasn't an encouraging sound. "Yes, I did. You asked me to find out whether Alex Beech had been transferred from a different school to Planter's Lane. I couldn't get direct access to the relevant records, but there seems to be no reason why he should have been. The Beeches were long-term residents in Orchard Court – they moved in about eight years before you did, when Alex was still a toddler – and that would put them dead centre in the catchment area for Planter's Lane school."

"That's not evidence though. It doesn't prove Alex never went anywhere else."

"I'm a lawyer, Jess. Believe me, I know what counts as evidence. I haven't finished yet."

"Sorry," she said. "Go on."

"Well, you said you were interested in one specific school – a school that had a goat and a flag on its crest and *dum spiro spero* as its motto. I found the school, after a lot of effort. It's a lamb rather than a goat, obviously – the Lamb of God. But it's real. It's called Bishop Borley. It used to be a Catholic school, then went all-comers in the eighties. But there are a couple of good reasons why Alex Beech couldn't have gone there. For starters, it's not in London. It's in Nottingham."

"Why couldn't Alex have relatives in Nottingham?"

"Have *had* relatives, you mean? I suppose he could." Paul shook his head, as though he was disowning his own words. "But it's in the Bridgeside. A really broken-down estate. Almost a slum."

"Do the Beeches strike you as upwardly mobile?" Jess regretted the comment as soon as it was out, but something about the way this conversation was going had unnerved her, and she was responding with aggression. She smiled and shrugged, trying belatedly to turn the crude jibe into a joke.

"I think they're what politicians call the squeezed middle," Paul said mildly. "But that's not the clinching argument."

"Good."

"The clinching argument is that Bishop Borley is a girls' school."

Jess blinked, caught out. "But . . . then . . ." she floundered. "Isn't there . . .?"

"What?" Paul's tone was still neutral, but there was weariness and maybe resignation in his face. "Any evidence that it used to be mixed? Or that Alex had had a sex change? No, Jess. I didn't find anything like that. And since you've never really been honest with me about what it is you're looking for, or why, there wasn't much else I could do at that point."

Jess cast around for an answer. It was no more than the truth. From the moment she'd detected Paul's interest in her, she'd used him to get what she needed. She'd barely given a moment's thought to him outside of that. *I believe you have a defocusing effect on Mr Levine.*

Impulsively and suddenly, she hugged him. He was the only person she knew besides Alex who might actually welcome her touch, but in that first second he stiffened, taken by surprise. A shudder went through him. Then he melted into it, pressed his cheek against hers – against her bad side, where the flesh had been rebuilt – and made a sound that was like a sob.

From behind them, Ratner swore. "No fucking way!" A hand came down on Jess's shoulder, but not roughly. "Hey," Corcoran said. "Come on, Moulson. Mr What's-your-name. I don't think this was meant to be a conjugal."

Ratner slid the van door open and Corcoran stepped back to let Jess climb inside. For a second longer, she held her ground.

"Thanks, Paul," she said. "Thanks for everything. I'm sorry if you think I've used you. No, I have. I have used you. I didn't mean to, I was just . . . trying to get something done. To keep a promise."

"Well, you're fine," Paul said, utterly flustered. "I mean, *it's* fine. *It's* fine and *you're* welcome."

"Enough of this fuckery," Ratner said.

She stepped in between Jess and Paul, forcing him to retreat. Then she put a hand on Jess's arm and turned her. Jess climbed into the van, still in Ratner's grip. Corcoran followed.

"Try and get a good night's—" Paul called after her. But the closing door cut him off.

65

All the way back to the prison, across the stark beauty of the fells, Jess didn't say a word and didn't look up from her lap.

Alex had asked two things of her – that she reunite him with his friend and that she find out the name of his enemy. He wanted to know them both, the girl who'd loved him and the girl who'd hurt him. Jess had failed completely in both goals. She had nothing to give him. Nothing to say to him.

And the package taped to her stomach was a burden almost equally big. Instead of clues, answers, revelations, what she was bringing back to Fellside was hard drugs for Harriet Grace's dirty little empire. How far from redemption could you get in a single jump?

She couldn't find a way to sit comfortably with the package. Folding her hands hid it from view but maybe drew too much attention to it, accentuating the straight line ruled across her midriff under the yellow tracksuit top. Leaving her arms at her sides was more casual but made her feel naked and defenceless. She was oppressively conscious of the package's bulk, the square-ness of its corners, even its weight, which had seemed slight at first but was now harder and harder to bear.

She felt as though she was being carried bodily towards a decision she wasn't ready to make. And once she got back to Fellside, it would be taken out of her hands as soon as she found herself between the rock that was Liz Earnshaw and the hard place represented by Big Carol Loomis.

The high wall of Fellside reached out to them and took them in. They parked up, and Jess was hustled through secure transfer. There were three separate gates to pass through. At the outer gate, Corcoran signed them all back in on a log sheet. At the inner one, Jess's return was registered manually by a guard and electronically by one of the secretaries on the duty desk.

"Can we have a different van tomorrow?" Ratner asked. "That one smells of piss."

"Shouldn't piss in it then," the secretary pointed out. She broke into chuckles. Corcoran joined her, Ratner kept a stony face.

The two guards walked with Jess across to Goodall, where there were more gates to pass through. Finally they opened the main door into the Goodall ballroom, where Jess expected to be left to her own devices. She stepped away from the guards and back into gen pop like a fishing boat disengaging from a couple of tugs. But it didn't take. Ratner tapped her shoulder and pointed to the stairs.

"Keep walking," she said.

Jess didn't obey. For a moment she didn't understand what she was being told to do. "It's free association," she pointed out. "I think I'll just . . . stay here."

"No, you won't," Ratner said. "Mr Devlin's orders."

Jess still didn't get it, although she was starting to. "But—"

"You're confined to your cell while the appeal's on. You know how popular you are, Moulson. Someone might think you've got a chance of getting out early and decide to do something about it. So you stay indoors and tuck yourself up warm."

Ratner's hand gripped Jess's forearm now and turned her bodily, just as she'd done at the courthouse but with a lot more insistence. "Give me a hand here," she said to Corcoran.

Corcoran seemed uncertain. "Dennis said this?"

"Yes, he did. Come on, take her other arm."

"Sorry, Moulson," Corcoran muttered. She did as she was told, and although her grip was a lot lighter than Ratner's, Jess was now trapped between them. They propelled her firmly towards the stairway. Ratner made the pace, which was a quick march. Jess almost stumbled as she was propelled up the stairs towards the next landing.

The women in the ballroom had turned to look at her, with speculative rather than hostile faces. To most of them, by this time, Jess Moulson felt like personal business. She had been in their dreams a lot lately.

Jess was almost too stunned to think but there wasn't much thinking that had to be done. This wasn't a random act of management — it was Grace: Grace needing to make sure that Jess delivered the goods this time and not trusting her to do it on her own. Earnshaw and Loomis would be loitering near her cell and would step in as soon as the guards left.

That thought hardened her resolve. She might have sleepwalked into submission all by herself, driven by fear or pragmatism or some kind of special pleading about staying alive so she could do right by Alex. But now she had something solid to push against. She did it without thinking.

Ten steps up, halfway between the ballroom floor and the level one landing, she accelerated and leaned back at the same time. Her feet kept climbing the steps, her body's weight sank back into the arms of the two guards.

She kicked and went over backwards.

They could have held her if they'd seen it coming, but they were bracing from underneath and Jess was shooting out horizontally. She fell back down the stairs, twisting to land on her side because she didn't want to break her spine. One arm came up to protect her head, the other clutched her stomach in case the drug pouch came free, but she couldn't maintain the crash position for more than a second or two.

332

She rolled and clattered all the way back down the stairs to the soundtrack of Corcoran's yell of surprise and alarm and Ratner's blurted "Shit!" She didn't quite have enough momentum to go head over heels: it was a messy, sprawling slither and a bruising crash on to the ballroom floor.

A whole crowd of women ran over to check out the damage, to offer help if they could, or else just to watch something more interesting than cockroach races.

Ratner grabbed Jess by the arm to haul her upright again, but a couple of dozen voices shouted no. Ratner hesitated and looked over at Corcoran, who was also shaking her head. "She might have a spinal injury," Marge Todd said. "If you move her, you could fuck her up for life."

"Call the infirmary," Corcoran said to Ratner. "I'll stay with her."

"She's fine," Ratner said.

"We don't know that. Go call the doc."

Ratner looked like she was going to say something more, but she swallowed it, whatever it was, and went to do as she was told. Jess lay on the floor trying to look like someone concussed and confused. When Corcoran asked her how she was, she didn't answer.

Patience DiMarta arrived a couple of minutes later, moving at a fast clip. She studied Jess's bloodied nose and scraped hand and then started feeling her over cautiously for other injuries.

"What happened?" she asked.

"She fell down the stairs," Corcoran said.

"Fell?" Ratner was indignant. "The mad bitch took a bloody nosedive."

"Can you feel your feet?" DiMarta asked her.

"Yes."

"Move them, then."

Jess did, evidently to DiMarta's satisfaction.

"How about standing?" she suggested.

Jess sat up, but she made a big deal out of it, moving slowly with a lot of wincing and gasping.

"All right," DiMarta said. "I'll take her."

"She's meant to be confined to her cell," Ratner protested.

DiMarta gave her a blank look, as though a piece of furniture had piped up at her. "That's nice," she said. And then to Jess, "Come on, prisoner. Nothing wrong with your legs, as far as I can see."

She helped Jess get herself upright, with Jess turning in a creditable performance as someone who'd taken enough knocks to forget where the vertical hold was.

Ratner again. "I've got my orders. She's meant to be—"

"I'm not arguing with you about your orders," DiMarta said across her. "She's hurt; I'm taking her."

Ratner was standing between them and the door. She stayed there for a moment or so, scowling, weighing up her options.

DiMarta spoke more slowly and distinctly, as though she was talking to an imbecile. "Go to the rulebook. Look it up. Don't you know anything? If you break this, you'll be the one to pay for it."

It was an unanswerable argument. A big part of the infirmary's function was making sure that Fellside, its managers and its corporate owners were indemnified if any of the inmates came to harm. As soon as DiMarta arrived on the scene, her jurisdiction was pretty much total. All Ratner could do was step out of the way, which she did now with seething bad grace.

"There you are," DiMarta said grimly. "Thank you so much."

66

Sylvie Stock was in the infirmary when DiMarta arrived with Moulson. She didn't take it well.

"What's she doing here?" she blurted.

"She took a fall," Patience said. "It's all right, Sylvie. I'll deal with it."

She sat Jess down in a straight-backed chair, disinfected her scraped wrist and cleaned the blood off her face. Jess's nose was still bleeding sluggishly so DiMarta gave her a tissue to hold under it.

"You'd better get your clothes off," she said. "Let's take a look at you, see whether anything's bent or broken."

Jess swallowed bile. The moment of decision had its own peculiar taste, sour and burning. "I need the toilet," she said.

DiMarta nodded. "All right. You know where it is."

"And I'd like to talk to Dr Salazar, if that's possible."

After Moulson had trudged through into the bathroom, DiMarta gave Stock a look with a big question mark in it. "That was an odd reaction," she said.

Sylvie shrugged it off. "I don't like that woman. Sometimes you just take against people. For example, if they murder an innocent child or something. I wouldn't ever let it affect my professional judgement."

"No," Patience agreed. "Of course not."

"I'm serious," Stock snapped. "I'm a nurse, Patience. I do my job. When have you ever known me not to do my job?"

"Never," DiMarta said. "Listen, why don't you go and tell Sally she's here and wants a word with him?"

"Fine," Sylvie muttered. She walked out, slamming the door behind her.

She got ten yards down the corridor and burst into tears. It was just too much. She'd done a terrible thing but it had been an accident and it wasn't fair that it should keep coming back again and again to torture her. And Sally knew everything. Sally could shake her off into the gutter with a word whenever he wanted to.

That was hard to live with. It made Stock desperate. It pushed her to the brink of an interior precipice, where she stood and waited to see whether chance or fate would push her over.

67

Jess walked into the bathroom, locked herself in and sank back against the wall, eyes closed. She felt so weak, she didn't trust herself to stand upright. The package of drugs against her stomach reflected back her body's heat like a baked brick. She was almost afraid to touch it.

But when she pulled up her tracksuit top and peeled the tape away, the plastic pouch was cold and clammy to her touch.

It took a long time to flush away the drugs. The pills in particular refused to surrender, bobbing back up to the surface two or three times over before Jess finally got rid of them by dropping sheets of toilet paper over them like nets.

"Moulson, what's going on in there?" DiMarta shouted through the door.

"My stomach," Jess muttered.

"What?"

"My stomach," she said again, louder. "I've got really bad diarrhoea. I'll be out in a minute."

DiMarta tutted and went away to make up a glass of ORT salts. "You're in the wars," she called out conversationally – the same thing she always said when a patient presented with more than one condition at the same time.

Jess flushed again and again until there was nothing left. She folded up the empty pouch and the zip-lock bags and stuffed them into the pocket of her trousers. Then she ran the tap for a long time, because DiMarta would expect to hear it. She splashed cold water on her face. Stared at herself in the mirror with the water trickling down her cheeks like tears.

She'd done it. There was no going back now. She was at war with Harriet Grace. Only she'd forgotten to bring any weapons.

She unlocked the door and went back out into the infirmary. "Drink this," DiMarta told her, thrusting the glass of salts into her hand. "It will rehydrate you. And then take your clothes off. I need to see how bad the damage is."

This time Jess did as she was told. She downed the salts. She stepped out of her clothes as DiMarta drew the screens across, and submitted docilely to an examination. DiMarta was thorough, looking for swelling and bruising – there was a *lot* of bruising, old and new – testing the rotation of Jess's joints, making sure her pupils were responsive, and generally exercising due diligence.

While she was still doing all this, Sally arrived and called out to them from the other side of the screens. "It's me, Patience. Sylvie said—"

"We'll be right with you, Philip," DiMarta said. She was the only one at Fellside who ever used Dr Salazar's first name.

Jess put her clothes back on. DiMarta folded the screens back.

"I understand you wanted to speak to me," Salazar said. He looked concerned. "This was the first day of your appeal, wasn't it? I saw it on the news. Would you like something to settle your nerves a little?"

Jess hesitated. This was her window, but whatever she said couldn't be unsaid. And if she made her plea to Salazar and he refused her, there would be no hope left at all.

"It's . . . Actually it's private," she said. And then, taking the plunge, "It's about drugs."

68

Sally fought an invisible battle against himself that lasted for several very long, very full seconds.

Drugs.

Why would it not be? A lot of Fellside's inmates were junkies or former junkies. Moulson might not mean illegal drugs at all. She might mean the drugs that he prescribed. She might have a medical condition she'd forgotten to disclose. She might have any of a thousand things to confess, to request, to reveal.

But something in her face warned him. Out of nowhere, he was terrified, naked under her asymmetrical gaze.

"Well," he said, "I don't think I'm necessarily the best person to—"

"You know Grace?" Moulson interjected. "Harriet Grace, in G block?"

Sally kept his face neutral with a colossal effort. He crossed to his desk and sat down because he knew his legs were shaking and he didn't want DiMarta to see.

"Patience," he said, shuffling some folders meaninglessly. "Would you mind leaving me and Ms Moulson alone for a moment or two?"

DiMarta stared at him, nonplussed. It was against regulations, of course. There was meant to be a nurse present whenever Salazar saw any of the inmates. Sometimes that rule had to go by the board in the barely coordinated chaos of their working lives, but actually to ask for privacy when privacy wasn't allowed . . .

"I was due a break anyway," DiMarta said, her tone a little stiff. It hurt her that Sally didn't trust her discretion. She'd thought they had a rapport. But it didn't matter. She was taking all the holiday she'd accrued to whittle down her notice period, so this was her last week at Fellside. Soon she and her family would be stepping off the plane in Monfortinho, and the Yorkshire moors would be a fading memory.

When the door closed behind her, Salazar turned back to Moulson. She was still sitting on the straight-backed plastic chair in which DiMarta had examined her. He faced her with daunted courage, like a Christian in the arena who's seen the lion limping and thinks a deal might be done involving thorns.

"What was it you . . .?" he invited her.

"Harriet Grace tried to use me as a drug mule," Moulson said. "She's going to kill me if you don't help me."

The doctor raised a hand, trying to ward the information off before it landed, but Moulson went on anyway. "I had to pick up a packet from the courthouse in Leeds. The toilets there. The middle cubicle. I think she does the same deal with everyone who's got an appeal coming up."

"But then . . . where is . . .?"

"Where are the drugs? I flushed them just before you came in. I picked the package up, but then I didn't want to deliver it. That was why I fell on the stairs. I made it look like an accident, but it wasn't. It was all I could think of. That if I got signed in here, she might not be able to reach me."

Sally listened aghast. Everything Moulson was saying fitted into the gaps in what he already knew like cogwheels locking their spiky little teeth and starting to move. This was the big secret, the part of Grace's operation that he was purposely locked out of. He knew it all now, the whole chain of supply. Apart from Grace and Devlin, he was probably the only one in the whole of Fellside who did.

But if Moulson wanted asylum, she'd chosen the worst place in the whole prison to look for it. He couldn't help her – not when Grace already had him on her payroll. When she found out Moulson was here, she'd send Devlin to fetch her, and Sally would have no option but to hand her over.

"I understand your problem," he mumbled, looking anywhere but in her eyes. "But there isn't anything I can do for you."

"Please," Jess begged him. "If you just sign me in here for a few days, until I think of what to do next. I made a promise. I made a promise to someone who needs me. There isn't anyone else he can ask, so if I . . ." She swallowed visibly, her gaunt throat bobbing. "If I die, he's alone."

"Yes, yes, I see that," Sally said. He didn't ask who this mysterious someone was – he thought the story was a fiction to give more weight to her plea. "I know what Grace can do. But I can't get involved. You should go to the governor. Tell him everything."

"You think he'll help me?"

Sally's mouth opened, closed, opened again. No sound came out of it.

Will he help you? In my experience, no. He'll smile in your face and leave you hanging. This was what he thought, but he didn't say it, because at that moment, Devlin walked into the room, throwing the door open without knocking.

The Devil didn't even look at Sally. His eyes went straight to Moulson and it was clear that he wasn't surprised to see her there. He must have heard from Ratner or Corcoran by this time, or seen the incident report.

"Just come to take her back to her cell," he said. "If you're finished with her." He walked straight towards Moulson, reaching out with his right hand.

That was what did it, if any one thing did it. Devlin's certainty. Devlin being so sure that finding Moulson in the infirmary

341

meant that he owned her and owned what happened to her next.

Sally planted himself in Devlin's way. It only took one step, which was probably just as well. The doctor might not have been capable of a longer journey right then.

"I'm not," he said. "Not finished. Not at all. I'm sorry, Dennis. This prisoner has a suspected concussion and I'm keeping her in overnight."

Devlin looked at Sally like he'd trod in a dog turd and the dog turd had tried to put the blame on him. "What?"

"I've signed her in," Salazar said.

"Sign her out again."

Moulson was watching all this with wide, scared eyes. Devlin come to bring her to Grace without pretence or subterfuge. The doctor standing in between them like the world's softest rock.

"This is my surgery, Dennis," Sally said. "And it's my call."

"Trust me, Sally," the Devil said, "it really isn't."

"Well, my clinical opinion is what counts here. Suspected concussion. It's written in the register, and there it stays."

Devlin's gaze was on the doctor now: the immediate obstacle, the matter in hand. His right fist came down to rest on the handle of his nightstick. "A concussion. You're sure about that?"

"No. But I don't have to be. I'm going to keep her under observation."

Devlin unshipped the nightstick, slowly and with great deliberation.

Sally gave a ragged laugh.

"What's funny?"

"It's funny that you think you can threaten me with that." Sally's voice was high and strained. "Are you going to kill us both, Dennis? Beat our brains out in the middle of the admin block? I don't think that would be a good idea."

Devlin raised the nightstick like a teacher's pointer. Sally tensed but all the Devil did was tap him on the shoulder, very lightly. "I didn't say a word," he said coolly, "about hitting anyone. A concussion. Fine. You're the doctor, Sally. You've got to take all the risks into account. You're doing that, right? Weighing up the risks?"

Sally stared into the other man's eyes for a second longer than he should have done. He saw what was boiling in there and almost lost his nerve.

But he still managed to get the word out. Somehow. "Yes."

"Then I'll leave you to it."

The Devil put his sidewinder back in its holster. He gave Moulson one more curious glance before he turned on his heel and walked out.

Sally ran into the bathroom where he threw his guts up into the sink. He did it for a long time, until all he was getting was a thin, clear trickle like saliva.

"Thank you," Moulson said from behind him.

"Lock the door," Sally told her, his voice slurred.

"I haven't got the key."

He fished in his pocket and handed it to her without turning around. He didn't want her to see him soiled and disgraced.

He counted her footsteps as she walked to the infirmary door. Heard the key turn in the lock there.

Just a gesture, really. A superstition, almost, like throwing salt over your shoulder or touching wood. It wasn't the door that would keep Devlin and Grace out (Devlin was senior on-block, he had a master set). It was the logistics. The awkwardness. The infirmary being where it was, in the broad human thoroughfare of the admin block. You couldn't commit a murder here. It would be madness.

But you couldn't live here either. Not for ever. And in Sally's case, not past eight o'clock. That was when his shift ended.

69

Devlin went back to Grace's cell and told her what had happened. That he'd had Moulson right there in front of him but couldn't bring her away. He wasn't happy about having to say it, and he was even less thrilled with Grace's reaction, which was of course to blame him.

"Salazar?" she echoed. "Salazar sent you packing? The man's a frigging meringue, Dennis!"

There was no gainsaying that. Soft and paunched though the doctor was, there had always been something brittle about him. A meringue was exactly what he was. But a thing can be easily breakable and still be a bastard to deal with. Ice is brittle, but try walking on half an inch of it. Devlin didn't bother to make that point: Grace would have accused him of making excuses. Instead he said, "I'll deal with Sally when the time comes. The question is what you want to do about Moulson."

"Nothing," Grace said. She picked up her iPod and fidgeted with it, scrolling rapidly through its menus. Devlin knew he was about to hear something heavily orchestral.

"Nothing? Are you serious? She's laughing at us!"

"Maybe she is. But nobody touches a hair on her head until I find out whether she's got that package."

344

"And if she hasn't?"

"Then someone has to go and get it, like last time."

She slammed the iPod back down into the dock. Keening violin chords oozed from the speakers.

"Someone? Don't be shy, Grace. Say it. You mean me."

"Of course it's you," she said. "We went over this. Anyone else we send gets to see how the connect works. You don't want that any more than I do."

"Okay, but I'm not going tonight. I'm on duty. There's no way I can go off-site for that long."

"Well, first things first. Let's see what madam has to say for herself. What time does Salazar's shift end?"

Devlin carried all the work schedules in his head. "Eight o'clock," he told her at once.

"And he's not down for any overtime?"

"Nope."

"Then he'll be out of the way by quarter past. Who's the night nurse?"

"Stock." He got where Grace was going and answered the next question too. "I know her pretty well. I think maybe we can get her on board."

"Really? In spite of the risk?"

"I'll talk the risk right down. And obviously I won't tell her any more than she needs to know. Afterwards she'll keep her mouth shut because she'll be neck-deep in it. She won't have any choice."

Grace nodded, her eyes flicking back and forth as she thought out the details. "It's worth trying anyway. Doesn't give us much time before lock-up. But the light will be starting to go – that'll help."

She told Devlin what she had in mind. Obviously the hardest thing to do would be to winkle Moulson out of the infirmary and back on-block. Stock (assuming she was amenable) would be well placed to do that as soon as Salazar was off the scene. Lizzie and Carol would take delivery at the Goodall end. All that was needed was a guard to play piggy-in-the-middle, and that couldn't be Devlin because Moulson knew not to trust him.

Devlin liked the plan very much – especially the part about him not being directly involved. He told Grace he approved and would do the necessary.

"Good to hear it," Grace said. Devlin thought there might be a trace of sarcasm in her voice, but this wasn't the time to vent hurt feelings. Grace knew she needed him. Maybe she was shocked that he'd allowed Sally to get away with treating him like that, but let her judge him by what happened to Sally next.

He took his leave of her and went looking for Sylvie Stock. He ran her down in Franklin block, where she was pretending to check and resupply the first aid post. What she was really doing was hiding from Jessica Moulson and from the terrible prospect of spending a whole night in her company.

"I need you to do me a favour," he said bluntly.

"I'm not in a giving vein right now," Sylvie warned him. But when he told her what the favour was, she changed her tune.

70

Up in the infirmary, Sally told Jess Moulson how Naseem Suresh had died.

He'd never told anyone else, and he didn't set out to tell her. It just happened. They were sitting up there together with the door locked against the world. Sally had ordered in dinner from the commissary and dinner had come – one bed filled, so one meal, which they shared.

Being back in the infirmary reminded Moulson of her first day at Fellside. The siege conditions placed them both inside each other's guard. They sat side by side on one of the beds in the quarantine ward, and they were honest with each other as if they were bound by some childish pact. Spit on your hand and swear.

"I wasn't ever brave," Sally said. "I think to be brave you've got to know what you're up against and carry on anyway. Being stupid or arrogant . . . that's not the same thing. I was about as stupid and arrogant as it's possible to be. So when Naz came to me and said she wanted to blow the whistle about the rackets that were being run in G block, I told her I'd help her in any way I could."

"Why did she come to you?" Jess asked.

"I had a name in those days. To be honest, I was a bit of a

troublemaker. In a good cause. I complained about things. Made a noise about bad conditions when I found them, or sloppy systems. I thought I had a mission here. Holistic health. Mind and body and spirit and everything, no limits. A lot of the warders hated me, and I didn't mind that at all. Word got around. It was natural enough that she'd come to me."

He shook his head in sorrowful amazement. "It didn't seem impossible at all. That we could fix the whole prison. I know it's hard to believe when you look at me now."

"You just sent Dennis Devlin packing," Jess reminded him. "That's what you're like now."

But Sally was still reliving the past. "Now Naseem . . ." he said. "Naseem was brave. She was seeing things in Goodall that reminded her of the shit she'd lived with on the outside. She'd been pushed into prostitution by an uncle. Someone her father owed money to. She was turning tricks at fourteen to pay her family's debts – can you imagine that?

"Then the police raided the brothel and she thought she'd been rescued. But they arrested all the girls. Treated them like they were the criminals. They said the trafficked women were going to be deported right back to where they came from. The rest would do time. That was when Naz assaulted one of the officers. Hit him with a bedside lamp and broke his jaw."

"She sounds like a real piece of work," Jess said, half appalled and half admiring.

"Oh yes," Sally agreed. "Well, Liz Earnshaw loved her. That speaks to her robustness, doesn't it? But she had . . . I don't know. A strong sense of how things ought to be. She hated unfairness. Bullying. Cheating.

"And one day she came to me and said she was ready to blow the whistle. She had chapter and verse on every bent screw in Goodall and every racket that was being run. She wanted me to talk to the governor and set up a deal."

"Some kind of plea bargain, you mean?"

"No, not that. Not that at all. Just a guarantee that if she talked, she'd be protected all the way to the trial. So she'd get to give evidence. And I said of course she would. But I didn't really know how to make good on that, so I was cautious. Or I thought I was. I went to Scratchwell. No names, no pack drill, but I put a question to him. If an inmate did come forward, what sort of systems would he put in place to keep her safe while he heard her out?"

"And?"

Sally's shoulders sagged and the corners of his mouth turned down. "Naseem died the same night. They murdered her in the third-floor toilets in G block. And Dennis Devlin came in here to tell me that if I ever said a word to anyone about Naz's little fantasies, he'd tell the governor I stole drugs out of my own cabinet."

Moulson frowned, not getting it. "But how did Devlin know? About Naseem, I mean. Did the governor . . .?"

"The governor is a fucking idiot. But I don't know. I asked him not to speak to anyone, and I didn't give him Naz's name. He said I could rely on his discretion. He said he wouldn't talk to anyone inside the institution. Anyone at all. It's hard to believe he would have gone straight to the senior warder in G block and told him that G block might be rotten."

"Did anyone else know?"

"No. Nobody. So it must have been Scratchwell. He must be even stupider than he looks. I suppose he said 'an inmate', and Devlin knew who that meant. Maybe Grace was already watching her."

Sally looked as though he was about to cry. Jess put a hand on his shoulder. "Either way, it doesn't sound as though it was your fault."

"I don't know. I could have gone to the papers first. Made it public so they would have thought twice about . . ." He shrugged, slowly and massively. "That's not it anyway. That's not the worst of it."

"What, then?"

He did cry now. Fat, greasy tears, chasing each other silently down his cheeks. "I could still have done it with what she'd already told me. I could have spoken up, and I didn't. I didn't say a word. I realised, after Devlin left . . . the . . . the only reason they didn't kill me was because they had the drugs as a handle to use on me. That was all it was. Otherwise I'd have gone the same way."

The doctor wiped his eyes with the heel of his hand. It just made them redder. "I can't tell you what it was like," he mumbled. "I saw her. Saw what they'd done to her. And instead of thinking they had to answer for it, I thought, That could have been me. That could *still* be me."

His hands were moving, describing in the air something he could see in his mind's eye. "She was . . . They didn't just hurt her, they disrespected her. Her body was wrapped in toilet paper, to say . . . to say, this is a piece of shit. A nark. So nobody would speak up for her afterwards. Nobody would mourn her."

"Earnshaw mourned her."

"Earnshaw went mad. I'm not sure that's the same thing. You know what? I wish now it had been me they took into the shower block."

"Sally . . . "

"No, I don't mean I wish I was dead. It's not self-pity, it's . . . I'm thinking of outcomes. If I'd died, Naz would have gone on and done what needed to be done. She wouldn't have let them scare her into line. Things could have turned out . . . very different."

They sat in silence for a while, and then Jess told Salazar about Alex Beech. The mystery she'd been set to solve. She didn't say she was keeping a promise to a ghost, but she told him that this was why she couldn't be Grace's errand girl. "I've got too much to lose. If I'm innocent of this, of the murder, but then I'm guilty of helping her bring the drugs in . . ."

Sally told her he understood. It was a half-truth, like when she said that Naseem's death wasn't his fault. Each of them was aware that the other was trying to climb up out of a pit. They gave each other what they each craved the most right then, and what both Brian Pritchard and Pastor Afanasy had prescribed: the benefit of the doubt.

At eight o'clock, Sally had to leave. Off-shift, off-site – that was the rule. If he didn't sign out, he'd be looked for. But he said he'd find Nurse Stock, who was in charge of the night shift, and make sure she knew about Moulson's status. "Nobody will move you before the morning. You can go to the court from here, and I'll be on duty again before you get back."

Jess thanked him, and briefly hugged him. It caught Salazar by surprise, and he didn't know how to respond. He patted her on the shoulder, one-handed, embarrassed.

"I'll see you tomorrow," he promised. And went off to find Stock.

Jess locked the door again behind him and lay down on the bed on top of the covers. She breathed in and out, shallowly, gathering herself.

Then she stepped out of her body and went to find Alex.

It didn't frighten her any more to wander through the spray of memories, along a beach where the tide was the past endlessly returning. If she felt anything, she felt relief. A sense of coming home, or at least coming back to a place that knew and welcomed her: coming back in a way to a childhood haven, like a tree-house or a pillow fort. The Other Place.

She saw her own face reflected in the world she walked through, ghost echoes of her floating in the air that wasn't air or drifting in the water that wasn't water. That was the Fellside women thinking of her. Most of them weren't even asleep yet, but they turned their inward eyes on Moulson as she passed by the little windows of their souls. As she walked abroad in the night where they all really lived.

You hurt yourself, Alex said. He had fallen in beside Jess without her noticing. She smiled as she turned to welcome him, but the dead boy's face was stern.

A little. You saw?

No. I'm seeing it now because you're remembering it. You fell down the stairs. It was dangerous, Jess. You could have died.

Says the dead boy. She put on a playful tone, trying to reassure him. But there were things weighing on her. She found it hard to hold his gaze. She knew he hated to be pressed, and she was going to have to press him. Either that or back away, as Salazar had backed away two years ago, from a truth that had become too awkward to negotiate. *It worked anyway*, she told him. *It got me out of Grace's way for a while.*

Really? Alex raised his eyes to hers, touched the back of her hand. It looked a lot more like a real hand now: she was starting to acclimatise.

Really, she promised him.

She told him a little about her adventures that day. Crossing the moors to Leeds, sitting in court while lawyers had a big argument about her future. It was displacement. She was putting off the moment when she confronted him with what she knew.

And if you win the argument, then you get to go away? he asked her.

Yes. Maybe. There are other things that could happen. Like they could say I was guilty of a smaller crime. Manslaughter instead of murder.

What does that mean?

It means I killed you, but I didn't mean to. If they decide that's what happened, then they might send me back but cut my sentence. Let me out in a year, or two years, or five.

Alex had been looking at her all this time, but now he looked away again and fixed his gaze on what passed for the ground. His face had a sort of trembling blankness to it. *After you get out, will you come back and see me?*

I'll find a way to take you with me, Jess told him firmly. *Alex, I will. I already promised. I don't think we found each other by accident. I think it was meant to happen. And whatever happens, I'm going to do what I said I'd do.*

Which was as good a segue as she could ask for. She brought up an image in her mind: something she'd never seen but could easily imagine. A red badge on a black blazer: the lamb-with-a-banner device that turns up in a lot of religious iconography because it's meant to represent the Lamb of God, the sacrificial victim who turned out to be a Trojan horse for Man's redemption. Alex had said a goat with a flag, but that was an easy mistake for a kid to make.

(And kid meant goat. And children had been sacrificed lots of times, in lots of places.)

You remember this? she asked him.

Yes, Alex said. *Of course I do.*

You said it was the badge of your school. And that the motto was dum spiro spero. *"As long as I breathe, there's still hope."*

Alex shook his head. *Miss Loach told us: "while there's life, there's hope."*

Did she now? What else did she tell you?

That it was Cicero who said it. He was a lawyer in ancient Rome, and he said it in a murder trial.

Of course he did, Jess thought. Where else?

Did Miss Loach call you by your first name or your last name? she asked. She was trying for a casual tone, but of course he could read her thoughts. He saw past the question to the intent behind it.

A second later, she realised that he wasn't beside her any more. She turned to find that he'd stopped and was staring at her hard.

I don't remember, he said.

"Okay." She held out her hand for him to come and join her, but he stayed where he was.

What were you trying to do, Jess? Trick me? Do you think I'm lying to you or hiding things from you?

"No. No, Alex. Not that."

Then what?

She braced herself. It was going to be hard to explain something that she didn't understand herself. But if there was any way of getting to the truth, then it lay on the far side of this conversation.

"The lamb and flag badge, and the motto. Alex, they belong to a girls' school."

So?

"So how could you have gone there? Did you have a past life where you were a girl?"

353

Maybe.

"What?" She laughed. It seemed to her that he had to be joking.

Maybe. Yes. I think I did. I think I was a girl until you came.

"But . . ." Jess protested. "That doesn't make any . . . Why didn't you ever say this?"

I was scared to. Alex's tone was level, inflectionless. *I kept remembering more, but I didn't want you to stop liking me, and you only liked me because you thought I was him. I was always a girl. You made me into a boy when you looked at me.*

There was no gainsaying that flat certainty, but Jess dug in her heels and tried anyway. "Alex, you said . . ."

No, I didn't, Jess. You said. *You told me you knew me. And I didn't know who I was, so I believed you. But before you came, I looked different. I was . . . I wasn't ever like this. You made me be like this!*

Jess almost staggered. Only the fact that this wasn't her real body, her physical body, kept her on her feet. Her mind reeled and raced at the same time. She'd heard his voice before she saw him – a high, clear voice, like a child's, but all children's voices have the same pitch. You can't tell a boy from a girl with your eyes closed until they hit puberty. And then when she did finally catch a glimpse of him, he was a silhouette, backlit by the ever-changing colours of the dream world. The detail resolved gradually. His face had been indistinct at first, then had come clearer and clearer as she . . .

As she *shaped* him with her mind, the same way she'd shaped this ramshackle body she now wore. The same way she'd given Tish wings and a magic necklace.

It was insane. But what was the alternative? Mr and Mrs Beech falsifying the birth records for their daughter? Dressing him as a boy? Raising him as a boy? Telling him and the whole world every day that he was a boy? And then sending him to a girls' school?

"Oh my God," Jess whispered. "Alex—"

But Alex was scanning the fractal landscape, suddenly alert.

"What is it?"

354

Someone's coming.

Abruptly, impossibly, the night world shook and lurched. No, it was Moulson herself who was shaking, her upper body riven by shudders of involuntary movement that made her stagger and lose her footing.

She tried to back away, feeling herself gripped by a force she didn't understand and couldn't fight. But it refused to let go of her.

"Alex!" she cried. But she'd been twisted round somehow. She had to turn her head as far as she could to get a glimpse of him, and when she did, she could only see a blur, an outline with all the detail left out. Its rudimentary shape wavered from one second to the next. She couldn't tell if it was male or female. If it was human, even.

"Moulson," a voice said. "Come on. Time to go."

Something took her by the arm. Pulled hard.

Lifted her like a fish caught on a hook.

71

After that little conversation with Devlin, Sylvie Stock headed back to the infirmary at a fast trot. She wanted to get this over with as quickly as possible. But along the way, she thought better of it and slowed right down.

Eight o'clock was when Sally was meant to be signing out, and regulations meant he couldn't hang around past his shift, but it wouldn't do for Stock to get there any earlier than five past eight. Better still, she should find a vantage point from which she could watch the duty desk and not go in until she'd seen him leave.

She chose the Goldstein room, also known as God Botherer HQ. While the prisoner blocks at Fellside were named after women who were scientists, the meeting rooms were named after novel-ists and poets and playwrights. Stock had no idea which of those three categories Goldstein fell into, and as far as she knew, nobody else on staff did either. The room had got its nickname because it was the biggest of the meeting rooms and nobody was allowed to call a meeting there except Save-Me Scratchwell, their beloved and devout leader.

What mattered to Sylvie right then, though, was that GBHQ had picture windows looking down into the open space (the equivalent of the commons in the prisoner blocks) where processing and registration took place, and where staff signed in and out at the start and end of their shifts.

Stock sat in the room with the lights-out until she saw Sally walk by below her. He took his time about signing out, talking for a good few minutes to the guard on the desk and wearing Sylvie's nerves to shreds before he finally scribbled in the book and headed for the main gate. Even then he hesitated. He looked at his watch, then away down the corridor, back the way he'd come. Yeah, Sylvie thought, keep looking. I'll come when I'm good and ready.

Technically the handover was supposed to be face to face, but the nurses didn't usually stand on ceremony. The infirmary was in central admin, locked up tighter than a nun's hope chest, and Fellside was a busy place. It wasn't unusual for Sally to leave without ever seeing the nurse who was carrying the night shift. Tonight he seemed keen to hand over in person, which meant he wanted to brief Stock about Moulson and make absolutely sure she was on-message. That was definitely not going to happen. She waited Sally out with a slightly vindictive satisfaction and gave him a little wave behind his back when he finally gave up and walked out past the duty desk. The barred access gate clicked shut behind him.

Sylvie waited a few minutes longer in case he changed his mind again. Then she ventured down from her little sniper's nest. She felt ridiculously nervous. Nothing she was going to do tonight was against regulations. That was the whole point of not meeting up with Sally and not having a formal handover. If she had, he would have given her a progress report which would have had Moulson in it. This way, she only officially knew what she saw with her own eyes.

But when she got to the bottom of the stairs, she heard her name called. Sally had pulled a flanker on her. He'd gone through the access gate but he'd waited on the other side of it. He shouted out again, and waved to her. "Sylvie! Over here!"

Stock thought about just walking away, but it was obvious that she'd seen him. Their eyes had met.

"I've got to go, Sally," she called. "I'm on duty now."

"Yes, but it's handover!" he said. "I need to tell you something."

Stock hesitated, but there wasn't any getting away from it. If she turned and ran, Sally might come back on-block and chase her down. So she walked over to the gate and told him to make it quick.

"I signed Jess Moulson in overnight," he said. "Suspected concussion. She needs to stay there. I don't want her to go back on-block until morning, even if it looks like she's improving."

"I'll see to it," Stock said.

"Promise me, Sylvie. It's really important." Sally actually reached through the bars and touched her hand. *Jesus!*

"Fine," she said again. "I promise. Philip."

She offered up that unfamiliar name to make him stop asking. To make him go away and leave her alone. It did the job, but it left Sylvie in a seething rage. She hated Sally for making her swear to him – for forcing her into a false position. In her mind she cursed his retreating back, his fat arse and his waddling legs.

This changed nothing, she told herself. Nothing at all. Sally's bleeding heart notwithstanding, all the big guns were on her side and so were the angels. So screw him.

"I just want to talk to her," Devlin had told Stock. "It's possible she picked up some drugs from a contact at the courthouse and brought them back into the prison. She could be in a lot of trouble. It's better for her if I have this little chat with her off the record. That's why I need your help, Sylvie."

And all the while he talked, she was nodding. Telling herself it might be true, and at the same time knowing it wasn't. Stock was nobody's fool. Even before Devlin handed her the little wad of fifty-pound notes, she knew damn well what had to be going on here. This was off the record because it was dirty business. She wasn't keeping Moulson out of trouble, she was delivering her into it.

358

And she was fine with that.

The infirmary was dead quiet when she went in. Patience had signed out at six. The medical staff from now until six the next morning was just her on her lonesome own.

Moulson was in the quarantine ward, lying on the same bed where she'd slept before. Old habits, Stock assumed. She'd taken her shoes off, but apart from that she was fully dressed. Her eyes were closed, one arm behind her head and the other resting on her stomach. She didn't stir when Stock looked in.

On the table in the consulting area there was a folded note with Stock's name written on it in Sally's beautifully neat script. She tore it up into a lot of very small pieces and flushed it down the toilet. She didn't need to read it because she already knew what it would say. And now nobody could prove it had ever been there.

She picked up the phone and called the main guard post in G block. Devlin picked up.

"It's Sylvie," she said. "We're all set."

"Moulson's there?"

"Sleeping like a baby."

"Great. I'll send someone over."

"How will I know him?"

There was a half-second pause which Stock imagined was filled with Devlin rolling his eyes. "He'll be a guard, Stock, and he'll tell you he's there for Moulson. Do you want a secret password?"

"All right," she said. "But give me a few minutes. I'll need to get the paperwork done."

"You do that."

The paperwork was minimal in fact, but she wanted to make absolutely sure she had her story straight. *I examined Moulson and I determined that her condition had improved significantly since . . .*

No. She could do better than that. She took one more look around the door of the quarantine ward to make sure her only patient was still out of it, then sat down and began a brief but masterful work of fiction in which Moulson signed herself out on her own recognisance.

The knock on the door came about ten minutes later, when she was reading through the discharge forms for the third time to make sure they held together. She vaguely recognised the man who walked in. Lovell? No, Lovett. Keith Lovett. He was skinny and blond and had a look that reminded her of the vivid American phrase "trailer trash".

"Moulson," he said. "For Devlin."

Good enough.

"All right," Stock said. "Wait here."

She went through to the quarantine ward. Moulson hadn't moved a muscle as far as she could see. The expression on her face had changed though: now she was wearing the look of idiot consternation that goes with a nightmare.

Stock shook her shoulder. When she got no response, she did it again, harder.

Moulson mumbled something. A name, maybe. Oh my God, it was *his* name. The kid's name. Alex. You bitch, she thought. You callous, callous bitch! You relive it in your fucking dreams?

"Moulson," she snapped. "Come on. Time to go."

She lifted Moulson off the bed with a two-handed grip – the woman was still lighter than her so it wasn't hard – and shook her more vigorously. That finally did the trick.

"What?" Moulson mumbled, her eyes blinking open. "I'm awake. What's happening?" She pulled free of Sylvie's arms, her hands coming up to ward her off. Stock stepped away. She wanted Moulson calm, not panicked. But she also wanted her on her feet. Moulson was still looking confused, but she was fully conscious now, just breathing a little heavily from that rude awakening.

"We're moving you," Stock told her.

Moulson's expression of puzzlement focused down to one of alarm and suspicion. "What? Why? Where to?"

Stock took the middle one of those three questions. "Dr Salazar thinks you might be at risk here. He said something about another prisoner having a grudge against you, or a quarrel with you? I don't know – he didn't name names. He was worried that the infirmary was too open. There's only me on duty now, and if I get called away, you'll be on your own."

Her face as she said all this was studiously deadpan. Devlin had given her the script to work to, but she'd thought long and hard about the delivery, which was brisk and efficient rather than kindly or concerned. She was trying to play to her strengths.

Moulson ran a hand through her hair, which was lank and tangled. She looked exhausted. Whatever sleep she'd managed to grab hadn't refreshed her much. "Where is he?" she asked. "Can I talk to him?"

"No, he's gone off duty," Stock said. "I just told you: there's only me. It's your call, Moulson, but I can't protect you here. Someone might be coming over right now from Goodall. Do you want to be here when they arrive?"

That did the trick. Moulson flinched and shook her head.

"No," Sylvie agreed. "You don't. So we're moving you to a safe room."

"A safe room?"

"It's another infirmary in . . ." – she covered the pause for thought by pointing – ". . . in Franklin block. Nobody will look for you there."

She was pushing Moulson's shoes into her hands as she spoke, trying to convey a sense of urgency. Moulson took the hint and put the shoes on. There was a weird kind of absence about her, as though part of her mind was somewhere else. She kept looking into the corners of the room, where as far as Stock could see there wasn't anything to look at.

While she was still doing that, and Stock was still scolding her to get up, get dressed, get out, Lovett walked in. Moulson tensed all over again and scrambled up off the bed, looking like she was prepared to fight her way out of this if she had to. Stock's money would have been on Lovett, but a fight in the infirmary wouldn't do at all.

361

"He's your escort," she told Moulson quickly. "Don't be stupid. You can't walk across the yard at night on your own; you've got to have a guard with you. Lovett's fine. He's a good friend of Dr Salazar."

"Yeah," Lovett said flatly. "We're like brothers. Can we get a move on?"

Stock could see that Moulson wasn't convinced, and it didn't surprise her. This knuckle-dragger was the very opposite of reassuring. She put a hand on Moulson's arm to calm her, but once again Moulson didn't seem to like that, so she took it away again.

"You'll be quite safe," she repeated.

Lovett opened his mouth to say something, and odds were good it would have been something stupid. Maybe something that started with "Mr Devlin said . . ." Stock jumped in first. "Do you want me to go with you? I can lock up here for a few minutes. I'm just afraid there might be an emergency while I'm out . . ."

Moulson raised a hand in surrender. "No. There's no need. I'll go."

"Right then," Lovett said briskly. "Let's bounce."

They went into the consulting area, all three of them. "Oh, hey," Stock said to Moulson. "Can you sign a transfer form before you go?"

Moulson scribbled her name on the piece of paper Sylvie pushed across at her. She didn't even look at it, which was just as well. She might have smelled a rat if she'd read how she'd insisted on checking out of the infirmary against the primary duty nurse's strongly worded advice.

"Thanks," Moulson said as she gave Sylvie back the paper and pen. "Thanks for helping me. I would have been in real trouble if you and Sally hadn't taken me in here."

"Well, it's our job," Stock mumbled. But she couldn't meet Moulson's eye.

After Moulson had gone, she sat down at Sally's desk, folded her arms around her body and rocked herself back and forth as though she were a baby in a cradle and the baby's mother, all in one. She did this for twenty minutes straight, feeling self-pity well up inside her like sap pouring out of a tapped tree. She'd never wanted this. Not any of it. She was the victim here more than anybody.

72

The evening wasn't cool exactly, but it felt that way after the overheated air in the infirmary.

Jess stepped out ahead of Lovett into the silent yard. It looked immense. She'd only ever seen it thronged with women, the horizon never any further than the next little wedge of humanity. This late in the day, with lock-up pending, it was a desert, lit by thirty moons: even though the sun wasn't all the way down yet, the big spotlights on the towers were already turned on.

"That way," Lovett said. He tapped her arm as he pointed. Either he hadn't seen how Jess had responded to Stock's touch, or he'd seen it and didn't care.

Jess tacked around the edge of the yard, staying out of the glare of the lights. She was still looking around in all directions, hoping Alex would appear from somewhere and fall in beside her. He didn't.

She followed the guard down the narrow space between admin and the first prisoner block, into a hinterland of wheelie bins and wooden storage sheds. The light from the spots didn't penetrate here at all. "No cameras," Lovett muttered over his shoulder, as though Jess had asked him a question. She had a momentary presentiment all the same. In the outside world, she would never have come into a place like this with a man she didn't know.

But Lovett was walking ahead of her really fast now, and he didn't even look back to see if she was following.

He's scared.

Jess looked down, expecting to see Alex walking next to her. He wasn't there.

Alex?

Over here. But the words just popped up inside her mind, the way his words always did. There was no vector, no sense of bearing or distance. She turned her head slowly as she walked, trying to locate him.

"Come on," Lovett said impatiently from up ahead of her. "Keep moving."

Alex was standing beside a battered metal dumpster from whose half-open lid black plastic bin bags spilled like entrails. Jess was past him before she saw him, and he made no move to follow her.

Scared of what? she called out to him in her mind.

Of being seen, Alex said. He was up ahead of her now, in the angled shadow of the prison's outer wall. He turned to keep her in view as she went by, but he didn't join her. *Well, of being seen with you.*

That makes sense, Jess thought back at him. *Devlin is his boss. He's got to make sure nobody finds out he helped me.*

It's Devlin he's thinking about. They were talking. Just a few minutes ago.

This time Alex was on her left side, peering through a stretch of fence that bore an electrical hazard sign. A squat bunker-like building behind him was presumably a generator or a switching station.

"What?" Jess asked, keeping her voice low. "That was in his mind? What did you see?"

"Don't talk," Lovett snapped. They had come to a steel door. It had no handle on the outside, but it had been propped halfway open with a fire extinguisher. Lovett gripped the edge of the door in one hand and opened it a little wider. He kicked the extinguisher on to its side and rolled it inside with the toe of his boot.

"Come on," he said. "Quick now."

Jess tried to look past him. A sudden stab of unease had made her slow to a halt. Inside the door it was completely dark: she couldn't see a thing in there.

What's he thinking now? she asked Alex.

"I don't have time for this, love. Come on!"

He's thinking . . . he doesn't get paid enough for this. Not to risk his pension and everything. That Devlin takes the piss sometimes.

As Alex said this, Jess finally saw what her eyes had been telling her all along. The door that Lovett was holding open bore a sign she'd seen before on her first day out of the infirmary. THIS IS NOT AN EXIT EXCEPT IN CASE OF FIRE.

By day, the colour of the stonework would have told her, but in this fading light all colours were muted to anonymous grey. They were at the back of Goodall block. Not Franklin.

She turned to run. Lovett's arm, skinny but surprisingly strong, whipped out and his hand caught her wrist. In a single movement he dragged her up against him, then his other hand closed on her shoulder. He turned on one heel and pushed her bodily through the doorway.

The door closed behind her, not with a loud boom but with a soft, irrevocable click.

Carol Loomis's voice spoke out of the darkness right beside her.

"Told you, Lizzie," she said. Her tone was cheerful but her voice had a dead echo to it. "She just lost her way, that's all. She gets there in the end."

73

There was no time to think. No time to scream, although Jess opened her mouth to give it a try.

The breath was knocked out of her as she was pushed jarringly against a wall. Hands at her waist hauled up her tracksuit top and groped underneath it. Jagged fingernails scraped her stomach.

"Nothing," Loomis grunted. "Oh dear, oh dear."

Something hard slammed into the side of Jess's head, filling it with light and static. Another blow and she went sprawling. Her palms and her knees hit cold concrete.

"Where is it, Moulson?" Loomis asked. "If you can answer in ten words or less, Lizzie may leave you some of your teeth."

Jess could barely see, even before they hit her. The darkness was almost total. A shadow loomed over her, just about visible against the slightly paler blur of a whitewashed wall. Something grazed her scalp, and a half-second later a metallic clang reverberated right by her ear. A kick that had missed her by a millimetre and hit something else. Something that rang like a bell. Earnshaw swore feelingly.

Hands fastened on Jess, started to drag her upright. She threw her weight backwards, broke the hold but lost her balance and fell down again with a jarring impact. That didn't matter. Down here was where she needed to be. She'd just realised what that metallic sound meant.

Jess! Alex was right beside her in the dark. He was shrill with panic.

Run away, Alex. Run away.

Why did she say that? There was no danger to him here. But plenty of things a kid his age shouldn't have to look at.

She squirmed across the floor, propelling herself with her knees, groping blindly ahead of her with both hands. The tips of her fingers touched the edge of something cold and hard, a curved surface. She groped for it and it rolled away, but she lunged and caught hold of it again, by the handle at the top and the thick rim at the bottom.

"Now then," Loomis grunted. She grabbed Jess by the hair and pulled her sharply around. Jess brought the fire extinguisher with her and used the momentum as she swung, two-handed. The steel cylinder buried itself in Loomis's body, somewhere around waist height. The big woman made a plosive *buh* sound like a baby's first word and suddenly let Jess go again.

Jess shifted her grip on the extinguisher and thrust it forward like a battering ram. This time she got a different result. The extinguisher hit something hard that stopped it dead. There was a dull, terrible crunching sound.

Something flailed and scuffled in the darkness. The fire extinguisher was knocked out of Jess's hands. She scrambled to her feet and fled.

Her eyes were just beginning to adjust to the dark, but it was too little, too late. She saw the blacker rectangle of a doorway at the other end of the corridor and headed straight towards it. She ran hard into the open door, which was edge-on to her and invisible. Her legs went from under her. A second impact, with the floor, took away what breath she had left.

For a moment she just lay there, staring straight up, concussion filling up her eyes with blurry lens flare. Then lights — *real* lights

– flickered three times above her, on-off-on-off-on. Jess blinked blood and fog out of her eyes. She twisted her head to see Earnshaw ten feet away, turning from the light switch to glare down at her.

Beyond her Loomis lay full-length, her forearm and shoulder one continuous curve, like the back of a beached whale.

Jess tried to stand, but she wasn't even sure where her legs were. Her feet scrabbled against the concrete floor, but she stayed where she was as Lizzie advanced, fists raised in front of her like an offering.

"I am going to fucking kill you," she growled. She took a step forward.

Alex moved in between them, facing Earnshaw with his small fists clenched. *Leave her alone!* he yelled. *Don't you touch her!*

Earnshaw stumbled to a halt, staring at the dead boy in bewilderment. Something strange and frightening happened to her face. Terror and astonishment passed across it in a sluggish wave.

"No," she said. And something that sounded like "isn't."

Isn't what? Isn't possible? *That was actually funny*, Jess thought. Who stands and argues the toss when the impossible rears up and smacks them in the face?

It was Alex who was advancing now, raging at Earnshaw at the top of his silent voice. *Go away! Get away from her! Leave her!* His arms windmilled like a farmer herding sheep.

Earnshaw took one step back, then a second. But she reached out a hand with the fingers spread wide. To touch the apparition? To push it aside? To supplicate it?

Alex was beyond caring and beyond thought. He swatted the hand aside.

No. Of course he didn't. But he swiped at it as though he'd forgotten, in the heat of that long moment, that he couldn't touch it. The tips of his fingers, for a tangled heartbeat, were where Earnshaw's fingers were. Neither of them seemed to like the result.

Earnshaw gave a keening wail, her mouth gaping asymmetrically as though she were undergoing a stroke.

Alex flickered like a candle flame in a strong wind. He seemed

369

suddenly terrified, panicked. He tried to dodge around Earnshaw, to the left, to the right, but the corridor was too narrow. Breezeblock walls presented no obstacle to him, but he acted as though they did. Finally, in desperation, he ran right through the shrieking woman.

Earnshaw's eyes rolled back in her head, showing – for a single sickening moment – pure white. She fell to the floor and lay twitching, a little white foam bubbling on her lower lip with each ragged out-breath.

Jess climbed to her feet. She did it very slowly. There was a continuous tone sounding in her ears, a dentist-drill tocsin. The day-bright neon that now shone down on the corridor showed Loomis lying still, her eyes wide and her lower jaw askew. One side of her head had gone from convex to concave. The fire extinguisher, smeared with blood, lay next to her. Earnshaw was moving without volition, in convulsive shudders, the steel toes of her boots tapping arrhythmically against the floor.

Jess let herself out the way she'd come, finding – thank God! – no trace of Lovett when she opened the door and stepped out. She vomited behind the overflowing dumpster, but there wasn't very much for her to bring up because she hadn't eaten anything since lunch.

She walked back across the yard as the sun dipped below the horizon, and found the fire escape door by which she'd left central admin. It ought to have slammed shut behind them, but somebody – most likely Devlin – had covered the lock plate with six layers of duct tape earlier in the evening to allow Lovett to come and go without having to swipe his ID card. The door was still open.

74

When Moulson walked back into the infirmary, Sylvie Stock almost had a cardiac event just at the sight of her. Moulson closed the door behind her, came on over to the desk and pulled up a chair. She sat down facing Stock.

Acting on pure instinct, Sylvie grabbed for the phone, but as soon as she had the receiver in her hand, she thought through the implications of Moulson's return to the fold and froze there, mouth half open.

Slowly she put the phone down again.

"Is there a Plan B?" Moulson asked. "Someone else coming for me? Or do you want to take me on by yourself?" The reconstructed side of her face was a snarl, the good side deadly calm.

Stock shook her head dumbly.

"Well, then, you'd better listen, because I'm going to tell you what you have to do now. There's a dead woman on the ground floor of G block, in one of the corridors behind the ballroom, and there's another one in a very bad way. I think you probably know who they are and what they're doing there. What everyone else gets to know depends on you."

Sylvie thought, Dead woman? Who could the dead woman

be? Where was Dennis Devlin? Who had died? "I'm not . . . I don't understand," she faltered.

"That doesn't surprise me in the least," Moulson said. "But try. I left my fingerprints on everything over there. A fire extinguisher. A door. Walls and floor and I don't know what else. I bled a fair bit too, as you can see. So there's a great big trail that leads from that dead body in G block all the way over here to me, and where do you think it leads after that?"

"Oh Jesus!" Sylvie whimpered.

"No, Jesus is clean. But you're in dead trouble, Nurse Stock. You conspired with Harriet Grace and Dennis Devlin and that other man – Lovett? – to have me killed. I think you should go on over there with a mop and bucket, don't you? Just as soon as you rip up all your paperwork and stamp whatever needs stamping so I'm still officially right here where I belong."

Stock stared at Moulson in blank-eyed horror, and Moulson stared right back. The woman Stock hated had up to now been a fairly abstract creation. This creature sitting opposite her, painted in her enemies' blood, was frightening in a very different and very concrete way. If this was how Moulson pushed back, then Stock wished to God she'd never pushed her. "But . . . I didn't kill anyone," she stammered. "*You* did it. You can't . . ."

But Moulson could. Of course she could. If there really was a woman lying dead in G block, then Moulson could unravel the whole story and there'd be evidence enough to blow all of them to the moon. From Grace to Devlin, Devlin to Lovett and Lovett back to Stock herself. One big fuse burning backwards, like the one in the title sequence from *Mission: Impossible*, until the final whiteout.

"Please." The word was forced out of her under pressure. "Please don't tell."

"Then go clean up your mess," Moulson said. "What are you waiting for?" But as Sylvie jumped up, Moulson pushed her down again – a violation that shook Sylvie to her core. "Wait. Leave me your keys. I'm locking the door. Nobody gets back in here until morning."

"I . . . I can't do that! I'm PD. Duty nurse. I'm meant to be here if anyone calls."

"Then you'd better hope no one calls. Keys." Moulson held her hand out.

Giving up the keys felt to Stock like surrendering the last shred of autonomy she had in the world. "You said one of the women was still alive," she blurted. "If she's hurt, I'll have to have her brought here!"

"That would be your problem, not mine. You told me there was an infirmary in one of the other blocks. Is there?"

"Franklin. An aid station. There's not much there apart from—"

"Make do."

Stock had taken it as far as she could. She surrendered without another word.

75

Grace and Devlin didn't realise right away that something had gone wrong with their Moulson trap, but they figured it out soon enough. They might have figured it out sooner if the Devil hadn't been so concerned about keeping the whole transaction at arm's-length. He'd escorted Loomis and Earnshaw down to that access corridor and unlocked the door, but he never had any intention of coming back for them. The deal was that they'd do what they had to do and then merge back into the general mêlée in the ballroom. The Devil would come in on lock-up and debrief them when he was doing the head count.

But they weren't there for lock-up, so of course all hell broke loose. And it was out of Devlin's hands from that moment. As soon as a single prisoner failed to answer to her name, a big machine was set in motion. Gates and guard posts were nailed down, search parties turned over the whole block and then – working outwards – the rest of the site. The next step would have been to call the regular police and put them on an emergency footing. Cue road-blocks and APBs, helicopters with 5K spotlights, dogs, summit meetings with the oversight board, contrite press conferences and a whole ton of pre-programmed damage limitation.

Things didn't get that far, though. It only took seventeen minutes for one of the search parties to run into Loomis and Earnshaw.

Nothing doing for Loomis. The skull fracture that had killed her had left a visible dent in the left side of her skull. It was scarcely necessary to take a pulse. And there wasn't much doubt about the murder weapon either, since the fire extinguisher was just sitting there in plain sight with a corresponding dent in it that made it look like the next jigsaw piece along. (No blood on it now though, and no fingerprints. Sylvie Stock had been and gone by this time.)

Lizzie was sitting up with her head buried between her knees. She was whining. Miserable, terrified sounds that she didn't seem to have any control over. The guards who found her couldn't get any actual words out of her, so they phoned the infirmary. A minute later, Stock got the message on her pager.

And came bustling along from nowhere at all, trying to look as though this was news to her. Devlin was already there. It was him who told her to check Earnshaw over and try to figure out what was wrong with her. He was keeping it together remarkably well, and that helped Stock to do the same, even though she felt like the next loud noise would make her break in pieces.

The first time she'd visited the access corridor to wash away the prints and Moulson's blood, Lizzie had been lying catatonically still, with her face against the wall and her knees tucked up to her chest, like a foetus in Doc Martens. It was hard to tell whether the mewling sounds she was making now were an improvement.

Stock did all the obvious things – mainly ruling out concussion, stroke and drug overdose. And at some point in all this, Earnshaw quietened down again. She still wasn't responsive – still hadn't said a word – but she was calmer and she seemed to be marginally more aware of what was going on around her, sometimes following Stock's movements with her eyes.

Devlin asked her what had happened, but she didn't give any sign that she heard him.

"Looks pretty clear to me," one of the other screws said. And really it did. It looked like Earnshaw had thrown a massive wobbly of some kind and hammered Big Carol flat in the course of it. Even knowing about the ambush and how it had gone wrong, Stock wasn't sure if she could buy the idea of Jess Moulson bringing down these two big, powerful women. She'd have to be a ninja or something. Anything made of flesh and bone would hit Liz Earnshaw and shatter. But it was Lizzie who looked broken.

There was a lot of back-and-forth about what should happen next. Devlin was for sticking Lizzie back in her own cell overnight, which would have kept her in circulation for Grace to interrogate her when she started making sense again. But the other screws thought Dietrich block offered a better range of facilities for a dangerous and emotionally unstable inmate who might just have beaten another woman to death. The infirmary was mentioned, but it didn't have many fans.

Then the governor rolled up and the answer turned out to be "none of the above". Scratchwell was a few frayed inches away from hysteria, and he wasn't hiding it very well. He regretted every one of those media interviews now. He'd made himself the face and the voice of Fellside so he was going to be tied to the stake now when this catastrophe hit the news, as it inevitably would.

His thoughts were so focused on his own survival that he saw the problem of containment as the most pressing one. He made the right noises (or some reasonable simulations) about Loomis's tragic death, but he wanted to be in control of how and when it got reported.

"I think the safety of the other inmates is paramount," he pronounced. "Put this prisoner in solitary." In the heat of the moment, he forgot to use his own mealy-mouthed euphemism.

"I don't think that's a good idea," Stock piped up.

Save-Me gave her a ferocious look. "I'm sorry?"

Sylvie was sorry too, but she'd been trained as a nurse and for most of her life she'd acted like one. The blind spot she had for Moulson didn't make her unfit for her job in other ways. "Earnshaw is really in a bad way right now," she said. She nodded towards Exhibit A, who was rocking backwards and forwards a little, staring down between her knees. "That sort of thing – those involuntary movements she's making – they're called autistic gestures, and they're generally an indicator of profound mental health problems. I seriously wouldn't advise locking her up and leaving her unsupervised. That's just asking for trouble."

"What's your name?" the governor demanded.

It was right there on Sylvie's badge, but obviously Save-Me was a busy man and couldn't be expected to read something just because it was right in front of his face. Or remember Stock from her job interview, for that matter.

"Stock, sir."

"And are you a mental health professional, Stock?"

"No, sir."

"No. And we have a large number of them right here onsite, in Dietrich. When I want my decisions to be second-guessed on mental health grounds, I'll go to them. In the meantime, you should confine yourself to issues within your actual expertise. Mr Devlin, please take this prisoner to one of the punitive withdrawal rooms. And the . . . the body to . . . well, just put it somewhere safe and out of the way."

Stock walked away quickly, shaking so hard that she thought her outline must be blurred. A lot of that was just anger at Scratchwell for being such a condescending, moronic shit-heel. She hoped he did move the body because then he'd lose his job for interfering with a crime scene.

All of this rage and indignation helped to quieten down the other voice inside her head. The voice that was saying, *She's dead she's dead she's dead. Oh God, you just got a woman killed.*

And it wasn't even the *right* woman.

76

Devlin delivered Liz Earnshaw to one of the half-dozen solitary cells on the top floor of Goodall. (There was a similar set-up in each of the five prisoner blocks, but G block's was the only one where you needed to book early to avoid disappointment.) Earnshaw went as quiet as a lamb.

When he got back down to ground level, the Devil found everyone still standing around waiting for someone else to tell them what to do. Even the governor, whose job it was to do the telling.

Devlin took Scratchwell off to one side. He said that while the governor called the West Yorkshire police (the governor started at this – he hadn't even thought of it until then), he felt that he himself, as senior on-block, should stroll around Goodall a little and make sure that everything was as it should be. The governor thanked him profusely and gave that plan his blessing. God forbid there should be any more nasty surprises waiting to be discovered.

So Devlin got to make an after-hours visit to Grace's cell. He couldn't go inside without opening up from the main control panel, but the two of them had a whispered conference through the cell door's Judas window. Grace was shaken when Devlin told her Loomis was dead, but when she heard about Earnshaw's mental collapse, she was utterly appalled.

"What the bloody hell happened?" she demanded. "Moulson didn't do this. No way did that scrawny little bitch do this. So who did?"

"Maybe Loomis and Earnshaw just fell out," Devlin said, voicing the majority opinion.

"My arse, they did! What about your man? Did he see anything?"

"Lovett? No, he dropped Moulson off and ran like shit."

"So where is she now? It's your prison, Dennis. Don't tell me you don't know."

"Best guess is she scuttled straight back to the infirmary. I know for a fact she wasn't signed back on to block. I wanted to ask Stock, but there were too many people around. And I can't go over there to check. Not with the whole place on full alert. We've got to clean up after ourselves, Grace. If she talks, what evidence is there that they can pin to us?"

"Nothing," Grace said at once. And then, "Well, nothing except that last package. We've got to see if she picked it up, and if she didn't, we've got to fetch it. With that gone, everything else is just her word against ours. That's for you to do, Dennis. You and nobody else. See to it."

"Courthouse is closed now."

"I know. You get yourself put on the escort run tomorrow. Go in with her. There's nobody else we can trust it to."

No blowjobs this time (although to be fair, the door would have got in the way). She just gave him his marching orders. In the general stress and strain, the niceties were falling by the wayside a little.

Devlin went down to the duty desk where he wrote himself on to the next day's escort run to Leeds, transferring Andrea Corcoran to the Goodall ballroom as acting senior. After that, he walked back over to G block in a gloomy and restless mood. Normally after a late shift he would have the morning off, but tomorrow he'd have to be here at 8 a.m. for an 8.30 start. And there was no way he'd even be leaving tonight until the sneaks and geeks from Leeds had finished poring over Loomis's dead body. He was looking at a maximum of four hours' sleep, assuming he could get to sleep at all.

As he walked across the yard, he looked up at the windows of the infirmary. They were dark. It pissed him off to think of Jess Moulson probably already asleep up there, snoring obliviously through the shitstorm she'd caused. She hadn't taken out Carol Loomis: that would have been ridiculous. But she'd slipped out of the trap somehow, and the trap had fallen in on itself. Loomis and Earnshaw must have had some kind of an altercation just before Moulson got there, and the sound of them fighting had alerted her in time to save her bacon.

Temporarily.

But in the fullness of time, he and Grace would see to her properly and appropriately. That thought consoled him.

77

In fact, Jess was very much awake. She was still sitting at Dr Salazar's desk, where she'd been sitting when Sylvie Stock left her two hours earlier.

She was waiting for Alex Beech to come back and talk to her. Except that she wasn't thinking of him as Alex Beech any more. She'd had plenty of time by then to think about what it was she'd done when she climbed out of the abyss and found him. And she knew that *found* was the wrong word.

She'd made him. Made him wear that face and be the thing she wanted most to see. Dr Carter may have been clueless about a lot of things, but she was right about that. *The imagination is a plastic power, Mrs Moulson. A* shaping *power. We make the things we need.* Even as a child, Jess had just had a gift for that. She made what she needed out of whatever raw materials came to hand, including other people.

There was something that had made its home down there in the dark, but it had only become Alex Beech when she looked at it. It had forgotten its own face by then.

Not it. She.

I think I was a girl until you came.

Until Jess put a yoke on her and harnessed her to the laden wagon of her own guilt. *Here, pull this for a while, kid. You look young enough, and strong enough.*

So who was she when she started out? The solution to that mystery was as far away as ever. But the answers to the ghost's questions were maybe becoming a little clearer. Jess had seen the expressions passing across Liz Earnshaw's face when Earnshaw saw Alex standing there, blocking her path. Something like terror. Something like astonishment. Something else she couldn't identify at all.

And not just that. Earnshaw had said something. Not out loud, because she didn't have enough breath left to push it out past her teeth, but Jess was sure it was a name.

Where Jess saw Alex, Earnshaw had seen a different face entirely. And she had known who she was looking at.

Alex had seemed to share that moment of recognition. He didn't panic and run away like that for nothing. He'd always been drawn to the other Goodall women. Had hovered around them and made up stories about the things he saw in their dreams and memories. So what had he seen in Liz Earnshaw?

That was a rhetorical question, obviously.

He'd found his nasty girl. That was why he ran. And that was why Earnshaw could see him when nobody else could. It was Earnshaw he was meant to be haunting in the first place, before Jess ambushed and redecorated him. Because it was Earnshaw who had killed him.

The night passed slowly, and Alex didn't come. Jess called out aloud to him every few minutes, but got no answer. Finally she screwed up her courage and stepped out of her body into the night world. She thought if she just went a little way, she might be able to catch a glimpse of him. But she had no idea where to look, or how.

She only realised then how much she'd relied on him in their previous excursions. She'd thought she was starting to find her way in this place, but without Alex at her side, she was as lost as ever. She wandered from mind to mind, from one sensory tempest to the next, shouting out his name. But there was no response.

No, that wasn't true. Of course there was a response. No answer from Alex, maybe, but in the dreamers she walked through there was alarm and perturbation, moans and starts and interrupted sleep. Jess left a wake behind her, and the wake was nightmares.

It wasn't anything she could help. Her mind was full of Carol Loomis's death and her own almost-death when Liz attacked her. Those things – the fear and the pain and the claustrophobic panic of being shut in with her killers – were still standing at the very front of her thoughts, vivid enough that everything they touched took their colour. It was a ripple effect, spreading out from Jess in all directions.

She'd seen the same phenomenon at work a few nights before, but it was still too new to her, and the logic was too strange. She didn't know she was spreading poison just by being there and remembering.

Every woman in Fellside dreamed of blood and violence that night. The ones Jess touched directly dreamed Carol Loomis's death – dreamed themselves smashing her head in with the fire extinguisher, the heavy heft of it and the sudden stop. The grating vibration, subtle and quick, as the raised rim on the extinguisher's base caught on some piece of impacted bone. The sound of Loomis's body as it fell and the grateful surrender as the heavy steel cylinder dropped from their numbed fingers.

There was a warder in those dreams too. Jess didn't know Lovett well enough to remember his face, but his uniform showed out strong and clear in her mind – and so did the moment when he had picked her up, helpless, thrown her into the darkness and slammed the door.

The women further away from Jess's fruitless searching saw and heard and felt some of the same things, but got them piecemeal. They experienced the manhandling and the panic and the shattering of Loomis's skull as a sort of semi-abstract jumble, a slew of unconnected impressions. They woke up choking, panicking, tasting blood from their own bitten tongues.

And slept again, still unsettled, to pass a diluted distress on to other women even further away.

It was like ink spreading through water. Except that the ink was murder, first-person shooter style.

78

Devlin got a kick out of seeing Moulson's face when Ratner brought her out through the checkpoint to the vehicle yard and she saw him waiting there. She actually stopped dead for a moment until Ratner gave her a push in the middle of her back and told her to get a move on.

Devlin held open the van's rear door, smirking as she went by. She didn't see it, though: she didn't have the guts to look him in the eye. "All aboard that's going aboard," he said cheerfully.

Well, he hoped it sounded cheerful. He was feeling like he'd lain down in front of a road roller. Those four hours of sleep he'd promised himself had turned out to be three hours of being horizontal with his eyes closed. The detectives from Leeds, two real charmers with pretty-boy good looks and Ermenegildo suits, had had a million questions. Some of them were even good ones. How was the corridor where Carol Loomis died reached from inside the block, and from outside it? How was access to it controlled? Who had keys to the intervening doors, or a staff ID that would swipe them open? Who saw the dead woman last, and where was she then? Who were her known associates? One of them even made a connection to the last death at Fellside.

385

"Dominica Weeks. We closed off on that, right? Did she and this Loomis know each other?"

By the time they finally went away to have a one-sided chat with Liz Earnshaw in solitary, Devlin was physically exhausted and emotionally wired. He drove home stewing in a potent mixture of worry and anger.

Actually he didn't drive straight home. He went to Salazar's house first. He was scared the evidence trail might lead back to the infirmary at some point, and he wanted to make sure Sally had a clear grasp of what he could and couldn't say to the nice men from the detective division.

He knew the way, of course. Being there brought back old memories. Leah in the window watching for him to arrive so she could open the door without him having to knock. Leah on all fours opening herself up for him while her husband was away off in Fellside changing bedpans. The time they'd used his handcuffs, which had been the best time by a country mile.

Now Leah was dead. That was a strange thing when he thought about it.

He knocked a few times, then rang the doorbell once. No answer. And he couldn't hammer on the door in the middle of the night without rousing a posse of nosy neighbours. He had to admit defeat at last and walk away, which did nothing at all to improve his temper.

But maybe it was just as well, he thought now, as he climbed in next to Moulson and swung the door to. Sally brought out the worst in him, no doubt about it. The mood he'd been in last night, he might have gone too far and killed the gutless bastard.

He'd tried to get through to Stock, too, with no better results. The infirmary was closed and locked when he left, but he called her mobile four or five times. She wasn't picking up.

So he was still completely in the dark about what had happened the night before, and how Carol Loomis had ended up dead. But he couldn't see any scenario in which Moulson had killed Carol and then walked away from Liz Earnshaw in one piece.

All he wanted from Moulson was an explanation as to what the hell had gone wrong with the package. Not even that, really. As long as the drugs were still in the toilet cubicle (and he was pretty sure they were), then that little matter was done and dusted. They wouldn't use Moulson again obviously, because she was sod-all use for anything, but bygones would be bygones at least until the cops went away. Moulson just needed to understand that if she talked to anyone – anyone at all – about anything other than the weather, then she would find out very quickly why silence was golden.

"Strap in," he said to her now, giving her arm a sharp nudge with his elbow.

Moulson said nothing. She just did as she was told and then sat with her hands limp in her lap. She looked as ragged as Devlin felt.

"Is she always this talkative?" Devlin asked Ratner. Ratner pursed her lips and said nothing. She was on Grace's payroll too, of course, and had a lot of reasons to be unhappy about the police setting up shop in Fellside.

The three of them kept that silence up all the long way across the fells to Leeds. And once they got to Oxford Row, they wouldn't have been able to hear each other speak in any case. The lunatic fringe were out in force today, waving their banners and shouting their stupid rhymes – complaining about the shape of the world, Devlin thought, because it was easier than getting your finger out and actually changing it.

Inside the courthouse, he got straight down to business. "I need to take a shit," he muttered to Ratner. "Look after Chatty Kathy, yeah?"

He went through security into the restricted area at the back of the building. He stalked along the corridor, past the gents' toilets and into the women's. That carried a small risk but there was nobody around to see him do it. All eyes were on the circus outside the front door.

But his day started to go downhill again as soon as he locked himself in the middle cubicle and reached up behind the cistern. There was no package there. Whatever Moulson had done, she'd taken the drugs away with her. So why hadn't she just handed them over? As far as Devlin knew, she didn't have a habit – and even if she did, anybody sane would just grab a little tiny helping of their favourite flavour and hope they didn't get caught out. Was it possible she was thinking she could sell the drugs on elsewhere and keep the money?

"Shit," he muttered.

He thought about checking the other cubicles. But there wouldn't be any point. This was a well-established routine and it always went like clockwork. The drugs had been here and now they weren't.

"Shit!" he said again, more loudly and more bitterly. He'd really believed until then that this time was the same as the last time. That Moulson had chickened out of making the pickup, and then chickened out of owning up to it through fear of the inevitable reprisals.

Now he had to wait until the end of the day to get the truth, and the package. And he had to find a way to talk to Moulson in private here, or else winkle her out of the infirmary once they got back to Fellside. None of it would have been easy, even without the Leeds detectives sniffing around.

In the past, Devlin had always managed to convince himself that his connection to Grace was invisible and deniable. That wasn't true any more, if it ever had been. There was a trail, and it wasn't made out of fucking breadcrumbs. It had Moulson in it, and Salazar. Sylvie Stock. Liz Earnshaw. That prick Lovett, and of course Grace herself. He had to sort this. He had to hold his nerve and sort it.

He rejoined Ratner. She'd brought Moulson through into the waiting area, where the two of them were now sitting. There might still be time for a little informal debriefing with Moulson before things got rolling, but this wasn't a safe place to do it. Anyone could walk past. Even if they didn't, the acoustics were amazing. You could eavesdrop from halfway around the building.

388

It irked the Devil to be right next to Moulson and not to be able to question her. The only consolation was that she too looked very far from her happy place. She was sunk in on herself, thoughtful and quiet and distanced from everything that was going on around her.

She really had been hoping to sell the drugs on, he decided. That was why she was so scared now. She was wondering if it was too late to scramble back out of the pit trap she'd dug for herself before someone filled it in and buried her alive.

Yeah, he thought. It really is. But it seemed like a bad idea to have her walk into the courtroom desperate and terrified. She had a big fucking audience here and she might get the idea into her head that she could use it. He opened his mouth to say something – a threat, a warning, maybe even a phoney reassurance – but right then the clerk of the court walked up. "We're ready to start," he said.

"On your feet, prisoner," Ratner said briskly. "Come on." They led Moulson over to the door and through it, Ratner on Moulson's right side and the Devil on her left.

The steps of the courthouse had reminded him of a circus, but what they had here was the eager audience come to see the clowns and the fire-eaters. The public gallery was packed, with the front two rows staked out for the media – reporters with notepads, artists with sketchbooks. The crowd behind them all had church faces on, but you could practically smell the excitement.

Moulson stopped for a second in the doorway. Less than a second actually, because Devlin and Ratner bore her onwards, hands pressing firmly against her shoulders. Ratner put her in her seat and gave the clerk a nod. *Over to you*. Then she and Devlin went back to their station by the door.

Courtrooms were normally really dull places for Devlin, and for the first hour or so this one was no exception. Just endless blather, endless talking. Men with whiny voices trying to look clever by saying the same thing a hundred different ways. Moulson's lawyer, Pritchard, was a jumped-up little prick about the size of a pint pot. The CPS men were robots who only came alive when the judge asked them if they had anything to add, as though they were frigging voice-activated.

Intent. Mental capacity. Motive. There was a consensus forming, and though they were taking their own sweet time, they were gradually coming to an agreement about the blindingly obvious.

But then Pritchard said something about calling a witness.

In a fucking court of appeal? What was this?

The clerk called John Street, who apparently was Moulson's former boyfriend. He came to the stand, and from that moment everything began to change.

In Devlin's opinion, it did not change for the better.

79

For Jess, the second day of the appeal was much worse than the first. It was a kind of death by a thousand cuts.

Everything that was being said about the night of the fire took her back there again and again, and she didn't want to go. On the first day, the proceedings had been wrapped in a thick, protective layer of legalese. But she'd been shielded from it in a deeper way too, by Alex's belief in her innocence. Now she knew that Alex wasn't Alex. She couldn't fool herself any more into thinking she'd been forgiven by the one person who had the right and the power to do it.

She stood alone, and the blows of memory rained down on her.

John Street was the hardest to bear. This was a man she'd loved, and then hated. The man who'd walked her down the dark road that had a dead child at the end of it. Even to look at his face was painful. It was a reproach to some part of her that went deeper even than conscience.

This was the first time she'd seen him since her original trial. She was surprised at how bad he looked. She'd taken it for granted that time inside was much harsher than time out in the world, but nobody looking at John could assume that the time he was doing was easy. There were hollows under his eyes and he was thinner than she remembered. He looked like a man who did most of his sleeping standing up.

His hands had healed a lot better than her face though.

"You understand why you're here, Mr Street?" Pritchard asked in the slightly solicitous tone of a doctor who's about to talk you through your X-rays.

Street nodded.

"Nonetheless, I'm going to explain it so that you have an opportunity to question me or to state any objections you may have. In Jessica Moulson's original trial, you gave evidence for the prosecution. But your cross-examination by me as defence counsel was never completed. I intend to complete it today. Do you consent to this?"

It was a trick question, obviously. The CPS lawyers would have explained to Street that if he said no, there would have to be a full retrial. He nodded again. "Yes. But I've told you all I remember."

"I'm sure you have. All the same, if you've no objection, I'd like to walk you through some of the pertinent points in your original testimony. To make sure the court is fully apprised of their significance."

"Fine," Street said. "Sure." His eyes stole across to Jess for the first time, and shied away again almost at once. But that at least didn't particularly hurt. She got the same reaction wherever she went, and she was hardened to it.

"On the night of the fire, you arrived at Ms Moulson's flat at or about eight p.m."

"That's right."

"Having left there two hours earlier to buy some drugs from an acquaintance, Gavin Matthews, known to you and to my client as Buster. The drugs in question were for your own and Ms Moulson's use?"

"Yes."

"And just to be clear, the drug we're talking about is heroin?"

"Yes."

392

"How much heroin, exactly?"

"Not a lot. Just enough for two good hits."

Pritchard affected polite surprise. "Was it normal for you to buy in such small quantities?"

"No," Street said. "But our credit wasn't good. That was all I could get."

"The trials and tribulations of addiction," Pritchard sympathised, without any hint of irony that you could actually point to. "Mr Matthews has confirmed that account. 'Two good hits' were his exact words, in fact. Now, what happened after that, according to your original deposition, is that you and Ms Moulson injected the heroin. Then, after a while, she went through into the flat's living room while you remained where you were."

"Yes."

"In the bedroom."

"In the bedroom, yes."

"And at some point you fell asleep."

"Yes."

"Obviously you wouldn't be aware of when exactly that was, so there would be no point in asking you. When you slip from a waking state into a doze, even without having taken a narcotic drug, the mind becomes gradually fogged. Perceptions lose their clarity."

One of the CPS lawyers, who had been scribbling in his legal pad, looked up at this point and tapped with his pen as though it was a judge's gavel. "Objection," he said.

The judges conferred and nodded. "Don't tell the witness what his mental state was, Mr Pritchard," Judge LePlastrier said.

"I beg your pardon," Pritchard said urbanely. "Let us assume, by all means, that Mr Street's perceptions were clear throughout these events unless he himself states otherwise. In fact, as we'll see, he's admirably precise about a great many things. For example . . ." – he consulted his notes – "He tells us that he woke at eleven o'clock. Is that true, Mr Street?"

"Yes."

"How did you verify that? Was there a clock in the bedroom?"

There wasn't. Jess could have told him that. She remembered going around the bedroom with a pillowcase in her hand, bundling the clock, the speaker dock, the bedside lamps into it all on top of each other. That had been a regular feature of their lives back then: turning household objects into cash, and then into smack. Junkie alchemy.

"I looked at my watch," Street said, sounding faintly irritated. It seemed to Jess that Pritchard was needling him on purpose with his dry delivery and exaggeratedly formal tone.

But the lawyer didn't press any harder on that point. "Very well then," he allowed. "At eleven o'clock, as verified by your watch, you woke up?"

"Yes."

"Perceptions clear? Muzzy?" The CPS lawyers looked up from their annotations again, but Pritchard raised a hand to forestall the objection. "Merely to build a picture, Your Honours. Not to cast doubt on the witness's testimony."

"Muzzy," Street admitted. "I didn't know where I was for a moment."

"Perfectly understandable. Perhaps we can pick up the story at that point."

Street frowned as he summoned the memory. "I didn't know what was going on, but there was a terrible smell. Really sharp. Like, chemicals and burning. Then I saw all this smoke hanging in the air and I thought, 'Oh my God, the place is on fire'."

"And was that in fact the case?"

"Yeah, it was. Of course it was. The smoke was from the carpet, and the sheets on the bed. They were already on fire, and the hallway outside the bedroom . . . you . . . you couldn't see a thing out there, just the smoke and this light like a big orange spotlight. The whole flat was going up."

"What happened after that?"

"I jumped up and I started to . . . you know . . ." Street held up his hands and paddled them in the air.

"You tried to put out the fire with your hands?" Pritchard interpreted.

"Yes."

"And how did that work out?"

"I got burned. Really badly."

"Badly is a relative term," Pritchard said. "My client lost half her face in that same fire. And Alex Beech, of course, lost his life. Can you show us your injuries, Mr Street?"

Street held up his hands. "They healed up, mostly. You can see the shiny bits where they did the skin grafts, but they look almost normal now."

"Indeed," Pritchard agreed. "Photographs were taken at the time though. Perhaps we can refer to them in support of your testimony." Paul Levine handed Pritchard a small stack of photographs – eight by ten, full colour. Pritchard left the desk and strolled across to the witness box where he showed them to Street, holding each one up to him for a few seconds before flicking to the next. "Here they are. Your Honours have copies labelled 1 through to 9, although I'm sure the witness doesn't need to have his memory jogged. Would you please confirm, Mr Street, that these photographs show the state of your injuries on the night of the fire."

"Yes. They do."

"Second- and third-degree burns to your hands and your forearms. Very severe on the right hand particularly."

Street nodded wordlessly.

"But now here you are, a great many skin grafts later. You've made a wonderful recovery. In your own eloquent phrase, almost back to normal." Street considered this and seemed about to make some reply, but Pritchard was holding up one of the photos again. "I'm curious about this one," he said. "This burn mark here, this very angry one on your forearm just above your right wrist, in a crescent shape. What do you think that was?"

Street stared dumbly. "I have no idea."

"Well, it's a trivial detail. Possibly you brushed against something.

It's mainly significant because it's on an area of otherwise undamaged skin. Separate and distinct from the other burns. It suggests you touched your hand against something hot at some point. Not a particularly unlikely event in a house fire, of course." Pritchard walked back to the desk and put the photos down. But then he turned to face Street again. "And that was all the damage your body suffered that night?"

"Yes."

"Apart, of course, from the damage that was self-inflicted."

There was a moment's silence. "I don't know what you mean," Street said, stony-faced.

"Your blood showed positive for heroin. Trace amounts but still, positive is positive. Remind me, Mr Street. How long have you been an addict?"

"I'm straight now."

"My apologies. How long *were* you an addict?"

"Almost three years."

"And after three years, what counts as a good hit?"

"I don't know. Hard to say. You judge it by eye; you don't measure it."

"But bigger than when you started out?"

Street gave a hollow laugh. "Only about twenty times."

"Because the body habituates to heroin, and it takes larger and larger doses to produce the same effect. I'm sorry, I interrupted your account. There you were, beating at the sheets to very little purpose. What then, Mr Street?"

"I got up and ran," Street said.

"Ran where?"

"To the door. The front door of the flat."

"Did you try to find Ms Moulson? Your girlfriend? You must have been surprised to wake up and find her gone from the bed. You must have been concerned for her, given that you'd woken up in the middle of this inferno."

Street shook his head, but he wasn't disagreeing. He seemed to be trying not to see what was in his mind. "I shouted out Jess's

396

name," he said in a low voice. "Again and again. Lots of times. But I couldn't see her. There was too much smoke everywhere. And she didn't answer me. In the end, I thought she must have already got out."

"So you did the same."

"Exactly."

"And then you called the emergency services. You told them there was a fire. Asked them to come and put it out."

"Yes."

"And then?"

Street didn't answer. He just stared at Pritchard, who was staring back at him with a look of polite enquiry. The silence lengthened. Pritchard let it.

"How do you mean?" Street asked at last.

"After the phone call, Mr Street. What did you do next? Obviously you knew by this point that your girlfriend had not, as you'd hoped, escaped from the flat. You might also, quite reasonably, have had concerns about the other residents. So tell us what you did."

Another pause followed, and again Pritchard did nothing to fill it.

"I waited," Street said. "For the fire engines."

"Quite right," Pritchard said encouragingly. "You did. We know this from the CCTV footage that was admitted in evidence during my client's original trial. Let's look at it now, shall we? With Your Honours' permission . . ."

"Proceed, Mr Pritchard," one of the judges said, sounding bored.

"A moment, Your Honours." One of the CPS lawyers was on his feet – the same one who'd objected before. "Mr Street is not on trial here. If the drift of this questioning is to establish that he could have done more to mitigate the harm that arose from Jessica Moulson's actions . . ."

"No," Pritchard said. "That's not at all what I'm trying to establish. But Mr Street's statement of his movements is absolutely key to establishing the actual sequence of events."

He looked to the judges, who waved him on. The court clerk dimmed the lights a little, and the screen – a permanent fixture – folded down out of the ceiling. For a moment it showed a computer desktop with files and folders, because the image was being relayed through a projector from a laptop on the lawyers' bench that Paul Levine was operating. Then it showed the front doors of Jess's block of flats and the street outside. The angle was steep and the colours were muddy. Edge noise turned the image into a restless cauldron.

But John Street, when he emerged running, was unmistakable. He didn't get very far. Levine froze the onscreen image just as Street slammed through the doors. Pritchard pointed to the time signature in the top left-hand corner of the screen. "23:00:58," he said. "One minute past eleven."

Levine unfroze the image. Street resumed his headlong run out of the burning building, but he slowed down as soon as he was out on the pavement. He was still moving, but with an asymmetrical lurch to his gait. His posture was unnaturally rigid. He was staring down at his hands, which he held at chest height, palms up and with the fingers spread. He looked as though he was cupping an invisible bowl, but actually he was in agony from his burns. He wore a bright blue shirt and red boxer shorts, hastily thrown on. He looked both absurd and pathetic.

"This is where you place the 999 call," Pritchard said, off to Jess's right. He moved across her field of vision to point at Street's hands in the video clip – in motion now as Street laboriously fished his phone out of his pocket and held it in cradled fingertips, each stab at the keys followed by a violent, trembling recoil. The skin on his hands had all been burned away of course. Every contact must have brought a fresh jolt of pain.

"And this is where you wait," Pritchard added in the same dry tone he'd used before. "Incidentally, Mr Street, I've watched this footage many times. I haven't seen any point at which you check your watch. And you're in full view throughout. It really is a mystery how you could be so specific about the time."

398

Street mumbled something that Jess couldn't catch.

"I'm sorry?"

"The stairs. I must have looked while I was on the stairs."

"Running for your life? Through a burning building? Well, possibly. Shall we see?"

Street's eyes widened. He started to speak, but choked on the first syllable, which was an ambiguous vowel sound. Pritchard seemed to enjoy the reaction. "Yes, Mr Street. Good news. Your role in this movie is a little bigger than a cameo after all."

80

When Sally got to Fellside for the start of his shift, he found the car park full of police cars. Nausea twisted his stomach as he flashed his ID at the gate. "Something happen?" he asked the duty guard.

"Inmate was killed," the guard said tersely. "Hell to pay."

Sally felt dizzy, almost weightless. Blackness flickered behind his eyes for a moment. "Anybody know who?" he asked. Echolalia made him repeat *who flew grew two new blue* inside his mind.

"Loomis."

"Big . . . Big Carol?"

"Yeah. Her."

Sally went straight to the infirmary, walking as fast as he could, trying hard not to break into a run. But the place was empty, which told him nothing.

Moulson not being there was fine. If everything was running to schedule, her escort would have had her in a van and on the way to Leeds half an hour before. When he looked in the daybook to make sure that had happened, he found that a page had been torn out.

He looked for the missing page in the wastepaper basket, a

little troubled now. He didn't find it there, but he did find the release form that Stock had forged and then – on Moulson's orders – torn up and thrown away.

It wasn't a difficult jigsaw. She'd only torn the sheet into four pieces.

81

The overlap between night and day shifts at Fellside was two hours. Sylvie Stock thought she could spend that time hiding out at the aid station in Franklin block the way she had the night before, then scuttle for home. Maybe ask Ron to lead her in a prayer or two.

But Sally found her as easily as Devlin had.

He had the torn pieces of the release form in his hand. He shook them in her face. "Look at this!" he said. "What is this? You signed her back on-block!" He sounded ferocious, full of righteous rage. It would have been hilarious any other time. Any time when her job and her life weren't hanging by a thread.

"She was fine," Stock said. Shame and fear made her brutal. "Your diagnosis was bullshit. She didn't have a concussion. The bruising wasn't even fresh."

"Sylvie, I told you—"

"You don't tell me anything, Sally."

"But I was trying to save her life. Grace wanted to hurt her. Probably to kill her. The only way to—"

"I said you don't tell me anything!" The words came out in a breathless yell. Stock couldn't help it. She'd been at snapping point all night, but the whole time she'd been hiding out, she hadn't come across anything worth snapping at. Sally was catharsis in a pear-shaped package. "What, did she give you a hand job behind the screens? You like them well done with crispy bits, yeah? You're not the fucking Pope. You don't get to give sanctuary. And even if you did, not her! Not that! You side with that, you get what's coming to you!"

She was right up in his face, spit from her rant flecking his cheek and his chin. Salazar backed away from her, speechless with shock. But not for long.

"What's coming to me? What does that mean, Sylvie? That doesn't sound like you; it sounds like Dennis Devlin. Did he put you up to this?"

Stock was exhausted by her own rage. She tried to push past Sally, but he outweighed her by a factor of two. "You have no idea what I sound like," she told him through her teeth. "You know nothing about me, Sally. You don't know anything about anything."

She could have stopped there. There was no reason to carry on. And Sally probably would have stood aside and let her go. But his stupid, reproachful eyes were staring into hers as though he had some kind of a right to judge her. And she had to push him off that perch even if it meant fighting dirty.

"Dennis Devlin was doing a bayonet charge up your Leah for years," she told him, not shouting now but measuring out every word. "He timed his shifts so he clocked off when you clocked on. He took photos of her with her kit off for bloody *Fiesta Readers' Wives*, she was that besotted with him. You thought she pissed holy water, and for ten years you were getting Devlin's sloppy seconds. If you were getting anything at all."

Sally's face registered blank astonishment. Then she could see him putting the pieces together – the cartoon shock of realisation.

"Devlin," he said. Childish. Bewildered.

"Oh, now the penny drops." Stock shook her head in bitter contempt. "You're a real saint, aren't you, Sally? A real Good

Samaritan. Everybody loves the Good Samaritan. But have you ever noticed how little pussy he gets?"

It was easy to elbow her way past the doctor after that. Suddenly it seemed like there was a whole lot less of him.

82

With the image on the screen freeze-framed once again for ease of reference, Brian Pritchard told the judges and the CPS lawyers in exacting detail what it was they were looking at.

"This window here is Ms Moulson's living room. And this one . . ." – he touched the tip of his finger to the screen, leaving no margin for error – ". . . this one is the landing in the building's stairwell. We're going to enlarge this portion of the screen in a moment, but before we do, I'd like to show you the layout of the space you're looking at."

He held up a badly framed, washed-out photo which had estate agent's listing written all over it. It was a perspectiveless shot of the landing outside the door of Jess's flat, exactly as it had looked before the fire and still looked in her memory. The drab space was dominated by a large mirror in an overly ornate frame.

"The mirror," Pritchard said, "is the pertinent fact. I'm going to play another piece of footage, starting at time point 22:47:13. That is to say, thirteen minutes before the witness, Mr Street, claims to have woken up. There's something very interesting there that escaped all of our notice during the first trial."

Levine tapped at the laptop's keys. The screen blacked out for a moment, then the same image came back – minus John Street, who had disappeared from his front-and-centre position on the pavement outside the block.

The shot was now devoid of life and movement. But as Levine ran the image forward in extreme slow motion, a flare of light appeared in the third-floor window that looked into the stairwell.

"There are two puzzling things about what you're seeing," Pritchard said. "One is place, and the other is time. Jessica Moulson's flat is here, on the right-hand side of the stairwell and well out of our field of vision. The light is coming from the opposite side, where the flat is empty and boarded up. Any thoughts about that, Mr Street?"

Street said nothing. He looked sick and unhappy.

"No? Well, the mystery is solved when you consider the position of the mirror. We're seeing the reflection in the mirror on the left of the landing of Jessica Moulson's front door opening on the right."

Pritchard paused and swept the court with his gaze. "Of course," he said, "that opens up a larger mystery. Why was Jessica Moulson's door opening at a quarter to eleven? Who was there to open it? In order to answer that, we'll need to go in closer."

Levine tapped keys. The image zoomed and adjusted, zoomed and adjusted until the window filled the visible area. It was just about possible to make out a figure standing out on the landing, framed in the light from Jess's open door. The detail was largely absent, but the blue shirt and red boxers made identification a whole lot easier.

Jess stared, stupefied. This made no sense.

Street stood on the landing for most of a minute before going back inside.

Levine froze the image. The courtroom was full of electrified silence.

"Would you care to alter your testimony, Mr Street?" Pritchard's voice rang out across the courtroom. "When did you wake up again?"

The prosecution lawyers started to rise at the question, getting into gear for another objection. But then they sat down again, conferring in inaudible whispers.

"When, Mr Street? What time was it?"

"I don't remember," Street said. He made it sound like a plea, or a protest. He'd stopped looking at the screen now. His eyes ranged across the faces in the public gallery as though he was trying to enlist them on his side.

"A long time before eleven o'clock, certainly. And you're not running yet. That comes later. In fact, you're going back into the flat, even though – by your own testimony – you woke up in the middle of an inferno. But there isn't any inferno yet, is there? That comes later too."

Street just stared – at Pritchard, at the prosecutors, at Pritchard again. "Let's move on," Pritchard suggested evenly. The onscreen image unfroze. The homunculus in the boxer shorts made a second sortie. This time when he came back, he was running. He sprinted right past the window and was gone.

"How do you explain this, Mr Street? What was the false start there? What were you doing going back inside?"

"I don't remember," Street repeated.

"I find that a little too convenient to be true."

"I was high. I was out of my head."

"On heroin?"

"Yes."

"Having shot up at eight o'clock?"

"Yes!"

"But you didn't take any heroin that night, Mr Street. So that can't be it."

"Objection," one of the CPS lawyers cried out, up on his feet. Ever since that earlier false start, he had been hair-trigger, ready to jump in as soon as he saw a suitable target.

Jess objected too in the privacy of her own mind. What was Pritchard doing? Was he trying to say that she and Street had both lied? That there was some sort of conspiracy between them?

The prosecutor addressed the bench, terse and indignant. "Mr Street's toxicology results clearly show the presence of heroin in his blood on the night of the fire."

"Your Honours, I'm coming to that. Those results are entirely pertinent to my argument."

The judges conferred, heads down and wigs bobbing. "Proceed, Mr Pritchard," Judge LePlastrier said at last. "But get to the substantive point quickly, if you please."

Pritchard bowed gravely. "Mr Street, let me rephrase that statement as a question. Did you take heroin that night, yes or no?"

Street's eyes opened so wide they looked as though they were going to fall out of his head. "I . . . Jess herself . . ." he stammered. "You know what she said!"

"Yes, I do. Everybody here does. In her trial testimony, she said you both shot up. But of course, and as a matter of custom and practice, you injected her first. Her testimony as to what happened after that can't be taken to be one hundred per cent reliable." Pritchard turned his back on Street. On the judges too. He walked back towards his desk, where Paul Levine was holding up a sheet of paper. Pritchard took it en passant and waved it in the air, still with his back to Street.

"The two of you," he said, "you and Jessica Moulson, were admitted to the same hospital. The same burns unit. At the same time. You both had your blood tested at the same time. You both tested positive for heroin, which at that particular juncture seemed like the salient fact. Nobody was exercised to enquire any further, particularly as there was no disagreement between you and my client as to the fact of your addiction. These are the toxicology results my learned colleague just mentioned. Your own, Mr Street, and Jessica Moulson's. Do you know what they show?"

Street made no answer. Pritchard turned around to face him. He was overdoing the theatricals a little, Jess thought in some dim corner of her brain that could still think. Mostly she was just listening, her mouth hanging open, her hands gripping the brass rail in front of her. Letting the words pile up in her mind into the shape of some edifice still to be defined.

"Murder," Pritchard said, drawing the word out, "is defined as the deliberate, willed and planned ending of another person's life. At one stage I had intended to stand up in this courtroom and argue that Jessica Moulson was innocent because she'd only tried to kill you, Mr Street, and not Alex Beech. That her crime was manslaughter, mitigated by the fact that she'd missed her aim.

"But she didn't, did she? She didn't miss her aim because she didn't take aim in the first place. You did."

Street shook his head violently, but didn't speak. Yells and gasps erupted in the public gallery. In a movie, the judges would all have drawn their gavels and started up a carillon, but the judges – and the crown prosecutors – seemed to have been caught off balance too. They only stared.

Pritchard talked right over the noise. "Exposure to heroin is measured by assessing the amount of free morphine in the blood," he said. He glanced down at the sheet in front of him, ran his finger along the lines of text with a frown of concentration, as though he was parsing them as he went, although Jess was sure he had all this by heart. "For you, that amount was barely perceptible. The doctors who treated you recorded a level of 0.02 nanograms of free morphine per millilitre of blood. The term is 'background positive'. Indicating a regular habit serviced in the not too distant past. Jessica Moulson's free morphine level, however, was recorded as 130 nanograms. The disparity, the ratio, in case your maths skills aren't up to it, is a factor of more than 50,000. Astonishing, if the two of you had taken an equal dose at the same time.

"But perfectly explicable if you bought two good hits and injected them *both* into my client."

Jess was already sitting down, but it was as though she had just tripped and fallen. The breath was pushed out of her in a gasp of what sounded like – felt like – pain. Her hearing faded out, then returned with a background hum that drowned the words. The

CPS lawyers were arguing with the judges. The judges were arguing back. She fought to make sense of it.

"Would you care to rephrase that as a question, Mr Pritchard?" LePlastrier asked.

"Did you inject the whole of what you cooked into Jessica Moulson, Mr Street?"

"No!" Street yelled. "That's bullshit. I did us both. Ask Jess! I did us both!"

"Then you weren't trying to kill her? I think you were."

"Objection." This time the CPS lawyer sounded like a poker player checking to stay in the round. He didn't even stand up. "No motive has been established for—"

"We have an abundance of motives," Pritchard said. "Almost too many motives. Mr Street was now in another relationship, were you not, Mr Street? With one Nicola Saunders, well known to my client as well as to yourself. Do you deny that you and Ms Saunders are now lovers?"

"No, but that . . . that was after . . ."

"You're under oath, Mr Street. And your mobile phone records make a liar out of you. But perhaps you're just polyamorous. Many people are. I'm more inclined to see money as the salient issue. You took out joint life assurance policies only two months before the fire, so my client's death would have been your pay day. A pay day you needed because you were in debt to the point where your credit wasn't even good with your drug dealer."

Pritchard was fairly in his stride now, and he'd abandoned the polite consultative tone altogether. He was a tidal wave of righteous rhetoric. Street was trying to speak up too to contest these points, but if anything was coming out of his open, working mouth, it could not be heard.

"So when Jessica Moulson refused to die of an overdose, you didn't give up. There was too much at stake. You decided to stage an accident. To be fair, she helped you with the staging. She was sitting in the living room tearing up photos. Trying to excise you from her life, which is an impulse I can easily understand. And you knew that photographic paper was flammable. Not as flammable as film stock though, which was why you had to go back inside to coax the blaze along. In the end, you were obliged to use lighter fluid."

"This is bollocks!" Street wailed. "I didn't even know there was any lighter fluid left! I'd given up smoking months before!" And nothing he could have said would have sounded more like a confession, Jess thought in scalp-prickling wonder. It was such a tiny thing to cling to. If you were innocent, you'd say, *I couldn't have* for so many reasons besides the logistical ones.

In the charged silence, Pritchard sighed long and loud. It was as though, after the thrill of the chase, he took no pleasure at all in the kill. "Which brings us back to your injuries," he said. "Not caused by beating at the sheets obviously. You seem to have been up and about long before the fire spread to the bedroom, so that little piece of fiction simply isn't tenable any more. It never was really, given the absolute absence of smoke damage to your lungs. You didn't wake up in a room that was already on fire. That was a preposterous claim.

"But a necessary one, of course. You needed an explanation as to how your hands came to be burned, and you couldn't really tell the truth, which was that you had an unfortunate accident while you were pouring lighter fluid on to the burning photos in Jessica Moulson's waste-bin."

"No," Street said. "No, I didn't do that."

"Objection," said one of the CPS lawyers – the same one as before, the poker player. "Phrased as—"

"Withdrawn," Pritchard snapped. "Temporarily. Let's talk about wounds, Mr Street. Yours were very consistent. Third-degree, full-thickness burns to most of your hands caused by direct exposure to flames. Extensive damage to subcutaneous tissues, destruction of nerves, complete evaporation of the subdermal fat layer. But on your right hand, you had a mark that looked like this." He held up a photo – the same one he'd shown earlier, showing the curved red-black line on Street's wrist.

"This is an oddity frankly. The tight, contained pattern of skin damage identifies it as a contact burn. You held your hand against something that was already very hot, and the damage was limited to the small area where that contact occurred. It's much more superficial damage too, because when we're taken unawares, by pain we're not expecting, our reflexes cause us to break contact with the source of the pain very quickly." He traced the line with his finger. "Part of a hollow circle. The rim of an object, clearly. An object of radius 28.2 centimetres, made of a substance that transmits intense heat while holding – at least temporarily – its original shape."

Pritchard held out his hand and Paul Levine, ready and waiting, put one more photo into it. "There was such an object in Jessica Moulson's flat," Pritchard said quietly. "Only one. It was this." The photo was of Jess's wastepaper basket. "You really need to be more careful when you're setting a fire, Mr Street."

There was shouting.

A lot of shouting.

People were on their feet in the public gallery as though they were going to rush the witness box. Uniformed security guards ran in to block their way.

Pritchard was still declaiming, but nobody could hear the words.

John Street was crying, the whole of his face drooping and distorting like the burned side of Moulson's.

The image on the screen now showed Porky Pig from the Looney Tunes cartoons doing his "Th-th-th-that's all, folks!" wave. This inappropriate levity on Paul Levine's part was seen by nobody except Jess in the last moment before she closed her eyes.

It wasn't quite fainting. She'd fainted when she heard about Alex Beech's death. This was different. She closed her eyes and the world went away for a while to an inaccessible distance. She was alone. As she'd been alone in the pit beyond the night world until Alex had plucked her out of the air and saved her. (Not Alex. The ghost. The ghost who wasn't Alex.)

But this was a kind of aloneness she'd never experienced before.

She wasn't even there herself. There was just a blankness. She felt as though she'd stepped out of her own life, leaving everything she'd ever known lying behind her like a discarded skin.

If the fire was a lie, if Alex was a lie, then so was everything. She was born in that moment, her past annulled.

Nothing as pure as that could last of course. Jess knew even as she stood in that empty, anonymous place that she could never truly be wiped clean. She was Janus-faced. Her burned side watched the past and would never be able to look away from it.

A ringing in her ears brought her back to a sort of consciousness. She was hunched over, her eyes an inch from the brass rail of the dock. There was a fingerprint there, not her own, perfectly clear and distinct. It was like the footprint on Crusoe's island. It meant she was back in a world that had people in it.

She took in a breath. Then another. After that, gradually, it got easier.

John Street was sobbing on the witness stand, hands clenched as though he was trying to bury his face in them but had frozen halfway. Paul Levine was smiling at her. *What did I tell you?* The woman at his side, the intern, was already tidying away the stacks of papers into arch files and cardboard boxes.

Pritchard was up at the bench, arguing with the judges and the CPS lawyers about times. Places. Procedures. The lawyers were nodding a lot but not saying very much. From the look of things, whatever Pritchard said was fine by them. Jess could only just hear him over the continued yelling from the public seats. And was that weeping? Was someone crying back there?

"Today," Pritchard was saying for perhaps the third time. "Now. I'm sure everyone here understands the workings of habeas corpus. If the conviction falls, you don't have any right to hold her."

No. No no no. She couldn't let that happen. She couldn't be free while Alex was still trapped in Fellside – locked behind someone else's face and name. She had promised him. If she didn't come back, he'd be alone again, probably for ever, and lost to himself.

413

The judges were leaning in together, speaking too low for her to hear. Her fate was being decided. She had to say something, and the truth was no use at all. The truth was broken and unserviceable.

But perhaps she could salvage some pieces of it. Put them to use.

She stood on shaking legs.

Nobody noticed her at first. Then one of the judges did, the woman, but she said nothing. It was only when all three of the judges and the CPS lawyers and Pritchard turned to face her that the hubbub died down far enough for her to be heard. Not completely. Not at first. But as she opened her mouth, cleared her throat, the last few voices faltered and tailed off. Only the sobbing was still audible. A woman's voice. Jess didn't turn around. She knew it was Mrs Beech who was crying.

"Can I speak?" she asked. "I'd like to speak if I'm allowed to. It's relevant. To the case."

The female judge, LePlastrier, nodded permission. "That would appear to be the very least you're owed," she said. She sounded sad, or perhaps just tired. Her job must hold few surprises, and almost no pleasant ones.

Jess nodded thanks to her. But it took her a few moments to scrape the words together in her ransacked mind. Her voice sounded hoarse and strange to her. "I didn't think I'd ever see . . . this," she said. "I didn't think it was possible. I believed what everyone believed. That I set that fire and killed Alex. That it was right for me to be where I was."

She had to stop and suck in a breath. She thought there would be more yells, more protests and curses. There was nothing. Almost no sound at all. Even the crying had stopped now.

"People said I was a monster, and I . . . I thought they had to be right. For a long time. Then I started to think they were wrong, but I never thought . . ."

She shook her head. It was all coming out twisted, ridiculous, but she had to push on anyway. She wanted Pritchard and Paul

414

Levine – especially Paul – to understand what she was about to do. "I never thought the truth would . . . that anyone could ever find it out. And I'm so grateful – so very, very grateful – to Mr Pritchard, and Mr Levine, for proving . . ."

She went on, forcing the words out. "I thought I'd done a thing that couldn't be forgiven, and I didn't. I'm free of that now."

She looked across at Paul. A last, beseeching look. This was going to hurt him. She wanted him to know she didn't do that lightly.

"But I *am* a murderer. Last night I was in a fight with another woman. Another inmate at Fellside prison. I beat her to death. I broke her skull in with the end of a fire extinguisher. So send me back to Fellside. Please. That's my home now and it's the place where I belong."

That was all she had to say. She sat down again and waited for the pandemonium to start. She turned away from Levine now, afraid of what she might see in his face. Unfortunately, that left her staring across the courtroom at Dennis Devlin.

Devlin's arms were folded across his chest and he didn't move them. But he slid the raised thumb of his right hand from right to left across the skin of his throat.

You're dead.

83

When it was finally over – when all the arguing and grandstanding and horse-trading had narrowed down to one anticlimactic nod of consent – the two guards took Jess Moulson away. Paul sat stunned, unable to process what had just happened on any level.

Moulson kept her head down as she walked by, but he would almost swear she smiled.

He stood.

"I could do with a hand here," Susannah Sackville-West said, hefting stacks of paper in both hands. Paul ignored her. He walked across the courtroom floor to the door through which Moulson had just made her exit. He caught it as it closed and slipped through.

"Jess!" he shouted. The female warder turned and stared at him. He pushed right past her. The man must have gone ahead to make sure the prison van was waiting where it should be.

He was a second or two behind Moulson as she walked down the corridor towards the back door. He ran to catch her up.

"Hello, Paul," she murmured. Her good eye was wet, her drooping one bone dry.

"Just tell me why," he said. He sounded angry, which was fine,

416

because he suddenly realised that he was. He was almost crying too. "After everything we did, you just . . . what? Are you scared, Jess? Are you just scared of being free, is that it?"

"No." She shook her head. She didn't turn to look at him and she didn't stop walking. They were through the doors now and out in the little yard where the prison van waited. The male guard loomed up and put a hand on Paul's shoulder to pull him back. Paul spun round and smacked the hand away.

"You want to assault me?" he asked the guard. The man towered over Paul and most of his mass was muscle, but that didn't seem to matter much right then. "I'm a lawyer. I'm *her* lawyer. Back off or lose your job."

He turned his attention back to Moulson without waiting for an answer. "What?" he asked her. "What then?"

She looked desperately unhappy, but he couldn't tell if that was for herself or for him. "I've got things to do in there," she said, her voice so low he almost couldn't hear it. "In Fellside. If I come out now, I don't know if I'll ever get back in."

"Things to do?" He was appalled. "You can say your goodbyes by post, Jess. Or go back on visiting day. You just threw away . . ." – he flailed for words – ". . . everything."

"No," Jess said again, calm now, or almost calm. "That's not true. You got my verdict overturned. I'm free now. That's what you gave me. But if it's a gift, you don't get to say what I do with it."

"I love you," he told her. It came out before he could even think. He only heard it in retrospect, when the echo of it was hanging in the air.

"No," Jess said. She smiled. A sad, bleak smile that was there and gone in a heartbeat. "You don't, thank God. Why would you want to? I'd just mess your life up and set your things on fire. But you've been a good friend to me when I haven't done anything to deserve it. I'm going to ask you one last favour."

A lot of answers, most of them sarcastic, boiled up in his throat. He only said one word. "What?"

"Tell Brenda what happened. I don't know what I'm going back to now. What's going to happen to me. It might be bad. Tell her—"

"That you're innocent."

Jess nodded. "Yeah. That. And that I love her very much. And that . . . I didn't throw myself away. I'm answering to myself, the way she said I should. Not to anyone else."

"I'll tell her."

Jess leaned forward and kissed him on the cheek.

Then stepped back quickly, out of his reach. For ever.

"Thank. you," she said. "Thank you for everything. I won't forget you."

She climbed into the van and the doors slid closed between them. She looked away from him, then down into her lap.

He stood there for a long time after the van drove away.

Eventually Brian Pritchard came and stood at his side. Put a hand on his shoulder.

"Take your triumphs where you find them, Mr Levine," he said gently. "You'll never have to look far for a tragedy."

"She was . . ." Levine said, and gave it up. If he said any more, he was going to start crying in front of his boss.

"Our client," Pritchard finished. "Look. Look at me."

Paul turned. The older man held up his hands, side by side, and then folded the palms in together.

"Case closed," he said.

PART FOUR

WE MAKE THE THINGS WE NEED

84

There was no way to talk to Moulson with the driver only a few feet away from them, so Devlin didn't try.

He wasn't sure what he'd say now, in any case. He'd been hoping he could still sort out this shit, get the drugs back and keep the lid on it all, but there was no lid. Not any more. Moulson's confession had thrown the lid up into the air and blasted it to pieces with a shotgun.

He didn't even know where she was going back to. The infirmary? G block? A padded cell in Dietrich? She'd just had her appeal upheld and then gone ahead and owned up to a murder. He didn't envy the governor, because whatever call he made, it was bound to be the wrong one.

So Devlin sat and brooded, and wished with all his heart it had gone the other way. If Carol Loomis had bashed Moulson's brains out, the world would be a much sunnier place. Next after that, he wished he hadn't let Moulson see him in Grace's cell. This could all have been Grace's problem, but he'd let her make it his.

Where the hell was the way out of this? The Leeds detectives would still be onsite, hoovering Loomis's corpse for DNA. A quick stroll over to admin and they'd have their sweaty hands on Moulson as soon as she touched the ground. They'd probably want to take her out of Fellside altogether and bang her up in one of their own remand cells, out of reach of anything he or Grace could do. That would put the last nail in a whole long row of coffins, with his own at the head of the parade.

He had to stop Moulson talking. So he had to give her some kind of incentive for keeping her mouth shut. He had no idea what that could be.

But once they were through the gates of Fellside, pulling into the vehicle yard, he snapped out of his daze. It was time to take charge and maybe salvage something out of this mess. "I'll sign her through," he said to Ratner. "You go grab a coffee or something."

Ratner looked surprised, but she could see from his face that it was a bad moment to argue the toss. She muttered a quick thanks and was gone. As they went in through the first checkpoint, Devlin slowed his steps and put a hand on Moulson's arm to force her to keep pace with him.

"You've really got a death wish, haven't you?" he said in an undertone. "Listen, what happened to the package?"

"I flushed it down the toilet," Moulson told him, not bothering to keep her voice down.

Five or six thousand quid's worth of sweets. Jesus shitting Christ! Devlin nodded, taking it on the chin and trying to look on the bright side. "Well, then, there's no evidence," he said. "Anything you say about me or about Grace, you won't be able to prove it. And you've seen what she can do. If you grass on her, you won't last a week. She's got friends out in the world as well as in here. You just keep your mouth shut and we'll call a truce. We won't try to use you again."

He had to stop talking when they got to the duty desk. He scribbled his name in the day book, distracted and clumsy. He did it one-handed, keeping a grip on Moulson's arm with the other, as though he still had a sporting chance of defending his claim to her.

422

But he really didn't. The whole scampering pack came around the corner at a dead run before he was even done signing in. Governor Scratchwell, the pretty boys from the Leeds constabulary and a team of lawyers from *N*-fold head office, who exuded an air of quiet, deadly proficiency. They swept down the corridor, seizing hold of Moulson in passing and carrying her away with them. They barely acknowledged Devlin's existence.

So now the fat was in the fire and there was no doubt in the Devil's mind what his next stop had to be. He pushed the day book back across the desk to the secretary, Marcela Robbins, who had watched this little command performance with big, hungry eyes. "Is Moulson mixed up in this too?" she asked him.

"I only know what I'm told," Devlin said, shutting her down with a cold stare. Then he registered what she'd said. "Mixed up in what?"

"They're saying Goodall's going to riot. It's been crazy over there all day. Everybody's being pulled in for overtime."

"A riot?" Devlin felt an atavistic chill at the word, as any screw would. But he was also bemused. "About what?"

"There's a rumour it might have been a warder who killed Carol Loomis."

"Is that what they're saying?" It was so wide of the mark, he almost laughed.

Robbins nodded. "In Goodall they are, yeah. They're running around like headless chickens. Standing out on the walkways and shouting at the guards. Saying they want police brought in from Leeds to guard the block. Save-Me was going to cancel free association, but he was scared that might just spark them off."

Might as well get the counter-rumour going, Devlin thought. It wasn't going to be a secret for long. "Moulson killed Carol Loomis, Marcela. She just stood up in court and copped to it."

Robbins' eyes and mouth became three perfect circles. "Moulson? But there's nothing to her! How did she . . .?"

"Must be ninja skills," Devlin grunted. "Anyway, you heard it here first."

He went to Goodall block. That was where he'd been going anyway, to check in with Grace, but now he had to see for himself. Robbins hadn't exaggerated. He could practically taste it as soon as he pushed open the doors and walked out into the ballroom. Suspicion and fear tainting the air. The cons all clustered together in little heaving knots, the guards circling aimlessly, like sheepdogs without a cause.

Corcoran was the first screw he saw. As acting supervisor, she was right where she needed to be, standing by the main console that controlled all the cell block doors. A lockdown was unlikely, but it was a real possibility.

Corcoran was exhausted, wired and utterly pissed off. "They're crawling up the walls," she told Devlin. "We're all on double supply and Scratchwell is pissing himself. You picked the right day to run escort, Dennis, I'll tell you that much."

Devlin shook his head and sighed. "I leave you alone for a few hours . . ." Corcoran laughed. She offered him the keys, but he wasn't ready yet to take back the senior role. It suited him to be free to come and go until he had some idea what he was going to do. "Finish the shift," he told her. "You might as well get the extra pay."

Corcoran put the keys back on her belt. "I'd just as soon be shot of it," she said. "They were barking like bitches when we unlocked and they've been barking like bitches ever since. Moulson's in the mix but don't ask me how. Either she killed Carol Loomis, or a warder killed her and Moulson saw it. They want the cops to come back in. They say they're not going into their cells until someone's been charged."

"Who starts these things?" Devlin asked, straight-faced.

"It's sweating out of the bloody walls, Dennis."

And she was right, it was. Devlin ascended to Grace's cell, feeling it everywhere around him. The air was bloated with some massy, heaving emotion. He knew right then that there was going to be trouble of a big, out-of-control kind. This much badness needed to be earthed in something.

424

Jilly Fish and a steroidal heavyweight with the unlikely name of Ashley had replaced Liz and Carol on the walkway outside Grace's cell. They made a point of not noticing Devlin as he walked in, which right then was exactly the response he wanted to inspire.

"What kept you?" Grace asked. She was lounging on her bunk with an account book and a pencil in her hands, looking like she was above the fray and not worried about anything. But the music that leaked out of the speakers was "Für Elise". Something of a giveaway.

"I just got back." Devlin heard the conciliatory bleat in his own voice. Fuck that, for once. "We've got trouble," he said in a louder, harder voice. "I mean, besides the obvious."

Grace wedged the pencil in the book as a placeholder, set it aside and sat up. No disguises now. Her face was set in a scowl. "You didn't get it?"

"The package is the least of our problems, Harriet. Moulson's decided to get herself right with God, and she started off by telling the whole courtroom that she killed Big Carol."

Grace shook her head, refusing to give that idea any headroom. "She didn't kill Loomis."

"It doesn't matter whether she did or she didn't! She's in with the governor and the sniffers from Leeds and a matching set of piranhas. Right now. Spilling her guts. We've got to get our story straight or we're completely fucked."

He turned the music off. He wanted to make Grace understand how bad this was. Things were falling apart, everywhere and comprehensively. It was time to draw a line. It was time to draw all the lines that should have been drawn already.

"All right, Dennis," Grace said, putting a hand on his arm and then on his shoulder. She drew him in close and kissed him – a big, generous kiss. "All right," she said again when they separated. She sat him down on the bunk and sat beside him. Her hands were holding his, pressing them tight against her thigh. "What's the worst-case scenario? It's still just Moulson. Take her out of

425

the equation and nobody knows anything about anything. It's business as usual."

It wasn't business as usual. Not on Goodall. On Goodall, it felt like Armageddon was coming. But Grace's body had its own gravity and her voice its own power. Devlin found himself calming.

"Unless she talked to Sally," he said. "Between the two of them, they could join up a lot of dots. She was certainly cosying up to him last night."

"They'd make a lovely couple," Grace remarked with a throaty chuckle. And yeah, it was grotesque to think of those two together. Salazar with his Mr Potato-Head bulk and Moulson with her shiny, twisted face. Devlin laughed. Grace stroked his shoulder affectionately. "There's my Dennis."

They talked it through. Each of them knew and tacitly admitted that they could have handled this better, that there had been lost opportunities. If they'd steered away from Moulson in the first place, because of her known instability. If, after her first failure, they'd either left her alone or shut her down for good.

Grace reproached herself with the terrible sin of half-measures. She had thought she understood Moulson better than she did, in part because of a totally superficial resemblance, a coincidence of their two backstories. That their faces had been taken apart and remade. She had been conned and disarmed, for the briefest of moments, by her own child self.

Devlin admitted that he should have stayed on point the previous night. Should have been there himself, along with Lizzie and Carol, when Moulson came back on-block.

They forgave each other. And in the end they came up with a plan. It complicated things a little that the whole place was hanging on the edge of a riot. But as Grace said, the trick is to think of every threat as an opportunity.

85

Most of the questions came from the two detectives, and most of the answers came from the *N*-fold lawyers. They had magically become Moulson's lawyers, insofar as the information she was offering touched on *N*-fold interests and *N*-fold property.

Jess said as little as she could. Her attention was a little distracted in any case. She was calling out to Alex in her mind – using that name because it was still the only one she had for him. But he didn't answer and he didn't approach.

He was the only reason she'd come back when the way out suddenly opened in front of her. The debt she'd once thought she owed to the real Alex Beech had dropped away, though her heart still ached when she thought about his wretched, lonely death. But this new Alex, who she'd trapped and dragged into her own tragedy without even meaning to . . . That debt was real and couldn't be escaped. The ghost had saved her, and she'd failed him – no, failed *her* – in every possible way. Thinking she was helping, she'd stolen her from herself, erased her face, left her even more badly lost than she was already. This was her last chance to put that right.

But all she could do for now was to dig in and wait the

detectives out. Her agenda couldn't get underway until theirs was finished.

"Tell us again," they ordered her.

She told them again. "I got out of the infirmary, and then out of the admin block. The nurse there must have been called away or something. And there weren't any guards in the corridor."

"How did you get out of the admin block?"

"The door had been left open. I just slipped through."

"And what – you just slipped into Goodall?" Both detectives looked politely sceptical.

"Yes."

"To find . . . what? Two inmates waiting there in the dark, on the off chance that you might stop by?"

It was a ridiculous story, but Moulson refused to add in any of the details that would have made sense of it. She didn't mention Grace, or Devlin, or Lovett, or Sylvie Stock. This wasn't cowardice or even mercy. She just wanted to make sure she got to spend the night at Fellside with Alex. She was certain that if she told the truth, or anything like it, that wouldn't happen. The detectives would widen their investigation, probably take her into protective custody. This way they might let her stay here rather than arm-wrestle with the N-fold lawyers who wanted Jess in Fellside so they could keep a toehold in the investigation.

"Are you protecting someone?" one of the detectives asked in exasperation. "Someone in here?"

Jess didn't answer. Trying to, she thought. Trying very hard.

Eventually the detectives gave up. They were sure there was more to Loomis's death than had come to light so far – that other people besides Moulson must have been involved. They were also sure that when they brought the big guns of the regional crime squad to bear, they could winkle Moulson out of Fellside in short order, and then they would see what they would see. One night wouldn't make any difference. It wasn't as though she was going anywhere.

428

They went back to the governor and made him agree to put Moulson in solitary for the night. They pointed out that if she were free to associate with the other prisoners, there was a real danger that they would then collude in a cover-up of some kind. It was much better not to allow that opportunity to arise.

Scratchwell agreed, very much aware that he was up against the wall. And he said he would make assurance doubly sure. He would assign to his most reliable senior supervisor the task of monitoring Moulson and keeping her safe and incommunicado.

Devlin was sent for, and arrived in due course.

"Yes, sir," the Devil said gravely. And, "No, sir. You have my word, sir, the prisoner won't have any contact with anyone at all. I'll make myself personally responsible for her."

Scratchwell took comfort from this, but he was far from a happy man. While the detectives were closeted with Moulson, the company lawyers had worked him over mercilessly. They had made it clear that if the Loomis investigation threw up anything that might embarrass the parent company, he was going to be asked to fall on his sword. When he said that he might be able to use his media contacts to put a positive spin on the situation, they told him bluntly not to go within a mile of a reporter. They said the company was battening down, not making itself into a target. They implied that if Scratchwell had heeded his original instructions to be discreet, the present situation wouldn't be nearly so bad.

He didn't tell them about the explosive atmosphere in Goodall. He was just too scared. He thought they might ask for his resignation right there and then if they knew there were other problems at Fellside besides Loomis's murder.

So what with one thing and another, Save-Me was praying to God for a quiet night and hoping that Dennis Devlin could deliver.

But God wasn't listening, and neither was the Devil.

86

Devlin didn't even bother to talk to Moulson as he took her over
to solitary. All that stuff he'd said before about letting her off the
hook was part of Plan A. Now, after his talk with Grace, he was
all about Plan B.

It was quite an eventful walk given how short it was. Moulson's
arrival on-block had a dramatic effect on every woman who saw
her. Some of them shouted to her as she passed. A few curses, a
scatter of accusations, but mostly questions. Did she do it? Did
she see who did it? "Moulson, tell us!" That was Marge Todd's
voice, rising in an anguished wail. "If you protect them, they'll
only turn on you!" "Was the governor in on it?" Sam Kupperberg
yelled. "Don't say anything, Moulson, just nod!"

"Must be nice to be so much in demand for once," Devlin
commented.

Moulson ignored him. The uproar and unease among the Goodall
inmates barely registered on her crowded thoughts. The one person
she really wanted to see wasn't there.

The solitary cell, an eight-by-eight-foot box, had been readied
for her. A bedding pack lay on the bunk in its paper wrapping
– no cellophane or plastic ribbon in solitary, because you never

knew what innocent object might inspire a suicide attempt. Moulson's name and number had been scribbled on the status sheet which slotted into a steel holder on the door.

On the way in, she glanced at the label on the next door along. ELIZABETH MARTINE EARNSHAW, 76123. Devlin saw her looking. "Yeah," he said sourly. "You want me to arrange a sleepover, Moulson? I'm sure the two of you would have a lovely time."

He pushed her into her cell and closed the door. Regular cell doors locked and unlocked from the master board, either individually or collectively. The doors in solitary had a board of their own, and even when it was set to the open position, they were default-locked. The closed doors could only be opened from the outside.

Jess fitted a bottom sheet over the bunk's inch-thick mattress and threw the rest of the bedding pack on the floor. She lay down fully clothed.

"Alex?" she called again. She didn't bother to raise her voice. She knew he could hear her: distance was meaningless where he lived. If he didn't come, it was because he didn't want to come (she kept trying to shift that pronoun from a *he* to a *she*, and it kept shifting back).

Something Alex had seen or remembered when he was right up in Earnshaw's face had terrified him – and left Earnshaw more or less completely disconnected from the world. They'd touched for half a second and both of them had turned tail and run in opposite directions.

Jess kept on talking, hoping that Alex was close enough to hear her. "This will help you to find what you wanted," she told him. "I know you're scared. I know this is taking you back to when you were hurt, and you don't think you can bear it. But I'll be with you. We'll bear it together."

No answer.

"We have to go there, Alex. This is the only way you're ever going to find your friend." *And yourself*, she added silently. *Because I put that face and that name on you, and how else am I going to get them off again?*

431

Alex still said nothing. But Jess had all the time in the world and nothing to do with it but wait. There were no windows in the cell, just a shadowless glare from three parallel strip lights set into the ceiling, so she had no idea how much time was passing. After a while, it felt as though she'd been in that tiny little box for ever. Maybe the light was too strong for Alex, she thought despairingly. Maybe he hadn't stopped running yet. Maybe he'd finally decided to hang out with somebody more his own age.

Of course, there was no telling what that age was. The ghost didn't have to be a child any more than she had to be male.

Jess's thoughts began to wander. She thought about her relationship with John Street and how it had ended. She turned it in her mind to look at it from different angles, trying to gauge how much it hurt. Not much at all really. Getting shot of him had cost her half her face, but she didn't consider that too bad a deal. Ridiculously, she felt free now. Or closer to freedom than she'd ever been. She had the one debt to pay, and then she was done. Nobody had any claim on her after that, or any reason to reproach her.

What's reproach?

Jess's heart jumped like a stalling car, but she didn't look up. She didn't want to spook Alex, and in the bald radiance of the strip lights she probably wouldn't be able to see him. *Her.* See *her.* "It means blame," she said.

Did people blame you before?

"They blamed me for you."

For the boy that burned.

"Sorry, yes. For the boy."

Slowly, carefully, Jess raised her head. The ghost was just about visible, but too faint for her to make out any details – beyond the salient fact that it still had Alex's face. There was no way of reading the expression that face wore.

"Will you come with me?" Jess asked.

Where?

"You know where. To visit Liz. The woman you met last night.

432

I think maybe you remember her from . . . before. From when you were alive."

I do.

"And you're scared of her?"

The vague shape that was the ghost heaved its shoulders, gave the ghost of a shrug. There was a long silence. As Jess finally opened her mouth to speak, Alex said, *I think I'm scared of remembering.*

I can understand that, Jess said. *You can get used to being nobody. To having nothing. Then when you have to go back to a life of some kind, it's frightening. It feels like it might be too much.*

She felt ashamed suddenly. She'd just been celebrating her own imminent release – not from Fellside, but from the burden of her past. She'd been looking forward to exactly that weightlessness and emptiness.

It does feel like that, Alex agreed solemnly. *But it's stupid to be scared of the thing you want more than anything. Remembering was the only thing I ever wanted, until I met you and wanted to be with you. So I'll do it. I will. As long as you're with me, I think it will be okay.*

It will, Jess promised.

She stepped out of her flesh again and took his hand in hers. It came naturally now. There was no uneasiness or sense of tearing.

They ran together away from the blazing strip lights into the night world and the seas of thought.

87

Salazar had spent most of that fraught and crazy day in the infirmary with the door locked. He had clinics in Franklin and Blackwell blocks, but he didn't attend them.

He didn't do anything else either.

He felt as though he'd been skating on a frozen lake and had fallen through, but all the ice water was inside him. In his brain. His brain was frozen solid, incapable of pursuing the smallest thought for more than a sluggish, hypothermic second or two.

Leah.

Leah and Devlin.

(Brown skin, glossy black blood, white toilet paper.)

Leah and Devlin intertwined, two halves of one thing.

His own voice, saying something (no words, just the rumbling rise and fall, the self-satisfied bleat), and Leah replying. "What's that about, then?"

Naseem in the infirmary, but not for a clinic. Naz wasn't sick. Naz was medicine.

What's that about, then?

Leah. Oh Leah.

What's that

What

What's that about

It was me that killed her, Sally thought. Just me. Not the governor. Not Devlin, or Grace, although they were certainly part of the chain reaction that led to her lying there on the floor in the shower block, broken and thrown away. But they didn't make Naz any promises. They just did what they were always going to do. Sally had killed her by going home to his wife and boasting about how he was going to make a difference, what a big man he was and how his conscience shone out in the dark.

"What's that about, then?"

And Sally spoke a name. A name he'd promised to keep secret and safe. And Leah went and whispered it to Devlin, because why wouldn't she? Something going on in G block right under his nose. Maybe she asked him what he knew about Naseem Suresh, whether he believed her, whether he knew any of the officers she was accusing.

And Devlin probably said no, nothing in it.

Then rose from her side and . . .

I've got to move, Sally thought. I've got to do something. I can't just sit here until the world ends. It will take too long.

His hands were heavy on the ends of his arms. Every movement felt exhausting and wasteful of energy as he booted up his computer and opened a document. The confession was long and rambling, full of false starts and repetitions. It jumped backwards and forwards in time. Even the sentences had no structure. They were coming apart in much the same way Sally was. He attached all the sound files from his secret store, his spy tapes, but forgot to reference them in the document or explain what they were.

When the document was complete, or felt like it was complete, he spent another hour looking for places to send it to. Newspapers. TV channels. Online newsfeeds. Blogs. The more the merrier.

He hit SEND and a bar appeared in the centre of the screen. It showed 0% complete, and for a long time it didn't change. Then the 0 ticked over into a 1. It was the sound files of course. They were colossal.

But he couldn't wait for them to finish. There were so many things he still needed to do.

Signing out, first of all. In the middle of his shift. Marcela Robbins was incredulous. "But . . . what if it all kicks off over in Goodall? Didn't the governor say everyone had to stay onsite?"

"Pharmacy," Sally said. "We need . . ." – he dredged up some words – "Blood. Bandages. Toilet paper."

"Toilet paper?" Marcela repeated.

Sally walked on, leaving her staring.

He drove to the Pot of Gold, where he ordered a pint of bitter with a whisky chaser – the first of many. He had to be drunk to do what he needed to do, but there were collateral benefits too. After three pints and three whiskies, his pain had a much duller edge to it.

It wasn't fair to canonise someone, he thought, alive or dead. To make them the keeper of your conscience or the apple of your eye or the guarantee that you'd actually lived. And it wasn't fair to hate them if they let you down. If his wife had needed to take six inches of solace from a brute like Devlin, that had to say as much about Sally as it did about her.

He felt as though he was spitting out dead parts of himself. The beer took away some of the filthy taste. He was having trouble standing now, but he didn't want to sit down. He was so unused to serious drinking that he might just put his head in his hands and fall asleep. That wouldn't do at all.

"Are you all right, love?" The barmaid, who was about twenty, was looking at him with pity and concern. Sally had no idea what she was reading in his face, but he tried to rearrange his features in a neutral configuration and told her he was fine.

He ordered another beer. Another whisky. As he drank, he looked around him at the early evening crowd. The pub was already filling up. It would take a long time to sift through so many strangers, even sober. There had to be a quicker way.

And there was, of course.

Sally stood and banged his empty glass on the counter. "On me," he called out. "All of your drinks. On me."

A few people looked at him, but only for a moment. One or two cheered. Most just turned away again, amused or contemptuous.

"I said it's my round!" Sally shouted. When they still didn't pay attention, he closed his hand on the glass he was holding. Squeezed it and squeezed it until finally it shattered, shards biting deep into his fingers and his palm as they slid and ground across each other. It hurt a lot more than he expected, but it did the trick. Everyone was looking now as the blood dripped down over his wrist and spattered on the counter.

The barmaid swore and backed away from him. She shouted out a name – the manager's name, maybe – but there was no immediate response.

"I would love," Sally said with ponderous dignity, "to buy you all a drink. That would be my privilege." He shook his hand gingerly, flexing his damaged fingers to dislodge bloody pieces of glass, which fell on to the bar, the floor, his jacket. He took a deep breath and went on. "I'm celebrating, you see. A drug deal. Big one. Up at the prison. That's who I am up there. Big man in the drugs. Smuggling. Get them in through the gate. Get them on to Curie . . . Curie block, especially. That's my particular . . ." – he waved his bleeding hand – ". . . thing."

He still had everyone's attention. Some of them were whispering to each other, shaking their heads. One or two had taken out mobile phones and were either dialling or else filming him. The barmaid was gone, headed for the hills. That was fine. Sally didn't mind being dismissed as a lunatic by everyone in the room who didn't know what he was talking about. As long as there was someone there who did.

"Harriet Grace," he said ringingly. "Harriet. Grace. You know who that is? I'm very, very friendly with Harriet Grace. She lets me in on all her little secrets. Dennis Devlin. Me and him are like . . . are like . . ." He tried to make his fingers connect. The blood was welling so freely now from his right hand that it made a constant pitter-patter sound on the wooden floor.

"Dennis is the one," he summarised. "Makes it happen. If someone needs to go, like that Minnie Weeks, Dennis just waves his hand and it . . . happens. And it's taken a long time, but I think I can honestly say I'm as big a man as he is. Important. Influential. Involved. All the way. All the way to the top. Enjoy your drinks and thank you for your . . . for your time."

That will do it, Sally thought. Or else it can't be done. Either way I'm dead so . . .

He staggered to the door, pushed it open with his elbow and went out. When the cooling evening air hit his face, he felt a wave of nausea rising inside him. He barely made it to the verge of the road before throwing up the entire contents of his stomach. The heaves were like someone's arms gripping his abdomen and performing a Heimlich on him.

Drained and tottering, he made it to his car and got it open, cradling his injured hand against his chest. He slid into the back seat, the world rocking around him. He couldn't drive in this state. He couldn't go back inside either. There was vomit on his trousers and his shoes. He was filthy, a disgrace. He would give himself a few minutes and then stagger down the road to the bus stop. There was nothing else left to do.

Both of the car's rear doors opened at the same time, and two men climbed in on either side of him. One was lean and hard and whippet-thin, with an army buzz cut. The other was huge, barrel-chested. Sweat made his shaved head shine like lacquered wood. He wore an apologetic smile.

They clicked the locks down on the car doors. The thin man wrinkled his nose at the sour smell of Sally's vomit. The other, precisely and without undue ceremony, took a straight razor from his pocket and unfolded it. He turned a cool, blue-eyed scrutiny on Sally.

"Evening," he said gravely. "My name's Kenny. Kenny Treacher."

"Is it?" Sally said. "Well. I do not give a flying fuck about that."

"No?"

"No." Sally started to shake his head, but had to stop at once as another wave of nausea sluiced through him. "You're as bad as she is. As they are. Poison. Sell poison, and get rich from people dying. Bad as I am, probably. But are you bad enough, Mr fucking Kenny fucking Treacher? That's the question. Are you bad enough to be any fucking use to me?"

"Well," Treacher said, pressing the razor up against Sally's throat, "I can only do my best. Tell me about this Devlin, yeah?"

88

While Devlin was waiting, he thought the waiting had to be the hardest part.

Three hours until lock-up, riding herd on six hundred women who were on the edge of rabid the whole time. He'd read in some tabloid once that women who lived together ended up going on the rag together. The image he'd conjured up in his mind when he read that article was something close to the way Goodall wing was right now. Whenever a warder even looked at a prisoner, it was a challenge. Every unguarded word flared up into a shouting match.

But lock-up rolled around at last. And that was the hardest part, no doubt about it. Forcing the rabid bitches back into their cells like ships into bottles. He kept thinking it was going to start, but time after time Corcoran was there to talk it down or bluff it out. The two of them went back to back. They kept poker faces, like nothing was wrong. Joked to each other and to the prisoners. Nonchalantly walked and waved and waltzed them through the doors. Nodded the count through.

Turned the keys.

CHUNK CHUNK CHUNK: done.

"Holy fuck," Corcoran said, leaning back against the wall. "I am going home and drinking a whole bottle of Bacardi. Someone can pour the Coke into me after I pass out."

"Bourbon any good?" Devlin said. And on her nod, "Follow me."

They went to the second-floor guard station. There was a camera there, but it only showed the left-hand side of the room. Devlin drew up two chairs against the right wall.

"Here." He took his hip-flask out of the first aid box, where he stowed it for use during night shifts, and handed it to her. They sat side by side, taking alternate swigs.

When Corcoran's head was thrown back, gulping down the sweet whisky, Devlin punched her hard in the throat. It was meant to be a killing blow, but he didn't hit hard enough. At the last moment, his mind wouldn't let him commit to what he was about to do.

Corcoran went down, but she was still trying to breathe, and she struggled in his grip when she realised what was happening. Devlin had her arms pinned but she used her head as a weapon, slamming it into his face so hard that he saw fireworks. So hard he let go of her.

But he caught her again as she crawled towards the door, and this time she was on her stomach so it was a lot harder for her to defend herself.

It took a long, long time to get the job done, because she was still fighting and he had to make sure that no part of her flailing body crossed the invisible line that was the camera's field of vision.

That was the hardest part. He cried the whole time he was killing her.

89

Physical distance didn't count for much in the night world. Liz Earnshaw was only a few feet away from them in waking reality – was Jess's next-door neighbour in solitary – but it still took her and Alex a long time to find her. When they did, Jess was surprised and disturbed at what she saw.

Earnshaw wasn't an ocean and she wasn't a tower. She was a ruin – inert and broken, the pieces of her mind lying in overlapping layers that hardly seemed to move or change. The trail that Jess and Alex had followed tasted of fury and violence and belligerence, but the ruin had none of those things. Emotionally, it was empty. Burned out.

Don't think about fire, Alex warned Jess.

"I'm sorry. I can't help it."

You have to try, Jess. If you think about fire, you'll get upset and you'll change things the way you changed me. You'll make everything look like what you remember.

She knew that was a real danger. She tried her best to calm herself – to pull her thoughts and emotions back inside her and lock them down. It was hard.

"Perhaps you should go in on your own," she said.

No! Alex was dismayed, pleading. *You said you'd stay with me. I'm not going unless you come too.*

Faced with that ultimatum, Jess surrendered. Alex took her hand – she did her best to make it firm and solid and real – and they stepped inside.

Once they took that last step, once they were inside Earnshaw looking out, everything changed. From the inside, Earnshaw – like anyone – was vast beyond any reasonable measurement. They weren't wandering in a ruin; they were lost in a world.

But they weren't lost for long. Earnshaw was catatonic for a reason, and the reason was Alex. She'd folded herself like a fist around some buried thing, some memory, some part of her lived experience. That folding had left marks on every part of her. They followed the only path they could see through that endless, scarred emptiness.

To the dense, impacted core of Earnshaw. A vast blotch of something and nothing, yellow-blue like a bruise, beating like a heart in a sky of brass.

Jess and the ghost that wore the shape of Alex Beech walked out across that sky, ignoring the drop below them because it wasn't real and didn't merit their attention. The thing they were walking towards knew they were there and it threw out snaking tendrils of itself to whip in the air above them.

GO AWAY GO AWAY GO AWAY GO AWAY GO AWAY GO AWAY GO AWAY GO AWAY GO AWAY GO AWAY GO AWAY GO AWAY GO AWAY GO AWAY GO AWAY GO AWAY GO AWAY GO AWAY GO AWAY GO AWAY, it shouted at them endlessly in Liz Earnshaw's voice.

"No," Jess said.

One of the tendrils lashed her across her face, exploded in her eyes in a flare of hate and rage. She flinched back, the pain taking her by surprise. A second blow hammered on her shoulders, and then a third in the exact same place. Earnshaw was trying to swat her out of the sky.

But Jess was pretty schooled up on pain by this point. After the fire, and the endless surgery to save her face, and what Stock had put her through with the needle, she was inoculated against random agony – especially if, like this, it was mostly "let's pretend".

"We're coming in," she said, trying to sound resolute and determined despite the tremor in her voice. "Nothing you can do will stop us, Earnshaw, but if you fight us, we might have to hurt you. It's up to you."

The bloated thing screamed and struck again – only against her, Jess noticed, not against Alex. Some of the tendrils hovered in the air over the boy's head but they offered him no harm. And Jess ignored the blows, only ducking her head as though the lashing filaments were heavy rain.

She knew they had to make a breach in this thing that towered over them, and she thought she might know a way to do it. It was brutal, but she had no particular reason to be gentle.

"You see who's with me, Earnshaw?" she shouted. "Does this face seem familiar to you? Maybe it doesn't because she's changed a lot since the last time you met. But I'll give you a clue if you want one. I'll tell you how you killed her."

She gathered her strength and shouted as loud as she could. Not just with her voice, but with her mind.

"You cut off the fingers of her left hand. You sliced her cheek open. Her

You cut off the fingers of her left hand. You sliced her cheek open. Her

right cheek, I think it was. You took her eye out. Then you stabbed her in the throat

right cheek, I think it was. You took her eye out. Then you stabbed her in the throat

and let her choke to death on her own blood. Is this ringing any bells?"

and let her choke to death on her own blood. Is this ringing any bells?

Alex whimpered at Jess's side. Clung to her arm like a castaway clinging to a spar.

She was describing the wounds he had told her about in their very first conversation. Told her about and – she knew now – tried to show her. He'd held up his hand, touched his eye and his cheek. But she had already been writing her own memories on to what she was seeing. The wounds were invisible to her because they didn't fit with what she knew about Alex's death.

444

The pulsing bruise above them made no response, but Jess felt that it was listening. The silence sucked at her.

"It sounds to me," she shouted, "as though most of the time you were just hurting her for the sake of it. Did you only decide to kill her right at the end? Or were you trying to draw it out as long as you could?"

The great dark blotch clenched and then expanded, again and again, as though it was a monstrous bird trying and failing to take off, hammering the air with useless vestigial wings.

Jess tried again, with Alex's own words this time. "You hurt her with sharp things. Cut her until she—"

The bruise screamed, and opened. For a moment it was everywhere. Pain and rage flooded the whole world. Then came the systole, the contraction, pulling it inexorably back into itself. Jess felt that furious anguish draw on her like a half-consumed cigarette, pull at her mind and her soul and what she wore by way of flesh.

Alex! she cried, wanting . . . what? To warn him? To reassure him? Just to remind him that she was there? It didn't matter. Alex was gone. The returning current had dragged his hand from hers and carried him away.

Then it carried itself away too. Jess was standing alone in the night world's vast nothingscape of endless shores and endless oceans.

90

First things first.

Devlin had a lot of work to do, but he had to do it systematically, in sequence, or else it was all going to fall apart on him.

The only reason he had killed Andrea Corcoran, who he liked as much as he liked anyone at Fellside apart from Grace, was to get at her keys. She was senior on-block, and the keys went with the job. If Grace hadn't made Devlin run escort for Moulson, it would have been him who had the keys. He wouldn't have been able to get away with this because all the inevitable concomitant shit would have come flowing back to him. Now it would flow to a dead woman in the second-floor guard station.

He took the keys off Corcoran's belt. He was still sobbing, blinking tears out of his eyes. Having met so many murderers and found them on the whole a pretty contemptible bunch, he hadn't expected murder to be so very hard.

He went to the main security panel and used the keys to unlock all the cells. He trusted in human nature to do the rest. The women of G block were foaming at the mouth already. Now they were foaming at the mouth and free as birds. Probably an hour kettled up in their cells had fermented their paranoid frenzy very nicely, but to encourage them to cast aside the last of their inhibitions, Devlin turned off the CCTV cameras.

He walked out of the block just as the shit was hitting the fan. Yells of jubilation, anger and alarm were sounding from all the walkways as the inmates checked out the full implications of that loud click in the middle of the still night.

Sally first, then Moulson. Locked up tight in a solitary cell, which wouldn't open on the general release, Moulson wasn't going anywhere. So Sally first.

But the infirmary was locked when Devlin got there. No sign of Sally or anyone else. He couldn't afford to be seen waiting there.

He still had Corcoran's keys, which like all the master sets worked for central admin as well as for the specific block they were issued for. He let himself into the infirmary, swiped a bottle of surgical alcohol, a pair of disposable gloves and some dressing pads, and was about to slip away again when another thought occurred to him. He smashed open the medicine cabinet with his nightstick and swiped a shitload of pethidine. When he did catch up with Sally, he was going to close that supply line permanently, so he might as well stock up while he could.

In the meantime, Moulson was now promoted to item number one.

The alarms were already ringing as he descended the stairs from the infirmary. Other officers were jogging along beside him and past him, having just been transferred from administrative duties to riot control.

The yard was a lot busier now. Warders were running from the other four prisoner blocks towards Goodall. The skeleton crews left behind, instead of staying on post, had come to the doors of the other blocks and were watching the shit-storm with troubled fascination. Riots were bad news for everybody. Warders had been known to die in riots. Scores were settled and debts were paid. Afterwards there were public inquiries that sometimes led to mass sackings. Despite the paid overtime, nobody was enthused.

447

The governor was standing in the middle of the yard, shouting orders that nobody could hear over the jangling alarms. Devlin walked past him without slowing.

He found Goodall in a very satisfactory state of chaos. Guards and furious women were brawling through the corridors, and the ballroom was like a rock concert in a war zone. Nobody spared the Devil a second glance. Po Royal, who didn't move out of his way fast enough, got a tap from his nightstick that she either wouldn't forget or wouldn't live to remember. Apart from that, he got through the mêlée without making a ripple.

The next thing he needed to do was to cover his arse. He fought his way up to the second floor, locked himself in with Corcoran's corpse and put the gloves on. He cleaned all around the guard station with the alcohol and the dressing pads. His fingerprints had been on the door, the hip-flask, the handle of the first aid cupboard and the chairs. Now they weren't. He didn't think they were on Corcoran's throat – he'd used his nightstick to choke her, not his hands – but he wiped her down anyway to make doubly sure. He'd have to remember to do the same thing with her keys when he was finally done with them, and to find a place to drop them that would seem plausible when people with some degree of expertise picked over the pieces of this.

He unlocked the door again and peered out. The alarms were still clamouring. The air was thick with screams, and hundreds of running feet made the walkways twang like tuning forks.

Devlin stuffed the bottle of alcohol and the pads into his trouser pocket. He was going to be needing them again soon.

He unshipped his nightstick again and went on up the stairs to solitary, to kill Jess Moulson.

91

Jess was in the night world when she saw Devlin coming. In that place where emotion stood in for physics, his fixed concentration on her was a field that bent the landscape around it. She felt it as a shifting of forces and volumes. Something was moving towards her and focusing its will on her as it came, projecting hate and malevolence and grim purpose.

The emotions were a vector she could follow. Jess turned to face them, listening with every inch of her skin. She silenced her own mind and let those other thoughts rain down on her, taking their measure and their meaning.

She recognised Devlin. She read his intentions.

Alex! she screamed. But this crisis was all hers. There was nothing Devlin could do to hurt the dead. All he could do was send Jess to join them.

There was no answer. No trace or echo of Alex's presence. Jess waited a few seconds longer, then ran headlong back to her waiting flesh.

92

Every prison riot is a chaotic system, tending to break down into its component parts but artificially sustained and concentrated by the narrowness of the spaces involved. It can seem to be petering out, to be dying down to nothing, and then surge again without warning into unpredictable and motiveless violence.

Devlin had uncorked this bottle with full knowledge of its toxic contents. He didn't even flinch when he stepped over Keith Lovett's sprawled body. Didn't stop to check whether Lovett was dead or only unconscious. Dead would be preferable, all things considered, since he was another potential loose end.

On the fourth-floor walkway, three guards were desperately trying to prevent a group of determined women from getting access to the stairs. Devlin walked on by quickly before anyone could call on him for help.

Finally he reached the top floor. It was deserted, as he'd hoped. The inmates from the lower levels had for the most part headed straight down to the ballroom as soon as their doors had opened. Devlin made his way along the walkway, down the short row of solitary cells. Moulson was in the furthest, number 5.

He took one last look up and down the corridor. There was

nobody in sight way up here at the top of the stack. Screams and impact sounds echoed from the ballroom below, where sixty or so officers were struggling to contain six hundred women.

Devlin also remembered to double-check the camera at the angle of the walkway, just to make sure that nobody had turned the CCTV system back on again. No red light on the fascia, so he was fine.

Devlin unlocked the steel cabinet on the wall and used Corcoran's keys again to release the doors of the solitary cells, but they still weren't fully unlocked. The doors were on a one-way latch, needing somebody on the outside to open them. He turned the handle of Moulson's door and stepped inside.

He was surprised to see Moulson still asleep. He thought the noise from down below would have penetrated this far and woken her. But the soundproofing was very effective. As soon as he stepped into the narrow space and pulled the door to behind him, all external sounds faded almost to nothing.

Moulson was curled up in what looked like a foetal position under the single blanket, only the top of her head showing. She didn't stir even slightly as the Devil approached the bunk. He'd given some thought to the question of how he was going to kill her. Throttling her, as he'd done Corcoran, would be easiest and quickest, but he didn't want to work to a pattern. It would be bad news if anyone got to think that the two deaths were linked in any way. So he'd decided on suffocation as the least worst option.

He bent and picked up the pillow from the floor where it had fallen. Which brought his head down almost to the level of the bunk.

Jess kicked out with both feet. She'd returned from the night world a few seconds before, had barely had time to take up the reins of her body again, but she knew the danger she was in and she put everything she had into that kick.

Devlin caught it full in his face. He was slammed back hard against the opposite wall of the narrow cell. Something – his nose

451

possibly, or maybe part of his jaw – crunched under Jess's heel. He slumped to the floor, stunned.

Jess jumped up as he went down. Two steps brought her to the door. If he had closed it all the way, she was dead. She knew there was no handle on the inside. As soon as Devlin found his feet again, he would dismantle her, and in those close quarters she'd have no chance at all.

Her clawing fingers found the edge of the door and it opened. She fled.

But she skidded to a halt almost at once. Alex was still here. Inside Earnshaw, swallowed whole by her rage. Jess wasn't thinking right then about the meaninglessness of miles and yards and inches in that other world: she just knew she didn't want to leave him after swearing to him that she wouldn't.

Fighting her own panic, she tried the handle of Liz Earnshaw's door. It gave. Her hand shook as she eased it all the way down and pushed the door open. She stepped inside, moving quickly and quietly. Then, as Devlin had done, she pulled it closed again as far as she dared, almost but not quite all the way, the latch a trembling thousandth of an inch away from shooting home.

A metallic boom told her that Devlin had thrown open the door of her cell and stepped out on to the walkway. She held her breath. His steps went by Earnshaw's door, but then slowed and stopped. He must be looking around, trying to get a sense of where Jess might have gone.

Or maybe he was looking at the door, seeing the tell-tale line where it failed to sit flush with the jamb.

Movement behind Jess made her turn her head, very slowly, terrified that a rustle of cloth would betray her.

Earnshaw had sat up on the bunk and was staring at her. The sheet fell away from her naked body, the harsh light of the neon strips shining down on a latticework of short, wide scars that covered her entire torso. Her jaw worked as though she was trying to swallow something. It was impossible to tell from her expression whether or not she was seeing what was in front of her. Jess

452

stayed absolutely still and – vaguely remembering that this was how you survived a confrontation with a wild animal – kept her eyes averted and slightly downcast.

Earnshaw swung her legs around and let them slide to the floor. Ponderously, inexorably, she climbed to her feet.

Devlin's boots clattered right outside the door. Jess braced herself. If the door opened, she would be caught between them. All she could do was fight until they put her down, which wouldn't be long.

Devlin's footsteps receded. A second later, she heard them clattering on the steps that led down to the next level.

So now there was only one homicidal maniac to deal with. Jess looked around for a weapon, but why would there be one in a solitary cell? Everything here was designed to be as little use as possible if a prisoner decided to try to hurt herself or anyone else.

Earnshaw strode towards her. Jess held her ground. "What have you done to him?" she demanded. "Where is he?"

Earnshaw put one massive hand on Jess's upper arm and moved her aside with no visible effort. She pulled the door open. Jess grabbed her wrist and tried to drag her back into the cell. Earnshaw ignored her, and she was carried along by the other woman's irresistible strength, jarring her shoulder against the door jamb.

"Alex!" Jess shouted. "Where are you? Talk to me!" Her feet slid and scrabbled on the steel walkway as she tried to get some traction and bring Earnshaw to a halt, or at least slow her down. And finally Earnshaw did stop.

But only to set her hand in the middle of Jess's chest and push her away with such force that she staggered and almost fell.

The wild animal comparison came back into Jess's mind, because that was what Earnshaw looked like right then: something that wore a human shape but had never learned speech and would rip your throat out if you crossed it.

She lumbered on and didn't look back.

Jess didn't try to close the gap with her again. She just followed her to the end of the walkway and down the stairs, staying a few paces behind all the way.

On the next level down, she found out what all the noise was. There were women throwing furniture and personal effects from their cells, or more likely other people's cells, into the ballroom below. They were screaming abuse at the warders down there, who were laboriously clearing the big central space by advancing across it in a double line.

Earnshaw didn't let anything slow her. The women who got in her way she violently pushed aside.

Jess moved in Earnshaw's wake, staying close to the wall to keep from being seen. But nobody was looking her way in any case. Their minds were taken up with the fighting. There was a warder who did see her and recognised her, and decided to strike a blow for incinerated children everywhere. He strode straight at Jess, his nightstick in the ready position. Jess had about half a second, seeing him coming, to throw up her hand in a futile defence.

Lorraine Buller barged into the man head-on and pitched him over the railings into the suicide nets. She gave Jess a nod, and then she was gone too. It was a passing courtesy in the middle of the chaos, from one cellmate to another.

Jess speeded up a little. The closer she stayed to Lizzie, the less likely she was to be molested. She was calling Alex's name in her mind, but there was no response. And now she realised with a sickening of the heart where Earnshaw was going. Not down into the ballroom, but left, and then straight along to the end of the level-three corridor.

To Grace's cell.

The two women on guard at Grace's door turned when they saw her coming, and moved into a defensive phalanx. Earnshaw slowed to a stop, and for a moment they faced each other without a word.

"I need to talk to her," Lizzie said. Her voice was raw, low, but it carried over the distant shouts and screams.

"She said not to let anyone through except Dennis," Jilly Fish said. She didn't say a word about Liz's nakedness, or the ridged, glossy lines of old scars that covered her from neckline to crotch.

Earnshaw twisted her neck to the left, then to the right, and flexed her fingers. "I need to talk to her," she repeated.

"What's it about?" Fish asked.

"It's private."

For a moment or two nobody spoke. Fish interrogated Earnshaw's stern, serious face and came to a quick conclusion.

"Time for our fag break," she said to her companion. "Come on."

"But Grace said . . ." The other woman, a tall blonde with a bodybuilder's overdeveloped physique, faltered into silence. Fish was already walking away, and now Lizzie was coming straight on. The blonde was the same height as Lizzie but out-massed her by twenty or thirty pounds. The muscles of her arms were like sculpted stonework.

She held her ground almost to the last moment, then threw up her hands and backed away. "Private," she said. "Fair enough." She turned and ran.

Grace was washing at the sink when Earnshaw walked into the room. Jess slipped in behind her, flattening herself against the wall.

Grace raised her eyebrows at the sight of them but then she welcomed them in with an ironic sweep of her arm. She walked around them to kick the door to, shutting out the worst of the noise from outside.

"I don't know what it is with this one," she said to Earnshaw with a nod of her head in Jess's direction. "I keep telling people to kill her and she keeps coming back into my field of vision not dead. Do me a favour, Lizzie, please. Put us all out of her misery."

Earnshaw didn't seem to have heard. "I had . . . a really awful dream, Grace," she said in the same rasping voice as before. She bowed her head into her own clenched fist. Pressed it hard against her forehead, grimacing with effort, as though she was trying to push through and grab hold of something in there. "I want to talk to you about . . . something that happened."

"Later, love," Grace said. "This is a busy time. Let's get the chores done first." But still Lizzie didn't move.

455

Grace turned to glance at Jess, her lips pressed into a thin line. "Well, I'll give you ten for balls and one for brains," she said in the same conversational tone. "What did you think? That you were on a roll after winning your appeal? That you could talk me into not killing you? You can't."

Jess didn't bother to answer. Grace seemed like an irrelevance right then. She was much more scared for Alex, trapped in Liz's dark heart, than she was for herself. She spoke only to Earnshaw, who was struggling in the grip of some emotion that was close to panic. "Earnshaw," she said. "Tell me who she was. The girl you killed. What was her name?"

Earnshaw didn't seem to have heard. Her shoulders twitched and twisted. "Please, Grace," she moaned. Her voice seemed to be on the brink of dying away altogether now, a broken instrument driven by inadequate breath. "I dreamed she came back. But now I'm awake and she's still here. She didn't go away when I woke up."

Grace looked perplexed. "Later," she said again. "Come on, Lizzie. You're no use to yourself like this. Clock that bitch and be done with it."

Earnshaw turned and took a step towards Jess, her big hands reaching out. But then she stopped as though she'd forgotten what it was she was meant to do.

"What was her name?" Jess shouted. "Who was she?"

"Why?" Earnshaw demanded in that same voice of agony and exhaustion.

"Because she deserves to be remembered! Nobody remembers her right now. She doesn't even remember herself. But you know who she was."

"It's not my choice," Earnshaw rumbled. Jess realised then that Earnshaw wasn't talking to her, or to Grace for that matter. She was talking to a voice inside her own head.

To Alex.

Jess laughed – a strangled sound of surprise and relief. He was still there, in Earnshaw's fractured soul. Still fighting.

Grace walked right up to Earnshaw, took her by the shoulders and shook her. "Come on, Lizzie! What do I pay you for? Sort her out!"

For a moment, Earnshaw only stared. Then she gathered herself, her whole body, by some huge effort of will. A shudder ran through her. She crossed to Jess in three strides.

"Tell me who—" Jess said again, and had to stop. Earnshaw's hand shot out and clamped on her throat. Her other hand reached round to grip the back of Jess's neck. The flesh there, like the flesh on the right side of her face, was burned and imperfectly reconstructed, but even through that barricade she could feel the calloused toughness of Earnshaw's grip.

She grabbed the wrist of the hand that was around her throat and tried to pull it away. She couldn't budge it. It started to tighten. Earnshaw stared at her at point-blank range, rigid as a statue, implacable as a hanging judge.

"That's better," Grace said. "That's my girl."

Earnshaw drew Jess close. One hand squeezed and the other twisted. Jess struggled as her airway closed. She might as well have been trying to dismantle a wall with her hands.

I remember! a voice said. It seemed to come to her across a great distance, almost drowned out by the sound, suddenly very loud, of her own heartbeat. It was Alex's voice. *Jess, I remember now! Can you see it?*

Jess thought she could. Dimly, and getting dimmer by the second. But she couldn't speak to say so.

93

What she saw was:

A prison cell, right here in Goodall block to judge by the floor plan and the colour scheme. Mostly anonymous, grimly generic, although there was a picture on the wall – a sketch of Liz Earnshaw drawn in blue biro. In the picture Liz was smiling, which had to make you wonder if the artist had ever met her or was just drawing her from a verbal description. The shaded areas were done by drawing in lots of short lines, horizontal and vertical. Cross-hatching, like an image in a comic book.

Nothing else about the cell stood out. There was a table. There were two chairs. There was a toilet without a seat, the cistern clamped to the wall with a thick steel bracket. There was a locker unit with two lockers, an upper and a lower. That was riveted to the wall too. On the windowsill, two ceramic giraffes intertwined their necks in an impossible caress.

And on the bunk – a real embrace. Liz Earnshaw, gaunt and gangling, was folded around another woman, both of them naked. This second woman was so short that for a second, cradled in Earnshaw's arms, she looked like a child. Or perhaps the ghost of a child still lingered, for a second, behind her eyes.

But she wasn't Alex Beech. She'd only worn his face for a while – from the time when Jess first saw her down in the abyss to the moment, less than an hour ago, when the two of them had stepped into Earnshaw's dreams. She wore her own face now. Dark skin, slightly angular cheeks, brown eyes with thick black eyeliner, and a flat nose like a blade. No breasts to speak of, and no hips either. She smiled as she pushed back into Earnshaw's embrace, settling herself there with a smug, proprietorial air.

"Settle down," Earnshaw growled. "You're keeping me awake."

"Well, as long as you're awake," the other woman said, "you can scratch my back."

Earnshaw did as she was bidden with a sigh and a long-suffering "Bloody hell!"

"Lower," the woman said.

"Any lower and I'll be in your arse crack."

"Yes please."

The scene broke up in front of Jess's eyes as her profligate brain burned through the last few molecules of oxygen that were sustaining it. Arcs and streaks of abstract colour replaced the vision of the prison cell. The colours swirled in the air irresolutely, as if they wanted to come together again but something was preventing them.

I remember! Alex cried again. Jess couldn't imagine now how she'd ever mistaken that voice for a little boy's. It was a woman's voice, with the burr of maturity behind the lightness of it.

Jess saw the outline of the truth, its angular, uncompromising shape, and it was so unlike what she'd expected that she was dazzled by it. She might have seen it before but she'd only ever known Earnshaw as a monster, a wrecking ball. She'd all but forgotten the story Shannon McBride had told her. The story of Naseem Suresh, of Liz's fierce love for her and how her death had broken Liz along some pre-existing fault-line, turning her into what she was now.

An incredulous laugh welled up from Jess's diaphragm, but it stopped halfway. Her crimped throat blocked all traffic.

It's not funny, Jess!

But it was, a little bit. Jess had been wrong on every count. Ridiculously wrong. She'd seen a ghost without a shape, without a memory, and stamped it with the seal of her own guilt. And then when its real identity was right in front of her face, she'd read it backwards. She'd been so sure that Earnshaw was the nasty girl, the one who'd hurt Alex. But she was Alex's friend. Naseem Suresh's friend, rather. The nasty girl was . . .

Someone else.

The grip on Jess's throat slackened. Her lungs had been dragging at nothing for most of a minute, and they were still at full stretch. Given something to work with, they managed to suck down a slender, burning filament of air.

Lizzie was my love. My big mummy bear. Nobody dared to touch me when she was there.

So obviously the nasty girl must have waited. Until Naseem was on her own.

Jess fell down on to her hands and knees, and into the here and now. She blinked tears out of her eyes, sipped air through her bruised and swollen throat. Earnshaw had dropped her, was turning away from her to face Grace again.

"Tell me what happened!" she said, desperation in her voice. "Grace, tell me. Naz is here, and she's listening. What did you do?"

"I don't know what you're talking about," Grace said. "Lizzie, finish that bitch off. Go on. Don't make me do it myself."

She didn't wait. She arranged it. She made it happen. And she got you out of the way so you couldn't help me!

"Who did?" Earnshaw bellowed. "How?"

Jess looked up groggily to see Earnshaw and Grace face to face, one on either side of her, like two dogs fighting for the same bone. But she wasn't the bone: Alex was. Naseem was. Earnshaw was worrying at the truth, and Grace was trying to snatch it back from her.

I'll show you, said Alex. Said Naseem.

460

Grace's cell blurred and went away again. Moulson fought against the vision this time, conscious of the danger she was in, but there was no defence against the ghost's vivid dreaming. Threads of colour knitted themselves into shapes. Shapes coalesced and acquired volume.

This time she was in the ballroom. Liz Earnshaw was up on her feet, a fallen chair next to her that she'd just jumped up from. Dennis Devlin was poking her repeatedly in the chest, yelling into her face, which was reddening with rage. "You know how to address a warder. Try again. Try again!" Naseem Suresh, dressed now like Liz and all the other women there in a yellow and black Goodall tracksuit, was holding on to Earnshaw's arm and stopping her from throwing a punch. It made no difference. Half a dozen guards descended upon Earnshaw and dragged her away screaming.

The vision blurred and broke apart, leaving Jess sliding on a slippery scree of afterimages.

"Devlin," Earnshaw muttered, sounding lost and amazed. "The Devil."

"Present," Devlin said thickly.

He closed the door behind him and advanced on Jess. He wore a bib of blood. The lower half of his face was a swollen mess.

Jess was watching his clenched fists, so she didn't see the kick coming.

94

Up in the solitary cells, Devlin had had a plan. Don't make a pattern, don't leave any presents for the forensics team, use the tools that are lying around. That had blown up in his face in every sense of the word. He was all done with plans now. Liz Earnshaw was standing in front of him stark naked and whimpering, so this was clearly the ending of days and a man had to respond accordingly. The first thing he did was to kick Moulson in the stomach, putting her down hard.

Then he went on kicking her with his steel-capped boots until, in his opinion, she was unlikely to have any more fight in her. It went some way towards relieving his feelings.

When Moulson wasn't moving even to try to defend herself, he hauled her up off the floor and threw her down unceremoniously on to Grace's bunk. Here he did revert to the plan, because this part of the plan was fine. He grabbed the pillow and pushed it down over Moulson's face.

Fight him, Jess! Don't let him!

Who the fuck was that screaming in his ear? It threw him off for a second. The voice was so loud and so close that he turned to swat away a hysterical woman who turned out not to be there.

Moulson was starting to revive a little. Her fingers clawed at the backs of Devlin's hands. Shit! That meant his blood and tissue would be under her fingernails. More work with the disinfectant.

Moulson was trying to squirm free. The Devil shifted his weight and bore down on her, teeth clenched with effort. As her movements got weaker and weaker, he thought, Where in the name of Christ did I leave the disinfectant?

Right then, as though to admonish him for losing concentration, something exploded against his skull like a depth charge against the hull of a battleship. Suddenly he was on the ground, without any idea how he'd got there. A large mass moved above him, a towering shadow in the stark illumination of the cell's strip light. Liz Earnshaw. Grace tackled her from the side, but Liz hurled Grace away with a convulsive one-armed shrug.

Reflexively, Devlin threw up his hands.

Earnshaw brought her arm around in a horizontal sweep, like a reaper, hitting him on the elbow of his raised right arm. He screamed in shock and agony. Her weapon was his own nightstick, which she must have swiped from his belt while he was wrestling with Moulson. She rained blows down on him, putting all her beef and all her hate into the task.

Devlin kicked at her legs but didn't connect. Another blow from the nightstick caught him on the base of the spine, and for the first time he was actually afraid. The mad bitch was capable of crippling him, or even killing him.

He rolled under the bunk. He couldn't think of anything else to do. Earnshaw gripped his ankle and dragged him back out into the light. He launched another kick and she let go – but only to start again with the nightstick.

Devlin was trying to get to his pepper spray, but another well-aimed smack from the sidewinder broke his wrist. After that, he just lay there. His best chance of surviving this was to pretend he was already dead.

95

Grace had a very pragmatic mind. She also had a shank which she kept to hand as a weapon of last resort.

It was taped to the inside edge of one of the legs of her bunk, and it had a cardboard sheath from which it would come free at a single tug. She had always felt ambivalent about having a weapon in her cell. If it turned up in a search, it was a mandatory two years on sentence. On the other hand, she had ways of forestalling searches, and she hated the thought of being defenceless if anyone of hostile intent came calling, or if, say, one of her own bodyguards switched her loyalties.

So there it was.

Grace tugged the serviceable little blade out of the cardboard. And cut Moulson's throat.

96

And then there were two.

Or three, but Dennis Devlin was playing dead.

Or four, but Jess Moulson was as close to being dead as made no difference. Her hands clutched to her throat. Thinking, *Why can't I breathe?* Then, *Oh.*

Right.

And if the dead were included, then Naseem Suresh brought the total up to five.

But Earnshaw was still on her feet, and so was Grace. Earnshaw was pounding away at Devlin with the nightstick. She looked as though she was never going to stop. She'd found a home at last for all the pain and sorrow that was inside her, and she was busy repatriating it.

Grace looked up from Moulson's sprawled body with the shank in her hand and a glove made of blood. One problem solved, and the shortlist getting shorter.

She made a run at Liz, who was intent on what she was doing and didn't see her coming.

Something crazy happened. Liz's left hand lashed out and knocked Grace head over heels. Grace was already stabbing out with the shank when the blow connected. The blade grazed Earnshaw's side, low down, but then Grace was on her back and the shank was rolling away across the floor.

Jess watched it happen – through dimming eyes, but still she knew. It wasn't Earnshaw who was responsible for that lightning defence. It was Naseem Suresh playing tail gunner. Naz in Jess's mind had only ever been a tourist. In Hannah Passmore's, a burglar. In Earnshaw's mind, she fitted like a piece of jewellery or a musical instrument into the case that was made to protect it. She was comfortable there. And she had the run of the place.

Grace tasted blood and raised her hand to explore her split lip – spreading a whole lot more blood, most of it Jess's, across her lower face.

Earnshaw turned to find out what her left hand was doing. She saw Grace sitting on the floor a few feet away. Saw the fallen shank, and Moulson on the bed with blood still welling sluggishly from her opened throat.

"What?" Earnshaw croaked. "What's happening? Naz, was that you?"

Yeah, said Naz. *Oh baby, I've got something else to show you. It's gonna hurt you, but you need to see it. You too, Jess.*

Another vision blinded Jess and deafened her, dragged her away from herself. This time she wasn't sorry to leave.

The ballroom again. Naseem elbowing her way through an indifferent crowd, anxious to avoid being seen.

Hurrying along one of the lower corridors.

Ducking into a shower room. Hiding in one of the cubicles, pressed flat against the tiles as though she wanted to sink into them. She peered through the gap in a plastic curtain, making sure she hadn't been followed.

But she had. Three women stepped in out of the corridor, their movements unhurried and casual. Two were strangers. The last one closed the door, then turned and put on a perfunctory smile. "Come on out, Naz. I just want to talk to you." It was Harriet Grace.

466

Grace's grim-faced bodyguards – clearly the Earnshaw and Big Carol of these olden days – took hold of Naseem and held her in place. She was a child again in their grip, just as she had been in Earnshaw's embrace. One of the two had an arm around her throat. Each of them held an arm, and had a leg hooked around one of Naseem's legs, locking them at the knees. They'd made themselves into a human torture frame.

Grace took something from the pocket of her tracksuit. Jess, still watching this scene from a queasy, bodiless perspective, recognised it at once because it was the same shank that Grace had just used on her: a workmanlike tool made from the metal hinge of a door, honed to an exquisite edge and embedded in a slightly tapering piece of wood that might once have been a drumstick.

"So," Grace said, "you wanted to have a conversation, is that right?"

"If you touch me, Lizzie will kill you." Amazingly, Naseem sounded arrogant as well as scared – as though she thought she had some kind of immunity that protected her even here. "You should drop this, Grace, before you—"

Grace put the shank to Naseem's cheek. She incised a short line there, the tip of the blade grazing the edge of Naseem's eyeliner. A red teardrop trickled down from Naseem's eye – which widened as she realised she wasn't invulnerable after all.

Earnshaw gave a bellow of anguish and tore herself free from the vision, in good time to see Grace crawling across the floor towards the fallen shank.

Liz got there first. Her hand clamped down on Grace's wrist and held it, an inch or two short of the weapon it was groping for. Grace looked up, and when her gaze met Liz's, something sudden and silent passed between them. A renegotiation.

Grace lost that battle, much to her amazement, but she tried it on anyway. "I made you," she reminded Liz, through clenched teeth. She tried to pull her hand free, but couldn't move it even an inch against Liz's implacable grip. "I picked you up when you were falling apart. The life you've got now – you owe that to me!"

467

"Yes," Liz agreed. Her voice was hoarse, breathy, full of jagged edges. "I owe you that. And what you took away from her, Grace. From both of us. That's what you owe me."

Grace lunged for the shank with her other hand, but Liz kicked it away.

Grace tried to get her thumb up into Liz's eye, but Liz dislocated her arm, slowly and remorselessly twisting it out of its socket.

Jess saw very little of what happened after that. She was dying, her throat filling up with blood and her mind emptying.

But she caught the gist.

97

Jess felt strong, gentle hands lifting her to her feet. Drawing her into an embrace that was warm and welcoming but stranger than anything she'd ever felt. It didn't begin or end at her skin. It was like being hugged by the sun.

She surrendered to the joy of it and to the sudden release from her body's many pains. She knew that the reason they were gone was because her body was gone. She was dead.

She pulled back at last, but only so she could look at Naseem face to face. It was the first time they had ever met like this, but they knew each other so well.

Naz had a scar on her chin, and a pitting of rough skin on one cheek, just as she had when she was alive. But when she smiled, as she did now, these blemishes fell below the horizon of Jess's attention. It was like the alchemy of her own ruined face, but in reverse. Naz's smile joined the dots of her features into a whole that was unexpectedly beautiful.

"Hey," she said.

"Hey," Jess muttered. She raised her hand to check that her throat was whole. It was reassuring to find that she had both, a hand and a throat, to a reasonable level of resolution. She seemed to have made the transition into death pretty well. But then she'd had a lot of practice.

Involuntarily she looked over her shoulder, as though she might find the cell there. Find her own body, and Grace and Earnshaw working out their differences without weapons or distractions. But they were in the night world now. Memories and echoes were their only companions.

Jess let her shoulders droop. If she'd had a breath to let out, she would have released it in a long-drawn-out sigh. Mostly what she felt was weariness and desolation, but she was surprised to find that there was some relief in the mix too. To be dead. Finally to be dead and done with. It didn't feel, right then, like anything she couldn't cope with. At least she had friends here.

"You did it," Naz said. "Jess, I don't know what to say to you. You found her and brought her back to me. Or me to her. Both. Everything I forgot, it's all here now. It's all . . ." She faltered into silence. She was staring at Jess in mute dismay.

The penny's just dropped, Jess realised. She thought I'd slipped away from the fight of my own free will. Now she knows. Somehow. Just by looking at me.

"It's all right," she said. "It's fine. Well, most of it is fine. If I regret anything, it's . . . him, Alex. He had such an awful life. I wanted to help him. I wanted that so much. And now I know for sure I'll never see him again." She felt a welling-up in her throat that wanted to be tears. She groped for more words that wouldn't come.

And then a monstrous sound broke over them like a wave, making speech impossible. It was a peal of thunder, and it was a scream. Both things at once. The air curdled and the world tilted, as though gravity was a pair of scales and someone had just put their thumb on the balance.

Harriet Grace when she was alive had been all about control. She burst into the afterlife like steam shrieking out of a pressure cooker valve. Her gaping mouth opened behind the sky. A second mouth opened within it, and then a third, her titanic rage coming now in three deafening, clashing registers.

"You can't do this to me! You can't! I won't let you!"

The storm slammed into them, knocked them off their feet and snatched the ground out from under them when they fell. For a moment, Jess found herself falling horizontally across the endless plain, as she had on the night of her involuntary overdose.

But she knew where that led to, and she fought her way back from it with quiet, deadly ferocity.

"You can't! You can't! You can't!"

Down is down, Jess told the world. And the world obeyed. She caught hold of Naz's hand as she tumbled by, reeled her in and set her on her feet. Naz clung to her, terror etched across her face.

"It's her!" she gasped. "It's Grace!"

"I know."

"Jess, we've got to run. We've got to hide until she—"

"No. Not this time."

A grey-black mass was rushing on them, reaching out for them with taloned hands.

Jess turned her attention on it like a cold spotlight. "You're not so big," she said tightly. And then again, in her mind, *You're not so big at all.*

She picked that thought up and hurled it. It hit the storm that was Harriet Grace full on and folded it in half.

When she had given wings to Patricia Mackie and a boy's face to Naseem Suresh, she hadn't known what she was doing. But her mind had been able to shape dreams like clay. And the dead were dreams that dreamed themselves alive. Maybe the living were too. Another time for that.

For now: *You're a tiny little thing. A speck. A dot. A dust mote in my eye.*

The churning madness of the storm shrank and shrank again, forced back into itself until it was a black shape no bigger than a pillow.

She took it in her hands, and she was surprised by the weight of it. Its surface was fractal, writhing like worms. It hurt to look at it.

I'll kill you, Moulson, Grace raved. *Keep killing you again and again and again.*

Naz was staring wide-eyed as Jess turned to face her. "We've got to," she said, as though Naz had spoken. "We've got to do it now."

Naz nodded. She didn't have to ask what Jess meant. The thought had occurred to both of them at once.

She grabbed hold of the dark mass that was Harriet Grace's naked soul and held it tight. Jess did the same. It twisted in their grip as Grace tried to squirm free. Tried to squeeze or thread herself through the gaps between their fingers. They started to walk, and then to run, gripping the dark, writhing mass at either end like firemen or stretcher-bearers.

The speed with which Grace adapted came as a nasty surprise to both of them. Jess had thought her first sucker punch might have ended the fight, but Grace was already fighting back. They had to dispose of her, put her where she couldn't do any further harm. And there was only one place that would let them do that.

But it was further away than either of them remembered. They lumbered on and on through the night world with their burden clasped tightly between them. Grace seemed to be getting heavier, but that had to be impossible. It was just that they'd never really carried anything here, and they didn't know what their own limits were.

But it was true, Jess realised. Grace was changing. Growing more massive in their arms. What had taken Jess days to learn and weeks to get any good at, Grace was figuring out in minutes. She had understood what Jess had done to her and she had learned from it. Squashed down as she was into this coiled, compressed essence, she couldn't attack them directly. But she was making herself denser and more massive, reconfiguring herself into an uncompromising weight that would slow and hamper them.

And when you stop, when you let go of me − oh, then you'll see. I

472

like this place. I think I can make something of it. I think it has possibilities.

"Which way?" Jess cried.

But right then she caught sight of it up ahead of them. They were approaching the lip of the abyss.

Perhaps Grace saw it too, or sensed it. She was applying herself with relentless focus. The shapeless lump that was her soul was growing again moment by moment. Growing and changing, becoming more solid and textured. Ropes of muscle and sinew swelled and stood out on its surface. It looked now like some sort of human embryo that had been kept from birth and fed on steroids for a human lifetime. It looked as though it was about to unfold, to open like a flower. Jess didn't want to see what might be inside.

Born again! Grace exulted. *It took Jesus three fucking days!*

They drew back their arms to hurl the terrible thing over the edge, but the edge receded from them. One moment they were almost there, the next they'd lost sight of it. The abyss's rim was pulling back like a Hitchcock dolly zoom faster than they could walk towards it.

They ran again, trying all the while to bear down hard on the dark mass, to push it back into itself. Trying too to concentrate on their destination and how close it was. Grace had outstripped them in mere minutes, and now they were learning from her, learning that where there was a will, there had to be a way. In the night world, your way *was* your will, and Grace applied that principle with berserker finesse.

They fought back. They struggled inch by agonising inch all the way to the pit, imagined it gliding to meet them as they came. But when they got there, when they drew back their arms to throw the seething mass over the rim, they couldn't let go of it. It stuck to them, flowed over them, welded itself to their hands and arms.

With a scream of disgust, Naz staggered back. The black blotch clung to her, stretched out into filaments of pulsing dark. Then

473

they snapped and she fell backwards. The tendrils groped for her, whipped like broken guy-ropes in a hurricane before wrapping themselves around Jess's forearms and burrowing into her flesh.

But of course it wasn't that. It wasn't flesh at all.

Desperate, losing, Jess turned her thoughts in a different direction. She stopped trying to get free. Her mind filled with Grace's gleeful, mocking laugh. She ignored it and thought instead about the pull of gravity. The dead weight of herself, from which she'd tried so hard and so often to escape.

Grace pressed hard against her, bit into her as though all of that dark smeared bulk was one big lamprey mouth. It was just the two of them now, balanced on the brink of the bottomless fall. Jess wrapped her arms around a part of Grace's squirming, mutating mass that might have been her waist or her chest or something else entirely. Whatever it was, it had just grown a row of serrated hooks like the heads of harpoons. That's fine, Jess thought. She hugged Grace close and ground the wicked barbs into her body as deep as they would go. Anchored herself in them.

Weight, she thought. Just weight. The weight of being me. She leaned forward, far out over that emptiness. Sent her centre of gravity out and out, past the tipping point.

And carried Grace over the edge at last, off balance, Grace so full of the ache and lust for life that she couldn't imagine someone weaponising suicide.

They dropped out of sight in a heartbeat.

Approximately. Hearts in that place by definition don't.

98

Dennis Devlin lay where he'd fallen until he was absolutely certain that Liz Earnshaw wasn't there any more. That took a while because Liz sat for a long time on one of Grace's comfy chairs, talking to herself in an endless rumbling monologue.

It was actually a dialogue but the Devil couldn't be expected to know that.

"I missed you so much, Naz," she said. "I went . . . oh, I think I went crazy! I didn't know what to do without you."

Well, I'm back now, Naseem told her. *And I won't leave you again. I promise.*

"You'd better not!"

Feel that? That's me touching you. I'm inside you, Lizzie. You can cut your hand off, or your foot, or any bit of you, but you can't ever cut me out, because I'm everywhere you are.

Earnshaw cried then. Great gulping sobs that Devlin, lying motionless on the floor and unable to see her face, mistook for grief. But it was the opposite of that. Earnshaw was so happy she felt it was going to burst out of her like a fire and burn the world up. She thought, I will never hurt anyone again as long as I live. Everyone should be like this. Everyone should always feel the way I feel now.

As part of that, part of the business of atonement that was going to take up so much of her time from now on, she picked up Moulson's dead body and carried it out of Grace's cell to the ballroom. It felt wrong to let her lie with the enemies who'd destroyed her, especially after Naz told her all the brave and kind things Moulson had done for her. How it was really Moulson who had brought them together again.

The riot was petering out into random skirmishes as more and more of Fellside's manpower and womanpower was concentrated in Goodall, and more and more of the inmates were corralled into service corridors which could be locked and turned into temporary holding pens. The ballroom was still part of a tiny free republic though, and Earnshaw's arrival there with Moulson dead in her arms caused something of a sensation. Or maybe the opposite of that. Everyone who saw Moulson had the wind whipped right out of their sails.

The dismay that struck them then was strange, considering how few of them had ever spoken to her, even in the casual coinage of good-mornings and how are yous. Every woman there had dreamed of her, and because of that each of them had come to think that she must hold some personal meaning for them and them alone. Now they felt, in a way that was even harder to define, that her death was a tragedy that touched them all.

Earnshaw set the body down on a table and kept vigil as the rioters surrendered to the warders or else went back to their cells to wait for the other shoe to drop. More than half of them were in tears as they went. Some hugged each other for comfort, or pressed hands on each other's shoulders as though to offer condolence.

The guards watched in absolute silence, not wanting to say or do anything that might derail this fortuitous surrender.

And through the middle of it all, Devlin slipped away. It wasn't easy. A riot makes good camouflage, but he was a mess and his appearance wouldn't stand up to scrutiny. He had a broken wrist and a broken jaw. He could barely walk. He was covered in blood,

476

most of which wasn't his. If he was found now and taken to hospital, his body and his uniform would be teeming with evidence of one kind or another that would link him to the bloodbath in Grace's cell.

He had to get out of Fellside on his own two feet, scrub himself sterile, ditch the uniform – no, burn it – and then deny everything that was deniable. The injuries would work in his favour, up to a point. He could say he was concussed. He'd wandered away from the prison without even knowing what he was doing. Had found himself at home, not knowing how he'd got there, and fainted because of the pain. Everything after that was a blur.

Playing up to that scenario, he walked past the duty desk without a word, ignoring the officers and secretaries on station there. Only one of them, Kate Mitchell, actually saw him; the rest were watching the riot play out on the CCTV feed from Goodall, which someone had finally managed to switch back on again. Kate called out to the Devil as he passed by like the walking dead, and getting no answer, she placed an emergency call. Ambulances were already on their way to Fellside, summoned by the governor when the first alarms went off, but she couldn't leave the desk and she wanted to make sure that someone knew Mr Devlin was injured.

Devlin exited through the main gate and crossed the road to the car park. The silence out there was almost perfect, only slightly spoiled by the faint clamour of distant alarms. Ambulances, police cars, fire engines, journalists and camera crews would soon be swarming thicker than flies on shit, but for now he had a window.

He was thinking that driving one-handed was going to be a bitch, and that he'd have to stick to back roads so he didn't meet that incoming armada. Have to take it really slow too, because he was hurting so much that he might actually black out from the pain.

He walked down the bank into the car park, too fast and off balance because he didn't have the strength to check his forward motion and he couldn't throw out his arms to stabilise himself: the broken wrist hurt too much.

As he reached the bottom of the bank, two men appeared from among the parked cars, one from either side of him. Hands closed on his arms.

"Minnie Weeks says hello, you worthless fucker," Kenny Treacher said.

The two men just pushed Devlin along in the direction in which he was already moving. Gripping his arms and twisting them up behind his back – the pain made his breath stall in his throat – they accelerated him until they were running on either side of him and he was stumbling, almost falling, a prisoner of his own momentum.

To the edge of the asphalt. Across the narrow paved verge.

They gave Devlin the bum's rush. Pitched him out over Sharne Fell, whose outstanding natural beauty he had about six and a half seconds to appreciate.

99

Dr Salazar's body was found the next morning. Someone – probably not the doctor himself – had driven his car from the car park at the Pot of Gold to a quiet and secluded place a few miles out on to the fell and then killed him, execution-style, with a single bullet to the head.

The unexplained murder was driven into sidebars and filler spots by the more dramatic events at Fellside itself. But then the balance shifted as various news organisations began to process the information that Sally had posted along with his confession. Hold the front page, the nine o'clock news, the whole damn internet.

Sally's whistle-blower emails were rambling and disjointed, but they were full of circumstantial detail. The drug allegations were exhaustively backed up by the sound recordings he'd made of his conversations with Devlin in the infirmary. Harriet Grace, her lieutenants and fixers, her retail staff and every bent screw in Goodall, they all got a mention one way or another.

Sally also offered a thrilling eyewitness account of Moulson's near-death from tramadol overdose. Stock might still have scraped up a reasonable doubt or two if her accomplice, Lovett, hadn't made a full confession as part of a plea bargain – revealing that having tried once and got nowhere, she'd conspired in the murder of Jess Moulson all over again.

Stock got twenty-to-life and as a supreme irony was sent to Fellside to serve it. Lovett got away with seven years on account of that plea bargain. If he was haunted by his past, he never gave any outward sign of it.

Sylvie Stock *was* haunted, in very short order.

It came on her first night as an inmate in the prison where she had formerly worked. The enormity of her reversal of fortune sat in her stomach like a slab of undigested gristle, and she didn't get to sleep until well after midnight. She just lay in her bunk listening to her new room-mate's snoring, and feeling somewhat bitter and unamused about most things.

When she did finally doze off, she slept fitfully and had unsettling dreams. She was struggling and sweating her way through the worst of these, in which she was performing open-heart surgery on herself in front of a live TV audience, when Naseem Suresh came strolling along and sat down next to her.

The laugh track tailed away into silence. The MC stopped commentating and the audience bowed their heads.

Could I have a word? Naseem asked Stock.

"Yeah, sure," Sylvie said. "Do I know you?"

You treated me for an ear infection once. It was a long time ago. I wouldn't expect you to remember.

Stock just nodded and waited for Naz to go on, but she was already starting to have a bad feeling about this. The texture of the dream had changed. She was sort of awake inside it, and wishing she wasn't.

You hurt someone I love, Naz said. *I'm not really big on vengeance any more, but I can't let this one go. Sorry.*

"I didn't mean to . . ."

Naz shook her head, and Sylvie left the sentence unfinished. Something in the other woman's face told her that she wouldn't be doing herself any favours by lying. *It's all right,* Naz said. *Things are better here than they used to be, in all sorts of ways. Nobody gets murdered now for not facing the way the wind is blowing.*

She was looking at Stock searchingly, expectantly, as though there was some sign she was hoping Stock would give her. *You understand me, Sylvie? If I could hate anyone, it would be you. But I can't. I can't afford to. Everything just runs in together here, and we'd keep drinking that hate until it made us all sick. I'm not prepared to do that.*

She stood up and waved away the furniture of Stock's dream with one hand. *So*, she said. *I'm not going to hurt you. And I'm not going to ask Lizzie to hurt you. I'm going to do something else.*

"What?" Stock asked, terrified for no reason she could explain. It's not a good thing to be awake in your own dream and then have someone walk in out of nowhere and hijack it. "What are you going to do?"

I'm going to show you everything − every last thing − about what happened here, Naseem said. *I want you to understand what you did and who you did it to. I want you to remember her the way I do.*

She took Stock's hand and they walked together through the memories of the women of Goodall. Everyone had seen something, and some people had seen a lot. But nobody had seen it all except Naz herself, so the last thing they did was to stroll, still hand in hand, into Naz's own soul. Stock walked that Möbius strip road with her, and it was the hardest road of all.

So she got to remember all these things she'd never seen. She saw her sins and regretted them bitterly. She knew that the harm she'd done couldn't ever be put right. That she'd have to carry the weight of it to her grave and find out after that if there was going to be a chance, ever, to put it down.

But the harm she hadn't done yet was still up for grabs, and it might yet make a difference. Who knows, really, how the system works? That was Naz's revenge on Sylvie Stock, and her mercy too. When it was all over, when Stock had lived it all and acted it all and suffered it all, Naz told her goodbye and good luck and went away. Stock would have to figure out for

481

herself what she did next. She wouldn't get to see Naz any more.

Stock wasn't sure if that last thing was part of the revenge or part of the mercy.

100

There were more aftershocks besides, some of them trivial, others not so much.

Save-Me Scratchwell survived the riots by two days and seven hours. He dug his heels in and refused to resign, claiming that he'd shown superb leadership during the disturbance and that he'd been on the brink of uncovering Grace's drug ring when Grace pre-empted him by dying. The N-fold directors sacked him and withdrew his pension rights, inviting him to sue them if he was feeling brave. He didn't take them up on that invitation.

N-fold itself was another casualty. In the wake of that one indelible night and the morning of revelations that followed it, all the new licences they were hoping to get vanished like shadows at noonday. Three successive quarters of negative profits were followed by a zero dividend and an abysmally unsuccessful share issue. A year after that, the whole company was swallowed by a Swiss pharmaceuticals giant which had whimsically decided to diversify into public utilities. They left Scratchwell's successor in place but made her answerable to a board of trustees, including a Howard League representative and the current editor of the *Guardian*.

John Street got a life sentence for setting the fire that killed Alex Beech. Nicola Saunders wrote a book about her relationship with him, portraying both herself and Moulson as victims of his Svengali-like charm. It sold in reasonable numbers, but her attempts to reinvent herself as a talk show host didn't come to anything.

Earnshaw is a lifer too now. They got her for Grace's murder and — on much more questionable evidence — for Moulson's. She didn't mind at all. Fellside is where Naseem lives, so it's Earnshaw's home too. The only home she wants or needs. If they ever try to take her out of there, they'd better send an armed response unit.

The two of them are happy together. Although *happy*, all things considered, is a pretty pale word for it. Naseem Suresh lives in Liz Earnshaw's soul. They're never going to be separated, not while they live and not in what comes after.

It's changed Liz. And Liz and Naseem between them have changed everything else. Women who've got shit happening in their lives that they can't deal with, whether it's going cold turkey (G block is about ninety-nine per cent clean now) or relationship hassles, or just the despair and stir-craziness that comes over you sometimes in a place like Fellside, they go to Liz. If they don't know to do that, some old stager will point the way. Po Royal, maybe, or Hannah Passmore. One of the women who were there when all this went down and who know what the deal is.

You come to Liz's cell in free association time and you wait outside until she calls you in. Then she sits with you, holding your hand in complete silence, while Naz takes you to places inside yourself that you didn't know were there. If a queue builds up, which it does most days, it's a very peaceable queue because nobody wants to do anything that will lose them their place in it. The women don't talk afterwards about what happened, but they come out of Liz's cell with a different way of looking at things. Sanity, serenity, solace, something like that. But not something you'd be quick to give a name to.

484

Dr Salazar's ghost never found its way to Fellside, and neither did Dennis Devlin's. Perhaps they both had other places where they needed to be. It was a women's prison, after all.

And then there's Moulson.

No news there really. There haven't been any sightings of her since that night of death and madness.

But Naseem still keeps a lookout for her. At night, when Liz is asleep – properly asleep, not walking in the Other Place – Naz will slip away from that endless, perfect embrace to go and sit at the edge of the abyss.

She never sees anything moving in there, but she knows it's a long way down. Days, months, years, there's room for that. Maybe Moulson managed to pull free before she and Grace hit the bottom. Maybe she's been climbing all this time, and one of these nights she'll haul herself up over the edge, brush herself off and come home.

Or maybe not. There was one time when Naz was walking a long way out in that silent immensity and she saw something. Footprints. Naked. Human. About a size 6, if she had to guess.

She traced them back to the edge of the pit, and forward as far as she could go. But the prints were heading away from the pit, and away from Fellside, in a direction Naz had never gone. You could get lost out there and she was afraid to risk it.

Naz didn't give up her vigil (to some extent she's also watching out for Grace; you can't be too careful), but when she thinks about those footprints, she thinks two things.

First, there's no *need* to leave prints in the Other Place. You would have to work hard to do it. So whatever feet those were, and wherever they were going, their owner most likely put the prints there as a signal. As a message.

Like, just for the sake of example, *goodbye*.

And secondly, that Jess Moulson takes her obligations seriously. Perhaps she's gone to see someone who she knew when she was alive and still cares about. A friend, say, or a close relative.

485

Or it might be something else again. There might be another ghost out there, a real boy this time, who died by fire after hardly living at all. Who doesn't know the ropes. Who's lost and waiting for her to come.

Across how many miles and years of distance?

How many lives?

If it is that, Naz hopes he'll still be there when Jess comes looking for him. She wants that happy ending for both of them.

I've been where you're standing, she whispers to the boy (and sound carries a long way in the dark, so maybe if he's out there he hears her). *I know what it's like. When the night goes on for ever and the little light of you is going out and there's nothing to grab on to.*

You just hold on tight, kid.

And keep saying your name until she comes.

About the author

M. R. Carey is a pen name for an established British writer of prose fiction and comic books. He has written for both DC and Marvel, including critically acclaimed runs on *X-Men* and *Fantastic Four*, Marvel's flagship superhero titles. His creator-owned books regularly appear in the *New York Times* graphic fiction bestseller list. He also has several previous novels and one Hollywood movie screenplay to his credit.

Find out more about M. R. Carey and other Orbit authors by registering for the free monthly newsletter at www.orbitbooks.net.